THE ESCAPE

AN UNBOUNDED NOVEL

BOOKS BY TEYLA BRANTON

Unbounded Series
The Change
The Cure
Protectors
  Ava's Revenge
  Mortal Brother
  Set Ablaze
The Escape
The Reckoning
Lethal Engagement
The Takeover

Colony Six Series
Insight (prequel)
Sketches
Visions
Travels

Imprints Series
First Touch (prequel)
Touch of Rain
On The Hunt
Upstaged
Under Fire
Blinded
Street Smart
Hidden Intent
Checked In

Other
Times Nine

UNDER THE NAME RACHEL BRANTON

Lily's House Series
House Without Lies
Tell Me No Lies
Hearts Never Lie
Your Eyes Don't Lie
Broken Lies
No Secrets or Lies
Cowboys Can't Lie

A Town Called Forgotten
Kiss at Midnight

Noble Hearts
Royal Quest
Royal Dance

Finding Home Series
Take Me Home
All That I Love
Then I Found You

Other
How Far
I Don't Want To Eat
  Bugs

THE ESCAPE

AN UNBOUNDED NOVEL

TEYLA BRANTON

WHITE STAR PRESS

The Escape (Unbounded Series #4)

Published by White Star Press
P.O. Box 353
American Fork, Utah 84003

Printed in the United States of America
ISBN: 978-1-939203-32-8
Year of first printing: 2013

To my daughter Cátia, who has been a loyal reader for more years than I care to count. I appreciate your sharp eyes and kind comments. I love our discussions on grammar and word tense. Most of all, now that you are all grown up,

I'm

glad

we

are

friends.

I LOVE YOU!

CHAPTER 1

I RUBBED MY HANDS TENSELY OVER MY BARE ARMS AS I STUDIED EACH person in the lobby, but everyone we passed was mortal. None of them was shielded or thinking about Unbounded. Their thoughts came to me loudly, their life forces glowing with the additional brightness I'd felt since Mexico, when I'd pushed my ability to its limits. The increased sensitivity made me jumpy since coming to New York, where there seemed to be a crush of people and stray thoughts everywhere I turned. My own mental shield was becoming conversely strong as I worked at keeping them out.

Keene McIntyre arched a brow, a question in his eyes, and I shook my head, indicating that I hadn't located any Emporium Unbounded or Hunters. Of course we had yet to see our target.

I wondered for the hundredth time how Ava had talked me into attending this swanky political fundraiser in New York City. She or Stella would have been a much better choice for hobnobbing with the rich and famous, as well as ferreting out the truth about our target. I'd agreed only because a prominent Hunter and his cronies would be in attendance and I was one of the few Renegades not in their database—the only one who also had the sensing ability.

"Cold, Erin?" Keene whispered, amusement thick in his voice. As luck would have it, he was the only other experienced Renegade in our group who was likewise not in the Hunters' database. In fact, before his defection from the Emporium, he'd worked undercover with the Hunters. That he was mortal was ironic, since it meant he was also one of the most vulnerable of our group, but he was good at what he did, coming by his fighting ability through sheer force of will and determination rather than by inheritance.

Not that we were left to ourselves. This mission was far too important. All the Renegades who could be spared were watching the grounds, ready to back us up if needed. Keene and I were here to gain information about our target, not take him out—unless we uncovered information that made his demise more important than our safety.

I rolled my eyes at Keene's comment. "A strapless dress like this in December doesn't make sense, and why did I have to check my fur coat?"

His eyes, their green color bright under the chandelier, roamed over the dress appreciatively. "Because people who spend five thousand dollars for a picture with the vice president of the United States always check their coats." Easy for him to say since he wore a tuxedo and couldn't feel the winter chill seeping into the gilded lobby.

Cold notwithstanding, I'd spent far too much time working lately not to enjoy wearing the dress. The silky folds hugged all the right curves and made me feel feminine and in control. Unfortunately, the last time I'd worn red, things hadn't gone so well, and right now there were a lot of other places I'd rather be. Particularly with our Renegades not involved in tonight's operation, who were several miles away keeping watch on the building where the Emporium had taken five of our people captive. We'd staked out the compound for three weeks since discovering their whereabouts, but so far we hadn't found a way to rescue them.

My eyes went past Keene and the reception hall entrance, where men in stiff white suits were helping attendees to their destinations. With so much power and money here tonight, the Emporium would likely be represented in significant numbers, though we had yet to verify the presence of any operatives. That fact contrasted sharply with the uneasy feeling in my gut that told me something would go terribly wrong before the night was over. The sensation related to my ability and was one I'd learned not to ignore. I wanted to warn the others, but it wouldn't make a difference to our plan. We all knew the danger. We were prepared for it.

"You ready to do this?" I asked.

For an answer, Keene extended his arm to me. He looked lean and attractive in his black tux, his longish brown hair combed back to expose the scar that ran along the right side of his face near his ear. He appeared comfortable, which was more than I could say for myself. At least my dress fell to the tips of my incredibly tall red heels, obscuring the knives in the sheath around my thigh, knives made not of metal but of plastic with 3D printers and nanotechnology. A couple of guns made of the stuff would have been better, but even we hadn't found a way around exploding barrels and the metal required by firing pins and decent bullets.

We passed the Secret Service agents and through the metal detector at the door in front of the reception hall without incident. As I was replacing my dangling earrings and the glittering gold bracelet Stella had lent me for the evening, a man in a white suit appeared before us.

"May I have your ticket, please?" He extended his hand. Keene gave it to him, and he checked it briefly before handing it back. "Thank you. The photos are being taken behind that backdrop. Please wait with the others. It shouldn't be long. After you pose for your picture with the vice president, please use the exit over there. However, if you wish to stay for the speech, you may still upgrade your ticket. I apologize, but all the dinner tickets have been sold."

"Oh, that's terrible news," I said. "I was hoping there would be a last-minute cancellation."

Keene almost laughed aloud. I'd been the one who refused to stay for the overpriced dinner. Not only was I an opponent of our current vice president, but I could think of a lot better ways to spend thirty thousand dollars, or the sixty it would have cost for both of us.

"I'm very sorry." The man gave a little bow and moved aside so we could pass.

A wave of heat welcomed us as we approached the midway point of the room where photographers had set up their equipment. We couldn't see Vice President Mann behind the backdrop from where we stood, but the line for photographs wasn't too long when you considered he was likely to be president after the next election. Clusters of well-dressed people gathered all over the room talking, some holding a small digital copy of the photograph they'd taken with the vice president. I understood that event organizers would mail larger copies later to attendees, and I planned to use mine for target practice.

"Cort, can you still hear us?" I said, testing to make sure I hadn't damaged the tiny microphone in the left earring when I'd removed them for the metal detector. Keene had another mic in a ring in case we were separated, but I didn't want to depend on him.

"Both signals at full strength," came the voice in my earbud. "And everything's still a go."

"Remember. In and out," another more forceful voice reverberated in my ear. Ritter Langton, of course, making sure we stayed on task. He'd take any failure as a personal one. "No dallying."

Dallying? I couldn't help smiling. Who used that term these days? Only old people—and long-lived Unbounded apparently.

"Yes, Your Deathliness." I'd started calling him that since our arrival in New York, in part because he was in charge of the operation to free our imprisoned Renegades but mostly because it bugged him. I was bugged, too. We were supposed to be figuring out our relationship, but all we'd been doing was working and training.

Ritter didn't respond to my jab, as I knew he wouldn't, but I'd probably pay for the remark later. I was even looking forward to it because I was beginning to see a downside to the possibility of living two thousand years. Decisions in non-life-threatening issues, such as intimacy and romance, seemed much slower to come by, and since my ability made me privy to his emotions as well as my own, I was pretty much a hormonal wreck. It didn't help that Keene had been hanging around so much, adding to the tension.

Cort laughed in my ear. "We'll let you know if anything happens on our side. So far everything looks calm."

"Great," I answered. "We're almost to our target."

Heads turned in my direction as we passed. Most Unbounded and mortals are unaware of the confidence exuded by all Unbounded, simply translating it as beauty or physical attraction, but to a sensing Unbounded like me, the pull was as clear as a neon arrow pointing out the identity of any quasi immortal. In fact, the early days of a Change were the only time I couldn't definitively pinpoint an Unbounded.

There was the strong possibility that some of these milling people were Emporium plants. The Emporium had many new operatives that we didn't know about, both Unbounded and mortal, a direct result from their active breeding program. Unlike the mortal Hunters, the Emporium was aware of my existence as well as Keene's. If we were noticed and identified, getting out of the hotel alive could become a serious problem.

"That woman wants to meet you," I whispered to Keene as we passed a brunette, whose black dress exposed most of her long, shapely legs. She stared at him intently from under long lashes. She was beautiful enough to be Unbounded, but a glance told me she was mortal.

Keene laughed and flashed me a crooked grin. "I'm more into blondes." His stare made me flush, though that might be more because of Ritter's possible reaction than my own. The men had a sort of uneasy truce at the moment, fueled by a grudging admiration for each other, but I worried that the fire simmering below the polite silences and gruff exchanges might flare into something dangerous at any moment.

We arrived at the end of the line, where two waiting couples turned to greet us. Mortals all, in their fifties, the men with thin, graying hair and expensive suits, and their coifed and expertly made-up wives dressed in silk and dripping expensive jewelry. They gave us falsely wide smiles.

One man wore glasses, and it was he who introduced the others. I nodded politely, hearing little of what he said; whatever corporation he and his partner owned didn't interest me, and I certainly wouldn't be having lunch with their wives.

Keene shook hands with the men and nodded at the women, giving our prepared spiel about some West Coast Internet startup that had made millions. The company was real, run by mortals we'd secretly helped with our advanced technology, but new enough that none of them should be familiar with the owners.

"Nice." The man with glasses smiled, but inside he burned with resentment of young geniuses that made more overnight than he'd accumulated in years of sweat and toil. I shut out his thoughts and continued scanning the crowd. With so many pinpoints that signaled life forces, the room felt positively glowing.

There. I'd found one. An Unbounded man hovered near the exit, talking to someone from the hotel staff and carefully examining those leaving before the speech. He wore a black tuxedo and a tie the color of fresh blood. I leaned over to Keene, catching his eye. He followed my gaze and then said to the others without betraying any concern, "So you're friends with Mrs. Mann, you say?"

"Oh, yes," said the blonde next to the man with glasses, her pointed nose twitching slightly. "I've known Carolyn Mann for many years. Our daughter went to college with their son. From what I've seen, he's following his father into politics. In my opinion, Carolyn will make a fine first lady someday."

The second woman leaned forward and said in a conspiratorial whisper, "Actually, it may happen faster than we think. I hear President Stevens is very ill. It's not been in the news, what with all those foreign conferences he has coming up, but I expect if things don't change, they'll have to make an official announcement soon." Her tone implied that the announcement was long overdue, and that she'd love to see Vice President Mann take over for the president immediately.

Keene and I exchanged a look. Unfortunately, this information went a long way toward confirming our suspicions. Three weeks ago, on a thumb drive we'd stolen from the Emporium, the same drive that identified the location of our missing people, we'd found references to the vice president taking over the oval office. The encrypted information hadn't been clear, simply citing meetings that had taken place earlier, but put together with intel we'd uncovered months back about a possible Emporium connection with the vice president's son, it was serious enough to check out. It became even more important with the quickly approaching election year when no one had yet announced whether or not President Stevens would run for reelection. There didn't seem to be any connection between the vice president and the Emporium, but that didn't mean they hadn't gotten to him, especially if the rumors about his son were true.

Keene chuckled. "Well, I'm sure an announcement will come through soon, or will if the press has its way. Is it me, or are there more of them than usual hanging around outside tonight?"

"Tell me about it," the second woman responded. "But even vultures sometimes have a use." She smiled, her dark eyes looking predatory, and I suspected she'd already had her say to the press— or planned to. Her annoying attitude gave me the urge to send a flash of light to her mind that would evoke a splitting headache, but doing so would seriously deplete my strength. The truth was, I didn't know how much damage I could do, and mortals were so fragile. Annoying or not, she was one of those we were trying to protect.

Outside in the communications van, Cort was probably already relaying this new information to Stella, who would be on her computers with her neural headset connected, searching for additional information. If there was anything out there on the president's condition, in printed or digital format, she'd find it within the hour.

The two couples ahead of us continued talking to each other, and we hung back slightly as the line moved forward, garnering a little space so I could report the Unbounded in the black tux to our listening friends. The man was still near the exit, though no longer talking to anyone.

"Well, we knew to expect them," Ritter said. "Just keep your distance. At least you know where he is." He was right. Finding the mortal agents was more problematic in a crowd this large.

The line moved again and we moved with it, nearly to the point where we could see the pictures being taken. One glimpse would be all I needed to decide our next move, though with the line growing behind us, I wasn't at all sure that we'd be able to leave even peacefully without being arrested for some kind of rich society faux pas.

I kept scanning the crowd. No more Unbounded or mortals who appeared to be operatives. Wait, near the entrance of the room where the vice president would be speaking, I sensed several life forces that glowed dimmer than the others in the large reception room, a sign of thoughts being blocked. Four people stood out, the most prominent a man in the middle, who walked with an exaggerated swagger. His short stature was made less so by the pristine dark brown cowboy hat that looked incongruous on his head, despite his matching tuxedo, and set him apart from the crowd. I couldn't see his front, or the insignia of a man with a rifle that was likely embroidered on his hat or lapel, but I was pretty sure I'd found the Hunter we were warned would be in attendance.

At his side walked a matronly woman with her grayish blond hair swept up into a tight bun. Her purple plaid dress might be ugly, but I'd crammed in enough study the past week to recognize it as one made by an expensive designer. She wore it uncomfortably, as though afraid she would trip on her high heels and ruin the dress.

Two tall men flanked the couple, broad enough to be body-guards and likely fellow Hunters. The only problem was that one of them radiated Unbounded confidence.

I swallowed hard, my hand moving instinctively closer to my knives.

Since Hunters' sole purpose in life was to rid the earth of Unbounded, the bodyguard had to be an Emporium agent who'd infiltrated the organization. It was a dangerous game he played; if he was caught, the Hunters would take joy in cutting him into three precise pieces that would assure no regeneration. Of course, the rewards he'd receive from the Emporium for a job well done would be astronomical.

"Hunters?" Keene asked in a low voice.

"That's my bet. But the bodyguard on the right is probably also working for our other favorite group. Definitely Unbounded, and he's not one of ours."

"Great."

"Do you know any of them?" There weren't that many Hunters in the world. At least I hoped not.

He shook his head. "I've mainly worked with groups on the West Coast, though the guy with the hat does look familiar. I've at least seen his picture before."

The Unbounded bodyguard's presence was definitely some-thing we'd have to look into further. Hunters had kept records of Unbounded genealogy since their mortal ancestors had been abandoned by the Emporium during their early phases of genetic experimentation. If this guy was working for the Emporium, we couldn't risk him infiltrating far enough to get the records that might also contain information about our descendants. Like it or not, we were often linked by blood to the Emporium.

"Copy that," Cort said in my earbud. "Describe them, and we'll start Stella researching their identities."

I did, beginning with the purple dress and the cowboy hat that would likely be mentioned by gossip bloggers covering tonight's event. "Maybe one of us should follow them."

"No," Ritter said. "Stay together. Keep your mind on the mission." It was difficult to believe he'd be willing to risk losing this lead. Maybe he planned to track down the bodyguard after we cleared the party and question him personally. That would be just like Ritter. He didn't kill Hunters except in self-defense, but his mercy wouldn't extend to an Emporium agent who had helped murder Renegades.

Anger radiated from Keene at Ritter's order. "Easy," I murmured. Keene frowned, his frustration quickly vanishing as his mental shield strengthened. Now his barrier was tight, but his lapse worried me. I hadn't spotted an Emporium sensing Unbounded nearby, but that didn't mean much because anyone with the sensing ability could mask life forces completely.

As if feeling our stares, the middle Hunter paused at the door and turned in our direction, scanning the room. I caught a glimpse of light red hair peeking from under the cowboy hat before I casually allowed my gaze to slide past them, pretending I was simply enjoying the crowd and the commotion. At the same time, I reached out mentally to the man. His shield was poorly erected, filled with gaps as though he didn't quite believe anyone could delve into his private thoughts, and despite the space between us, it crushed easily beneath my onslaught. There was no sign of suspicion. He'd stopped only because his Unbounded bodyguard had paused.

My thoughts shifted to the bodyguard, who was searching the crowd. He was several decades younger than his employer, a handsome blond who looked smart in his tux. Not your typical uneducated Hunter. *He has to be an Emporium agent,* I thought. Yet his shield was as poorly constructed as his boss's, and I swept it aside to find that he was simply searching for a fifth member of their party—a young lady, if I had it right—to make sure she was safe. Even as I found the answer, a red-haired girl detached herself from a young man and made her way over to the woman in the purple dress.

The others turned to enter the next room, but the bodyguard's attention drifted to the reception room exit, pausing on the Unbounded in the black tux. A signal to a cohort? I started to check the bodyguard's thoughts, only to find him now staring at me. My heartbeat increased, the pumping loud in my ears. If he recognized me or Keene from his Emporium briefings, he might choose to point me out to the Hunter, which would endanger our mission. Before I could decide what his scrutiny meant, he smiled and I received a strong impression of eagerness and curiosity. Nothing more. With a nod in my direction, he turned on his heel and followed his companions.

Keene gave a little chuckle. "Look who has an admirer. Do you think you could lure him into a dark room for me?"

"No!" The bark in my ear came from Ritter and caused me to wince.

That made Keene's grin stretch wider. He put his hand up to the side of my face, tucking a strand of hair behind my ear, and said, "Emporium agent or no, I don't blame that bodyguard one little bit. For the record, I'd go into any dark room with you." His hand left me as he stepped forward with the suddenly moving line. "Hey, we're almost there."

"Stop it with the feedback," Cort crackled in my ear. "Remember, you have to keep the earring and the ring apart or all we hear is static."

Keene gave me a wink. I glanced back at the bodyguard, who passed through the double doors, disappearing from sight, his thoughts fading. My range still wasn't as far as I'd like, though it had improved drastically since Mexico. If I pushed, I could follow him a bit longer, but I needed my full attention for the task at hand.

"I'm pretty sure he didn't recognize me," I said. "But the way he was staring could have been a signal of some sort to the guy near the door."

Keene's eyes went past me. "Uh, speaking of the guy at the door, where'd he go?"

Sure enough, the Unbounded in the black suit was missing. Keene turned his body slowly, casually searching the room.

Ahead of us, the woman with the pointed nose uttered a soft exclamation and lifted a hand to wave at someone behind the backdrop. I stepped forward to see who she was looking at, and finally a balding Vice President Mann came into view. He was smiling widely for the camera, his arm around one of the guests like a best friend. His wife stood on his other side, her gaze leaving the woman who'd waved and going back to the camera just in time for the bright flash. Tonight, apparently, the pictures were a two-for-one deal: the Vice President and Mrs. Mann.

Next to me Keene's body radiated readiness, but I shook my head. Whoever the vice president might serve, the man himself wasn't Unbounded. Neither was Mrs. Mann with her pale, regal face, wide-set eyes, and chestnut hair. Both of their life forces also gleamed brightly, without any sort of barriers, so it was likely they'd never heard of mental shields. Of course, that didn't mean the vice president was innocent of all connection with the Emporium. I pushed my thoughts toward the couple.

He was thinking about his speech and wondering why his son had been acting so strangely the past year—and if there was any way to fix whatever had gone wrong between them. She was wondering what the daughter of the woman in front of me was up to these days, and if she still had a habit of chasing older men for their money. While the vice president exuded strength, weariness leaked from Mrs. Mann like water from cupped hands. She wasn't going to last the whole night, not without the help of drugs. Maybe her doctor was here somewhere behind the half dozen Secret Service agents.

"Keene?" I asked, wanting to know if he'd spotted the Unbounded in the black tux.

"No sign of him."

I nodded, trusting Keene to keep watch while I did my job. I tried to delve deeper into the vice president's mind, but the cacophony of voices and thoughts around me made it difficult to distinguish his thoughts from the others that pushed in around me. "I need to get closer."

"The line should move soon," Keene said.

I joined him for a moment in scanning the room but refocused on the vice president as a small group of friends finished their individual pictures and left together, leaving a large gap in the line. We stepped forward.

I pushed harder, and a throbbing began at the base of my skull, something I hadn't felt in weeks. It only meant my brain was tiring from all the scanning, but I was nowhere near ready to give up. I began absorbing from the air, regaining my strength. A posh hotel right before dinner was a great place for absorbing, all those molecules with expensive, organic nutrients floating about begging to be taken in through my pores. In seconds, the throbbing eased.

Focusing more tightly, I watched the vice president shake hands with another couple and smile for the camera. More worry seeped from him. Something wasn't right. The fact that he worried so much about his adult son, who was supposedly holding his own in politics, seemed to underscore our intel.

"Erin!"

Keene's voice, but the warning came too late. Hard fingers bit painfully into the flesh of my shoulder.

CHAPTER 2

STIFLING AN URGE TO REACH FOR MY KNIVES, I TURNED TO STARE into the face of the Unbounded who had been at the door. He had dark brown hair and was tall enough that I had to look up to meet his gaze. A pleasant, average sort of face, but his mouth was tight and his pale blue eyes hard. The hand that wasn't causing me discomfort was in the pocket of his pants, probably holding a weapon. At his side were two Secret Service agents, who appeared ready to draw their guns.

"Hello," he said in a curiously flat voice. "I thought I recognized you."

Unlike the shields of the Hunters, this Unbounded's barrier resembled a thick black wall, strong and unyielding. Practiced. Definitely Emporium. I rammed my thoughts against it, seeing a momentary white flash that sent a trail of electric shocks through my temple. Ignoring the pain, I pushed with more force. If I made it inside, I could use my ability against him. I'd also be able to use his talent—whatever it was. So far I'd channeled Ritter's combat ability, as well as my younger brother Jace's. Channeling other gifts in our group, I'd also managed to teleport, or shift as we called it, and I'd had one lesson in technopathy. I was far from adept at any of these talents, but all of them were more instinctive than anything else, so the key was a good mental connection with the possessor of the ability. The drawback, of course, was that the Unbounded whose ability I was borrowing needed to remain in sensing range, and some abilities were more complicated than others.

"Oh?" I said to the man with a calm smile that belied the hammering of my heart. I didn't shake off his fingers because contact only heightened my attack on his mind, and I hadn't yet managed to force my way inside his shield. "I'm sorry, have we met?"

"No, but I know *of* you." His attention went briefly to Keene. "And him."

Keene shook his head, his voice calm despite the dangerous glint in his eyes. "You must be mistaken. We've never met. Who are you?" That told me Keene didn't know him because Keene never, ever lied, except by omission. Some might argue that was every bit as bad, but given the world of intrigue that surrounds the Unbounded, it was something I admired.

Unlike Keene, I recognized the man now that we were so close from the pictures Stella had shown me, though he appeared significantly different in real life. Plainer somehow, despite his overpriced tux and flashy scarlet tie. Dread came with the recognition. No way should this man be Unbounded.

Keene dropped his eyes to the hand on my shoulder, his nostrils flaring slightly. I knew his tight control was the only reason he hadn't started throwing punches. This was why Ava had sent him with me instead of Jace. Though my brother's combat ability made him a better fighter, his rashness and inexperience might not have allowed him Keene's restraint.

"Oh, look," squealed the woman with the pointed nose, motioning to her companions. "It's Patrick Mann." She took a few steps toward us. "Do you remember me? I'm Sophie Brinker, Finley's mother. You and she were so close in college."

Patrick's hand dropped from my shoulder, but I had already used his touch to help pound a tiny hole in his barrier and wriggle inside. If he wasn't a sensing Unbounded, he wouldn't know I was there as long as I didn't insert any thoughts or try to communicate mentally. I wouldn't be able to sift through his memories as I could if he were unconscious, but I should be able to get a sense of what his purpose was in confronting us.

"Mann?" Keene mouthed at me.

Patrick Mann, the vice president's son to be exact, and given his Unbounded condition, his father had every right to worry about him. I knew from the data that he was thirty-six, which put him at Keene's age, but he looked at least five years younger—and aging at only two years for every hundred, like most Unbounded, he'd still look the same at his parents' funerals. If he continued on in politics like his father, and became the president of the United States, he wouldn't be the first Unbounded to do so, as Kennedy had also been one of us, but Patrick's possible connection with the Emporium might mean that a mortal would never again hold the position.

Now that I was inside his mind, I could see Patrick was lying. He hadn't recognized us. Someone had pointed us out to him, a man who'd seen us arrive, a sensing Unbounded posted to watch for Renegades. Whoever it was had used his ability to mask his presence because I hadn't sighted him.

"Finley. Of course," Patrick murmured. Mentally, he dismissed the woman and her comment. His concern was us; she didn't matter at all.

This was worse than our intel had hinted. We'd thought maybe Vice President Mann had been offered a deal in exchange for advanced medical care by an Emporium healer after his son's near fatal skydiving episode a few months earlier. We hadn't considered the possibility of the son being an Emporium agent himself. That fact only spelled trouble for the entire nation, and eventually the world.

Yet Keene didn't recognize him from his years at the Emporium, so what did that mean? Perhaps not much. Keene's father was a member of the Emporium Triad, their ruling body, but even while he'd served them, Keene's mortality would have prevented him from being privy to their most important secrets.

"Oh, yes, I recognize you now from your pictures." I extended my hand to Patrick Mann. "Nice to meet you in person." I waited several heartbeats before adding with a glance at the reddened finger marks now quickly fading from the skin of my shoulder, "I think."

Jumbled thoughts came from the sand stream of his mind. Surprise and wariness. Worry that he'd made a mistake in challenging us without Emporium backup, especially given our known prowess in combat. While he could expect the aid of the Secret Service agents, we might not choose to go with him peacefully. Two agents plus the half dozen others close to the camera weren't nearly enough to subdue us unless they opened fire, and that would start a stampede of guests and negative publicity they didn't need.

These images were followed by more scrambled emotions I couldn't separate. Then finally a clear thought: *They don't seem to know about me or the plan so they aren't here to eliminate dear old Dad. I'll let the others deal with them.* The thought disappeared before it ran to its conclusion, the jumbled sand stream taking over again. Multiple images careened past me, but none of them seemed related or worth examining.

I needed to know more. What was it Patrick thought we didn't know? That he was Unbounded? But how would that relate to a possible assassination attempt on his mortal father? Unless the vice president was also working for the Emporium. While that was exactly what I'd come here to determine, I could tell from Patrick's thoughts that he didn't know I could sense, so he wasn't worried about me discovering whether or not his father was an agent. No, he thought we'd come to kill his father because of intel we already possessed before our arrival—and now he'd decided we didn't have it after all. Interesting.

Only a second had passed since my remark, though it seemed much longer to me from the viewpoint of our joined minds. Patrick took my proffered hand in a firm grip. "I believe I mistook you for someone else," he said with an easy laugh that was echoed by the two couples in front of us, who were avidly watching the scene unfold. "Someone who's created a tad of difficulty for my father in the past." He let my hand go, leaving behind a touch of nervous moistness.

"Couldn't be them," said the man in glasses, stepping closer to his sharp-nosed wife. "They're from out west with—what did you say your firm's name was?" This last to Keene, who relaxed marginally with the question.

I let the chitchat slide over me as I pushed farther into Patrick's mind, not touching the sand stream of thoughts but examining them closer. I clearly saw images of known Emporium agents, so his allegiance was clear, but there were no more mental references to his father or any type of plan—only the determination to play out this game so we wouldn't suspect. Or at least not until it was too late.

Too late for what?

Something in his mind caught my attention. A shiny, black, snakelike cord stretching the entire length of his visible thought stream, but unlike the other thoughts and images, it didn't slide forward and disappear with the rest, only moved up and down inside the sand, mostly buried and out of sight. Chill spread through me as I recognized the black cord. I'd created a similar substance in a corner of my own mind, a box where I'd locked up my fear of heights. While I wasn't completely cured, I could function when it mattered. This black cord, however, was far more elegant, undulating with a hypnotic call. I moved closer.

Was he a sensing Unbounded after all? Had he created this to hide important thoughts? No. I hadn't been quiet or careful getting past his barriers, and he would have noticed me. Besides, this black cord wasn't quite the same thing as my box. The signature was different—and I recognized it.

With a shudder, I pulled away. I'd felt this mark in my ex-boyfriend before his death, and I'd suspected then that something had been done to his mind. Now I was sure. It belonged to Delia Vesey, a member of the Emporium Triad and also a sensing Unbounded who had the ability to control people using mere thoughts.

I could feel the cord pulsating, seeming to beckon me to take it into my hands, to caress its length and steal its secrets. Except not only would disrupting the stream alert the Unbounded to my mental presence, but everything in my mind screamed out that Delia wouldn't go to such effort unless she was sure no average sensing Unbounded would be able to extract the hidden information safely.

No average Unbounded. What about me?

I backed off, staying in his mind but keeping clear of the thought stream. We didn't know much about how the sensing gift worked, but I'd learned that mental damage sometimes didn't heal like our physical bodies did, and for all I knew the cord could contain some sort of a mental bomb.

"I do apologize for the interruption," Patrick said.

"An honest mistake, I'm sure." I was trying to decide how to handle this. A fist to his jaw would be my preferred manner, but that would blow our cover entirely. For now we appeared safe, his thoughts revealing his desire to signal his Emporium cronies to come deal with us. Either we kept him from doing that with conversation or we made a run for it, which might be impossible given our place in line and the presence of so many Secret Service agents—even we could be temporarily incapacitated by their guns.

An idea occurred to me. "I know how you can make it up to us, Mr. Mann, and I'm sure Mrs. Brinker here will agree. Will you stand in my picture with me and your parents? My friends will never believe that I met the entire family if you don't." I tried to force enough enthusiasm into my voice to make the request sound real, but Keene's pained look told me I fell short.

Mrs. Brinker's nose twitched. "What a wonderful idea! Would you stand in ours, too? I would love to send a copy to Finley."

Patrick took a step back. "Well, I was about to—"

"Please, I insist." Mrs. Brinker put her arm through the hook made by his elbow. "We are one of your father's largest contributors, you know, and I anticipate that we will support you as well when it's your turn." She patted his arm. "Oh, it *is* good to see you. I don't spend enough time with Finley these days. We were all so worried when we heard about your skydiving accident. What a miracle you survived."

A rush of anger from Patrick jabbed into my mind, and I rubbed the base of my skull to relieve the throbbing. Yet now that I'd backed away from the thoughts and emotions in his sand stream, something else was bothering me about him, something familiar. I could almost hear a mental humming speeding through his synapses. Was this another side effect of my breakthrough in Mexico? I couldn't be sure. But there was a clear pattern to the humming.

Could I follow it? The impulses were going far too fast for me to trace without inserting my thoughts into them. Maybe if I just reached out and—a bright flash momentarily blinded me, and suddenly I felt connected to Patrick's entire body, as if I'd sprouted a million arms and legs that connected everything together. Then just as suddenly, it was gone, and I was outside Patrick's shield again, with no little hole in sight.

"You okay?" Keene touched my elbow, his voice soft.

"Yes."

"Do we need to come in?" Ritter's voice sounded tense coming from my earbud, but the reminder of his presence made me relax, and my confidence reasserted itself. If it came to it, I was sure I could disable most of the Secret Service agents with my mind, and while that would seriously deplete my energy, Keene could wipe up any that were left. Afterwards, Ritter and the others would do their best to see that we got out.

"Just think," I murmured to Keene, "a picture with the whole family. What luck."

Mr. and Mrs. Brinker were lining up for their picture now. The vice president slapped Patrick on the back and the men smiled but I was sure I didn't imagine the flicker of pure hatred in Patrick's eyes. Or did I? My head was pounding now with the effort of having broken into his mind, but it was a small price to pay for having glimpsed the information there, as well as that black cord. I hoped Ava would be able to explain its purpose.

Mrs. Mann and Mrs. Brinker had their arms around each other like old friends, though the thoughts radiating brightly from both clearly denied that premise. This was all for show. *Smile for the camera.*

They smiled, the lights flashed, and it was finally our turn. I stood between Patrick and his father, while Keene slipped between the vice president and his wife. Vice President Mann beamed and worried, Mrs. Mann wilted, and Patrick stood like a board, his mind dark to me except for the irritation pouring off him like water. This close it was easy to delve into the mortals' minds and see no knowledge of the Emporium. There was also no sign of any shiny black cord in the stream of their thoughts, which gave me a moment of relief.

So why had Patrick thought we'd come to remove his father? That he thought we had, probably meant it was a good idea, but for all my dislike of the vice president and his policies, he seemed to be innocent—or at least innocent of Emporium conspiracy.

"Thank you," I said to the vice president after the flash.

"No, thank *you* for coming." Vice President Mann patted my hand, already turning to greet the next people in line.

Patrick spoke as we left the lights and the backdrop together, heading for the exit. "You're not staying?"

"Not this time," I said.

His eyes met mine. "That's too bad."

"Yes, isn't it?"

A few more strides and we were through the door, leaving Patrick behind.

"That was close," Keene said.

"We're not in the clear yet. From what I saw in his mind, he'll be talking to his Emporium cronies. We need to get out of here."

"Not the front," Ritter said in my earbud. "They're out here already. Have been for some time. Though they don't seem to know—wait, scratch that. They're heading inside."

I walked faster, swaying ridiculously in the high heels. "Heading to the parking garage."

"No!" Ritter barked. "They'll be there already. Too easy to trap you."

"Try the exit on the opposite side of the hotel," Cort said. "If you go through the courtyard, it's almost as close as the side exit we discussed earlier, and it might throw them off. You may have to get through them, but at least you'll have an avenue of escape. With Secret Service watching every entrance, they may wait until you clear the hotel to attack."

"Heading there now." Ritter again. "Marco, Jace, you copy?"

Brief static, and then Marco's voice. "On our way."

"Save some for me," Jace added.

I smiled. "We'll see."

Welcome excitement thrummed through my veins as I anticipated the coming battle, blotting out my earlier unease. While we had hoped to get in and out without attracting undue attention from the Emporium or Hunters, I was itching for a fight. After the frustrating weeks of watching the Emporium compound, unable to do anything to help our captive people, I finally had a chance to strike back.

Slipping off my heels, I discarded them in a garbage container. Next, I unfastened the long skirt under the first ruffle at mid-thigh, throwing it into a planter.

Keene smirked. "Nice."

"Stella's design." I retrieved my knives, one in each hand.

"So you were able to get into his mind," Keene mused as we entered the courtyard. "I'd think he'd be trained enough to keep up a shield. They know you have at least two sensing Unbounded."

The icy cold of the pavement stung my bare feet, but I ignored the discomfort and hurried forward. "They know *we* have Ava," I corrected. "Don't talk like you aren't a part of us."

He shrugged. "Delia knows about you, too."

As far as we could figure, Delia still hadn't told anyone at the Emporium about my real ability. I believed she planned to take control of my mind and use me to tighten her reign over the Emporium and control her partners, so it made sense on some level, but not knowing also weakened them as a group.

I grabbed his hand and held it next to my earring so the others couldn't hear. "He did have a shield. I got through it."

Keene's step faltered. "You got *through* it?" Mixed feelings of horror and admiration came from him as I dropped his hand. Since I wasn't making an effort to probe his mind, I knew he'd purposely allowed his own barrier to fade. Or had he? I reached out, but his shield was solid. Only his surface emotions seeped through. I didn't push further. I didn't want to know what kind of a monster he thought I was becoming. Being mortal, he could never understand. I picked up the pace, sprinting to the far side of the courtyard and yanking open the door to the hotel. Keene kept up.

"You're close," Cort said in my ear, and I knew he was following the tracking chip embedded in my arm. "Turn left at the next hallway and then right at the end of the corridor. There'll be an emergency exit to the street midway down that hallway on your left."

The carpet was warm on my feet after the icy courtyard, and incredibly soft. It felt wrong to hurry across such luxury. We rounded the bend but had only gone a few feet when two men appeared at the end of the corridor, one a big man with blond hair and the other a compact Asian.

"Unbounded," I whispered. I couldn't tell their abilities but given the years of battle, the odds were that both were gifted in combat. Only in the past fifty or so years had the Emporium begun to recognize that brute force wasn't always the answer.

Should we fight here or try to find another way out?

The decision became moot as two more Unbounded appeared in the hallway behind us. One I recognized, though even after all our encounters, I still didn't know his last name. "Hey, Edgel," I called. "What are you doing here? And your three friends. Nice hotel, isn't it?"

"We copy," Cort said. "Four attackers. We're en route now to your location."

Edgel glared at me as he approached, the whites of his eyes bright against his black face. In his muscled hand he held a weapon, but it wasn't a gun. Apparently they hadn't been successful at sneaking one inside the hotel any more than we had. At least that evened the odds slightly.

"You killed my daughter," he accused.

I found his barrier and pushed at it. It appeared strong and solid, but like with Keene, I could feel his surface emotions—mostly anger, which would make him more dangerous. Outside his barrier, I wouldn't be able to use his combat ability. I had to get inside. We couldn't take all four men, but if I was successful, we could stand long enough for our people to get inside the hotel. Maybe.

Edgel's barrier felt familiar because I'd been inside it before, but pushing against it bore no result. Probably because of the energy I'd wasted on Patrick Mann. I needed to distract him.

"Your daughter's dead?" I asked.

His jaw clenched and unclenched. "You knew it would happen. All of you did."

"We didn't have the information you wanted. Your people erased it, not us. We would have given it to you." I didn't want to feel sorry for him, but I knew what it was like to worry about mortal family members.

Edgel didn't speak, but disbelief radiated from him.

Keene shifted his weight, getting ready to act. "She's right. They didn't have the information."

Edgel had served under Keene and knew his distaste for untruths. Would it make a difference? I didn't think so. He was a soldier who always followed orders, except for the one time when he had asked for our help and Keene had brought him to our safe house.

Edgel dipped his head, a signal to his men. *Showtime.* I slung one of my knives at Edgel's face. He anticipated the move, as I knew he would, but I accompanied it with a mental assault. There, I was in. For a moment, I considered sending a pulse of light to try to disable him, but that meant expending strength that would leave me vulnerable to the others and prevent me from utilizing his gift. Instead, I channeled his combat ability and hurled my remaining knife at the big blond behind me. To my surprise, the knife embedded deeply in his eye and he crumpled to the carpet. Not dead, but out for now. No combat ability there, or he'd have moved aside.

As Edgel flung a knife in my direction, I ducked and used my momentum to push off the wall and deliver a kick to the Asian, striking a knife from his hand. He countered with a jab to my face that sent pain reverberating throughout my entire head. My earbud fell to the ground. Instinctively, I rewarded him with a kick to the knee, followed by a punch to the gut and another to his jaw. He blocked these with lightning speed.

Edgel was coming at me from behind with another knife in his hands. I retreated past the Asian, darting a glimpse at Keene. He'd dispatched the fourth Unbounded and now lunged at Edgel.

A fist hurtled in my direction, and I barely managed to dodge. It was odd exchanging blows with the Asian, while the part of my mind connected to Edgel followed his fight with Keene. If I didn't concentrate, I was going to lose. Unlike Edgel, the Asian was closer to my size, so if I kept my wits, I had a shot at besting him. While Edgel had several inches on Keene, Keene was larger than me and better trained, and he'd fought with Edgel and would know his weaknesses. Keene had also spent years trying to prove to his father that he was good enough. I believed he could keep Edgel occupied until I finished with the Asian.

But where was our backup?

The Asian scooped up his knife from the floor and rewarded my distraction with a vicious slash on my upper left arm. Pain turned the world red.

That was when I felt Edgel sink his knife deep into Keene's belly.

No!

Reaching deeply for reserves of energy I didn't know I possessed, I pushed outward. Edgel grabbed at his head as my flash seared his mind.

CHAPTER 3

THE NEXT INSTANT I WAS DOWN ON THE CARPET AS MY ATTACKER slammed his fist into my temple. I tried to get up, but my strength was depleted from my mental effort. Even if I could find the strength to move, with Edgel incapacitated, I could no longer channel his ability. The Asian cracked me in the face again. Blackness nibbled away my sight.

I reached for the Asian's mind, finding a barrier there and flinging myself against it. No luck. The pounding in my head was growing, though my sight was stabilizing. I tried to move away, but the Asian grabbed my wounded arm and yanked me to my feet, spinning me around until he had an arm around me and his knife at my throat. His breath was hot on my ear.

"Edgel?" he asked, pulling me several steps toward where Edgel knelt on the floor.

Edgel shook his head. "I'm okay. Just give me a moment."

Twisting my head to look for Keene, I found him lying beyond Edgel, blood welling through the hands he clenched to his stomach. His eyes closed. It didn't look good. I had to get him out of here to Dimitri, our healer.

I began absorbing consciously, pulling more sustenance from the air. I couldn't give up, not when Keene looked close to death.

The Asian turned me around and shoved me against the wall. His mental barrier was black and thick, and though it was hard to tell his age, I knew he'd practiced shielding for hundreds of years. "It'd be easier if we took her unconscious." Sweat beaded on his forehead.

Edgel stood up, his blunt features looking haggard. "Too hard to explain to Secret Service." Frantically, I tried his shield, but it was over his mind again, tight and unyielding.

"We could take her upstairs to the room. Give her some drugs."

"No. She's wired and probably has a tracking device. They'll come for her soon." Edgel strode over to me and pushed back the curls Stella had so artfully arranged in my hair. He removed both earrings, twisting them in his hands before tossing them to the ground. My bracelet followed. He did a thorough search of my body, his hands rough over my flesh. "That'll have to do for now. If we can get her back to headquarters, we can disable the tracking device there." He gave me a flat grin. "Delia will be happy to see you. So will your father."

By father he meant Stefan Carrington, the third Triad member. Except Stefan wasn't really my father, and I suspected Delia knew the truth about that, too, but if so, she'd kept silent to further her agenda.

"Let's go." Edgel started down the hall, but I resisted the Asian's pull.

"I'm not going anywhere without him." I pointed at Keene.

Edgel turned. "Don't you think your people will get to him faster if we leave?"

I wasn't sure of that. After all, they hadn't arrived yet. Secret Service must have the place locked down even tighter than we'd thought. Without my earbud, I had no way of knowing if they were close or if they'd run into trouble of their own.

I tried another approach. "He's Tihalt's son. Doesn't that mean anything?"

Edgel was back at my side in an instant, his movement a blur. He brought his face close to mine. "He's mortal and a traitor. The only reason I don't bring his head to Tihalt myself to collect the reward is because he never once lied to me. He can keep his head. For now."

"And if he dies?"

"If he dies, it will go a tiny bit toward avenging my daughter's death."

"I told you that wasn't our fault!"

Edgel's big hand wrapped around my left arm just below the knife wound, uncaring of the blood running down my arm, and squeezed hard. "Shut up and move!"

I could hardly breathe through the agony. "Over. My. Dead. Body." It wasn't so much that I was brave, but I felt him coming: Ritter. I'd always been able to feel glimpses of his emotions, but since Mexico I had become more aware of him than ever. He was close. Very close. Anger preceded him, a burning for revenge.

I needed a distraction so the others would be caught completely off balance at his arrival. Arching my body forward, I slammed my head into Edgel's with a satisfying crack. The Asian pulled back his fist, readying for a blow that would probably knock me unconscious, but abruptly his face went slack and he pitched forward to the carpet, his raised fist thudding against the wall. A kitchen knife sprouted from his back.

Edgel whirled to face Ritter who had appeared behind him, breathing hard, his black hair falling forward on his face. He looked big and strong and sexy and completely in control—or would have if he hadn't been wearing a silly burgundy hotel uniform that was obviously two sizes too small. I reached for his mind and found it without barriers, a dangerous thing with Emporium agents nearby, but I knew he'd left it that way for me.

Channeling Ritter's speed, I ran toward him. Edgel anticipated the move and lunged, probably hoping to use me as a shield, but I evaded him. Then Ritter was between us and they began exchanging blows, both of them beauty in motion. Strange how such a deadly ability could also be so magnificent.

Keene groaned from his place on the ground, and I knelt next to him. I had nothing to stem the blood, so I picked up one of the fallen knives and began cutting off his jacket, balling the material and placing it under his hands. His eyes flickered as I pushed down, adding pressure. His life force still seemed strong, but I wasn't sure how long that would last.

A loud crash scattered my thoughts. I glanced up to see a hotel worker near the bend in the hallway, standing next to an overturned room service cart. A scream wrenched from her throat as she turned and fled.

Ritter and Edgel fell motionless, staring for several long seconds at each other. Then Edgel leaned over, pulled the Asian over his shoulder, and sprinted down the hall.

Ritter came toward me, his anger dying away as he knelt on the carpet. "You okay?" His eyes went to the blood on my arm.

I nodded. "Yeah." My wound looked worse than it was and would stop bleeding in a few moments. By morning it would be only a memory—one to add with all the others I tried not to recall. "Thanks for coming." My eyes fell down his outfit. "But I really hope this isn't when you confess you have some kinky fantasy about hotels."

A laugh rumbled in his throat. "Not hardly. Long story, but it got me to you." He put his cheek next to mine, breathing deeply. I knew how he felt. We were alive and okay. If we'd been anywhere else, we wouldn't be doing any talking at all.

"We have to get Keene out of here," I said after what seemed like less than a heartbeat.

Nodding, Ritter felt for his pulse. "It's holding steady, but there's too much blood." Red still oozed from under the scrap of black jacket, staining Keene's white shirt with gore. If he'd been conscious a minute earlier, he wasn't now.

As Ritter leaned over to scoop up Keene, footsteps thundered down the hall. Three hotel employees appeared, accompanied by half a dozen armed police officers and four Secret Service agents. Ritter and I stood up to meet them.

"What happened, Miss?" an officer asked me.

"My friend and I were attacked." I indicated Edgel's two fallen men. "By those guys and two others who ran away." Their security cameras would actually reveal that I'd thrown the first knife. But wasn't that understandable when Edgel and his men were so obviously threatening? The bigger issue would be their reaction to how fast we moved. "Fortunately, this man saved us." I sagged against Ritter in mock distress. "But I've got to get my friend to the hospital." I gestured to where Keene lay on the carpet.

"Looks like you both need to go." The officer began speaking into his radio, while two of his companions came forward to look at Keene. One of them appeared to have advanced medical training. The other officers and Secret Service personnel began checking Edgel's men.

"We have to get Keene to Dimitri," I whispered to Ritter. I'd been checking out avenues of escape, but neither end of the hallway looked promising, not with so many people around.

He nodded and spoke into the hand containing a mic ring similar to Keene's. "You got that, Cort? They're sending an ambulance. Probably several."

I ordered myself to relax. We weren't through this yet, but as long as the Emporium didn't have agents among these officers, we might not have to fight our way out. Our people would put an alternate plan into play. I just needed to be patient and trust them, in spite of my worry for Keene.

"This one doesn't seem to be breathing," said an officer squatting by the big blond Emporium agent. "Weird thing is, he still has a heartbeat." Several of his buddies hurried over to verify his findings.

After sending hotel security for a copy of the video feed, the first police officer, who seemed to be in charge, continued to question us. Minutes ticked by as I worried about Keene. A pair of soft slippers appeared on my bare feet and a blanket around my shoulders, but I didn't remember who gave them to me. More blankets covered the unconscious men. Around the time someone put a bottle of water in my hand, my anxiety began to crank up, in part because I was sure the hotel manager had pegged Ritter as an imposter. Surely in a hotel this size, he couldn't know every employee. Then again, they'd probably reordered background checks on everyone in light of the vice president's visit.

We heard the ambulance gurney before it rounded the corner from the direction of the exit we'd been trying to reach, and I almost exclaimed as Dimitri Sidorov came into view. The Russian was a short, broad man with a narrow nose, wide brown eyes, and a trim mustache. His brown hair was swept back from his face, and he exuded a sureness that came from living over a thousand years. I'd known him only three months, but I trusted him with my life, and not because he was also my biological father.

Tears pricked my eyes. Keene was going to be okay—or at least had a fighting chance. A certified medical doctor, Dimitri was also our healer, and his touch could keep even a fatally wounded mortal alive.

Pushing the back of the gurney was Jace, his short blond hair slightly spiked in the front, his eyes glinting with excitement as he assessed the officers. With Jace and Dimitri here, our chance of escaping through sheer force became a serious possibility, despite the two additional Secret Service agents who accompanied our people. Still, it would be difficult with Keene, and we really didn't want to injure anyone not connected with the Emporium. That meant we needed to follow protocol. I gritted my teeth against my impatience.

Dimitri went directly to Keene, placing one hand on his chest, the other checking his eyes with a light Jace shined into them. "We need to get him into surgery now," Dimitri announced to no one in particular.

"He does look bad," said the officer in charge.

Jace stored the light in his blue uniform and helped Dimitri load Keene onto the gurney. Then, with a glance at Dimitri, Jace crossed the few steps to me and Ritter. "You look ready to pass out," he told Ritter, who appeared as healthy as ever. "Were you hit repeatedly?" When Ritter nodded, he said, "That's what I thought. You may have internal bleeding. You'd better come with us, too. No telling how long before the other ambulances arrive."

The officer in charge shook his head. "We have questions for him first."

"You can ask them at the hospital." Dimitri's tone brooked no argument. His gaze drifted to me. "Miss, you'll definitely need stitches for that cut. Come along, and we'll get you taken care of."

The police officer opened his mouth but apparently thought the better of objecting when Dimitri's bushy eyebrows furrowed in his direction. Jace put his arm around Ritter, who leaned on him, nearly pushing him to the ground with his bulk. Ritter's mouth twitched, but he managed not to grin. I bit the inside of my lip to keep my own expression suitably upset.

"What about an IV?" The officer with medical training pointed to Keene. "He shouldn't be moved without an IV." His eyes slid to Ritter. "And if that man has internal bleeding, he shouldn't be walking."

"Do you want him to bleed out while he waits for another ambulance?" Jace said, feigning offense. "Let us do our job, man."

Dimitri was already pushing Keene down the hall, trailed by the two Secret Servicemen who'd arrived with him.

"What about these other men?" asked the officer in charge.

"The other ambulances will be here soon," Dimitri said over his shoulder, apparently unconcerned at how his words contradicted Jace's. "We can't help them all at once. This is my patient, and I have to do what's best for him. He needs surgery now."

The officer nodded. "Okay, but one of my men will go with you to the hospital. Until we clear up exactly what happened here, we need to make sure we have contact information from everyone."

Dimitri shrugged and continued walking. We followed him

around the corner and halfway down the hall where two more Secret Service officers stood guard. They held the door open for us as we left.

"Nice playacting," Jace murmured under his breath to Ritter. "But can you stop leaning on me so hard?"

"Why? You think you might puke?" Ritter teased.

Jace scowled. "Man, are you guys ever going to forget that?" It was in large part my fault that no one let it rest. Jace seemed to be on a permanent high since his Change and I'd found that reminding him of his reaction to the first deaths he'd seen at Emporium hands was a good damper.

All four agents walked outside with us. Ava O'Hare, the leader of our group of Renegades, and also my fourth great-grandmother, jumped lithely from the driver's seat, her chin-length blond hair pulled back from her unlined face in a short ponytail, one hand inside her long jacket. I knew it wasn't a simple pistol she gripped there—and a good thing because I sensed at least a dozen life forces in the dark, just out of sight. All of them dimmed with their mental shields in place. Emporium agents.

"They're here," I said softly to Jace and Ritter. "A lot of them." Ritter stepped away from Jace and went to my other side, forgetting he was supposed to be ill. I saw the dull gleam of our nanotech knives in his hand. Jace looked around intently, his hand going to his own weapon hidden in his pocket. But what good were knives against so many guns?

Dimitri and three of the agents carried the gurney down the few steps to the sidewalk and over to the ambulance. Were our enemies willing to risk a shootout with the Secret Service here in the street? Was capturing us that important?

Apparently not today. I breathed a sigh of relief as the ambulance doors closed with all of us inside, except the police officer and Ava, who sat in the front. As Ava drove through the dark streets, Dimitri kept his hand on Keene's chest. "I wasn't joking about the surgery," he said. "We need to get him to the safe house immediately."

"Keene's mortal," I said. "Wouldn't the hospital be better?"

He shook his head. "I don't have operating privileges at any of the hospitals here, and I can't leave him alone right now, or he won't make it. I pulled in a few favors to borrow this ambulance, but that's pretty much the extent of my influence."

Ritter nodded and spoke into his ring. "Cort, are you still there?"

I couldn't hear the response, but Ritter looked outside the back windows. "Good, I see you. As soon as we're sure we've shaken our tail, we're going to pull into a street and make the switch. Ava, try to keep our friend occupied while I get him a sedative." As he spoke, he peeled off the tight hotel uniform, revealing a blue V-necked T-shirt that hugged his muscles like a second skin.

Jace shook his head. "I should have been the one to go with you," he said to me in an undertone. His eyes were troubled, almost resentful, and that worried me. Especially when I still kept secrets from him. Secrets that ate at my conscience.

"Maybe." I didn't know anymore. Jace's hot head might have gotten us into trouble, but the switch would have prevented Keene's injury. Seeing Keene lying on the gurney gave me the oddest feeling, a numbness with a sharp edge that felt like a razor blade. He was mortal. I'd come to think of him as permanent, like the other Unbounded Renegades, but no matter how well he fought, he would age and die and leave us all behind. I didn't know exactly how I felt about that, but it wasn't good.

"How's your arm?" Ritter asked me.

"Fine." I lifted my eyes, hoping he couldn't see the turmoil there. A shock ran through my body as our gazes connected. Emotion threatened to drown me, to overcome who I was and destroy the independence I'd worked for. It was as scary as hell. And more enticing than a needle full of curequick. My emotions and his swirled together. I wanted him and he wanted me and eventually we'd have to do something about it.

After a few sharp turns, Ava pulled into an alley and came to a stop. Ritter stepped out the back, meeting Cort who'd jumped from a brown van, followed by Marco Collins, one of our mortal security men. Cort handed off something to Ritter before hurrying toward us. Dimitri was already jumping down and pulling the gurney after him.

"Erin," he said to me, "grab my bag and as many of those supplies as you can carry."

"How is he?" Cort's voice was tense, and I could feel the sorrow emanating from him as he stared down into his brother's face. Keene had taken years to follow Cort's defection from the Emporium, and the brothers often didn't agree on issues, but their loyalty to each other ran deep. Cort had lived five hundred years, and he'd seen numerous mortal half-siblings die, but Keene was different. Everyone who knew Keene understood that. He lived by his own rules, regardless of the consequences, even while working for others. He saw things no one else saw, and he wasn't afraid of making tough choices.

Filling my arms with medical supplies, I glanced through the window to the front of the ambulance and saw Ava talking to the police officer. His words cut off as Ritter opened the door and fired a tranquilizer into his neck. The man struggled for a few seconds, his hand going to his gun before slumping over.

Ava and Ritter came to help us move Keene over to the van. "I'll take the ambulance back," she said, her gray eyes like steel. "I'll have to remove the officer's memory of the tranquilizer and tell someone in the emergency room that he became ill. Hopefully it will be enough so he won't lose his job."

"Should I go with you?" Ritter asked. "Or Jace?"

She shook her head. "Marco and I can handle it. The Emporium doesn't know where we're heading, and if I sense anyone nearby, we know how to avoid them." Her sensing ability might not be evolving as mine was, but she had three centuries of experience that I envied.

Marco was already walking to the driver's side of the ambulance, his dark hair and olive skin blending into the night. He looked to either side as he moved, his eyes constantly roving.

The man might be mortal, but his time in black ops with the government had made him as tough as they came.

"Will Stella be able to get a hold of that video recording from the hotel?" I asked. "If not, our faces will probably be plastered on the late evening news." Whatever happened at the hospital, there were going to be questions at our disappearance.

Ava gave a short laugh. "I'm betting the Emporium will get to it before we do. They have just as much at stake and a lot more plants in the police department." She turned and strode after Marco.

"We can't wait any longer," Dimitri said as I climbed into the back of the van. He was slathering his arms with antiseptic, his jaw twitching in exactly the same way mine did when I was forced to confront something I wanted to reject. "I'll have to put a clamp on that artery. We're lucky it was only partially severed or he'd be dead already. Erin, help me take off his shirt. Cort, I'll need some of your blood. You're the same type, right? You others, stand guard. If they come on us now, we're sitting ducks."

"Jace, get ready to start the van on my signal." Ritter pulled an automatic rifle from the back of the van and stalked to the end of the street. Jace grabbed another gun and went to stand halfway between the van and Ritter.

I couldn't sense anything suspicious nearby, so I dropped my blanket and grabbed a pair of scissors from my supplies and began cutting Keene's shirt, keeping pressure with one hand on the cloth over his wound. A sort of desperateness crept over me. I felt guilty that he might die of a wound that in the rest of us would eventually heal by itself. Removing the shirt revealed an ugly scar curving from Keene's left kidney to the middle of his chest. I'd seen it once before, but I hadn't learned the details of what had happened, only that it had occurred in a fight with the Renegades when he'd worked for the Emporium. It was a wonder he'd survived. After tonight, he'd have more scars to add to his collection.

Cort had grabbed two needles from the supplies I'd brought.

In seconds, he had a makeshift infusion taking blood from his arm into a bag, which in turn filtered down to Keene.

Dimitri injected Keene with a sedative before removing my hands and the cloth from his wound. "Dab away as much blood as you can," he told me, "but don't be too concerned. I'll be working mostly through my gift not sight. For now I'll clamp it off and stitch it up once we arrive. Get ready to let the others know when to go. This shouldn't take long."

He cut the wound open another two inches and sank his fingers inside. He wasn't wearing gloves and I remembered that he needed direct contact for his gift to work best. I understood because my ability was enhanced the same way. I watched in gruesome fascination as he delved inside Keene's stomach, at one point closing his eyes.

"There it is. Hand me that clamp."

I ripped open the top of the package and held it out on my palm. The clamp disappeared inside Keene's body.

"Let's go," Dimitri said, his bloodied hands spread over the wound. "Put the blanket on him and tell the others. Jace needs to turn up the van heater as high as it will go."

"Is he going to be okay?" Cort's worry seemed to deepen his physical resemblance to his brother, though his hair was shorter and his eyes a piercing blue instead of green. He was also a little on the nerdy side in his demeanor and dress, an oddity when his assurance rivaled that of any other Unbounded.

Dimitri's face was grim. "I'm doing everything I can."

If Cort made a response to Dimitri, I didn't hear it as I jumped from the van and called to Jace. As with many Unbounded abilities, healers had limits. They couldn't repair mortal organs damaged beyond repair, though they could often keep the person alive until a replacement organ was found. They couldn't heal instantly or bring back the dead, but they could slow bleeding, immediately pinpoint a problem, and repair damage in the most efficient way. Most healers chose to become medical doctors, their talent enhanced further by study. I hoped tonight all of it together would be enough.

Moments later, we were once again careening through the streets, this time with Jace at the wheel. What had the night accomplished? For the moment it all seemed useless. I knew we'd uncovered some important information, but was it worth Keene's life?

Not to me it wasn't.

But we had a duty to humanity, as Keene would be the first to remind me. I placed my hand on his cheek. *Live,* I told him. *Please.*

CHAPTER 4

THE SAFE HOUSE WAS AN OLDER BUILDING LOCATED AT THE NORTH edge of Midtown Manhattan and was one the New York Renegades had renovated. As this had been accomplished after one of our own had leaked information about our other safe houses to the Emporium and betrayed us during a worldwide gathering of Renegades, we were fairly certain the Emporium had no hint of our presence here.

The Emporium had slaughtered twenty of our people in the aftermath of that devastating betrayal. They'd had a sensing Unbounded with them to identify their victims' natures because the eleven dead mortals had been shot or stabbed through the heart, but each of the nine murdered Unbounded had been cut so that their focus points were severed from each other: the brain, the heart, and the reproductive organs. That was the most efficient way to permanently kill Unbounded. It had been an inconceivable horror, a bloodbath the New York police had no way of explaining. One that still haunted me—haunted us all.

That the betrayer had been a member of our small group and Dimitri's direct descendent made us all feel responsible for the loss.

Five other Unbounded Renegades had gone missing at the time of the slaughter, prisoners to the Emporium. Two had belonged to the New York group and three from other groups in Europe. To help the depleted New York group recover the prisoners was the primary reason we were here now. Their location wasn't the only information on the thumb drive we'd stolen in Mexico, but it was the most urgent.

Jace drove into a driveway leading to a garage under the building and punched in a code on a small panel. Everyone remained tense and alert until the doors closed behind us. We screeched to a stop near the elevators, and Ritter had the back doors of the van open before the sound of the engine died. Holding my blanket once more around my shoulders, I jumped down. Pain radiated from my wounded arm, but it would heal soon enough.

Stella emerged from the elevators as we approached, her neural headset blinking, though the eyepiece on the headset was twisted upward so both her dark eyes were visible. She was also wearing the wireless booster and the small power pack, a signal that she was still connected to her computers on the next floor. The slender, delicately boned woman was our link to the outside world, her ability as a technopath allowing her to compute and sort data at a rate I could only begin to comprehend. Most of the monitoring we did of the world's communication systems we accomplished through her and several other Renegade technopaths living in Europe. They warned us of possible Emporium activity, researched leads, created false IDs and backgrounds, and were currently dissecting the rest of the information from the stolen thumb drive. Stella was half Japanese and half Italian, the Japanese side considerably more prominent, and the third great-aunt and fifth great-aunt of our two newest Unbounded. She was also the most incredibly beautiful woman I had ever personally known. That her beauty was enhanced by nanites she, as a technopath, used to constantly adjust her appearance was nothing short of miraculous.

"The infirmary is ready," she said.

"I'm going to need an assistant." Dimitri walked beside the gurney, his hand under the blanket near Keene's wound. "Cort?"

"Of course." His scientific ability to decipher patterns at the atomic level made him the best choice, regardless of his relationship to Keene.

"I'll come, too." This from Ritter, and his concern for Keene surprised me.

"Ava's on her way," Stella told us as we squeezed into the elevator. "She called Tenika so we can talk about where to go from here. We have to figure out what the Emporium is planning. I can't believe Patrick Mann is Unbounded. How did we miss that?"

"Because Washington has been under Tenika's group," Dimitri said, "and they don't have a sensing Unbounded."

"But still." Stella shook her head.

"We'll have to take him out," Jace said. For once no one corrected him.

The elevator opened on the second floor, where Dimitri, Ritter, and Cort wheeled Keene into the hallway. I started to follow, but Stella put her hand on my arm. "Let them go. You're upset, and I think Keene will do better if you aren't there telegraphing your worry."

Jace nodded. "She's right. They'll let us know when the surgery is over."

I had my shield up, so I didn't think my feelings would bother Keene or anyone else, but there was nothing I could do in the infirmary that the others couldn't do better. "Okay, fine."

We rode down to the first floor and headed to the conference room. "I just heard from your brother," Stella said to us, seating herself at the long table in front of four computers. One was a laptop, two were personal computers, and the fourth was a hard drive hooked up to a large new monitor on the wall, a state-of-the-art gift from a local mortal ally. The computers were linked so Stella could interface with them all at once using the neural headset.

"Oh, what did Chris have to say?" Jace sat beside her but

almost immediately bounced up again to pace. Energy seeped from him like steam from a pressure cooker. He'd need to work off some of that energy tonight or his combat ability would drive him insane. Normally I'd take him up to the gym on the fourth floor and spar with him, but I felt exhausted. Besides, I wanted to think about what I'd learned tonight and what it meant for the Renegades. Sinking onto the nearest chair opposite Stella, I upped my absorption rate. Unbounded didn't need to eat, but I seemed to be craving something.

"He was just reporting on the refurbishing of the safe house." Stella glanced at her computers longingly but sat back in her chair and folded her arms over her stomach. "Actually, I think he called to make sure you two got out of the hotel safely."

Jace laughed. "Sounds like our big brother."

"Anyway, now that Benito's back on his feet," Stella continued, "they're moving right along, especially in mapping the underground tunnels. The more Chris tells me about it, the more I'm sure this will be a good move for all of us."

I hoped so. After our last safe house had been compromised, we'd made a pact to create someplace safe for Chris's two young children. The house in San Diego was one Ava and the others had abandoned over fifty years ago when the Emporium had stepped up activity in the area. Now, with modern technology and surveillance methods, we'd all agreed it was our best option for a permanent residence. The Emporium might eventually discover its location, but by then the safe house would be impenetrable by anything short of bombing—and that would attract worldwide notice.

"It'll be nice to put down some roots for a while," Stella added. "We've been moving around too much these past few years."

"I'm just glad Chris is somewhere safe," I said. At first Chris had protested at being kept out of the rescue attempt in New York, but he was mortal and I'd been grateful to keep him and our recently hired maintenance man, Benito Hernández, out of the line of fire for a while. With two of our former black ops employees providing security, they were as safe there as anyone connected with the Unbounded could be. I pulled the blanket tighter around me. "It's a bonus that San Diego is warm."

"You can say that again." Jace continued pacing as silence fell over the room.

How was it going with Keene? I wanted to go upstairs and check, but my backside seemed rooted to the chair. Besides, I'd only be in the way. Better to focus on something I could do. "So what do we know?" I asked, ignoring the urge to lay my head on the table.

Stella gazed at me and blinked. "You sounded just like Ava there for a moment."

I grinned. "Well?"

Sitting up, Stella plugged a cord into her neural headset and twisted down the eyepiece. "First, the vice president's son being an Emporium agent came as a total surprise." Words began scrolling on the large wall screen but ran too fast for me to read them. "Often when the Emporium is working to get someone into politics, we can catch them while they're still in the stage of creating backgrounds that will withstand scrutiny. It's an involved process, but they have enough technopaths to make it possible. Usually identities are created years before they need them. So for instance, when they can no longer hide that an Emporium senator isn't aging, they have him retire, fake his death, whatever, only to have him resurrect some years later in disguise under the new identity. We try to expose new identities whenever we find out they're being created, but the Emporium has a growing number of agents in high positions."

"To what end?" Jace asked.

Stella frowned, taking her eyes briefly from the monitor. "Sorry, I forget there's still so much of this you two don't know. We're pretty sure their goal is revealing the existence of Unbounded to the world, but only once they have enough votes to effectively run the country. Since we know their ultimate idea of utopia is to create a world where Unbounded form a caste system supported by a mortal workforce, we've been fighting against this. At the same time, we can't preempt them and announce our presence to the world and elicit help from the mortals without having certain safety measures in place to protect all of us from the violence we believe will ensue. We aren't there yet."

"Patrick Mann could eventually become president." My arm was hurting again, and I laid it on the table, holding the blanket tightly over it. "Especially with Emporium support. He seems to be following in his father's footsteps." I hoped Unbounded could make their announcement to the world sooner rather than later, but I'd seen enough of the Emporium's hunger for power to worry about this new development.

"That's exactly the problem," Stella agreed. "With that kind of influence, he could change a lot—health care, taxes, presidential term limits. But what's bothering me at the moment is that he can't be one of those false identities the Emporium set up—he's too prominently in the public view for that—and there are absolutely no Unbounded genes in the vice president's ancestry. Or in his wife's. And there's no sign of record tampering or of adoption. Patrick Mann can't be Unbounded."

"Yet he is." Jace finally sat across from me.

"So that means," I said, "the Emporium must have doctored their genealogy records too far back for you to trace and set their family on the political trail in the hope they would someday come to power. Either that or they've figured out a way to create new Unbounded."

Stella shook her head. "Not necessarily. If the Manns underwent fertility, the Emporium could have tampered with the sperm."

"You have a point." That was how I'd become Unbounded. My brother, too, though he was still unaware of it.

"They could have also killed the real Patrick Mann and had someone take his place," Jace put in.

"Uh, his parents probably would have noticed that." I took my hand from the blanket over my wound long enough to knead a pounding in my left temple. "Even if the Emporium had a sensing

Unbounded remove memories of Patrick when the Manns were unconscious, they couldn't cover a lifetime of memory gaps. And there's nothing in his parents' minds that doubts Patrick's identity."

Stella's attention wandered back to the screen. "I'm going to keep looking, but if it turns out the Emporium has figured out a way to create new Unbounded, or to impregnate women in prominent political families, Patrick Mann might not be the only one we need to find. Hopefully by the time Ava gets here with Tenika, we can come up with some idea as to what we should do next."

That's right. I vaguely remembered Stella saying something earlier about Ava bringing the leader of the New York Renegades back with her. I rubbed my face, feeling cold despite the blanket.

Stella looked up at the door, though I hadn't heard or felt anyone coming. "Ah, there you are, Ritter," she said. "How's Keene?"

"Good, now that Dimitri's given him the antidote for the poison that was on the knife."

"Stinking Emporium bastards," Jace muttered.

Stella cocked her head in apparent interest. "Was it one of the poisons I found listed on the thumb drive?"

"Yes. Lucky for Keene we already had the antidote." Ritter came around beside me and pulled out a chair, placing a syringe with a needle on the table, followed by a mound of gauze and a roll of medical tape. He reached for my blanket, but I pulled back so he couldn't take it away.

"Hey, it's cold in here."

"No, it's not." He tugged off the blanket, his eyes going to my wound.

Odd that it was still drizzling blood.

"See that green tinge around the edges?" Ritter asked. "That's from the poison. Not something that would kill you, of course, but it's going to prevent healing for a good long time. Fortunately, we have something better than an antidote." He mopped up the wet blood and began injecting the clear substance we called curequick, a sugar-based substance containing proteins reduced to their most usable form, which sped up even our accelerated healing by as much as five times. Eight different injections went into my flesh around the slash that looked more gruesome than I remembered at the hotel. His hands were gentle, but the needle felt like fire.

"You should give her the antidote as well," Jace said, coming over to watch.

"It's mixed in." Ritter finished and mopped up more blood before taping a patch of gauze over the wound. "You should be feeling better in a bit."

"Why don't we get you upstairs to change before Ava arrives?" Stella removed her headset and placed it on the table. The numerous metal protrusions on the bottom and inside, usually hidden by her smooth dark hair, gleamed brightly under the light.

"I'll take her." Ritter stood, looking far taller than I recalled. And why had he suddenly started swaying back and forth?

"Good idea." There was laughter in Stella's voice. "She looks like she might pass out."

Ritter leaned over. "Want me to carry you?"

"I'm fine." I stood, my scowl daring Ritter to try.

"I can see that." His eyes traveled down the length of my body and the scrap of red that hugged my breasts and waist like a second skin, flaring at my hips. His emotions burned and heat flushed through me.

Just the buzz from the curequick, I told myself. The substance was as addictive as narcotics for Unbounded, and I tried to avoid using it on a regular basis.

Ritter moved his arm in a sweeping motion toward the door. "After you, then." His lips twitched and I stifled an urge to smack him.

I didn't really want to hit him, but given the Unbounded rate of reproduction and likelihood of mortal offspring—not to mention his old-fashioned ideas of commitment—anything else might lead to frustration or an obligation I wasn't prepared for.

"Don't be too long," Stella called after us. She'd already replaced her headset.

Ritter paused at the door. "Jace," he said, "go to the gym. Take the stairs. Work through your forms—all of them—and hurry back down. Or you'll be no good to us."

"But I—"

"Now." Ritter's voice left no argument.

I was already moving to the elevator when Jace sprinted by me and disappeared through the door to the stairs. "Thanks," I told Ritter, as the elevator doors slid open. "He's strung tight." I wasn't sure if it was the poison or his care of my brother that made me feel weepy.

"Not his fault. It's hard not to be in the action."

He meant for someone with the combat ability, but in that instant his words took on quite another meaning. Decisions loomed in our future, but there had been no real time to work anything out. We'd been alone only a total of two times in the past three weeks. Plus Keene had been around. Or was that an excuse? The leader of the New York Renegades was a psychologist. Maybe I should ask her.

"You feeling better?" His voice was gentle, almost a caress that made my breath catch.

"Yeah." Thankfully, the fog did seem to be trickling away. "Strong stuff, whatever was on that knife." The elevator dinged as it reached the third floor where we had our living quarters. I moved through the doors before him.

"Enough poison to incapacitate even us for a time. Takes a bit to start working. It increases bleeding—that's why Dimitri had to clamp off Keene's artery." He shook his head. "I've seen Dimitri prevent a man with a severed leg from bleeding out with only a couple of rags and his touch alone, but poison complicates things. Keene must have gotten a lot of it."

The thought chilled me and I stopped walking. "He's going to be okay, though, right?"

Ritter's eyes wandered over my face, as if searching for hidden innuendo. "I'm predicting he'll be up by tomorrow, annoying the hell out of me as he always does."

I started walking again, falling silent. The carpet felt sensual on my bare feet, or maybe that was the way Ritter was looking at my legs. I stopped again, turning to him. Now probably wasn't the time for relationship dialogue, but would there be a better one? The last three weeks didn't seem to indicate there would be.

I realized I'd stopped outside my own room when he reached past me to a door, his bare arm brushing mine and sending a jolt of current rushing through my veins. He pushed the door open and crossed the bedroom to my adjoining bathroom as though he'd been here many times before, which he hadn't. Not yet. Taking a towel from the rack, he wet it and came toward me. "Come sit down. Let me see that arm."

I followed him wordlessly to the couch that sprawled before the flat screen television on the wall. A television I'd never even turned on. He sat next to me, reaching for my arm. The towel felt warm and slightly rough on my skin as he wiped off the dried blood.

My body suddenly felt heavy, and I settled back on the cushions, letting my eyes close halfway. It felt good being close to him, having him take care of me. Even the pain created by the pressure of the towel somehow added to the sweetness of his touch. I wanted to curl up next to him and sleep for the next hundred years.

"Tough night," Ritter commented, amusement in his voice. It was a tone I hadn't heard enough of these past few weeks.

I opened my eyes and found him watching me. My stomach turned in anticipation. "It was all going fine until Edgel and his poisoned knife. He was going to take me to Delia." I hated the way my voice wavered on her name.

Ritter dropped the towel to the carpet, his eyes holding mine. "I would never have stopped until I found you," he said, the timbre of his voice going deeper.

I knew that. The connection between us was too strong for me to pretend otherwise. At least to myself. That didn't mean I had to admit it to him. "You might have found me too late." I looked down at my hands, stifling a shudder.

"You're stronger than you know. And getting stronger."

My eyes snapped to his. "How did you know?" I hadn't told anyone but Ava about my growing abilities particularly because I didn't want the others to be wary of me. Ava had shared the information with Cort and asked him to create some experiments that would be able to scientifically measure my progress, but no one else should know.

He grinned, resting his hands on his knees as he angled toward me. "Part of my ability is to measure an opponent's strength. That way I know who to attack first. Your strength has grown."

Yes. When I was fighting the Asian and using Edgel's combat ability, I'd known all along that Edgel was the greater challenge and that I couldn't beat him.

"It would also help," Ritter added with a hint of mockery, "if you stopped doing things before people ask. Like passing the salt at dinner or answering a question before they finish speaking."

I sat up rigidly, hurrying to explain. "Surface thoughts come to me now without trying, and I've been able to break through mental barriers, even some strong ones." I hesitated. "Not our people. Not without permission."

He gave a quick shake of his head, furrows appearing on his forehead. "You're thinking about this all wrong. Maybe you can use this to teach us to create stronger shields. The Emporium has at least two sensing Unbounded, and they could have more. They've been breeding for it. Ava doesn't believe they can penetrate our shields yet, but they could be training to do so. Like you have."

Leave it to Ritter to see my ability as a defensive weapon for everyone. He was right, though. "Okay, I'll work on the shield thing," I muttered. "But you sure have a way of destroying the mood."

His left eyebrow arched. "There was a mood?" The teasing was back in his voice.

"I was definitely feeling it." My words were a challenge, one I knew he couldn't resist.

He scooted over, closing the space between us. "I think I can do something about that."

"Oh? Is that your ability talking? Because I didn't know mood fell under the combat instinct."

"With you it does." His lips came down on mine and despite my exhaustion, I pushed closer, opening my mouth to his pressure. His hands ran down my back, the thin material of my dress feeling almost nonexistent. I rubbed my hands along his chest, letting them slide around to his back. The desire in our minds melded into one thought.

It was crazy to feel safe in his arms when everything was uncertain between us, but I did. He wanted to be here holding me more than anywhere else, and I wanted the same. The issue of fertility and two thousand years of posterity didn't matter for the moment.

After a long while, we drew away. I felt stronger and oddly content as I arose from the couch, my lips tingling from his kiss. "I'd better change before Ava comes back."

His eyes took in the stains on my dress. "Do you need help?" He sounded almost hopeful.

I turned my back to him. "You could undo the zipper."

He stood and unzipped it steadily, trailing his finger down the opening, infusing my skin with heat.

"Ritter . . ." I swallowed hard, turning toward him.

He grinned, as though my obvious reaction amused him. "Erin . . . I . . . we—look, I have something for you." His uncharacteristic hesitancy sparked my curiosity. "I'll get it and come back to walk you down." He was already moving away with the grace and speed that came from his ability. He was so beautiful that I wanted to call him back, but I decided I was more interested in what he wanted to show me.

Having no time for a proper shower, I used two precious minutes to rinse off, keeping a towel over my wound to protect it from any spray. What was it Ritter had for me? The memory of his touch was almost as powerful as the actual experience and it made me want to linger in the water.

After drying off, I slipped on what I called my catwoman suit, especially designed by Stella for carrying numerous weapons. This one was sleeveless and worse for wear, but Stella had others on order for me. I zipped the front up all the way, frowning at the bit of cleavage still exposed. Stella was a romantic at heart.

Next, I tied my ancient machete and scabbard around my waist. There was a pocket for the machete in my suit, but since I'd be wearing a coat anyway in this freezing New York weather, the leather tie would keep it handy. I'd gone through a lot to retrieve this weapon a native had given me in the Mexican jungle, and I wore it every chance I got. It was easier to carry—and sometimes more useful—than the swords the others strapped to their backs whenever there was a possibility of meeting Emporium agents. Besides, there was a legend attached to it, that if stolen, it would turn on the thief, becoming the object of his demise. I didn't exactly believe it, but the last two people who'd stolen it had been killed, helped to their doom in a large part by the machete.

Then I put on my ballistic knife and my nine mil Sig. I didn't know if I'd be heading back to the Emporium compound tonight, or if Ava had something else in mind, but it paid to be ready. Thankfully, my interlude with Ritter had returned my strength. Well, either that or the curequick.

I'd finished restocking my other knives and was strapping on my backup pistol when Ritter rapped on the door. I could feel him there waiting, his body tense. Swallowing hard, I pulled on my calf-length leather coat and strode to the door. *Don't get distracted,* I told myself. I'd felt two new life forces enter the building as I'd dressed, and I knew Ava would be waiting.

My plan to hurry faltered as I came face-to-face with gleaming metal. Ritter held two three-prong weapons, one in each hand. The middle blade was a foot long, the handle another six inches, and two side blades curved up and out on either side of the main blade, about four inches each.

I was fascinated. "What are these?" They reminded me roughly of a trident without the long handle.

"They're called sai." Ritter lowered the weapons several inches, my eyes following the movement. "I got these in China a few years ago, and I thought you'd like them."

Was he flushing? My heart lurched, though I wasn't sure why. I knew Ritter had a soft side. He just didn't show it often. What did it mean that the softer side was showing now? No hint came from even his surface emotions, so I knew he'd clamped down on them.

"Now that you have the machete well under way," he said, "it's time for you to master another weapon."

"You mean because you're tired of the machete." It was all we'd been focusing on these past few weeks whenever we weren't watching the Emporium compound.

He laughed. "Maybe a little."

I took one of the weapons, running a finger along it. Ritter did the same with the other. "Notice the edges aren't sharp. Or the point. Sai are used mainly for striking and blocking. The idea is to disarm or repel your opponent so you can get away. They work well against clubs or any stick weapon."

"Like the bo staff?"

He nodded. "It's used for striking, catching, and stabbing. You normally hold it like this." He rotated it so the blade lay along the inside of his arm. "This is for blocking with your arm and for thrusting with the handle. Keep your arm straight or it'll bounce back and hit you. And this"—he slowly pivoted the blade out—"is for striking and for blocking swords and the like. Make sure your fingers aren't still over the guard or they'll be cut off. There's another way to strike and a hold where you use the handle as a sort of hammer, but we won't worry about those right now." He stroked the blade of the one in his hand again before passing it to me.

"They're beautiful. Thank you." I turned to put them in my room, but his hand grabbed at the flap of my long coat.

"They go in these inside pockets. Stella orders all of the coats and jackets with them, but not everyone carries sai. I haven't even trained Jace on them yet, though I know he grabbed some from the armory."

I'd fleetingly wondered what the oddly shaped pockets were for—it wasn't as if I went around looking inside everyone's coats when we were out on duty to check what weapons they carried. The sai fit perfectly, the main blade emerging from a hole in the bottom of the pocket, pointing toward the ground. "Nice."

"Yeah." He opened his black jacket, which was shorter and thinner than my coat but still long enough for his own pair of sai. I could see other bulges in his black clothing, and a sword rose from a back sheath, so apparently he'd taken the time to restock as well. Nothing more attractive than a man dressed to kill.

Silence stretched between us. Ritter opened his mouth, but closed it again without speaking. Was that uneasiness I felt from him? I stifled the urge to push into his mind. Despite his earlier assertions about me helping to strengthen shields, he'd hate the uninvited intrusion.

I broke eye contact first. "I guess we'd better get down there. Ava's in the conference room."

"About time."

"Yeah."

As we hurried to the elevator, I wondered what he'd wanted to say.

CHAPTER 5

THE MEETING WAS WELL ON ITS WAY WITHOUT US WHEN WE ARRIVED in the conference room, with Ava, Dimitri, Stella, and Jace all seated on one side of the table, staring up at the huge screen. A live stream of local news coverage filled one corner, the sound turned low, and the rest was taken up with different websites. Behind our people stood Tenika Vasco, leader of the New York Renegades, a line of worry on her prominent forehead. Tonight, her many small braids were pulled from her face into a large black mass at the nape of her neck, and her dark clothing told me she'd come directly from staking out the Emporium compound.

"Hey, Erin, we're going to be on the news," Jace said, looking up at me. "Or at least what happened at the hotel is going to be. They keep mentioning breaking news and live coverage before every commercial break."

"Great." I really hoped they didn't show any video feed of the attack.

Tenika walked toward us, and it said something for my state of mind that I was glad she was too preoccupied to give Ritter the kiss she normally gave him on the mouth. She simply hit her fist with each of ours in the customary Unbounded greeting, dipping her head in acknowledgment. "I hear you had quite a time tonight." Her voice held the slightest Angolan Portuguese accent.

"It was eventful." My eyes went to Dimitri as I spoke. That he was here had to mean Keene was out of immediate danger.

"Cort's with him." Dimitri answered the question I hadn't voiced. "He'll join us when Keene wakes."

"Maybe we shouldn't have gone tonight," I said.

"Of course we had to." Ava's voice was firm. "There might never have been another chance to get you close enough to the vice president to look into his mind."

Tenika nodded. "I agree."

"So what do we know?" Ava tented her hands on the table.

A smile tugged at Stella's mouth, and I knew she was remembering her earlier comment about me sounding like Ava. "Well, besides the conclusions Jace and I have filled you in on, I think we need to find out what we can about Patrick Mann's birth."

"Agreed," Dimitri said. "We must learn how he got into place, especially when Erin says his parents seem unaware of the whole Unbounded issue."

I took a chair at the head of the conference table where I could still see the screen. Ritter sat kitty-corner next to me with his back toward it.

"If they've done it once," Ava began. She didn't need to finish. However the Emporium had accomplished Patrick's positioning, we all realized it wouldn't be an isolated incident.

Tenika paced a few steps, her lean body and tight movements betraying centuries of training. Her ability wasn't combat, but I wouldn't want to meet her in battle alone on a dark street. "My biggest concern is getting my people back from the Emporium."

Before the slaughter, Tenika's group had been the largest organization of Renegades in the world. They'd had fourteen Unbounded and a dozen mortal family members and employees. They lost fifteen people the night of the slaughter, five of them Unbounded. Our visiting European allies lost four more

Unbounded and one mortal. Twenty people in all. By piecing together the remains found at the scene, Tenika discovered that five of the lost Unbounded hadn't been killed, two from her group, and we assumed they were the prisoners in the Emporium compound listed on the recovered thumb drive.

She stopped pacing and turned at the foot of the table, leaning over and placing her hands on the gleaming mahogany. "What I haven't told you is that of our seven remaining Unbounded we lost two more that same week."

"What?" Jace interjected. The question could have come from any of us, judging by my own reaction and the surprise on my companions' faces.

Tenika nodded. "It's not what you think. They left on their own—they just needed time away . . . from everything. Both are gifted in combat. One is very young, only a couple centuries, the other over five hundred. Their wives were killed that night. One was expecting. The other had a teenage son, who was also killed. So many deaths. It was hard for all of us."

Standing straight, she pulled back the chair in front of her and sat. "Sometimes people need to distance themselves in order to recover from a traumatic event. I see it all the time in my practice. I know where they are. They haven't removed their transmitters, but they won't come back, not yet. I believe they will eventually. Unfortunately in the meantime, that leaves me with only two Unbounded I can depend consistently on, Yuan-Xin and Eric Halden."

"What about the other two?" Jace asked.

Tenika rubbed her temple. "They have helped where they can. In fact, tonight they're with Eric, Yuan-Xin, and your two new Unbounded watching the compound, but the truth is, their minds are elsewhere. They're gifted in the arts." She smiled, nostalgia entering her voice. "When Chloe dances, you forget everything else exists. And when Noah sings, the tune makes you cry with its beauty. In another age, they would be our blessing, but for the moment, I confess that I worry about protecting them."

Ava put her hand over Tenika's. "You should have told us."

Tenika shrugged. "I thought I had it covered, especially once we had two more of our descendants Change, bringing us back to seven, even without the two who left, but they . . ." A frown grew on her face. "Well, let's just say they lack training."

Tenika was being generous. I'd heard from Yuan-Xin that their newest members were more interested in thrills and close encounters with death than protecting mortals. Hopefully they'd get over themselves soon.

"Anyway," Tenika continued, "this past November we were able to block several Emporium Unbounded from being elected to important political positions here in the east—mostly by uncovering flaws in their fake pasts and alerting the media, but we know for sure at least one was elected. The cover story was too perfect and attacking her openly and planting some false information was beyond our ability."

"It'll get worse if they have more like Patrick Mann," I said.

Tenika blew out a long breath. "Yes, but let's not assume anything yet. I believe if we can free our people, they will be enough to keep us active here in the east. Their return may even be enough to bring the others home."

"We all agree that freeing them is of primary importance," Ava said, "but so far the odds have been too great that we'll lose more than we'll gain. We must do this at a minimum cost to both our groups. That means waiting for the right opportunity."

Ritter spoke for the first time. "I think I may have a plan, but I need another day or so to work out the details. You know me, Tenika, and I assure you that freeing them is my first concern. Your people are our people. We work together. It has always been that way."

Tenika inclined her head. "Thank you. Yuan-Xin did tell me you were considering a new option, and perhaps these developments tonight will help us find a solution. Maybe even give us some leverage against the Emporium."

"What about long term?" Ava said. "We're moving far too

slowly getting our own people into place. When we eventually do announce our presence to the world, we'll need a face, someone people can trust. At my last count we have fewer than a dozen Renegade sympathizers in prominent political positions. That's not enough. And none are Unbounded so they couldn't be the face for our cause."

Sorrow crossed Tenika's features. "We'd have three Unbounded in place if not for the massacre. I really don't know what we can do about that right now, but there's a limit to the shootouts and murders we can continue attributing to the drug world or gang activity. Between the Hunters and our battles with the Emporium, we've already drawn too much suspicion. Especially after the slaughter of our people. Throwing down a couple packets of drugs and known gang paraphernalia didn't begin to cover it up. Nearly all of us were questioned and it was only my hypnosuggestion that prevented police from making a more thorough investigation. We should lie low for at least another three months, but I don't see how that's possible as long as the Emporium have our people."

Ava put one elbow on the table and tapped her finger on her lips. For the space of several long seconds no one spoke. "Okay," she said finally, "this is what I propose. Dimitri and I will visit the medical facility in . . ." She looked at Stella.

"Worcester, Massachusetts," Stella supplied.

Ava nodded. "It'll take some doing, but we'll come up with some reason to hold a medical consult with personnel who were there at the time of Patrick Mann's birth. We'll probably have to track those who've left or retired to wherever they are now. Once we get close enough, I should be able to learn something from their minds, even if they don't tell us willingly. Stella, you may have to break into their records as well."

"I've already tried," she said. "I think I'll have to do it from the inside. Even for a hospital, they're paranoid."

"That works in our favor most of the time." Dimitri took out his phone and began touching the screen. "I bet I can find someone who can get us an introduction." He shook his head.

"Or at least get us an introduction to someone who can get us an introduction."

Having worked in many hospitals all over the country under several different identities, I was sure he could do better than that.

"Good," Ava said. "Ritter, you will continue to work with Yuan-Xin to plan the rescue of our people. You'll have everyone except—"

"Wait," Jace interrupted, gesturing toward the big screen. "Turn it up, Stella. This is the interview they've been promising. Better record it." We all turned our attention to the screen, Ritter pivoting his entire body.

"Hey, that's Patrick Mann," I said.

Someone at the news station had pull if they could get an interview with the son of the vice president on such short notice. Or maybe he was trying to further his political career and had gone looking for the publicity.

On screen, he appeared like any other confident, attractive man. Nothing told me he was Unbounded. For my ability to work, the subject had to be in view, and it was odd seeing him as others did, looking like an ordinary mortal.

"So we understand there was a commotion at your father's fundraising event tonight," the blonde reporter said, smiling at Patrick as though she considered him the most important person at the event. "What can you tell us?"

Patrick shook his head. "Unfortunately, not much. There was an altercation in a hallway at the hotel, and some people were taken to the hospital."

"We understand there were weapons involved. How did those get past the tight security?"

"I'm sorry. I can't speak to that." His pursed lips radiated disapproval.

"Any clue as to the identity of the people involved?"

"None." Patrick shook his head solemnly. "Apparently there was some interference in the camera feed for that hallway in the hotel. I understand that's under investigation now."

I grinned. The Emporium was certainly quick at covering up their messes.

The reporter hesitated a dramatic moment before saying, "Was the vice president in any danger at all during the course of the evening?"

"That's uncertain. Everyone in town knew my father would be present tonight, so my feeling is that he may have been the target." Patrick flashed a tight smile. "But whatever these people wanted, they didn't succeed. My father is safe and ready to continue his job, as always."

"That's good to hear." The reporter nodded as if any other vice president would have tendered his resignation. "How does it feel to know your father could have been in danger?"

Patrick looked directly into the camera. "Well, we knew when he took office that the American people came first. This won't change anything. His family is behind him one hundred percent."

"Thank you for your very valuable time," the reporter said. "Please give our best to Vice President Mann."

The scene switched back to the news anchors, and Stella lowered the sound.

"Smart," Tenika said. "Creating sympathy and a feeling of outrage for the vice president, even though he was nowhere near the attack."

"If President Stevens really is sick," I put in, "this will smooth the way for the vice president to step in for him until he's able."

"If he's ever able," Jace muttered.

Something shifted inside me. "Do you think that's part of the plan? To get the vice president in control even before the next election?"

"I don't see how that would help the Emporium," Ava said with a frown. "The vice president doesn't appear to be connected with them. And with all the protection President Stevens has, how could they have made him sick?"

"There are ways," Dimitri said. "Poisons that can't be detected. Or an Unbounded healer who damages instead of heals." His dark expression told all of us what he thought about that idea. "Maybe the vice president isn't connected with the Emporium but has his own agenda."

I shook my head. "I saw nothing like that in his mind. Or in anyone around him."

"Not even Patrick Mann?" asked Ritter, his black eyes meeting mine.

"No. But I did learn something odd about Patrick." I recounted finding the shiny, black cord in the sand stream of his thoughts. "It reminded me of a snake, and it was definitely put there by Delia Vesey."

"Show me what it looked like," Ava said.

Opening my shield to her, I pictured it. After a moment, she nodded. "I've heard of this. It's called a binding. With bindings, a sensing Unbounded can place important information in someone's mind, either to pass it on to another sensing Unbounded or to hide important secrets from anyone who might break through a mental shield." Her gray eyes, so like my own, became troubled. "It worries me to see this now. There haven't been Unbounded who can break through shields for many years, so what's the point?"

She hesitated, her eyes meeting mine. She knew I could break through some shields, but there wasn't any way the Emporium could know it, so this could only mean they'd discovered for themselves it was possible.

"I can create something like that in myself," Ava continued, "but I wouldn't know how to go about doing it in someone else. Not without damaging them."

"Maybe that's the point," I said. "I can't see Delia worrying too much about damage to someone else."

Ava inclined her head in agreement. "The Emporium has never concerned itself too much with the individual. You were wise not to attempt penetrating it. There's no telling what might have happened. Although, maybe it's a new application of an old concept. Something different altogether." Silently she added for me alone, *We know Delia recognized your potential when you were captured by the Emporium. This might be connected. She'll not stay away from you long. She won't let you grow too powerful.*

Normally, I would have tried to show Ava my confidence, but it was a little shaky where Delia Vesey was concerned. The woman was frighteningly powerful.

Ritter's knee touched mine under the table, freeing me from the thought. "We need to find out more about Patrick Mann. The sooner the better."

"Stella, can you play that piece with Patrick Mann again?" Tenika asked. "Maybe there's something we missed."

The playback was halfway through when a black-clad person burst into appearance near the conference room door, wearing a knit face mask. Ritter was up in a blur, his gun ready. But it was only our shifter, Mari Jorgenson, emotions pinging from her in every direction. It had only been a few weeks since her Change, and sometimes she forgot to use her mental shield.

Mari pulled off her mask, revealing a heart-shaped face and black hair winding down her back in a thick braid. She looked more American than Japanese, but she still shared a family resemblance with Stella, her fifth great-aunt. "The Emporium's got another prisoner!" she said. "Another Unbounded. They just brought him to the compound. Yuan-Xin sent me to tell you."

There was more she wasn't saying, particularly that she'd been glad to leave because Oliver Parkin, our other newly Changed Unbounded and also Stella's descendent, was being his usual obnoxious, egotistical self. I liked to console myself that if he didn't have such a valuable ability, we'd have tossed him out weeks ago. It wasn't true because Stella had waited too long for someone in her family line to Change, but imagining it sometimes helped. I was glad Stella had Mari, whose childlike enthusiasm made her everyone's favorite.

"Did Yuan-Xin recognize the Unbounded?" Ava asked, coming to her feet.

Mari shook her head and stray hair that had escaped from her braid fell into her dark eyes. "No, but he's Unbounded all right.

We heard the guards talking, and they gave him curequick." Tonic, she meant, the Emporium version of our curequick.

Stella replaced her eyepiece. "I'd better contact all the Renegade groups to see if anyone's missing."

Mari glanced up at the television as Stella turned down the sound. "Maybe he's new."

Ritter shook his head. "They'd be trying to turn him not imprison him. What did he look like?"

Mari's gaze went back to the television interview of Patrick Mann in a belated double-take. "Actually, he looked kind of like *him*."

"When did they bring the prisoner in?" I asked. Could the Emporium have decided that Patrick Mann was a problem? They often turned on their own when it served the greater good.

Mari didn't hesitate, her gift with numbers coming to her as naturally as breathing. "Eleven minutes and forty-two seconds ago. He struggled with them at the gate and that's where they gave him the curequick. They, uh, broke his leg."

I saw it in her mind, the vicious strike and the guard glancing around to see if his comrades objected to what he'd done. The tonic would help the prisoner heal quickly in case anyone at Emporium headquarters was told about the break. It created deniability.

"Then it couldn't be him," I said. "This interview was live and it would have been going on then."

Mari went around the table to take a better look at the screen, where Stella had frozen an image of Patrick Mann. "The mouth is different," Mari said, "and maybe the hair wasn't quite so dark. It was hard to tell with just the street lights. But he did kind of have those features."

"So a white, American-looking guy with blue eyes and brown hair?" Jace said. "That could be anyone."

"Sorry." Mari glanced back up at the screen. "Yuan-Xin or Oliver might be able to tell you more. I was so mad that I wasn't really paying attention to details. I wanted to shift over there and shift out with him, but Yuan-Xin wouldn't let me."

"I wouldn't have either," Ritter said. "You've only been able to shift a few yards with another person and that situation would be far too dangerous. We can't risk you that way."

The Emporium had one aged male shifter, and we all knew they were anxious to breed the ability back into their family lines. Worse, if Delia could use others' abilities the way I could, Mari would be the Emporium's ticket to all kinds of mischief. Few documents or computer files would be safe, no lineage records secure. Assassinations that much easier. Normally shifters could only shift to places they knew, but sometimes they could also shift to people they were close to or had a mental connection with. Mari had so far been able to shift to places unknown only if Dimitri or I was there. Or if I showed her the place in her mind. But I believed it was only a matter of time before she was able to "find" the rest of our group.

Mari blew out a sigh. "I know. I know."

Ava resettled in her chair. "This brings up another issue we need to address. We're all aware of how the Hunters kept genealogical records since before their abandonment by the Emporium. These include connections with Renegade descendants. Lately, they've been researching and finding these extended connections and are watching them to see if they Change. Then they attack to kill. So far we've been lucky to have no casualties, though Keene reported that the Emporium hasn't been so fortunate. While that might be good news for us, we can't allow this to continue, especially as we have several more descendants approaching the age of Change."

As Ava spoke, I was watching Mari, who stood behind Jace, her fists now clenched. Her husband had been a Hunter, sent to watch her for the Change, and he'd betrayed her before being brutally murdered by the Emporium. While she'd rebounded more quickly than anyone imagined possible, there were still nights when she came into my room tortured by nightmares.

I reached out to her mentally, pushing soothing emotions her way without delving into her thoughts. *It's okay. You made it.*

Her eyes flew to mine and her hands relaxed. I refocused on Ava's words.

"That a prominent Hunter," she was saying, "showed up tonight at the fundraiser with an Unbounded is something we can't overlook. If the Emporium has managed to get a plant in that deeply, they may be close to obtaining the Hunter records, which we know they want every bit as much as we do."

"There is another possibility," I said. "I mean, the man had no shield to speak of. He didn't seem Emporium trained."

"He could be new." This from Jace, who could create a tight shield—but couldn't maintain it without repeated effort.

"That could be, but"—I shook my head—"it seemed different somehow. What if this cowboy Hunter is recruiting Unbounded now instead of killing them? He has money and position—that alone is different than most Hunters we deal with. Maybe he's also learned to work differently."

"I can't imagine Hunters overcoming that kind of hatred," Ritter said. "They don't even differentiate between us and the Emporium."

Jace perked up. "Yeah, but if they have their own Unbounded, they could get more of us, right? It's the smart thing to do."

"That's just it. Hunters aren't smart." Ritter paced a few steps. "They're racists, which generally means poor and uneducated. Most of them barely graduate from high school. And those who have gone to college are steeped in so much prejudice that they never see past it."

I leaned back and put my foot on the table, adjusting the left side of my coat so the sai inside lay lengthwise down my upper thigh. "Well, some would call Unbounded racists against mortals, especially Emporium Unbounded." Was I speaking for myself or saying something I knew Keene would say?

Ritter's eyes narrowed. "You know what I mean." His eyes dropped to where I was stroking the leather-wrapped handle of the sai. Satisfaction rushed from him. What did that mean? I pulled my hand away.

"The Hunter's name is Davis Emerson," Stella said, looking up from her laptop. "He was pictured on one of the news blogs. No mistaking that hat or his wife's dress. Not poor by any means, though he was once. He's a self-made man from right here in New York. Born on a small cattle ranch in St. Johnsville about two hundred miles north of here. Married his high school sweetheart after graduation. Only took a few classes at a community college and then worked his way up in the business world creating marketing videos. Barely saved his parents' ranch from repossession. Eventually he hit a couple of lucrative contracts that made him a quick two million. He kept working, got into several fast food franchises, and invested in the stock market the day before it took a huge dive, but the check didn't arrive at the broker's until after the plunge, so he made a lot of money when the market revived. He bought his parents' ranch and four other properties surrounding it."

"Living the American dream," I mused. That explained at least why Mrs. Emerson looked so awkward in her designer dress. "Any children?"

Stella nodded. "Two. Boy and a girl. Thirty and twenty-five respectively."

"I think the girl was there last night," I said. "She had red hair like her dad."

"More Hunters in training." Ava sighed, shaking her head. "That brings me to the next assignment. Erin, I want you to take the night off. Get some rest." She meant no going to the rooftop, as was my nightly custom, to see how much further I could push my thoughts, all the while beating back my acrophobia. "Tomorrow morning," she continued, "I want you and Mari to find the Emersons and feel them out. Even if the Unbounded bodyguard is with the Emporium, he didn't seem to recognize you as a Renegade, so there's no reason for you not to go. In fact, it might become an opportunity to set you up with a cover inside the Hunter organization that we can use later."

"But Mari's in their records."

"Only as a descendent. They don't know that she Changed." Ava rubbed her chin in thought. "But it might be good for her to go in disguise anyway."

"I always wanted to try being a blonde," Mari said, "and there are some really cool glasses in our costume boxes."

"Maybe Keene can set up a meeting with Emerson using some of his Hunter contacts, assuming his cover is still intact and that he's well enough." Ava glanced at Dimitri as she spoke.

He shrugged. "The poison is out and the bleeding stopped. I stitched the slashed artery and healed it as much as I could. He should be able to do some calling at least."

"Good." Ava's gaze now swung toward Ritter. "As I was saying earlier, you will have everyone else, including Tenika and her people. Freeing our Renegades remains the priority. If you need any more help, just ask and we'll juggle the other assignments."

"But shouldn't I go with Erin and Mari tomorrow?" Jace asked. "What if there's fighting? Erin and I together are unbeatable."

Ritter arched a brow, but he didn't challenge Jace's assertion. "A fight is exactly why she's sending Mari. If they run into anything Erin can't handle, Erin can channel Mari's ability and the two of them can shift out." Funny how he said the words and I could tell he wanted to believe them, but his vivid surface emotions told me he was more worried than he let on about what happened tonight. Whatever his feelings, he'd better not go all macho on me, and insist on coming with me himself.

"We won't need to shift." For the moment at least, I felt perfectly confident of my own ability against so few Hunters and only one Unbounded. And as Ritter had said, Mari and I could always shift out.

"So do we all know what we're going to do?" Ava asked. "Questions?" Heads shook as we all arose. Everyone but Stella, who was busy with her computers once again.

"I'm heading back to the compound now," Ritter said. "You up to it, Jace?" It wasn't really a question. Even after going through his forms, Jace was so tense that everyone could see it.

My brother nodded. "Oh, yeah. I can't wait to hear about this idea of yours. But do me a favor, huh? Send Oliver home. Another night of listening to his whining might be more excitement than I can take."

Ava stifled a sigh, but I could see it on her face. "Don't worry," Dimitri said, a hand on her shoulder. "It's nothing that won't resolve itself in a hundred years."

"Yeah," she replied, "we just have to make sure we all stay alive that long."

CHAPTER 6

"THE BEST THING ABOUT TODAY," MARI SAID AS SHE AND I RODE the elevator down to breakfast the next morning, "is that Oliver isn't going with us. Growing up I longed for cousins, but since meeting him, I take it all back."

"Well, you've got all of us now, especially Stella."

The elevator opened, and the delicious smell of bacon pulled us along to the dining room. Our cook, Janice, provided a nice buffet breakfast every morning at six, right after our morning workout. Technically no Unbounded needed food because absorbing gave us all the nutrients and calories we required, but sitting down to eat with the mortals in our group had become a ritual, one that bound us together more tightly and created a sense of normalcy that was missing from our lives.

Besides, I loved the taste of waffles with syrup.

Today, with three of our mortal employees in California and Marco still watching the Emporium compound with Ritter and Jace, only a few of us—all Unbounded—were present. I'd taken longer than expected in the shower, and Ava, Dimitri, and Stella were already finishing their meal when Mari and I entered.

Stella came to stand with me by the buffet as I picked up a plate. She looked the perfect business woman in her crisp, black pin-striped suit that couldn't hide her slender curves.

"Dimitri told me you did well with the sai this morning. Well enough that you should keep them on you."

"I have them." I opened my long coat and showed them to her. Today I wore black skinny jeans that I'd dressed up with a silky blue top and high heeled boots in deference to a possible meeting with the Emersons. The outfit wasn't as conducive to battle as my bodysuit, but any weapons I couldn't hide in the boots, my pockets, or under my blouse, were stuffed into inner pouches of my leather coat. That included the sai in their special pockets.

"They're fun," I told Stella. "I thought the dull tips would make them useless, but I took away Dimitri's staff every time."

"Too bad I missed it, but I was doing more research on the Emersons for you. I've forwarded everything you need to know about them to your phone."

"Thanks." I started to close my coat when Stella reached out to touch one of the sai.

"These remind me of the sai Ritter has. We haven't trained with them lately, but that leather wrapping is similar."

"He gave these to me, so maybe that's why they look familiar."

Stella blinked and glanced over her shoulder at the others who were chatting near the dining table. "He *gave* them to you? When?"

"Last night. They're Chinese. Said I needed to train on something new. I think he's tired of my machete." I grinned but Stella didn't return the smile.

"I see."

Her knowing tone annoyed me. Normally I'd let it pass, especially since she was still recovering from losing both her husband and her unborn child, but something about Ritter giving me his sai did seem rather odd. Why hadn't he simply found a pair in the arsenal we always carried with us?

"You see what?" I asked.

She leaned in and took my hands. "Has he given you anything else?"

"A ballistic knife last week. Seems to think I'll do better with that since throwing knives isn't my thing. Why?" I could feel the weight of the knife in my boot. It could shoot an easy eighteen feet at the press of a trigger.

"Is the blade black and does it have a dragon on the hilt?" she asked.

"Yeah. Is that significant?"

"Stella?" Ava called from near the door. "Are you coming? We really should get going if we intend to arrive in Providence on schedule."

That must mean Dimitri had been able to get some kind of appointment. "Wait," I said. "What about the knife?"

Stella squeezed my hands. "We'll talk when I get back. Good luck today. Be careful."

"You, too." I watched them leave.

Mari sauntered toward me. "What was all that about? You and Stella."

"I don't know." I scooped eggs from the warmer onto my plate.

"Are you going to take all those weapons to the Emersons? What if they ask for your coat?"

"First of all, we don't know we're going to wherever the Emersons are staying. Cort said during workout that Keene was still calling. So if we're out stalking the city for them, I want to be prepared."

Mari put five pieces of bacon on her plate. "This is so great. I never used to be able to eat this way. Always worried I'd gain weight."

I took three waffles, and then added a fourth. Why not? I'd work it off in less than half an hour or my body wouldn't absorb any more until the extra calories were gone. A healthy serving of syrup and a glass of fresh orange juice with plenty of pulp topped it all off.

We'd barely sat down when Oliver entered, wearing dark brown pants and a multi-colored button-up shirt with the cuffs open and turned back. His dark face was newly shaven and his curly hair cropped short. Though he also had Asian blood and his mother was half white, his African American heritage was more prominent. He was tall and muscular, a fine specimen of a man—if he didn't open his mouth or if you didn't watch him in training. Even Mari, who was a lot smaller and several weeks newer than he was, could best him.

"Good morning, lovely ladies," he said, strolling to the buffet.

"Aren't you supposed to be back at the compound?" I asked.

He shrugged. "Ritter hasn't called, so I'm waiting."

Mari looked at me and rolled her eyes. By unspoken agreement, we began eating faster. "Maybe I should call Cort and see if Keene has anything for us," I said.

"Good idea." Mari pushed a full strip of bacon into her mouth. "I'm almost finished."

Almost wasn't fast enough, and before long Oliver sat opposite us, his plate loaded. "Girls, I need your opinions."

I groaned internally. When Oliver started asking for our opinion, invariably it would be about women and would gross us out or make us want to kill him. Maybe tomorrow, I'd work out with him. Accidentally slip with the new sai and give him something real to talk about.

"It's Chloe." He stopped talking to shovel in a forkful of eggs, followed by a quarter of a waffle.

Chloe was the New York Unbounded gifted in dancing. I hadn't seen her perform, but I hoped I'd have the opportunity. Some people believed dancing was actually a variation of the combat ability, which in turn was a derivative of one main physical ability. A thousand or more years ago before the worst battles began between the Emporium and the Renegades, the artistic abilities had been highly valued.

I drank my juice and waited until Oliver swallowed.

"A woman like that," he mused, "must have a lot of experience. A hundred years of experience. I wonder if she'd give me lessons."

Dare I ask? Mari beat me to it. "Dancing lessons?"

Oliver shook his head. "I mean in the bedroom. All those admirers and her incredible sex appeal. I'm sure she knows things I've never dreamed of." He leered. "And I'm a pretty good dreamer. Maybe I'd even teach her a thing or two."

"Ooooh!" Mari jumped up from the table. "Every time I even begin to think that you can't stoop any lower, you prove me wrong." She looked at me. "Erin, I'm going to find Cort."

Even as she spoke, Cort appeared in the doorway. He wore nothing but black pants, and his bare chest looked more than twice its real size. His brown hair swept back from his face, and he didn't look nerdy in the least. "Mari, you called?" he said. "Don't worry. I'm here. Yes, I'll give you lessons in the bedroom."

No real emotion emerged from the apparition, and it acted so unlike Cort that Mari and I both knew it was a fake, despite the heady aroma of expensive cologne that the real Cort did wear, though never so much of it.

"Or how about this?" Oliver snapped his fingers and a new Cort replaced the old. This time he was fully dressed, slightly hunchbacked, and wore glasses. His shirt was buttoned clear to the top and his dress pants were a little short. It was Cort as he might have been if he were a contemporary mortal.

"Mari," said the image, not quite meeting her eyes. "Would you . . . uh, consider going out with me?"

With a frustrated growl, a flushed Mari ran past the apparition to the door.

"Come back, come back," the illusion shouted after her. "Please don't leave me!"

I glared at Oliver. "What's that all about? Are you ever going to grow up?"

"Why?" He shrugged. "I have enough time, right? Besides, if she'd only admit to herself that she likes him, it wouldn't bother her."

Mari liked Cort? I wasn't aware of any attraction between them. In the beginning, Jace had tried to flirt with Mari, and she'd rebuffed him. I told him she needed time to mourn her jerk of a husband.

"Don't do it again," I told him.

"Who's going to stop me?" He said it casually, not really a challenge. That he should have such a useful and powerful ability made me furious.

I pushed my thoughts out to him, swiping at his shield, which he'd never completely mastered anyway. *I will*, I said in his mind. I was tempted to do more, to thrust my hands in the stream of his thoughts to warn him, but I hesitated at touching anything. I didn't like Oliver, but I didn't want to damage him permanently.

Now he was glaring at me, and trying to push me out. I smiled. He couldn't get rid of me, and I knew just the way to teach him a lesson, one taught me by the master of control herself, Delia Vesey. I concentrated hard on his hand and it shot out toward the juice, knocking it over.

A horrified expression filled his face. "You!" he said, yanking back his hand.

I nodded. "Yes, me. You aren't the only one with an ability." I wanted to do something more, but I felt guilty already. He was an idiot, but he was our idiot, and I preferred to practice on people who had consented. Besides, I still wanted to try channeling his ability—when he calmed down—and doing so would be easier if he could walk me through how he created his illusions. I had an idea that might help us free our prisoners, if I could get Ritter and Ava to sign off on it.

"Goodbye, Oliver." I pulled my thoughts from his, ignoring the anger. A little humiliation was good for the man. Good for all men, in fact. But I'd probably have to apologize later to gain his cooperation. "Try not to annoy anyone else today."

He brought up his middle finger and flipped me off, a smile plastered on his handsome face.

"How very human of you," I couldn't help saying.

In the hallway, I reached out again, searching for Mari's mental signature. I found her down a floor, probably looking for Keene in the infirmary. But there were no other life forces on that floor. I hurried to the stairs and sprinted down them, taking two at a time. When I emerged, she was already heading back to the elevator.

"Hi, Erin." She didn't quite meet my gaze.

"I think Keene is upstairs in Cort's office."

"I should have checked there first."

I laughed. "No, he should be here, but since he's an idiot, like most men, he's probably not resting."

We'd reached the elevator and she jabbed her finger at the button. "I'd say you pretty much described all Unbounded, not just the men." Her smile returned. "You know, I used to like vacations, but now the idea of sitting around on a beach seems rather dull."

"Give it a few months." Because sitting around on a beach without worrying about what the Emporium was up to sounded like heaven to me.

"Okay. Then maybe we'll go together. Somewhere warm."

I waited until the elevator opened on the third floor to say, "I warned Oliver to keep his trap shut."

Her face whipped to mine. "You threatened him?"

"Kind of." My muscles tightened waiting for her disapproval.

"Oh, Erin. You're the best!" She hugged me before exiting the elevator.

"I don't know about that." I wanted to ask about her and Cort, to know if she really did have a thing for him, but I'd just pay attention and wait for her to come to me. She'd been seriously broken up by her husband's death, and I wasn't about to add to her pain. Hopefully, his betrayal was helping her get over him quickly.

In Cort's office, Keene sat on the shiny brown leather couch, fully dressed in gray jeans and a long-sleeved, white V-necked T-shirt, topped by a gray suede vest. I was relieved to see him looking so well after last night's adventures.

Cort looked up from his desk and cleared his throat. "Ah, there you are."

I took a seat on the couch while Mari ignored the chairs and perched on the arm next to me. "Missed you both at workout this morning," I said.

Cort shrugged. "I did it last night. Couldn't sleep with all the excitement."

"As for me," Keene said with a lazy expression, "I was just playing hooky."

I stifled a smile. "How do you feel?"

"Fine, thanks to Dimitri and Cort." He met my gaze briefly before looking away.

"Should you be up?" Mari asked.

"Well, we have a visit to make, don't we?" Keene stared down at the phone in his hand. I couldn't see what was on it, but apparently it was fascinating.

"Sorry," I said. "You're not going. Ava's orders. Mari and I can shift out if we have to, but you'll be a liability."

"Then you grab me and take me with you. I know shifting is limited to what you can carry, but if you're linked with Mari and shifting together, the two of you should be able to take us at least to the next room."

During our practice the past few weeks, we'd been successful at doing that with Jace, but it hadn't been easy. Alone, Mari hadn't shifted Jace more than a few steps. "What if that's not far enough? You can't fight anyway. Not with that hole in you. What if you get us all killed?" Or worse, captured.

Keene's eyes narrowed. "I won't. But if that's the way you want to play it, good luck. Let me know how it goes." He shut off his phone, put it in his pocket, and arose, the stiffness in his body belying the casual words.

"What about the introduction?" Mari said.

Keene smiled. "Only if I go with you."

"No," I said at the same time Mari said, "Okay."

I glanced at Cort, lifting a hand in appeal, but he shook his head with obvious enjoyment. "I've given up trying to talk sense into him. He has never listened to his older and wiser brother."

"My *ancient* brother is too conservative," Keene retorted. "Besides, you need me, Erin. There are certain handshakes and so forth that you don't have time to learn."

I rolled my eyes. "What are they, Masons?"

"Kind of."

I came to my feet, facing him. "You almost died last night. You should be in bed, not visiting Hunters. What if that Unbounded with Emerson attacks us?"

Keene took a step. "Then I'll watch you dispatch him." He shook his head and blew out a sigh. "Look, with me there, nothing will go wrong—we'll be their allies not their enemies. Besides, Dimitri patched me up great. I'm at least as well as I'd have normally been in three or four days with any ordinary doctor."

"Really?" This I put to Cort, because while Keene didn't lie, he might not understand Dimitri's ability.

Cort nodded. "Dimitri is that good, and my brother is that stupid."

Mari let out an amused snort.

"Besides," Cort said, hesitating, "we also tried out some other things we've been working on with nanites and regeneration since he couldn't protest."

It was Keene's turn to roll his eyes. "Guess I'm a guinea pig. So what's the verdict? Are you coming or am I doing this alone?"

I could call Ava and she'd set this to rights in an instant, but I didn't want to be someone who always went running to her. I had to learn to fight my own battles, and that meant weighing Keene's stubbornness against my desire to fulfill the mission. The mission had to come first.

"Okay," I said. "You come. But after we're in, you follow my lead. I'll know what they're thinking."

Was that worry emanating from Cort? Did he feel I'd made the wrong decision? Or was he simply tired of losing siblings?

Cort caught my gaze and the emotions vanished. He had one of the strongest shields in our group, and if I wanted, he'd let me try to break in, but now wasn't the time to practice.

Grunting in approval, Keene swept up his coat from the couch and headed for the door. He moved carefully but without any visible sign of pain. His torso had more bulk than I remembered, probably from the layers of bandages under his shirt. Mari hurried after him.

I followed them, pausing at the door. "You watching Oliver today?" I asked Cort.

His mouth twitched. "Yes. We're going to run through a few practice illusions before we take our turn at the compound."

"That's actually something I've been meaning to talk to you about." I glanced at Keene and Mari. "Can I have a moment? I need to run something past Cort. I'll be right down." Curiosity peeled from both of them, but neither voiced it, so I pretended not to notice.

"Sure, I need to get a gun anyway," Keene said.

"And how about more of those nano knives?" Mari suggested.

Keene shook his head. "I doubt he'll have a metal detector, so regular knives will do, and if I give him the right codes, we may not even be searched."

"After what happened at the hotel last night, he might be more careful," Mari said.

"We'll see."

I shut the door as they turned away. Cort leaned back in his seat, watching me as if I were one of his science projects, which I supposed I was. He'd been a constant in my life since my Change, drilling me on my experiences as a sensing Unbounded, teaching me about my new life, and planning multiple tests for my ability. But most of all, he was my friend.

"About Oliver," I said, walking to his desk and placing my hands on top. "I've been thinking how Stella can change her appearance by communicating directly with the nanites in her body, which in turn are the only things that can keep up with our regeneration and healing abilities."

Cort cleared his throat. I didn't usually notice how many times he did that before he talked, but sometimes it could be annoying.

"Nanites have been used on other Unbounded but simply aren't advanced enough to work on programming alone. We've been able to keep our bodies from rejecting the tracking chip, but it's too complicated for so many nanites to change someone's appearance without constant updates."

"Basically, you need a computer in your head."

He grinned. "Yep. Or to be a technopath. Or in your case to be connected to one. But even then the appearance doesn't change much. That would require more sophisticated nanites, which is still far down the road, even for us."

"Okay, but in that same vein, what about an illusion instead of a physical change? Could Oliver create a realistic enough illusion over his own body to pass himself off as someone else?"

Cort rubbed his chin, his gaze intensifying. "And could you do the same by channeling his gift?"

"Exactly. As a temporary measure, or course, like during an assault. Or some other operation."

"I don't know. It's been so long since an illusionist existed that no one really knows what they're capable of. I'll do some research and a few experiments with Oliver." He coughed. "I might have had an answer for you already if we hadn't been so occupied since Oliver and Mari joined us."

I understood. He'd been presented with two new abilities, plus my own developing one. Unlike Stella with her connection to computers all over the world, Cort had to find information the old-fashioned way, a piece at a time. "Maybe Stella could help?"

He rubbed his chin. "Maybe." He was already lost in thought, studying patterns that only he could see. If anyone could help Oliver do what I wanted, it would be him.

"Thanks, Cort." I was pretty sure he didn't notice me as I left. Five hundred years, and you'd think he'd be a little better with women. Perhaps he'd given up. I knew he'd been married several times and had children, including two Unbounded who lived in Europe. I wondered if he might decide to try again with Mari. She wouldn't die and leave him like the mortals had.

Unless the Emporium killed her.

Pushing back the thought, I strode to the elevator. I could sense two life forces heading for the garage, so I punched that level and waited for the doors to close.

My mind shifted to the pending meeting with the Hunters. If they had any idea who we were, they'd shoot us on sight. We had to be ready. Whatever happened, we couldn't leave the Unbounded bodyguard with them for long, even if that meant exposing his nature. The choice didn't leave much room for my conscience since revealing that he was Unbounded to the Hunters he was infiltrating was the equivalent of ordering his death. The alternatives were almost as brutal. I didn't know if I would ever become accustomed to choosing not between good and evil but between evil and worse evil.

Regardless, the Unbounded bodyguard could be close to retrieving the Hunter records that would lead him to Renegade posterity. We had to protect them at all cost.

CHAPTER 7

USUALLY WITH THE UNBOUNDED GENE PULSING THROUGH MY veins, I felt like the nearly immortal that I was: confident, bold, and a bit arrogant. Not today. I was too nervous. Gone was my assurance of last night. There were some things Unbounded feared, and the truth was that I'd nurtured a private unease about Hunters since my Change when they'd attacked us and I'd ended up sharing space with my first bullet. Subsequent encounters had gone downhill from there.

It didn't help my worry that even this early on Saturday there were a lot of people in the streets, glowing life forces filled with unshuttered emotions zinging around and begging to be noticed. Love, hatred, greed, and worry. The stronger the emotion, the more it pleaded for recognition.

As I drove to the address Keene put into the GPS on the dash of the white rental sedan, I clamped down on my emotions and strengthened my mental barrier. *In and out,* I told myself. *Nothing to worry about.* Ritter's philosophy hadn't worked all that well at the hotel last night, but that didn't mean things wouldn't go smoothly today. I'd feel better if I weren't taking either Mari or Keene along. It was one thing to risk my own life, but I felt responsible for them.

"I told them I was bringing my girlfriend," Keene said from the passenger seat. "They think we're all Hunters from Arizona. And don't forget that my undercover name with them is KC Farrell."

I scowled. "You talked to Emerson? Why didn't you say we were just friends?"

"I talked to him about an hour ago. And I didn't mean you. I meant Mari." He smiled at her in the backseat. "You don't mind, do you? Hunters tend to get their families and such into the business."

Mari shrugged. "I guess not. If it helps."

Why did that make me more irritated? I stopped myself from honking as the driver in front of me slammed on his brakes for no apparent reason. The traffic was terrible for a Saturday morning, but I should have expected as much of downtown Manhattan.

"I thought you never lied," I muttered.

"Cover stories are different. For today, we *are* our cover stories." A fine example of why even Keene's truth was sometimes not really the whole truth.

"My Hunter contacts gave me such glowing recommendations," Keene continued, "that Emerson agreed to meet with me. Fortunately he happened to be free this morning."

Happened. I didn't like the sound of that. Coincidence usually meant trouble.

"Relax," Keene said. "No one has plans the night after a big fundraiser. Too busy sleeping off the booze."

"Then why's he awake?" Mari asked, leaning forward so much that the ends of her blond wig fell over the front seat.

"Liver trouble." Keene shrugged. "Or so they say. Not much of a drinker at any rate."

That meant three of us because Unbounded didn't usually waste their time on alcohol that never stayed in our bodies long enough to do anything wonderful or destructive.

"Commuting to his ranch outside the city isn't always a

great option," Keene went on, "so he owns a thirty million dollar townhouse in West Village. That's where we're going."

Mari whistled. "Must be some townhouse."

At least it wasn't the hotel from yesterday, where we might be identified this close to the night of the attack. "We're almost there," I said. We'd entered an upscale area where a variety of townhouses lined both sides of the streets—brick, brownstone, stucco. Some looked alike, while others screamed out individuality.

The GPS directed me to a large, red-bricked corner building, but I drove past several equally impressive townhouses and parked down the street. Keene gave a little groan. "So far away?"

"Hey, you're the one who decided to come along." Like always, I checked the mirror for pursuit, but there was nothing suspicious. "If things go bad there's no use making our vehicle noticeable." The traffic here was considerably less than near our safe house, which would be nice if we had to start shifting. Or if Mari had to shift. Because I knew I wouldn't be able to leave Keene behind.

"I think you should leave some of your weapons here," Mari said to me. "In case they ask for our coats. It'll be weird if you refuse, won't it?"

"Okay. Okay." I opened my coat and took out the sai, placing them in a black duffel Mari retrieved from the trunk. I hoped Ritter never knew I'd left them. After Stella's comment, I had the sneaking suspicion they might be worth more than I thought. At least they should be safe in this part of town.

Keene's green eyes followed my movements as I laid my machete in its scabbard on top of the sai. I almost wished I'd left the weapons at the safe house, but I might need them if things turned nasty.

Moments later, I felt positively naked as we walked down the street. The air was crisp and cold, searing my throat, and the slight smell of ash wafted down from several nearby chimneys.

"So," Keene said, keeping pace with me, "those aren't your ordinary sai."

I tucked my hands inside my pockets, holding the leather of

my coat closer to my body, glad the top part was lined with a flannel-like material. "They're Chinese."

"Did *he* give them to you?"

"Who?"

"Ritter."

I stopped walking and faced him. "Yes. He thought I should learn a new weapon. Is that a problem?" I expected Keene to laugh and make some witty comment, but he didn't. His expression remained sober as he studied my face.

"They're at least a hundred years old. Maybe two hundred. Definite antiques."

"Funny, they don't look that old."

"And very valuable."

"Good thing Unbounded have a lot of money." I started walking again, telling myself the cost of the sai didn't mean a thing. I would have a fortune myself someday, once the modest monthly allotment Ava, as my ancestor, had given me matured in the stock market. A century or two did wonders for the pocketbook.

Keene hurried to catch up with me, and I slowed my pace slightly. No use wearing the man out before we arrived at the townhouse. "The point is that he gave them to you."

I lifted a brow. An odd emotion emanated from his surface thoughts, something that seemed an awful lot like jealousy. Yet it wasn't like Keene to exhibit such emotion. In fact, one of the reasons I liked him so much is that he didn't push or expect more from me than I was willing to give. Not like Ritter. I didn't have to lose myself in him. But Keene was mortal, which added complications while at the same time taking others away. I had to admit that in the months Ritter had been gone before our mission to Mexico, I'd started thinking that maybe it would be a good thing to fall in love with a mortal instead of an Unbounded. No worries about staying together for centuries or bitter breakups. Of having dozens of children and even more posterity to look after.

Of course, losing out to death was the end play of such a relationship, and I didn't think I'd ever come to terms with that finality.

Keene grinned suddenly, as if at a private joke. "Never mind. I'll show you some moves with the sai later, if you'd like."

Relief ran through me. "Sounds good. Provided you can still walk after we're finished here."

"Oh, I'll be able to do a lot more than walk."

His word flirted with desire, though his emotions were unclear, and I didn't want to decipher them. Instead, I pushed out my thoughts along the streets, searching for anything unusual. I could sense the life forces inside the buildings as we passed, and I hadn't always been able to at this range, which meant my nightly practice had paid off.

"Man, it's so stinking cold," Mari said, pushing up her costume glasses.

I had to agree. "At least there's no snow. We're almost there."

Another minute and we reached the outside stairs. Keene rang the doorbell as Mari and I waited tensely, ready to act. Mari wasn't too skilled as a fighter, and once she'd actually fired a gun, she'd taken a dislike to pistols, but unlike me, she was good with knives. In part because she could shift within inches of her target, shove in the knife, and shift instantly away. It was a close and personal way to kill—and it made me appreciate even more the ballistic knife that allowed me more space. In fact, next to my nine mil, it was the most useful weapon Ritter had ever arranged for me.

The door opened to reveal the woman from last night with the gray-blond hair. Charlaine Emerson, according to Stella, Davis Emerson's wife. No purple dress today, but a comfortable yellow pantsuit that gave her smile added cheerfulness. The outfit was still an expensive piece like the plaid monstrosity, but the designer had opted for comfort rather than flash.

"Yes?" she asked, her wide-set eyes falling across us. Her forehead was also wide, perhaps a little too wide, but her hair swept low to cover it, kept in place by several yellow clips.

"I'm KC Farrell," Keene said. "I have an appointment with your husband."

"Oh, yes, he's expecting you. Come on in."

Heat rushed out at us as we stepped inside. The entryway wasn't vaulted, but was high enough that I didn't feel the ceiling would fall on us. Elegance called attention everywhere I looked, from the travertine on the floor to the gilded picture frames, but it all appeared new, as though no one really lived here. I wondered what Charlaine's house in the country looked like and guessed it would be more casual.

"Please let me take your coats." Charlaine opened a door to the left, which revealed a large walk-in closet, perfect for entertaining. Only a few coats hung on the metal bar, and one on a coatrack in the corner.

Mari cast me a triumphant look as she shrugged out of her coat. With brief hesitation, I gave mine up as well because already the heat of the house threatened to strangle me. There were only five life forces inside, and as long as they weren't all Unbounded, Mari and I could handle them with the weapons we carried in our jeans and boots.

Charlaine led us down a hallway to where the Unbounded bodyguard stood outside a doorway. "They're here," she announced unnecessarily. To us, she added. "Brody will take care of you. I'll bring in some coffee and croissants in a bit. I hope you enjoy them. My grandmother was from France and the croissants are a family recipe." She turned, leaving us alone with the Unbounded.

Brody stuck out his hand toward Keene, and they began a series of handshakes, occasionally exchanging a whispered phrase or two. Something about good hunting and three passes of a sword.

No doubt about what that meant. I pushed my thoughts toward Brody, prepared to break through his weak shield, but today he wasn't even blocking. Nothing important stood out in the sand stream of his thoughts except making sure we were legitimate. He finished with Keene and his eyes met mine. He was handsome with deep blue eyes, blond hair and sideburns, and broad across the shoulders like someone accustomed to working out in a gym.

The men finished their strange ritual and turned to us. "This is Jessie, my girlfriend." Keene put his arm around me and pulled me close.

I blinked at him. *What?* He gave me a tight grin. I looked at Brody and said in a flat voice, "Yeah, we're practically engaged." Next to me, Mari bit her lip as she tried not to laugh.

Brody nodded solemnly. "Good morning." He held out his hand. I really hoped he wasn't going to repeat that whole rigama-role because I wouldn't be able to do it. "It's great that you're both Hunters. I hope I find the right girl someday."

That was laying it on a bit thick.

"Nice to meet you." It seemed the polite thing to say.

"You were there last night." He held my hand longer than necessary, as if trying to remember something he couldn't quite grasp. For the first time I wondered what his ability might be. Probing his mind for the answer brought up nothing, yet he'd picked me out of a crowded room last night, and it was more than a man simply noticing a woman.

"Yes, I was." I noted the pistol at his side, probably a .45 by the size. Pushing closer to his thought stream, I could see nothing that told me he was lying, and no hint of the Emporium. There wasn't any shiny black snake hiding in his thoughts, either.

Yet I was sure he'd singled out Patrick Mann last night, and Patrick was definitely working with the Emporium. So either he knew Patrick, somehow suspected Patrick was Unbounded, or he'd discovered some other way to hide his thoughts from me.

Stop, I told myself. While it paid to be open to new ideas, constantly second-guessing my ability would only get me into trouble.

Brody led us into a sitting room—or across it, rather. The room was large and connected to a library with floor-to-ceiling shelves on three walls. Unlike the other areas we'd seen, the library was more inviting and appeared lived-in, if rather overheated by the roaring gas fireplace nestled between two windows on the only wall without books.

Davis Emerson was seated on a leather easy chair facing us, his brown cowboy hat still perched on his head, but he arose as we approached. Brody nodded at him subtly, and one side of Emerson's mouth twitched in a brief acknowledgment.

"Welcome, friends," Emerson said, sounding a bit loud like the cattle rancher he was. He had an average build and was even shorter close up. His pale, freckled face wasn't remarkable, except for the blue eyes that glowed with intelligence. I pushed out my thoughts and saw that he was shielding and doing a better job at it than he had the night before.

"Thank you." Keene shook hands and made the introductions, giving me a last name I'd never remember and calling Mari his friend Laurie, which at least rhymed.

Emerson nodded at us. "Please sit." He waited until we dropped to the couch before retaking his chair. "So, did I hear Brody say you were at the fundraiser last night? That must mean you're fans of Vice President Mann, as I am."

"Well." Keene glanced at me, and I remembered my demand to be the one who led the conversation.

"Actually," I said, "after last night, we're not sure."

Emerson's brows rose so high they disappeared under the brim of his hat. "What do you mean?"

"Didn't you catch the news? There was a problem last night, and our sources say it involved Unbounded."

"Emporium or Renegade?" Emerson asked.

I didn't bother to hide my surprise. "You're the first Hunter I've ever heard make a distinction. Unbounded are Unbounded, right?"

Emerson leaned back in his chair, his hands folded over his stomach. "Why don't you tell me what happened last night?"

"We identified Emporium agents, who seem to also support the vice president. In fact, we witnessed a run-in they had at the hotel with agents we believe to be Renegades." Nothing like a little truth to give credence to a lie. "We are now in the process of identifying any Unbounded who might be close to the vice president."

This last I added in case we needed help with Patrick Mann. For many years the Emporium had used Hunters against us. Maybe it was our turn to reverse the trend. As I finished speaking, I pushed harder at Emerson's mind shield, having found no apparent hole. Nothing left but to use brute force. Harder, harder, I pushed until it crumpled and vanished. Not nearly as thick as most shields I'd seen.

"Ah, honey, thanks," he said, as his wife and another woman I recognized from his mind as their live-in cook and housekeeper entered the room with trays.

"Never too early for croissants," Charlaine said. "And you'll have to try Josi's coffee. Everyone loves it." The women set down the trays, and Josi began pouring. There was a cup for Brody as well, which I thought was strange, despite the love of croissants prominent in his mind. Did bodyguards eat with their employers?

Concentrate, I told myself. Back to Emerson, who didn't touch his cup but was staring at Keene. I set down my coffee and laid my hands unfolded on my lap, my right just a bit closer to the top of my boot.

"Eat up," Emerson invited.

"I'd really like to hear why you think there's a difference in Unbounded," I said as the others reached toward the plate of croissants. Emerson's suspicion of Keene was clear in his mind, but Keene's shield was up and strong, so I could only warn Mari without becoming too distracted. *He suspects,* I told her.

Crap. She frowned at her croissant but didn't look at me.

"I think KC here can tell us that," Emerson said.

Keene's eyes rose to his as Emerson smiled. I noticed one of Emerson's hands was no longer on his stomach but had fallen to his side near his pocket where his thoughts told me he had a gun. Behind the couch, Brody stood ready, his hand moving toward his own weapon. Slowly, as if reaching for a mint.

Mentally, I reached for Mari. *Emerson has a gun. Can you take care of him when I tell you to?* Seated, he would be the weakest target, and I trusted Mari to be able to disarm him. We'd practiced a million times. Brody would be more dangerous. I didn't even want to think about him getting a bullet into Keene.

"You see," Emerson continued, "I've been doing a little research on you, KC, and discovered that while you've been involved in several Unbounded captures, only a few resulted in their deaths, and those were only Renegades, as far as I can tell. Is this a coincidence, I ask myself? I don't think so."

He hesitated before adding, "In fact, quite a few captured Unbounded have gone missing under your command, the last being at a raid here in New York almost three months ago. We lost one of our good operatives, and a new Hunter came back to us with no memory of the event." His words were almost casual, but his mind screamed with accusations against Keene, whom he considered responsible for the crime.

Keene scooted toward the edge of his seat. "I asked your Hunters here for help because I wasn't able to get to New York in time. I sent someone later for the Unbounded, and I can vouch that she and her human helper were taken care of. I'm sorry about your operatives, but we all know it's a dangerous line we walk."

"I don't believe you." Emerson's pistol was in his hand now, though not in plain sight. "Not about that or about last night."

Keene lifted the front of his T-shirt, revealing the bandages. "This is what those Unbounded bastards did to me last night, and regardless of the conclusions you've come to, this is why I'm going to work *against* the vice president. Something doesn't smell right. He's somehow connected with the Unbounded. I know it."

"So you say." Emerson regarded Keene's bandages with interest, and while he didn't sound impressed, doubt wedged its way into his mind. "Convince me further," he invited.

I glanced at Keene. "If you take off that bandage and the bleeding starts again, I swear, the engagement is off. I'm not watching you bleed to death to prove anything to this man." I was serious about not standing by to watch him bleed. I'd shoot Emerson first.

Emerson's mouth twitched as mirth entered his thoughts.

"Why don't we address something more important?" I said.

Emerson inclined his head, urging me on.

"I'm talking about the records from the days before Hunters separated from the Emporium."

"You mean when we were abandoned?" His voice rose with each word. "Kicked out with no money and no homes when we didn't undergo their precious Change?"

"You're not old enough to remember," I countered.

"No, but my dad and grandaddy remember, and I learned from the day I was born what happened. There is no doubt we have to get rid of the Unbounded—all of them. They think of mortals as little more than intelligent monkeys." Bitterness laced his voice. "If we let them live, they will take over and only heaven will be able to help us then."

"I agree with you—for the most part." I did, at least as far as the Emporium was concerned. "But about the records? You have access to them, don't you? You and a few others? You're the ones we get orders from. Who to watch, right?" *We* meaning Hunters, of course, though saying it left a nasty taste in my mouth.

Emerson didn't answer, and I felt his finger go to the trigger of his gun. "I do have access," he said shortly, "but I won't let you see them. I give out names only to heads of chapters."

"We didn't come here for that." Without looking, I felt Brody step closer to the back of the couch, seeming as fascinated at the idea of the records as I was. Of course, he'd want to take them back to the Emporium. "I think the Emporium has been infiltrating our organization," I added, "and I think they're planning a move to get the records from you." To Mari, I silently said, *Get ready.*

"Ridiculous." Emerson gave a sharp jerk of his head. "All my people are thoroughly investigated. Even my own relatives. Because as much as we love them, we know their genes give them the possibility of becoming monsters."

"You're sure you have no Unbounded working for you?" I pressed.

"Absolutely." He was finished with us. I could see his decision even as he made it. He didn't trust Keene, and he was realizing that having a copy of the records in his safe here at the townhouse might put him in danger. His gaze rose to Brody, giving him one steady blink. A signal.

Now! I pushed the word mentally at Mari as I reached for my ballistic knife, whipping it around to point at Brody, leaving my back exposed to Emerson's pistol. I felt a slight suction of air as Mari shifted at the same time a solid *click* signaled my knife had left its housing. This close, I wasn't worried about accuracy. I'd have to be way off not to hit him.

The knife left my hand at a slightly upward angle, coming at Brody even as he brought out his gun. It slammed into his throat. He gave a muffled, wet gurgle, his eyes staring at me in disbelief. As he fell, I was already diving to the side, reaching for my backup .380 in my other boot. I twisted toward Emerson, whose gun was on his lap, but useless as Mari's knife pressed against his throat. His cowboy hat had fallen to the side, revealing longish pale red hair that swept to the side and tried to hide a receding hairline.

"Show offs," Keene muttered.

Emerson let out a sob. "Brody!" His eyes went to me. "Please let me go to him." His pistol slid off his lap and onto the floor.

I stared at him. The emotion he felt threatened to overwhelm both of us. Not the ordinary feeling of an employer for a body-guard but something far deeper. I looked into the sand stream and there it was, the information that might have prevented this entire confrontation.

I nodded at Emerson, mentally kicking myself for not seeing the connection earlier. "Mari, let him go."

"What?" This from Keene.

"Let him go," I repeated. "It's his son."

CHAPTER 8

"KEENE, WATCH THE DOOR. I'LL COVER EMERSON." ALL WE NEEDED now was for Mrs. Emerson to return. Keene nodded and moved across the library into the sitting room, a pistol in one hand, the other over his bandaged stomach.

Mari released Emerson, who arose and shakily came around the couch, stumbling as he reached the fallen Unbounded. "Brody, Brody," he wept, his hand going to the knife and hesitating. "Please, let me call the ambulance. Oh, my son, my son. God, help him. Help my son!"

Mari shifted and appeared on the other side of Brody, her face solemn. No doubt remembering when she'd found her husband with his throat slashed by the Emporium.

"There's no need for an ambulance." Passing the gun to Mari, I knelt by Brody and pulled out the knife, stanching the blood flow with a pillow from the couch. "Hold this here," I told Emerson, taking back my gun. "Mari, if you could get my coat."

Nodding, she shifted, leaving me momentarily breathless as the air around her also vanished. Emerson didn't even notice. He was shaking and crying and praying. I felt terrible, even though I knew

Brody was fine. I had to remind myself of how many Renegades Emerson had killed. He deserved this for every spouse or child or parent who had lost their loved one to the Hunters. Wiping off my knife and replacing it in my boot, I shut my mind against his pain.

Mari popped back into the room, handing me my coat. I traded the gun for it, and from the pocket, I retrieved a syringe full of curequick.

"What are you doing?" Emerson tried to stop me, as I removed the pillow, but I was stronger. "You'll kill—" He broke off as he saw that the blood flow had already decreased.

I slid the thick needle under the flesh and slowly pressed in some of the liquid, removing it and beginning all over again in another place near the wound.

"He's not breathing," Emerson said, still sounding panicked.

"He doesn't need to. He should be around soon enough." Finishing with the needle and syringe, I squeezed together the edges of his wound.

"Who are you?" Emerson asked.

I snorted. "Not the Emporium, if that's what you're thinking. Or you'd be dead. No, we're Hunters like you. But your son may be with the Emporium."

"He can't be . . . he wouldn't have . . . will he really be okay?" Emerson had relaxed since my assertion that we weren't Emporium, which told me he knew there was a difference between Unbounded groups. Yet over the years he'd continued to condone the murders of all Unbounded.

We sat watching Brody in silence until Keene whistled from the sitting room. "Someone's coming," I guessed. I waved my pistol at Emerson. "Better get over there and stop them or things could get ugly."

He staggered to his feet, and I followed. "Drag him over there a bit, if you can," I told Mari over my shoulder, worried that even in the next room we'd see Brody's legs and feet.

Charlaine Emerson appeared in the doorway to the sitting room, puzzled to find most of us standing by the door instead of seated in the adjoining library where she'd left the coffee and croissants. "Is something wrong?"

"Not at all, dear," Emerson said. "Just showing them around. But we have some sensitive Hunter matters to discuss, so we'll be closing the library door."

"I see." Her gaze ran over her husband, pausing on his bare head. From her thoughts, I could see his words weren't completely unusual, as he often entertained Hunters, but the only place she ever saw him without his hat was in bed. "You don't need any more coffee? Croissants?"

"No, dear." Emerson assured her. "What you already brought is perfect."

"Okay. Well, if you're busy here, Josi and I are going to take Sierra shopping. She's actually up, if you can believe that. She's excited about finding something to wear for her date tonight."

"I'm sure she'll find something beautiful with your help." Emerson swiped a hand over the moisture beading on his forehead.

After Charlaine left, we all returned to the library, with Emerson stopping where the rooms adjoined to pull out pocket doors on either side of the wide doorway. I hadn't noticed them before, and they were flimsy enough to still give me worry, but the lock should at least give us warning if anyone approached.

Mari had moved Brody, and blood stained the white carpet where he'd lain. Two spots several inches wide where the blood had leaked down on either side of his neck. Not a lot, but enough that it would cause immediate notice. Emerson stepped over the marks and knelt by his son, taking his hand. "He has a pulse." Amazement filled his voice.

"You accuse me of working with Unbounded," Keene said, "and here you have one in your own household."

"Apparently, I was right about you." Emerson looked up at Mari with a pointed stare. "Want to tell me how she can move so fast?"

Things were growing more complicated by the moment. Before

we left, I would probably have to knock him unconscious and remove his memory of Mari.

"Let's focus on your son." I put acid in my voice. "You have some explaining to do."

Emerson's gaze dropped to Brody. The wound was noticeably healing now, and relief vied with horror on Emerson's face. "He's not my son."

"Yes, he is." I wanted to shake him.

"I mean, he is, but he's adopted. Both our kids are. We couldn't have children, and I admit, I was worried about passing on the gene. I know with each generation it becomes less likely, but it's happened, and I've seen good men have to . . ."

The scenes of carnage in his mind made me sick. "The Emporium must have had a hand in your adoption process."

Emerson frowned. "Why would they? I'm well-known in Hunter society, and they listen to me, but I'm a busy man. I haven't been on an actual hunt since before Brody was born."

"But you do pass on orders to others." Amazingly, I kept the bitterness to myself.

He shook his head. "I'm in the Hunter Circle, and I do give orders, but there are many others who are far more active. We made sure that no one man would have total control. We couldn't risk that the Emporium would be able to put an end to us, to our work."

Emporium. He'd singled them out again.

"So," I said viciously. "He's unconscious now. You can call your friends. They can dispatch him for you."

Emerson's eyes grew wide and his expression contorted. "No, no. Not my son. I can't." His voice grew stronger, his eyes hard. "I won't."

"Even if he's not working for the Emporium already, they'll be watching, waiting for him to Change." Keene leaned against the back of the couch, looking considerably worse for wear. Not at all like his usual self.

Emerson's head swung back and forth. "No, they won't know."

"Of course they will." Keene's lip curled in a sneer. "The Emporium has been foisting their offspring on mortals for years, tampering with genetics to get a higher rate of Unbounded and checking back to see if they Change. Likely they picked you because of your position with the Hunters. Probably trying to get a man inside. Your son's about thirty, isn't he? The Change usually takes place between thirty-one and thirty-three. Oh, yeah, they'll be watching and waiting to pounce, to convert him to their cause."

"Brody would never—" Emerson began.

"You'd be surprised what people will do to survive, especially once that gene kicks in. Like you, I've been hunting Unbounded all my adult life," Keene said. "I know."

Renegade Unbounded, he meant, but a chill ran over me that had nothing to do with his former allegiance. That sensation I sometimes had in my gut was screaming warning. With a sinking feeling I realized we shouldn't have come here at all. Because while the Emporium might not have noticed Brody's Change before, it was likely that the sensing Emporium agent from last night had noticed him as I'd been noticed, and while the Emporium might delay contacting him because of more pressing matters, they'd keep a closer eye on him. Especially knowing Ava had sent us to the hotel last night. They would worry that she'd have identified Brody's nature, and Keene and I were well enough known by the Emporium that our coming here would set off all kinds of alarms.

I pushed out my thoughts, passing the walls of the townhouse and into the street. Life forces gleamed as people careened by in cars or moved more sedately on the sidewalk. The blocked life forces were easy to locate: two seated in front of the building, probably in a car. Two more across the street. They hadn't been there when we'd entered, but at least one of them had been nearby to alert the others. Or they had the place on electronic surveillance.

Only four agents? I doubted it. Not for three of us. They'd want to be sure—and that meant at least one more, a sensing Unbounded who could hide from me and could possibly hide other agents as well.

If Keene hadn't come, I'd shift out with Mari. As it was, he'd created a liability we might not survive. I stepped over to Keene, motioning for Mari to join us.

"He's not with them, I tell you," Emerson insisted, fear showing as red blotches on his face. "He'd never join them."

"Shields," I said in an undertone to the others as we ignored Emerson. Mostly I spoke for Mari's benefit and I was relieved when the worried excitement she'd been broadcasting vanished. "They're here. At least five. Possibly more."

Keene's face looked pained. Any other day, I'd tease him, but this was too serious.

"I can shift to the compound and tell Ritter," Mari said.

"He won't be able to get here in time. I'm betting they'll wait to attack until we leave, to see if we have Brody with us." At least the four seemed to be staying in place. I wished I knew where the sensing Unbounded was. Or was I only imagining the additional trouble?

"What is it?" Emerson asked, looking up at us from his place on the floor next to Brody.

I stared at him, an idea coming to me. "I think they might have noticed your son's Change. Maybe that's why the Unbounded were there last night. For him." I didn't believe that last part was true. The Emporium's primary purpose for being at the fundraiser had to be to protect Patrick Mann and also his father, though we didn't yet know why the vice president would be in danger. Still, it didn't hurt to plant the idea in Emerson's head.

Emerson's breath came faster. "Please, help him. Help us."

"Of course we will." I reached for my coat over the arm of the couch, removing a syringe with a smaller needle and handing it to Keene. By the size, he'd know what it was for. "They probably want Brody to give them your genealogy records, but as long as those records aren't here, they have no reason to break in right away. The records aren't here, are they?" Of course, I already knew they were upstairs in his safe, and my whole premise was absurd, because the Emporium's main goal would be to get Brody and convince him to work for them, knowing he could get the records later. Only our presence—Renegade presence—would make them act earlier, but in Emerson's highly emotional state, I doubted he'd notice details.

Emerson choked. "They're—they're . . . oh, they're in my safe." He thought about the safe behind the picture above the fireplace in his upstairs bedroom, and I could see the combination in his mind. Interesting what a little suggestion could do.

"Don't worry," I said. "We'll help you. We're all in this together."

A sudden gasp cut through the silence in the room. All heads turned toward Brody, who was breathing now, his eyes rolling in fear. A ghastly hoarse sound came from his throat.

"It's okay," his father soothed, patting his hand. "It's okay. Rest. You'll be fine."

"Don't try to talk yet." Keene was already in place behind Emerson. "You'll heal soon enough." He lowered the needle into Emerson's neck, pressing the plunger.

"What? Wh—" Emerson keeled over, sprawling across his son.

Keene dropped to his knees next to Brody. "Sleep," he said, injecting a larger portion of liquid from the syringe into Brody. "This will help with the pain."

Brody lapsed back into unconsciousness, though with his accelerated metabolism and the curequick, it wouldn't last long. I knelt between him and his father, placing a hand on Emerson's forehead and pushing my thoughts down. Instantly I was in his mind. Instead of the sand stream of thoughts that existed during consciousness, a lake glistened below me. I dove inside the liquid, swimming deeper. Most unconscious minds were symbolized by lakes, but a few weren't and I was happy not to have to learn a new system. Bubbles containing thoughts circled around me and I carefully extracted a few: Mari shifting, his later thoughts about her, the needle going into his neck. The memory segments were short and his attention so riveted on his son, that I doubted he'd even notice their absence. I was tempted to remove the entire meeting, but that would leave a black hole he'd certainly question. Besides, he needed to know about his son.

Seconds later, I was diving into the lake of Brody's mind, extracting only the very last memory of seeing his father drugged. It wasn't more than a glimpse and he wouldn't miss it. I could see from the memories that he'd been conscious for a few minutes before he'd started breathing and the sensation had terrified him. I left that. He needed to learn that part of being Unbounded as well as the rest.

As I searched for the memory of Mari's first shift, something interesting caught my attention. In his mind, I was glowing in the hallway and as I sat on the couch. Odd that I hadn't noticed this before when I'd been in his mind. Energy seemed to pour off me. I resumed my search and found more energy, this time leaking from Mari as she shifted over to Emerson.

Only when she used her ability. I'd been using mine almost the entire time.

Curious, I moved further into his past, dodging memories as they floated by. I quickly found what I was looking for: me at the fundraiser when our eyes met. I was glowing, though less noticeably. More brightness came from the electric cables, floodlights, and other equipment around the photographer's backdrop, the greater the energy expended, the more the object glowed.

Odd.

Back further. This time Brody was looking at Patrick Mann by the fundraiser door. Patrick was also glowing, brighter than I had been. Using his ability?

At least that explained why Brody had singled us out. Something about energy translated to him as light. This could relate to his Unbounded gift—whatever it was. Maybe he really wasn't involved with the Emporium. Not one of the memory bubbles hinted at such.

A crash reverberating in my physical ears broke my concentration, and I stroked upward, out of the water and opened my eyes, removing my hand from Brody. Checking mentally, I saw that the four Unbounded watching the townhouse from outside were still in their original places.

"That came from upstairs," Keene said.

"The safe!" I leapt to my feet and grabbed Mari's hand. If I'd been able to see the combination to the safe in Emerson's mind, could the other sensing Unbounded have done the same? "Drop your shield. We need to shift upstairs. I'll show you where."

She nodded eagerly. "Okay."

"But—"

Before Keene finished we were gone, appearing in the room I'd seen in Emerson's mind. I kept my link with Mari, throwing up a shield for both of us and hoping such a thing was even possible. It *felt* possible, if the ache at the base of my skull was any indication.

Another fireplace was alight here, this time a real wood one with a chimney. A large picture lay against the wall, and the safe was open. A slight figure with short, tight blond curls turned from the safe, completely dark to my mental senses. I was so accustomed to seeing life forces in every living being, even blocking ones, that for a moment my mind wouldn't register the presence.

The figure turned, its movements exuding confidence like any other Unbounded. At first I couldn't tell if it was a man or a woman, but by the lack of breasts, I decided on a man. Or an older boy. His crunched features told me he was a product of a forced early Change, so though he looked seventeen or eighteen, he could be over a hundred by now. Because his Change was forced, his life expectancy would be closer to four hundred rather than two thousand. At least that was how it worked with the other forced Unbounded I knew.

I pushed my thoughts toward him, finding a tremendous black wall shielding his mind. I'd never seen the like. The surface of it whorled as if it had a life of its own.

"Hello," the man said. "I guess you heard the crash. You didn't see me there in his mind, did you? I'm good at that. I saw you, but not what you were thinking, so that was kind of impressive. Not as impressive as me hiding from you, of course. But I bet not even Delia could break into your mind without a serious distraction." His voice wasn't deep, but definitely male and slightly nasal.

"Too bad you're so clumsy." I slid my finger onto the trigger of my gun.

He shrugged. "Who knew the painting was so heavy?"

"Give me that disk." We couldn't let him take the information back to the Emporium. I didn't want more deaths on my hands.

"No." His smile held no amusement. "I've heard so much about you from Delia, but besides the shielding, you aren't much, are you? I think she's made a mistake not telling the rest of the Triad the truth about your ability, but she won't listen to me." He waved the disk. "Maybe after today she will."

Something was odd about his shield. A thick cord ran from it, leaving the Unbounded's body and trailing to a broken window some ten feet away. The cord reminded me of the black snake I'd found in Patrick Mann's thoughts.

But what's it connected to? I guessed the answer even as the thought came. *To his partner.* Unbounded didn't usually work alone.

I skimmed along the cord, finding the other Unbounded seconds before he climbed into the room. With all my force, I sliced at the cord, felt it sever. I shoved my thoughts at the Unbounded. Without the protection of the sensing Unbounded, his mind was all mine.

A knife hurtled past me, but I was already moving, anticipating the movement. The new Unbounded was about Keene's size and his ability was obviously combat. A fair match for me given that I could use both his ability and my own.

Wait. I whirled, jumping behind a chair as the sensing Unbounded near the safe fired in my direction. With a crack, his silenced bullet buried itself in the wall behind where I'd been standing. I raised my pistol, but Mari was already there next to him, slicing with her knife. His pistol fell to the ground. I turned back to my own opponent—only to have my gun kicked out of my hands.

I threw up a block and snap kicked at his stomach, following with a right hook. He slammed a kick to my thigh and a blow to my shoulder, but the movements left him wide open. I jabbed my fingers into his throat. Too bad I couldn't get to my ballistic knife at the moment. He fell, and I kicked hard, readying myself to pounce, but a silent cry burst from Mari's mind.

Spinning, I saw her, the disk from the safe in her hands, but she was unmoving, her face grimacing in pain. *The shield!* I'd dropped it with my concentration, and the sensing Unbounded was in her mind, holding her in place with an impressive show of mental force. Physically, he was several feet away, his chest bleeding from her knife. I saw Mari's gun on the floor by the fireplace poker.

I thrust out my thoughts, crashing into the Unbounded in her mind. Shoving a pulse of light at him, I threw up a shield around Mari, mimicking the thick one I'd seen around his own mind. His fury lashed out as his thoughts careened backward, but slammed uselessly against the outside of the shield. Mari's relief made me momentarily weak. She took a step.

Shift! I told her. *Get out now.*

Even as I thought the words, agony dug into my back. I sucked in a breath filled with pain—or tried to. My lungs no longer seemed to work. White hot agony filled my awareness.

Everything seemed to happen at once. Mari arching and falling toward the fireplace. Me sending a pulse of light to the combat Unbounded behind me. His wrenching pain. The sensing Unbounded running toward Mari, a recovered pistol in his hands. Mari tossing the disk into the fire. The Unbounded reaching for it. Burning his hand. Dropping the blackened, melted disk once more into the greedy flames. Keene appearing in the doorway and more silenced shots as the sensing man sprinted toward the window, dragging his companion with him. More pain filling my mind as Keene's bullet found a target.

Blackness consumed my physical sight, but I was still mentally with Mari as she shifted next to me. "Are you okay?" she asked.

I couldn't answer. Why wasn't she bleeding? I'd seen her hit, hadn't I?

"Erin," Keene spoke close to my face, "you have to shift out of here with Mari. She can't take you all that way on her own. Concentrate. Can you do it?"

I nodded. Mari and I were still so strongly linked, that I doubted I could separate myself from her if I tried. Something to do with my mega shield that still covered her mind. Almost, it seemed to be keeping me inside her.

"Shift to the car," Keene said.

"What about you?" Mari's breath came in gasps. "They'll be back with reinforcements."

"I'll meet you out front, but if they're in view, don't stop for me."

Mari gripped my hand. "Ready, Erin?"

Ready, I told her.

The next minute I saw numbers. Lots of numbers. I felt Mari's joy in how they fell perfectly into place. So easily. Here and there . . . and then we were gone from the bedroom and in the car, with perhaps half of a heartbeat of time in between.

"I hope you have the keys," Mari said.

"My pocket." The pain had miraculously eased during that half heartbeat when we were neither here nor there, and I could see clearly again, but moving would probably restart the agony.

"Where are the Emporium agents?" Mari asked, digging for the keys. "Are they outside the building?"

With effort, I pulled my mind from hers to check, the shifting seeming to have righted my sense of self. "Yeah. Still in the same place. No. Two are moving now. They're crossing and going around the corner. They can't be leaving."

"Bet they're going to help those other agents. That's where the bedroom is located."

I took her word for it. She could also add pages of numbers without a machine and she pretty much always knew the time from a running count in her head.

Mari started the engine with too much gas, the roar sounding like a beacon that shouted out our location. "Keene shot at least one of them," she said, "and the one who had the disk is bleeding pretty badly. The jerk. He deserved it. Not sure how they got up to the second floor window."

"The other two are still in their car out front. Let's get going before their friends come back."

Our car lurched forward. "I'm sorry about the disk," she said, a catch in her voice.

"They didn't get it. That's the important thing." I also felt sick about the disk, but it was only one of several copies, and if Mari hadn't thrown it into the fire, it would be in Emporium hands now, which was far worse.

She picked up speed as she drove toward Emerson's townhouse. Through my slowly returning vision, I could make out the car where the Emporium agents sat, not twenty feet from the stairway to the house. This was going to be close. The only thing on our side was surprise. Hopefully their companions who'd been inside had told them that both of us had been shot. It was possible they didn't know I could piggyback on someone else's ability, so even if Mari was sound enough to shift out, they would still expect me to be inside.

Not that I'd be much help to Mari in my condition. Every movement was torture, and I was having a problem breathing. Then again, maybe I could reach the Emporium agents' minds, maybe stop them if they tried to get out of the car.

First I had to find the strength. I began to absorb as fast as possible.

"Hurry, Keene," Mari muttered as she came to a stop.

I wondered if he was coming at all. Maybe he wanted us to get away and had told Mari to leave, knowing the Emporium agents would be in front waiting and hoping she would obey him and not stop. Yet neither of us were prepared to leave him behind. At the same time, I didn't dare expend energy trying to find him mentally. I was already close to collapse.

The agents' shields were nowhere near as strong as the sensing Unbounded's—a good thing since shards of glass seemed to be nestled inside my back and chest, making it difficult to focus.

I pushed hard but the shield of the first agent only bounced back. I had nowhere near the energy it'd take to break it down. If only I had something strong to hit it with. In frustration, I conjured up a mental image of my machete and hit the shield again. I was in!

"There he is." Mari's voice came from far away.

Not daring to move my head and lose my concentration, I saw Keene not with my eyes but as a life force moving down the stairs. Far too slowly. He wasn't going to make it. The second agent reached for the door. I slammed my machete again and I was inside him, too. His foot stepped onto the pavement as he reached for his gun. Keene was at the bottom of the stairs.

I mentally grabbed at the agent's arm, much as I had pushed at Oliver's hand that morning. But I was too spent, and he hesitated only briefly before the gun started rising. The other agent stepped from the car.

No! I swung the imaginary machete at them and light pulsed from the tip. I felt more than saw them grab at their heads.

The next second our car was in motion, tires squealing on the pavement. The last thing I heard before I lost consciousness was the door slamming.

CHAPTER 9

THE SOFT SCRAPE OF A SWORD LEAVING ITS SCABBARD WOKE ME. I was lying on my stomach naked from the waist up. Grabbing at the sheet covering me, I sat up too quickly, trying to see in the dark. I felt Ritter before I recognized the infirmary, and I let out a sigh of relief. Mari had gotten us to the safe house.

"Did I wake you?" Ritter asked, his tone too casual. In the dim light coming from the open door, I could see the gleam of his sword as he rubbed it with a cloth.

"What happened?" There was no pain in my chest, but I felt a buzz that told me I'd been given curequick, and probably more than once if I was healed and the high remained.

His hand stilled on the sword. "What part? When you disobeyed Ava's order and took Keene with you this morning? Or when you almost got yourself killed trying to get the Hunters' records? What happened to shifting out at the first sign of danger?"

"I did what any of us would have done to preserve our cover and mitigate damages." I swung my bare feet over the edge of the bed, adjusting my position. No pain meant someone had operated on me and taken out the bullet so I could heal faster. It sometimes took days to expel bullets on your own. With Dimitri away in Massachusetts, I was betting Ritter had done the operation. He seemed to excel at taking bullets from my body.

Ritter didn't respond, so I continued, "Look, I made a decision I felt would give the fastest return. As for the records, at least we stopped the Emporium from getting them."

"It might have been our last opportunity for months to grab those records."

"Don't you think I know that? But if I was able to get the combination from him so fast, don't you think the Emporium would have as well once they made contact with his son?"

In two steps Ritter was next to me, moving so fast I didn't see him put down the sword. He smelled of soap and clean clothes, so at some point he'd had a chance to wash up after his day of work and my operation. As usual, he was dressed in black and looked as dangerous as any weapon. He opened his mouth to speak but closed it again. Frustration leaked from him. What did he want?

"I used the ballistic knife," I said. "You'll be happy to know it works great. Shot out of the housing perfectly."

He sank beside me, a reluctant smile curving one corner of his mouth. "So I heard. Good shot, by the way."

"Thanks."

A buzz in the sudden silence had him reaching for his cell phone. "It's Ava texting from the garage, asking if you're awake. They're on their way up." He handed me a shirt. "Guess you'll be wanting this."

"Man, and I really liked my blue one." I seemed to have the worst luck with clothes. Maybe I'd start ordering them by the dozen. Mari had ruined my favorite pair of jeans in Mexico, and I still hadn't found time to find a decent replacement.

Voices down the hall signaled Ava and Dimitri's arrival. Quickly, I pulled the shirt over my head, threading my arms in the holes and letting it slide down before releasing the sheet. The older Renegades in our group didn't worry much about nudity, but I wasn't casual with my nakedness. Besides, with what hung unsettled between me and Ritter, the more clothes between us, the better.

Ritter hit the light switch on the wall by the bed and came to his feet. "I hope they have good news."

I did, too. And I hoped someone had already explained to them what had happened at the Emersons' townhouse so I wouldn't have to. Glancing down, I saw the shirt was a dark gray with a V-neck I'd seen Ritter wear before, made of a thin, stretchy material that caressed my skin like a touch. All at once, accepting the shirt felt far more personal than if I'd kept wearing the sheet.

"Is she awa—" Dimitri broke off as he saw me. He crossed the space between us and leaned down to give me a hug. "Sorry I wasn't around to take care of you."

I laughed. "You mean put my pieces back together?"

"Something like that. I hope Ritter did a good job."

Ritter paced to the other side of the room. "Wasn't me. Keene took out the bullet."

Oh, so not only had I disobeyed and gotten myself shot, but I'd had the gall to get better with Keene's help. "Guess I'd better thank him," I said lightly, turning to Ava. "Did you find anything?"

"Actually, no." She frowned. "Everything, and I mean everything, was in place. We talked to dozens of people at the hospital, pursued leads all over Worcester and several other cities in Massachusetts, and interviewed more people over the phone. Stella hacked into computers, I spied on people's minds, and Dimitri consulted on several cases—he even saved two trauma patients in the emergency room."

"They were children," Dimitri said somewhat apologetically. "All I did was give them enough strength so they would survive their surgeries."

Ava met my gaze. "Try explaining to frantic parents why a strange man was touching their child in such an intimate manner."

"Oh, I thought you filled in rather well with all that talk about pressure points and blood flow." Dimitri smiled. "As always."

Ritter and I exchanged a glance, and I was relieved to feel the tension between us dissipate. "There has to be something," I said. "Patrick Mann got those genes somewhere. Isn't there a chance he could be adopted like Brody Emerson?"

Ava shook her head. "The doctor who delivered him died a few years back, but we talked to two nurses who were there that day. For one woman, it was her first week on the job, and it was a big deal to her. They both verify that the Manns had a son that day. The only slightly interesting thing we found was that on the same day another woman had a baby boy and placed him for adoption, but that's not unusual in a hospital of that size."

"Did you talk to the birth mother?" I asked. "Is she Unbounded?"

"I wish. Then we might have some reason to think there was a switch." Ava sat on the bed next to me, her expression grave. "After some digging around, Stella found her name, but there is no Emporium connection that we can see. Same with the listed father. We talked to the mother on the phone and she became quite upset. Said she saw her baby after he was born and that he had black hair, but he had problems breathing so they rushed him away. When she saw him again his hair was lighter and he looked different."

"That seems promising," I said. "Maybe there's something to her claim."

Dimitri pulled a chair from against the wall and straddled it, resting his arms on the back. "Babies are always wet when they're born. That makes their hair darker. Depending how long they've been in the birth canal, their features are often squished and their color odd, and this mother had been in labor for over thirteen hours. It's also likely she was trying to emotionally distance herself from the baby she wasn't planning to raise." He sighed. "At any rate, if she were Unbounded or had any connection to them, I'd be more suspicious, but unless she's lying about who the father is, she can't be Patrick Mann's mother."

"Well, something happened at that hospital, unless you think Patrick Mann just suddenly became Unbounded on his own." I frowned at the white sheet on the bed. "Is there any way to trace that baby? Maybe test blood or something, just to check the woman's claim?"

"Good idea." Ritter stood by the bed, his arms folded over his chest. "It's a long shot, but if it's the only abnormality you found, we have to check it out."

I drew up my right knee and rested my arm on it. "I don't suppose the Mann baby could have been exchanged later, after they left the hospital."

"No." The look in Ava's gray eyes was intent. "If that baby was taken and another left in his place, it would have had to be done in the first hours. Parents, even busy political ones, spend a lot of time staring at their newborns. By then a switch would be noticed."

"We'll have to check out the adoption agency that placed Brody Emerson." Ritter paced to the door. "And his sister. For all we know, she was placed by the Emporium as well."

"We'll cross-reference all the names at the agency and where Emerson was born with the people we researched today," Ava said. "Another long shot, but any connection would give us a lead."

Ritter stopped pacing. "One big problem now is Brody Emerson. The Emporium knows we were there. Is he going to be safe?"

"Nothing we can do about that now," Ava said. "We'll bring him in as soon as possible. You sent Cort there to watch him, right?"

"Cort and Oliver." Ritter's voice showed a decided lack of enthusiasm.

Poor Cort if he had to endure Oliver all day. I'd rather take another bullet.

"Is Jace back?" Dimitri asked. "I can grab him and relieve Cort when we're through here."

Ritter nodded. "He's upstairs working through his forms again."

"Look, that reminds me," I said. "Brody Emerson has an odd sort of gift that I've never seen before. When he looks at Unbounded who are using their ability or at something using a lot of electricity, he sees a sort of glow around the thing or the person. He doesn't seem to know why it's happening, but it must relate to his gift. I didn't notice it when I was in his mind, but it's obvious in his unconscious memories. That's why he singled out Patrick Mann and me at the fundraiser. We were both glowing. And so were all the lights around the camera."

Ava looked at Dimitri, one brow raised. "Have you heard of such a thing? I haven't."

"Sounds like a blaster," Dimitri said, his head shaking back and forth. "I knew one once, and he went missing too many years ago to count. Centuries." We waited for more, all eyes riveted on his face. "Blasters see energy," he continued. "At first they can only see big energy, but as they mature and develop their gift, they can pinpoint increasingly smaller amounts. I'm not surprised you didn't notice the energy before, Erin. You were probably still using your own physical eyes to see the world. As I understand it, connecting with him mentally isn't the same thing as looking out through his physical eyes, though I know that's possible for you."

"I remember hearing Cort talk about something like that," Ritter said. "Can't blasters gather energy and convert it for other uses?"

Dimitri nodded. "That's why they're also sometimes called converters. It works a lot like absorbing, but they can use that gathered energy to literally blast things. Huge explosions or tiny isolated ones—whatever is needed. Very useful. One blast at the front gate and you're inside the castle. Or a blast to a pile of old armor laid outside the gate and the heated metal seals an entire castle regiment inside while you take over the land around. It's particularly effective." He laughed. "My age is showing, isn't it? Anyway, in this day and age I imagine the gift would be even more valuable."

I could imagine. "Can they draw power from people?"

"Yes, but only if those people are using an ability at that moment, and strong mental shields can prevent the transfer. Problem is that with people blasters seem to expend as much energy drawing it in, so usually they learn to take it from easier, non-living sources like electricity, storms, rivers, and so forth. They can even take it from fire. When they do, the hottest blaze won't heat up a small room. But once my friend managed to do quite a number by stealing the power from a dozen young Emporium Unbounded gifted with combat." Dimitri laughed, his wide chest expanding. "He almost died doing it, but it was a glorious win, I tell you. We were outnumbered."

How much he'd lived, all in a different time and place. I wondered what the world would be like a thousand years from now when I was his age. What marvels the world would have seen and what battles I would have fought. Surely by then we would no longer be hiding in the shadows, hoping humans didn't find out about us and murder us as we tried to save them from the Emporium.

"We have to make sure we recruit him for our side," Dimitri added. "I can only guess at how long it's taken to breed back that ability. Blasters have always been exceptionally rare, and while they can take a long time to regain strength if they discharge completely while using their gift, they can be extremely valuable."

Ritter was at the foot of the bed, his hands once more folded over his chest. "What I want to know is what ability Patrick Mann was using when Brody Emerson looked at him and saw him glowing."

"I don't know." I bit my lip in thought. "I couldn't see anything in Mann's thoughts about his ability. I sure hope it's not another one we're not familiar with."

Ava shook her head. "It's unlikely, given the odds, but let's talk to Cort and see what gifts he could be using just standing there—beyond sensing, of course."

"What about communication devices?" I released my leg, letting it hang over the edge of the bed with the other, the buzz from the curequick making me anxious. "Patrick had a way to contact his friends. Wouldn't that register on Brody's ability?"

"No," Dimitri said. "I mean, those things will eventually register as he grows in skill, but if they were registering now, he would have seen glowing from everyone there—cell phones, hearing aids, pacemakers. No, for him to pick out Mann, it had to be that he was using some stronger energy."

"So not only do we need to figure out what Mann is planning, we have to figure out what he is." I hated the uncertainty. "I've racked my brain and I just don't see what they're planning. Let's say the rumor about the president being sick is true and Vice President Mann becomes acting president or whatever. That still doesn't help Patrick because I don't believe he has a lot of influence with his father. His father may be worried about him, but there seems to be some bad blood between them."

"Yet it's kind of coincidental that these rumors begin just when Patrick Mann suddenly turns out to be an Emporium agent." Ritter's scowl wasn't meant for me, but the intensity made me shiver.

"I'll talk to a certain Pennsylvania senator," Dimitri said.

"You mean the one who's your descendant, right?" I was curious because that meant she was also some sort of relative to me.

He nodded. "Seven generations removed from the last Unbounded in her line. We knew she wouldn't Change, but since her family has always been in politics, we kept her grandfather, and now her, in the loop. She also knows about the Emporium and has helped us out a time or two already. Maybe she can verify what's going on with the president." Dimitri stood and replaced his chair against the wall. "To protect mortal America, we need to do what we can to protect both President Stevens and the vice president from the Emporium. Depending on where our search leads, that might mean removing Patrick Mann by any means possible."

We were all quiet a moment, and I began swinging my bare feet as they dangled off the bed in an effort to alleviate the effects of the curequick. Ritter paced to the sink on the far wall and back again. Ava and Dimitri were motionless.

"How about the compound and the prisoners?" Ava asked finally.

Ritter faced her. "If we force our way inside, we will have casualties. If we use Mari and Erin to shift inside while we attack outside, we will still have casualties." The hollowness in his voice betrayed his discouragement.

"It's a chance we are all willing to take," Ava said gently.

Ritter shook his head. "For three weeks Yuan-Xin and I have done nothing but go over this. Our numbers are too small and our enemy too protected. In every scenario, we believe we would lose more Renegades than we would save."

"We could ask for backup from Europe. After all, three of the prisoners are theirs." Ava slid off the bed, standing close to Dimitri. Really close. It made me wonder at their relationship. Just old friends, or had they decided to take the chance we all hoped they would take?

"No." Ritter's voice was inflexible, echoed by the physical stance he took with his feet apart and arms tensely folded. He looked like a rock that would never move. But the emotions coming off him told me of his agony at not being able to act. "Our allies in Europe aren't ready to trust us again so soon. We are the reason the Emporium found the safe house. Besides, they have their own battles there."

Ava sighed. "You're right. Some of their problems are more serious than what we're facing, and we can't send them help, either. Not yet."

"We can't just leave our people there." I dropped to the floor, the tile cold on my feet.

"Of course not." Ritter unfolded his arms. "Our best hope at this point might be to let the Emporium know we've found their compound. Get them to think we're going to attack and that we have more people at our disposal. But we hold off on the actual attack until they move our people to another location."

"Like a siege." A slow smile spread across Dimitri's face.

Ava rubbed her chin, her gaze going to the floor in deep thought before finally nodding. "Yes, that could be effective. Attack them coming or going, damage the building, cut the electricity. As for an illusion of more combatants, maybe Oliver will finally be able to help."

"Maybe later on," Ritter allowed.

Ava brought her hands together. "When does our siege begin?"

"In two hours. At midnight," Ritter said. "As long as you're all in agreement."

"Then I'd better keep Oliver with me when I relieve Cort outside Emerson's townhouse." Dimitri gave a sigh. "I'd rather have Jace, but if we let him beat someone up near the compound, he'll be so much more fun to live with."

I stifled a laugh. "He's coming now," I told them. "Must be finished with his forms."

Ava looked at the ceiling and concentrated. "He's barely leaving the fourth floor." Silently, she added, *You really are getting stronger.*

Minutes later Jace appeared in the doorway. "So, what's the plan for tonight?" he said. "Any chance of getting a little action?"

Ritter grinned. "I think I know just the thing for working off a bit of frustration." He didn't look at me, but I knew he was talking to me every bit as much as to Jace.

"Okay," I said. "I'm in. But I need to change."

Ritter regarded me seriously. "What you have on looks fine."

"Not really." Jace made a face as he examined me. "Whose shirt is that anyway? A gorilla's?"

"Yeah, one who probably needs it back." I spied my boots in the corner and went to get them.

"Don't worry about it," Ritter said. "This particular gorilla buys them a dozen at a time."

Of course he did. That's it. The next article of clothing I found that worked, I was going to buy out the entire store or send it to Stella's seamstress to replicate. "I'll only be a few minutes," I said. "That's plenty of time to fill Jace in on what's happening tonight."

"Oh, and Erin," Ava said as I walked to the door. "You and I need to talk."

I'd known it was coming. From the moment she'd walked in, she'd kept back her anger at my decision to take Keene along, but

I hadn't escaped entirely. Everyone studiously looked elsewhere, even Jace whose expression told me he was glad for once not to be the one in the hot seat. My mouth opened to explain Keene's obstinacy, but she shook her head. "Later."

Only Ritter met my gaze. I expected to see amusement or even satisfaction at Ava's words, but instead I glimpsed a sadness I didn't often see on his face, a heaviness usually masked by strength and competence, a weight caused by this centuries-long war. What had he been like before becoming Unbounded? Obviously he'd felt an urge to protect others since he'd chosen to be an officer of the law in colonial America, but what else had he done? Had he gone on picnics with his family? Had he participated in games of skill that were popular in the day? All I really knew about that time of his life began on the day his family was slaughtered by the Emporium.

Ritter saw my gaze and winked, his strength back, the weight lifted—or at least willingly borne. Warmth inched over my body, filling me to bursting and blotting out all thoughts of Ava.

With effort I left him there with the others.

CHAPTER 10

STELLA JOINED ME ON THE ELEVATOR AT THE NEXT FLOOR, HER FACE looking weary and her pinstriped suit slightly disheveled, which for her was unusual and testified of a fruitless day. As usual, her neural headset was on and occasionally blinking. "Glad to see you're recovered." She turned up her eyepiece and smiled. "Mari told me what happened today. That's tough about the disk."

"Thanks." I could always depend on Stella to say what I needed to hear.

"Keene should have known better than to force you to take him along. He was nothing but a liability in his condition."

"Well, he did get us in. Mari and I would have spent hours looking for the family and figuring out some excuse to talk to them." I don't know why I was defending him because I was angry about the way things had turned out.

"Instead you spent the entire day recovering." Stella rolled her eyes. "He should have set things up and let you take over. The question is why didn't he? And don't defend him. I like it better when you two are at each other's throats."

I laughed. "I'll keep that in mind."

The doors swung open and we continued down the hall together. "You heading to bed?" Stella asked.

"I've had enough rest." I explained Ritter's idea of scaring the Emporium into moving the prisoners. "Wanna come?"

"If he needs me, but I'd rather keep researching. A few of the technopaths in Europe are helping me sift through data." She stared into the distance at something I couldn't see. "And Ava and Dimitri just sent me texts with additional requests."

Requests I suspected she was already jumping to fulfill, if the increased blinking of the lights on her headset was any indication. "You should get some rest. From what I hear, I'm not the only one who had a rough day, and you're not fueled by an overdose of curequick like I am." I stopped in front of my door. "They must have given me too much."

That made her smile. "You just seem to be more sensitive to the stuff. As for me, I'm fine, or will be after a bit. I think what you're seeing is a problem with a couple of my nanites."

"A malfunction?"

She nodded. "I tapped into a computer at the hospital and I got my wires crossed with some nanite research they've been involved with. Good thing I noticed before I shorted out more of them and my appearance reverted completely. I had to reprogram the remaining nanites to temporarily do their job, but their replacements are back in now. Nothing a little time won't cure." She sighed. "Sometimes I think I'm too vain, but this version of me has become so familiar that I don't really recognize the other me."

I'd never seen Stella without her nanites slightly altering her appearance, but I suspected she was still an attractive woman. "Want to talk while I change?" I asked, twisting the knob on the door to my room.

The brow over one slanted eye rose. "Is this about Ritter?"

"Hey, I'm the one who's supposed to be able to sense, not you."

She chuckled and followed me inside. "I can spare a moment."

Dropping my boots by the door, I began undressing as I walked into my bathroom, tossing my clothes into the hamper. I would have liked to take a shower, but I contented myself with a rubdown using a hot, wet towel. In the large mirror I could see the skin in the middle of my back was pinker than the rest, but otherwise there was no sign of the bullet. I grinned.

As I finished washing, Stella came in carrying my bodysuit. "Might be a little cold, but you'll need it if you're going on the offensive. Too bad the jacket part was ruined in Mexico. Well, the other sets we ordered should be here soon."

"Better add in another long coat," I said to her retreating back. "We all left ours at the Emersons' townhouse." Pulling on the suit, I returned to my room to restock my weapons.

She flopped on my couch, though on her it looked more like a seductive flourish. "I already ordered you another long jacket and a short version. I like everyone to have a backup, so after I make sure it works, I order more. We tend to outlive our clothes." She paused. "Or most of us do."

She was thinking of her mortal husband and the unborn baby she'd lost, both three weeks gone. The loss was huge, a thing that filled up all of who she was and everything she might have become. She would get over Bronson and the baby in time, but for now it felt as if she never would. No wonder she worked so hard. It must help her to forget.

She looked up at me, her olive skin darkening with embarrassment. "I'm doing it again, aren't I? Projecting emotion. I'm sorry."

I shook my head slowly. "It's me. Something happened in Mexico. I would have told you before, but we've all been a little busy."

"Go on," she kicked off her shoes and pulled her feet under her.

"I can feel surface thoughts without really trying. I mean, I could somewhat before, but now I always do, and mind shields . . ." I stopped before making myself continue. "When I'm rested, I've been able to break through everyone's except for the sensing Unbounded we ran into this morning. Well, everyone that I've tried." I hoped it went without saying that I didn't pry in my friends' minds.

She stared at me, her dark eyes wide. "That will be very useful. Try breaking through mine."

I was pleased that, like Ritter, she still considered me more useful than intrusive, and I was almost teary that she hadn't asked me if I'd already breached her shield. That showed her trust more than anything else she could have said.

I sat beside her on the couch, pushing out my thoughts and finding her familiar shield. She wasn't making it easy for me. As a technopath, she was more adept at directing her thoughts than most Unbounded, and she had centuries of practice. There were no holes anywhere and her barrier was every bit as thick as Ritter's or Cort's, though hers was a shimmering dark gray.

Remembering the Emporium agents outside the townhouse, I pulled out my imaginary machete, wielding it in both hands, and slammed it into the gray. Three hits and a glowing hole appeared. I shot through it. *I'm here,* I told Stella.

"Impressive," she said. "So tell me how I can keep you out?"

I saw in the sand stream of her mind that she didn't mean me but someone like me. "I'm not sure yet, but it can be done, at least by a sensing Unbounded."

"Can you show me?"

"Yes." I called up the image of the black shield I'd seen inside the sensing agent, trying to include details. I pushed the image into Stella's sand stream, careful not to disturb the flow of the stream itself with any part of me—or any part of the representation I made of myself.

"It's more shiny than I usually see," I said, "and it felt far thicker. There was also a cord and another shield he'd thrown up around his companion. I was able to break through the cord and it shattered the other agent's shield but did nothing to the one over his own mind." That reminded me of the mental shield I'd thrown up around Mari. Had I seen her shot? Maybe I'd ask Ava to go back with me in my memories to see if I had it right. Mari seemed totally fine. Perhaps she'd shifted in and out in that very instant.

I held the image in Stella's mind as she tried to mimic the

construction. The problem was, I could only show it to her from the outside and neither of us really knew how it worked. After several attempts, she sighed. "I think you will have to figure out how it's built and then teach us."

"I'll work on that as soon as I get a moment."

The dryness in my voice didn't escape her. She laughed. "Life does seem to move at breakneck speed, doesn't it? Good thing we have so much of it left."

"So when do we get to sit on a beach and sip exotic drinks brought to us by gorgeous, half-naked men?" I asked.

She laughed again. "Maybe after we figure out what Patrick Mann is up to."

I started to leave her mind when a familiar mental humming stopped me. Where had I felt that before? There was a pattern to the humming, a pulsing pattern that I—

"Erin?"

I pulled my thoughts back to myself, realizing I no longer had permission to be in her mind. "Sorry."

Arising, I headed to my closet to see what weapons I might have stashed there. "I lost my guns at Emerson's townhouse, and my sai and the machete must still be in—" I stopped talking. The missing weapons sat on a shelf, and the coat I'd reported lost to Stella was inside as well. *Okay.*

"Is something wrong?"

I lifted the coat from the hook and pulled it on. "Apparently, someone's been busy while I was off in dreamland." I sure hoped it wasn't Mari, or I was going to rat on her. Weapons were replaceable; she was not. All the shifting in the world wouldn't help her if someone got lucky with a bullet.

Stella watched me put the sai into the coat's special pockets. "So what's going on with you and Ritter?"

I let my hands drop to my sides and turned to face her. "I'm not really sure. I mean, I know he's attracted to me and it's all I can do to keep my hands off him, but . . ." I groaned.

In the past I'd told him to get lost, but even then my body

begged him to stay. It didn't make sense on the surface, but when I remembered that all regular forms of birth control for Unbounded failed, it made perfect sense.

I called it the end of the sexual revolution. Vasectomies healed in a day, an entire uterus regenerated in forty hours. Unbounded genetic material had a longer life span, so keeping track of a woman's cycle was a challenge, and naturally occurring body acids rendered most barrier methods inconsequential. The only sure method of birth control was a relationship with a sterile mortal, unless you were a healer, and then you might heal your partner without realizing it. While healers couldn't replace a missing womb, they often untied tubes and healed vasectomies. They could extend the life of a failing organ just by proximity.

Great for the propagation of the species, but not so great for a developing relationship.

Add that to the fact that the normal rate of Unbounded offspring between two Unbounded was thirty percent, which meant a seventy percent chance of burying your child before you physically aged two years. Even with genetic manipulation, the rate was only nearing fifty percent. It was a sort of Russian roulette.

No wonder I was in such conflict.

"Aren't you going to ask me about his giving you the sai?" Stella asked.

I wanted to, but part of me was afraid of what she would say. My tongue felt suddenly thick. "You seem to think it's weird that he gave them to me, but he gives everyone weapons."

She arose and came to stand in front of me. "Yeah, from the arsenal, not his personal collection." She put her hands on my shoulders and stared up into my eyes. "Erin, it's a mating ritual that combat-gifted Unbounded have practiced for millennia. They give their most prized weapons to their intended. Combat Unbounded understand the significance immediately, and the rest of us have learned to appreciate it. Of course to mortals and to you, so recently Changed, it must seem odd." She let her hands drop from my shoulders but held my gaze. "Anyway, by giving you weapons, Ritter is making a declaration."

"What? It's a proposal?"

"Of sorts." Stella's grin was ridiculously wide.

"Why are you so happy about this? You're the one who told me Ritter is too angry to participate in any kind of romantic relationship."

She shrugged. "He's different now. I don't know if it's because Justine's death in Mexico finished his quest to find all the Unbounded who murdered his family, or if it's because of you. But I suspect it's you." She hesitated before adding, "Maybe it's because now he has something to live for. Loving someone makes near immortality a lot less bleak." The pain in her heart had come to the surface again, and I shut my eyes momentarily against the onslaught.

"I don't know if I'm ready for that." There. I'd spoken the truth I'd never dared to say aloud, especially not to Ritter. "It's a lot of commitment."

"I know." Her hand came up again, resting on my arm comfortingly. "But the only thing worse than deciding to commit and losing is never taking the risk. Erin, you have something I wish I had. I know it's a lot to work through, but finding someone to spend your life with . . . I would have given anything if Bronson could have been Unbounded. Or even if I . . ." She looked away before finishing. "If I could have been mortal with him."

That was silly, because even if she'd been mortal, it wouldn't have prevented his death.

Stella crossed to the door and picked up my boots. "I know you may think that's stupid, but can you imagine how horrible it's been these past few years to go out in public? I looked like his grand-daughter, not his wife. Even before he became weaker, he couldn't go on vacations because of his special diets. He couldn't work in the yard or go for a walk. If I sent him to the store, I worried that he would be too weak to get back alone." She walked toward me and pushed the boots into my hands. "All the while, I didn't slow down. I felt stronger than ever. Even his desire for intimacy steadily decreased at a time when I only seemed to need him more. It drove me crazy not to share that intimacy." Tears glistened in her eyes. "Several times . . . I'm ashamed to say I sometimes thought about cheating on him. I never did, and I'm glad I didn't, but it was hard. You know how Unbounded genes are. Survival of the species."

I knew exactly what she meant. Even being near Ritter made me feel crazy sometimes. Except when I was in his arms and then somehow it was okay.

"Aw, Stella." I hugged my friend tightly.

After a few moments she pulled away. "I'm okay. Or I'll be okay. Working helps. While you guys have been out casing the Emporium compound, Cort and I have been occupied with some nanite improvements. Most are for technopaths, and one will be of interest to you, but I don't want to get your hopes up yet. We're not entirely sure we can get it to work even for true technopaths, much less anyone channeling our ability." She walked toward the door, the sadness dropping away from her demeanor, or at least becoming adequately masked, and the hopelessness I was experiencing at my own situation lessened considerably. I really needed to work on my shield.

"So about Ritter," I called after her. "How serious is it? All the weapons, I mean."

She stopped and turned, one hand on the knob. "As serious as it gets, and you know Ritter. It's all or nothing with him."

I swallowed. "What do I do about the weapons?"

"Have you used them?"

I nodded. "Once. Today."

"Then I think you've already made your reply."

"That's crazy! I didn't even know what it meant."

She tilted her head. "You can probably claim ignorance and get out of it, if that's what you want. The question is, do you want to get out?" With that she opened the door and left the room.

I stood there alone, all dressed, weapons ready, curequick

running through my veins. There was a battle ahead of us tonight with the Emporium, but all I could think about was Ritter and how his touch made me feel.

A rap sounded on the door, and I moved toward it, tugging on my boots as I went. Or trying to. "Come in," I called, thinking that Stella must have forgotten something.

I was bent over trying to pull on the last bit of my left boot when Keene appeared in the doorway. He gave me a mocking smile. "Did I catch you at a bad time?"

I gave a last little hop as the boot slid into place. "Ah, no. I am heading out, though."

"I see you found the coat." His eyes ran over me slowly, sending warmth to my face.

"That was you?"

He shrugged. "I called Emerson and had him send our things by messenger to Central Park where Mari shifted in to grab them. All of our stuff was there, plus a few extra guns the Emporium agents left behind."

"Emerson did that?"

"It was the least he could do after we told him about his son."

"Wasn't he mad at the way we left?"

"Not after I explained. He was angry when he realized the danger his family was in, but happy the Emporium didn't get the disk. He's called in backup to protect his son."

"Good thing. Cort and Oliver are watching him, and I think Dimitri is heading over there now, but it's possible Brody's a blaster and the ability is rare. If the Emporium suspects, they'll retrieve him as quickly as possible."

Keene shut the door and my room suddenly felt small. "I only hope his father doesn't change his mind and kill him first."

"He won't. I'm sure of it. Thanks for taking out the bullet, by the way."

"No problem. I've had to do it enough for others." He chuckled. "Be different if I actually worried about killing you. Or scarring you for life."

I grinned. "Right. So, how are you feeling?" There seemed to be a difference in him now, a strength that wasn't there this morning.

"Good, surprisingly. Dimitri is better than the healer I've had work on me before." Keene took two steps, closing the space between us. "Going to the compound?"

I nodded. "You've heard the plan?"

"Yeah. A siege might work as long as the Emporium isn't connected by tunnels to the outside like our new facility in San Diego." He took another step. Now he was in my space and my heart thumped more rapidly. What was he doing?

"Stella would have let us know if that were the case."

"Computers can't tell us everything." His eyes held mine, brilliant green even in the average light of my room. His hair was pushed back and I glimpsed the long line of darker red on the edge of his face. I thought the scar looked different. Maybe it was finally fading or changing colors, or Dimitri's healing had helped speed recovery. "Erin," he said.

I swallowed hard. "Yes?"

"Here." He handed me a small folded knife.

"What's this?"

"A switchblade. Be careful. Remember that poison from last night? Well, something like that is on the blade. It's small enough to hide, but the poison gives it more punch." The knife was smaller than any switchblade I'd ever seen, the handle some kind of white material decorated with a carved blue-painted dragon riveted to a metal base.

Silence stretched out between us. At last he spoke. "I'm not Unbounded but if I have any ability, it's for combat, and I wanted you to know where I stand. In case it matters."

If Stella hadn't told me what the weapons meant, I would be completely confused right now. "Keene, I—"

He put a finger over my mouth. "Not now." In a swift movement he removed his hand and bent down, pressing his lips to mine. He felt warm and inviting. Desire rushed over me, but with my heightened sensitivity, I couldn't tell who drove the emotion. Before I could figure it out, he drew back and walked toward the door.

I didn't reply, still stunned. Despite his flirting and half joking comments, I was pretty sure he'd been resigned to my feelings for Ritter, but maybe he wasn't as content as I'd thought to sit back and wait until I made my decision.

At the door, Keene paused. "Be careful out there tonight." A second later he was gone.

I stared at the knife, shaking my head. I burned for Ritter, but I'd be lying if I said Keene didn't have a place in my heart. In many ways he was safer. Losing myself was something I was very much afraid of doing.

Locating a narrow pocket sewn in my bodysuit along the side, one of the outfit's many hiding places, I stored the switchblade. I waited two more minutes to make sure the hallway was clear before I headed downstairs.

CHAPTER 11

THE EMPORIUM COMPOUND WAS LOCATED ACROSS THE BAY IN Brooklyn on the west side near the water but not right on it. We always passed a Costco warehouse on our way, and as usual Jace said he wished it were open that late because there were some things he'd like to pick up. Before his Change, he'd been a huge Costco fan. I think he'd bought all his clothes there. Now he didn't have time to shop, so he used magazines or relied on Stella's contacts. He didn't care about the perfect pair of jeans.

The compound was a big, ugly, rectangular building surrounded by other big, ugly, rectangular buildings. Compared to Manhattan where we were staying, the buildings here were flat, most reaching only four or five stories, though there were eight-story buildings scattered among them. The compound was three stories surrounded by yards of cement. There were no plants or grass anywhere, unless they were in some interior courtyard we couldn't see. A huge chain-link fence dotted with construction signs encircled the property, but there was no evidence of construction except for a single backhoe and a small trailer parked near the entrance.

Four Emporium soldiers with assault rifles were always on guard near the trailer, and two of them walked the entire perimeter with regularity. Security cameras were everywhere, most focused toward the building's doors and windows and the approaching grounds. The building itself had at least ten other guards on duty at all times, two outside each entrance, and every time we'd seen them, they wore headsets connecting them with the others. While this wasn't a luxury safe house for high-ranking Emporium Unbounded, they were obviously protecting something they considered to be of high value. We knew from observation that at least one healer and two scientists were working there on manipulating the Unbounded gene. By the deliveries that came to the place, and the glimpses we'd managed to get of the inside with our technology, they weren't living a life of squalor.

We parked several blocks over and walked through the silent streets, making ourselves scarce whenever a car drove by. The cold was biting and the darkness heavy, but it was better than watching in the daylight when we had to be more careful of being sighted.

"Anything we should be aware of?" Ritter asked me as we approached the building from the right side.

I shook my head. "Not a thing." I'd been pushing so hard and reaching so far out that my head already pounded, an odd contrast to the rest of me that felt alive and ready to fight.

"See if you can sense the new prisoner when we get close," Ritter said. "We haven't seen him removed, but you never know."

Never know if he had been smuggled out or if he'd been killed? I didn't want clarification.

"I'm so glad we're finally doing something." Despite working through his forms twice, Jace was still wound tight.

I shot a glance in his direction. "Remember there's a sensing Unbounded in the area. Keep your shield up." The last thing I wanted was that Unbounded in my brother's mind. It disturbed me that I hadn't noticed the man spying on Emerson while I'd also been in his mind. I had to be more careful.

"I'm with Jace," Mari said. "It's good to be doing anything at this point. I wish I could just shift in and talk to our people. Let them know we're out here and not giving up on them."

I wished she could, too, or that my connection with the prisoners was clear enough for me to guide her inside. But I'd only been able to catch occasional glimpses of the prisoners at all.

"They know we're coming for them." This from Ritter and it was nearly a growl. The others fell silent but I felt his frustration and knew the growl was directed more toward himself than at their chatter.

"He's right," I said. "If it were any of us, we'd know someone was coming for us. Or I hope you know that."

They did. So odd feeling that from them without trying.

We usually watched the building from several locations, including from behind a grouping of storage sheds near the building next door, which was where we were headed tonight. Our primary goal in watching had been to make sure the Emporium didn't move the prisoners while we gathered information that might aid in their escape. So far, we'd kept our presence a secret, hoping to find some way in without risking a direct assault. But we'd come up empty, and after three weeks of waiting, the collective frustration was beyond high. We didn't forget our people had probably been tortured—perhaps still were being tortured—and that their genes were being studied and used by the Emporium.

As we approached, a figure separated itself from one of the storage sheds. A short Asian man talented in combat moved toward us with the sinewy grace of an acrobat. He had very short hair and looked to be in his late thirties, which made him closer to three or four centuries. His name was Li Yuan-Xin, the surname Li hinting at the moniker he'd once used as the famous mortal, Bruce Lee. Yuan-Xin was the only Unbounded famous in America who hadn't relocated elsewhere after faking his death. His son, also Unbounded and another faked death, was in Europe working with Renegades there.

Yuan-Xin smiled, taking my hand to gallantly kiss the back of it.

"We missed you last night. Heard you ran into trouble today. Good to see you're not letting it hold you back."

I returned his smile. "Never."

He kissed Mari's hand and bumped fists with the men in greeting. "My people are watching the other sides of the building, so I'll be joining them."

"You aren't staying for the fun?" Jace asked.

Yuan-Xin nodded. "Yeah, but we'll be on the other side in case they try to use the back gate. I'd rather be here with you guys, but someone has to keep an eye on our young ones. They've been talking about letting themselves get caught just for the experience. They don't yet understand . . . anything." He bowed to us. "Regardless, I'll be watching and waiting for the signal in case you need my help."

With that, he faded into the night. I was glad to have him for backup. I'd never seen him in an actual fight, but Ritter's respect for the man told me all I needed to know. Thinking of him saddled with two new reckless Unbounded and two others who cared only for their art was a little sad, but for all their irresponsibility, at least his new Unbounded weren't as arrogant and unlikable as Oliver, and their ability was combat. Eventually Yuan-Xin would live long enough to see the pendulum swing back the other way. At least if we could stave off the Emporium long enough.

"Okay," Ritter said as we made our way behind the sheds. "We know they change the guards at two. They are never late. Two new guards arrive and two leave. The others rotate. That's when we're going to act. We need to stop the guards from pulling their car into the gate. We hit them hard and fast. Use your silencers. Shoot out the tires and windows. Shoot *them* if you have an opportunity. We grab hostages if we can. Mari and Erin, if their people do get out of the car and make it inside the gate, I want you both to shift close enough to fire at them, but get out within five seconds. Got it?"

"What if they get the car inside?" Jace asked.

Ritter pulled a rocket launcher from the duffel bag he'd dropped on the ground. "This is our backup plan."

Jace's face lit up. "So much for silencers."

"The objective is to make it cost them every time they come or leave. No deliveries in or out. No people in or out. A literal blockade. In between, we'll hit their electricity and other utilities. It gets pretty cold at night, and without running water, they'll get desperate soon enough. No doubt it will get harder to maintain the blockade as the days go by, and we'll have to become more creative. During daylight it will be far more difficult, and if they bring in anyone they have on the local police force, that will complicate things. Yuan-Xin and his people have booby-trapped places in the street that are controlled remotely, if it comes to that, but our hope is that the Emporium will try to deal with this on their own first and not officially involve local authorities until they decide to move the captives. When they do move our people, we follow them as far as we can and, at the best opportunity, hit them with everything we've got."

"That's your plan? Really?" I asked. Now that he'd explained the so-called siege, it didn't seem at all like something that would work long enough to get our people to safety. "I can drive a semi through that plan. They have far more people available than we do, and we may be able to stop them for the first few days, but we all know they aren't above involving the local authorities. In fact, I'm betting that's the first thing they'll do. They'll probably have the vice president's son conduct a press conference right here with the media while they bus our people out in the background." I'd been emotionally close to bursting for days, and it was good to have an outlet.

Ritter's eyes narrowed. "I agree, but it's still our best chance—as long as they do eventually move our people. If we go in there now, we'll lose both of Yuan-Xin's new Unbounded as well as his other two, no matter how well they sing and dance. They'll be nothing more than cannon fodder. Even with all our people here, we aren't strong enough to take that building from fourteen experienced men armed with assault rifles."

The sinking feeling in my gut told me he was right, but there had to be another way. A better way. Two of the captured Renegades were women, and after nearly being raped myself for the so-called Emporium good, I worried most about them. While Unbounded sperm could be removed from its owner and manipulated to increase the possibility of Change, tampering with the ovum had not yet been successful, and neither had implanting an Unbounded-bred ovum in a host body. That meant Unbounded women were vital to the Emporium breeding program. They wouldn't let these two go easily, especially if they had any unusual gift or ancestry.

The Emporium's success at sperm manipulation had led to our own testing. We didn't, however, experiment on unwilling participants or kidnap Emporium agents for their genes. We also didn't try to force early Changes. I told myself that was because the resulting damage, defects, and even death caused by the failed experiments was immoral, but part of me wondered if it had anything to do with numbers. We had fewer than a hundred Renegade Unbounded in the entire world and significantly fewer healers and scientists. The Emporium had a least four times that amount, possibly more. They could afford to lose one or two potentials to an experiment that might reap far more. We couldn't.

Ritter took my silence as capitulation. "Can you see inside the building? Are they all still there?"

He meant the prisoners. Of the five, we'd sighted only two in the last three weeks, one when she'd briefly been allowed to walk around the grounds, and another when he'd made a break through the front door. The building was made of heavy materials and was large, but I should be able to see inside better. Unfortunately, an occasional glimpse of the five huddled life forces was all that I was able to receive. I'd broken through many shields outside the building as the guards came and went, but so far that hadn't been useful. The last time I was here, I'd considered trying to access the roof because it might get me closer to the Unbounded inside. Unfortunately, their soldiers and cameras made that impossible.

"I can't tell," I said.

Mari squinted into the night. "What about the new Unbounded? The one they brought in the other night? Any sign of him?"

I concentrated. "Nothing. Sorry."

"Not your fault," Ritter said. "It's a long way." I felt slightly placated, though I was still mad at him for that stupid plan. Still, he had to know what he was doing, right? He'd been fighting the Emporium for more years than I'd been alive.

"Someone's coming." I turned to stare into the street behind us. "Two, on foot. Coming from that direction." Everyone reached for a weapon, Ritter fading into the night to circle around. I pushed out my thoughts, touching the newcomers. "Stand down. It's Cort and Oliver."

"Oh, did he have to bring Oliver?" Mari muttered.

Jace snorted a laugh.

Ritter reappeared at my side as Cort rounded the shed, Oliver two steps behind him. "So, couldn't stay away from the fun, eh?" Ritter said.

"I came to give you another option." Cort nodded at me. "Actually, it was Erin who suggested it."

Me? I was brilliant, but I didn't know what he was talking about. "How's that?" I asked.

"Show her, Oliver."

Oliver's satisfied smile vanished and a cold menacing one took its place—an exact mirror of the one on Ritter's face. No, it *was* Ritter, and I was standing next to him where Cort had been, except my bodysuit was nowhere near that tight or that low. And did I really have that much cleavage?

"Wow, that's pretty neat," Jace said, moving around them. "It even looks real from the back, though not exactly like the real thing."

"Well, I didn't see them from behind." The Ritter that was really Oliver took several steps and peered behind the real Ritter, keeping a safe distance, which I thought was pretty smart, given that the real Ritter's expression had hardened even more.

"Oh, that's much better," Jace said. "Now try to do me."

Jace's blond hair slowly replaced Ritter's black, followed more quickly by the rest of Jace's face and body. Fascinated, I reached out to see how Oliver did it, to see if I could mimic his ability.

Mari looked back and forth between the real us and the illusions. "Wow, that's incredible. So how many can you do at one time?"

"Only two if I want them to look just like the real thing." Oliver morphed back into himself. "Cort says I should be able to do more eventually."

"Maybe I can do it." My thoughts were churning. If we could pose as someone who belonged inside the compound, it would be a lot better start than that ridiculous plan.

Oliver frowned at me. "I don't think you'll be able to. It took me all day to—hey! Get out of my mind!"

I glanced down and found myself looking at Oliver. It looked real enough that I had to touch myself to see that it was an illusion.

"I can't believe you'd do that," spluttered Oliver.

"You didn't have a shield." At least not one of any note. "Anyway, I'm not in your thoughts, exactly. I'm barely inside. I just watched how you did it." I let the illusion drop, taking myself from his mind. I really hadn't meant to go inside him, but what a discovery. "There, I'm out."

Oliver glowered. "Don't do it again."

"Shut up, Oliver," Cort said. "You finally have a way to help us. Don't blow it. Or are you saying you don't want backup?"

"I'm just saying she shouldn't—" Oliver broke off when he glimpsed Ritter's face. "All right. But if we're both going to do it, she'd better watch me again to make sure she's got it. There's a particular problem with the speech."

Ritter exchanged a glance with Cort. "The question is how can we use it?" Ritter asked. "Three or four people won't be enough to take the compound over, even from inside. Not without a plan and a simultaneous attack from outside."

"No, but it'll be enough to give us a peek and see what the setup is," Jace said. "We could even plant some booby traps inside."

"Go inside?" Oliver made a sour face. "What if we're caught?"

"Then we free you when we free the others." Mari gave him an insincere smile as she added, "Cousin."

Oliver flashed teeth that seemed almost too bright against his dark skin. "Sure you would. Cousin."

"Kids, kids." Jace placed a hand on each of their shoulders. "Let's call a truce, eh? Oliver, I'm amazed. That's a useful trick. And if we get caught, you can fake that SWAT team like you did in Oregon. They were detailed enough to cause a distraction. Maybe not from behind, but who cares?"

Oliver seemed mollified at the praise and Mari knew when to keep her mouth shut. That left Ritter to decide what to do since Ava had given him total control over what went on at the compound. He paced to the end of the storage shed and back. "If we take out the new guards that are coming tonight and fake being them to get inside, we'll tip our hand when they pull out early. Because no way am I leaving our people there all night, especially if we begin the siege."

"We couldn't fake being the guards anyway," Cort said. "We know nothing about their protocol except what Erin and Ava have seen from their minds. That won't be enough."

An idea was forming in my head. "What about visitors? They've had at least two surprise inspections that we know about. One we even witnessed." I used the term *we* very loosely because I hadn't actually been there at the time of the visit.

Ritter's face snapped to mine. "What are you thinking?"

"I'm thinking we forget the siege for right now and some of us go in there with Oliver, posing as another inspection team or visitor. We take note of the setup, see if we can give our people weapons, and let them know to watch for a signal."

"What if something goes wrong?" Oliver asked.

"We know they're blocking radio signals from going outside the gate," I said, "to make sure their guards aren't overheard, so we can't use radios. But we have detected cell phone signals. We can call out if we need to."

"If they don't take our phones." Oliver's voice was a mutter.

I shrugged. "Well, if it's just you and Mari and me, Mari and I can always shift and take you with us at least some of the way."

Jace arched a brow and I knew he was remembering our practices with him. "You may need to fight your way out. Maybe someone else should go, too."

I opened my mouth to tell him that was ridiculous, but I couldn't because he was right, and I was suddenly dreading going in with only Mari and Oliver. Even if the two didn't kill each other, they would be next to useless in an actual fight. Oliver's illusions certainly couldn't fight, and Mari's knives wouldn't be much protection against experienced Unbounded. At least she could save herself by shifting out.

"I don't think—" Oliver began.

"The question is, can he do it?" Ritter ran over Oliver's protest, looking intently at Cort.

"Oh, yeah. He does it rather easily, in fact." Cort's voice told me he wished it were otherwise. "He should be able to grow stronger with practice. There's even a possibility that—" He shook his head. "Never mind." But I had already seen in his thoughts that he thought Oliver might learn to imbue his projections with substance.

Wait. I pulled back mentally from Cort, shocked at myself for spying, but unlike with Oliver, I hadn't penetrated his shield, only picked up his surface thoughts, perhaps even meant for me. I gave an internal sigh of relief. I hadn't lost myself to instinct entirely. I really needed to talk to Ava about this increase of my abilities. I didn't want to lose what few friends I had in this new life.

"Look, if it fails," I told Ritter, "you can always go with the original plan. I know it's a risk, but what we stand to gain far outweighs what we might lose."

Our eyes met, neither of us speaking. Everyone else seemed to vanish until we were alone. A tremor slid down my back.

"Okay," he said finally. "You go in now, before they change guards." He looked at his watch. "You have one hour. If you're not back by then, we'll attack the guards, cut the electricity, blow Yuan-Xin's booby-traps, and hope that provides you with enough distraction to get out." In other words, he'd show all his hand instead of doling it out bit by bit as the original plan called for.

"Maybe we should wait," Mari said, "and do it all at once. Free them and attack from the inside and out with all our strength on the same day. We'd keep the advantage of surprise. We'll lose that if they discover us tonight."

Ritter shook his head. "We need to know what we'll be walking into. We have the original building plans but no idea how the inside might have been modified. We have no clue about locking doors or what kinds of experiments have been done on our people and how able they are to defend themselves. They could be drugged and useless for all we know, or their minds could have been damaged."

This last he said because of Delia Vesey. The Triad member had been one of the visitors to the compound before we'd arrived. Her machinations were not limited to enemies, as verified by the distinct fear the guards had of a possible return visit. It was she I planned to impersonate.

A sense of excitement replaced the trepidation in the pit of my gut. Ritter had signed off on my plan and that meant he thought we had a real chance at success.

"In and out," he said.

Sometimes he was so predictable. "Of course, Your Deathliness. No dallying or fancy stuff. I promise." Not even Jace laughed at my comment. Probably too afraid of the beating he'd get at their next training session.

Ritter scowled. "Good. Now just try to remember that."

"Will they let them in with weapons?" Cort asked, giving me a subtle wink.

"They will if I'm in the Triad," I said.

Ritter's mouth twitched. "Delia Vesey?"

Oliver paled. "If she finds out, she'll kill us."

"She'd kill us anyway." Mari looked at me. "Who should I be?"

"How about that guy at Emerson's?" I said. "The sensing Unbounded. He's obviously a favorite with Delia so they might have been seen together."

"Oh, I like that." Venom laced her voice. Apparently, she knew how to hold a grudge. So did I because a perverse part of me was looking forward to being Delia. She scared the hell out of me and I didn't like that one little bit.

"Oliver and Jace can be a couple of their Unbounded guards," Cort said. "Someone prominent enough that they are recognizable, but no relation to anyone we've identified at the compound. Stella should be able to send us profiles. Oliver will be able to remember the information long enough to mimic them tonight. He has a good memory." That was an understatement. Oliver's memory was a lot better than any of ours—as he enjoyed reminding us every other day.

"Jace?" Ritter said.

Jace looked over eagerly, and for a long moment they exchanged a measured stare. At last, Jace sighed and shook his head. "Normally I'd be all over this, but it's too risky to send four. Not when Erin and Mari can shift only one. Even a few feet could get them free. If Erin has to mask two people, she won't be able to concentrate on getting information. Besides, I'll need to be out here if things go wrong." Jace met my surprised gaze. "Don't worry, Sis. I have your back. I'll plow through these guards and come get you if you run into trouble—no matter how many guns they shove in my face." That was more like the Jace I knew.

"Erin can fight well enough if it comes to that," Ritter said. Well enough was high praise from him, but the fact that he'd been willing to let my unpredictable brother go inside told me he was more worried than he let on about us making it out without incident.

I was both relieved that Jace had finally started listening to his ability's internal warnings and worried that I'd need him inside. Clamping down on the emotions, I turned to Oliver. "What was it you were saying about voices?"

Ritter reached for his phone. "You two practice while I let Yuan-Xin and Ava know what we're doing. Ava and Dimitri will want to be here just in case."

"Not Dimitri," Cort said. "He and Keene are watching Brody Emerson."

"Right." Ritter put his phone to his ear. "Remember the clock is ticking."

Ticking fast, it turned out. By the time we drove up to the compound gate in a sleek black Mercedes produced by Yuan-Xin, we had only fifty minutes left before the guard change. Mari was at the wheel, looking like the sensing Unbounded at Emerson's townhouse. I sat next to her, with Oliver in the back, resembling a man I vaguely recognized from our Unbounded files.

"They're letting us go in because we're expendable," Oliver muttered. "That's why they've lived so long. They sacrifice the newbies."

Mari snorted. "No way. No one can do what we can. Ritter's letting us go in because he knows we're the best for the job. He would have come himself if he didn't need to organize out here in case we screw up."

"Let's make sure we don't screw up," I said. To Mari, I added, "If I say shift, you get out. You'll need to tell Ritter everything. Don't hesitate."

"I know. He told me I'd be on probation if I didn't." She waited several seconds before adding, "What does that even mean?"

"No action," Oliver said. "Sounds good to me."

Mari's hands tightened on the steering wheel, but she didn't respond. "They're coming."

Sure enough, the guards from the trailer had come out, their weapons pointed at the car. One opened the gate and stood in front of us, while the other approached slowly. Both wore green uniforms and hard green helmets.

Mari pushed the button to roll down the window. "Let us through," she demanded. "I have Delia Vesey with me." Her voice was more nasal than the real man, as Oliver was doing her illusion and he'd never heard the voice, but it would pass. Jace had been right about not coming because at the moment I didn't know if I could have masked him well enough while pretending to be Delia.

The Unbounded guard leaned over to look inside the car, a tablet in his very white hands. "We weren't told of your visit." He tapped the screen, taking a picture of Mari.

"I don't have to tell you anything," I snapped in Delia's strong, aging voice. She was physically in her mid-sixties, which made her seventeen hundred years old, one of the oldest Unbounded still alive. With the ongoing war, too few lived to two thousand these days. "Do you need proof it's me?" I pushed aside his shield and said silently in his head, *Well, here it is. Let us through now. Or should I have you moved to somewhere less comfortable? I hear we need a contact inside the mortal prison.*

The man dipped his head as if trying to shake me loose. His shield strengthened and I could see he believed he'd pushed me out, but I was still there observing. Interesting that he thought he could push her out. Could he really or had she let others believe they were protected? "Sorry. Triad Vesey. Just protocol. I need to verify your companions. You understand, I'm sure."

"Hurry, then, if you must." My voice dripped sarcasm, while I silently applauded his backbone. In his mind, I saw a clear desire to do his best. More than a soldier following orders, he was someone who believed in the cause. People like him obscured the lines between our organizations, and I felt that in other circumstances, he'd make a good Renegade.

The tablet in his hands beeped and he nodded at Mari. "Mr. Roberts." *Lew Roberts,* his mind said. He glanced in the backseat at Oliver and recognition flooded his mind. I watched the sand stream of his thoughts as he found the memory: the two had worked together during an operation in London fifty-odd years ago.

Pretend you know him from fifty years ago. I pushed the thought into Oliver's mind. He wasn't shielding so I could use his ability, though he was resentful about it. *Ask if he's ever been back to London.*

Oliver stiffened and cast me a quick look before addressing the guard. "Hello," he said, using a voice that to me sounded just like the one we had on file. "Long time no see. You been back to London recently?"

The man relaxed. "No. You?"

"Once or twice. Been busy."

"I hear you," the guard said with a hint of a smile. "Been a bit busy myself."

"All for a good cause." Oliver dipped his head and looked at me again. The guard followed his gaze, suddenly remembering my presence.

"I just have to take your picture." The man pointed the tablet at Oliver as he spoke, tapping the screen. Seconds later a beep came. "You're cleared," he said, signaling his companion. "Drive on in." To Oliver, he added. "Good to see you."

"You, too."

With that, we drove through the gate and into the compound.

CHAPTER 12

"WHAT WAS THAT?" OLIVER SAID, USING HIS OWN VOICE.

"My bet is recognition software." I glanced back at the two guards who were standing close now, one of them tapping on the tablet. "Probably double checking to see if there are any notices out on us."

As Mari parked the car in front of the main entrance, two guards opened the front doors, one large with skin darker than the night, the other slightly less dark, a thin man who must trace his ancestry from India, or maybe came from there himself. They were combat Unbounded by the way they moved, the big rifles in their hands held with the ease of familiarity.

Instinctively, I felt for my own weapons. They should expect us, as Emporium Unbounded, to carry weapons, but if they frisked us for some unknown reason, it would all be over. Oliver and I might be able to hold realistic illusions, but they had no substance and our real bodies wouldn't match up with the illusions. Not for the first time, I wished I could manipulate conscious thoughts without signaling my presence. Delia had nearly succeeded with me, but I'd been so intent upon resisting, that I hadn't paid attention to how she'd accomplished it. Ava didn't know how, either, but we had better figure it out soon.

I forced myself to be calm as we walked toward the guards. Mari's step was confident, which I expected from someone who knew she could shift out at any moment, but Oliver's fear was choking me. "Oliver," I said, sending him soothing emotions, "try to relax." The last thing I needed was for him to drop our cover from sheer terror.

A surge of resentment came from him, but the fear cranked down a notch, and I breathed a sigh of relief. Blocking him out wasn't an option as long as I was channeling his ability.

"Greetings, Triad Vesey," said the Indian. "Nice to see you again. Is there any particular reason for your visit?"

"That is my own business," I said with acid in my voice. I pushed at his shield. It wasn't as strong as Lew Roberts' but constructed more solidly than most I'd seen.

He bowed. "I only meant how I should guide you? Do you wish to visit Director Tunns or with the other doctors? I have already notified them of your visit."

"The director will do," I said. "But I also want to see our guests."

He blinked. "Guests. Uh, yes."

I'd chosen the word because when I'd been held prisoner at the old Emporium headquarters in Los Angeles, Delia and the others had been all too polite, pretending I was there for a long-awaited visit with my supposed father, that I wasn't actually a kidnapped victim. Apparently no such pretense existed here.

"Please follow me," the Indian took one hand from his rifle and motioned us through the door.

"We'll want to see the new prisoner as well," Mari said in the wide foyer where couches sat in front of a long reception desk full of computer equipment. "You haven't damaged him too much, I assume?"

"No. But he has been difficult." This from the dark-skinned Unbounded, who fell into step behind us. "He's still adamant about not helping."

I waved a hand. "No matter. He will change his mind."

"I thought that was no longer necessary," the Indian said over his shoulder. "Wasn't that why they brought him here?"

This gave me pause. Was the new prisoner connected to the Emporium's plan with Patrick Mann or Emerson's son? Or were they working on yet another way to further their control over the world? At any rate, I had no intelligent way to answer the question unless I could break through their shields and the big Unbounded's mind was equally protected. Why couldn't I get through? Maybe I needed my machete.

To the Indian I said, "My plans for him do not concern you or anyone else. You will focus on your job."

He stopped walking, pivoting in my direction and bowing again. I envisioned pulling out my machete and swinging it against his shields, but the black barrier remained impenetrable.

"If you will come this way?" The Indian made a sweeping motion toward the door. "My partner will call to ask the director to meet us in the lab."

I pushed harder as he turned to lead us deeper into the compound. The instant we stepped out of the foyer and into the hallway, the shield gave way and I practically fell inside his mind, scrambling not to touch the sand stream of his thoughts and give myself away.

How odd, I thought. *Almost as if something had been blocking me from getting inside. Something outside him.* The more I thought about it the more implausible it seemed. Yet it would also explain why Ava and I had both been able to get so little from those inside the compound, especially when at least part of the compound was within my known range. Yet at the same time, whatever it was hadn't interfered with the connection I'd already forged with Oliver before we entered the building. I reached for Ritter. I'd been connected with him when I entered the building, but I couldn't feel him now. I filed the observations away for future reference.

I could find no suspicion in the guard's mind, though resentment was there aplenty. He and his partner were supposed to be relieved within the hour and he worried my visit would keep him here longer than expected. He wished there was someone to complain to, but the Triad could do whatever it wanted. He reminded himself, not very convincingly, that my visit was to further the good of all Emporium Unbounded. Besides, no one complained about Delia Vesey. No one. He'd heard rumors about those who had dared defy her. About people disappearing. Just being this close to her was nerve-wracking. He only wished he knew more of what was going on with the new prisoner than what the agents who'd brought him here had let slip.

Excitement welled through him, momentarily blotting out his nervousness. It was important. He could practically *feel* it. Utopia, where Unbounded were out in the open and mortals in their rightful place of servitude, couldn't come too quickly as far as he was concerned. Meanwhile, keeping watch over prisoners who were going nowhere fast was a tedium he had no choice but to endure. He almost hoped Delia would take notice of him and move him up the chain of command, but the thought alone brought all his nervousness crashing back on him. He abruptly felt like vomiting.

For a moment, I toyed with taking advantage of his nervousness to question him about the prisoners and their condition, but the more exchanges we shared, the more chance I had of messing up.

Down one corridor and then another. I paid close attention, though Mari would be able to reproduce it better than I would later. For the most part the halls were bare and old paint flecked on the ground, but this contrasted with the occasional pieces of luxury furniture we glimpsed through partially open doors.

Finally we arrived at an inconspicuous door where another guard stood with a bored expression on his chiseled face. He came to attention as he noted my presence. "Triad Vesey," he said, nodding once but not quite meeting my eyes. I reached out to his mind, breaking through his weak shield. Nothing out of the ordinary caught my attention.

"I need to see your prisoners," I told him. "Now."

"Yes, ma'am." Strange that we had so many customs unique to Unbounded, but we still used this mortal term.

As he fumbled with keys in his pocket, I tried again to reach my thoughts across the distance to Ritter and Jace, but I couldn't feel them anywhere.

Mari's hand brushed against mine, her anticipation clear. I understood all too well—finally, we'd get a good look at the prisoners. Behind us, Oliver glanced up and down the hallway, as if expecting an ambush. He knew if that happened, he was supposed to call up more illusions while Mari and I fought the others, but he was completely untried in battle. I felt a twinge of unease.

The door opened onto pitch black. One of the guards reached for a switch and the room bathed in light. I stifled a gasp. The walls, floor, and ceiling were covered with silver sheets that were riveted into place, some stained by huge black scorch marks. Thick steel bars stretched across half the small room like a jail cell, and behind the bars, five people sat or lay on the carpeted floor, blinking at the light. There were no pillows or blankets, and a stinking bucket in the corner testified that they hadn't been allowed a bathroom or privacy. Several of the Renegades looked recently beaten, their cuts sealed and their bruises mottled green as they rapidly healed. The two women looked untouched, though the mistrust in their eyes spoke volumes. Since they couldn't help but absorb from the air, none of them looked malnourished, but despondency leaked from them. Even so, they had their shields up tight and their expressions were defiant.

One muscled man stood and faced us, his paleness testifying of confinement. His right eye was a puffy reddened black and one hand held the other arm as if it hurt. "To what do we owe the pleasure of this visit, Triad Vesey?" His voice was a sneer on the last two words. I recognized him from Tenika's files as Willis Tyrone, one of the New York Unbounded, who was talented with combat. Enclosed in such a small space, he must be near breaking.

"Shut up!" The Indian guard kicked against the bars, his boot clanging loudly against the metal. "Or do you want another go-round?"

"Enough," I told the guard. "Leave us. Do not lock the door." With Mari here, I wasn't really worried about getting out of the room, but I wanted to make sure they understood and obeyed. Of course, the rooms were probably bugged to find out anything the prisoners might know, so I had to be careful.

"But are you—?" the Indian began.

Leave, I said in his mind.

His eyes widened in shock as he realized his shield hadn't kept me out. He dipped his head and hurried from the room, taking the other guard with him. The door clicked shut and I heard no key in the lock.

"They've probably got the place bugged," Oliver muttered.

I scowled at him and he shut up. Everyone waited in silence as I studied the room, looking for cameras. I couldn't see any, but I knew there had to be one. I wished Stella were here. As a technopath, she'd be aware of anything electronic or computerized, and with a few twists of wire could even communicate with it. I could see or hear nothing but the buzzing of the florescent lights overhead.

"It's freezing in here," Mari said.

I knew why. Cold would keep the prisoners more docile and more eager to visit the lab or wherever else they were needed.

All the prisoners were still sitting on the carpet except Willis, who stared at me with his disheveled brown hair and angry blue eyes. Edging closer to the bars, I let my gaze wander over the Unbounded. I knew them all from the files. Besides Willis, there was Guenter Simon from Germany and Mandalyn Sharp from England, both combat Unbounded, and another man from Austria who simply went by the name Dragon. He was a pyro, which now that I remembered him, explained the silver layers on the wall. Fireproof, I was guessing. The scorch marks must be where he'd touched the walls as they took him in and out of the room because I knew he hadn't yet learned to throw his fire.

The last prisoner was Francis Bennet, the other New York Unbounded, a blonde with close-cropped hair, a narrow face, and muddy, almond-shaped eyes. I hesitated on her, finding something I'd hoped not to find—a tiny life force glowing inside her belly.

"You're pregnant," I said to her.

Coming to her knees, she threw herself at the bars, gripping them with white hands. "As if you didn't know."

I looked back at the other woman. She was also expecting, but she didn't radiate the desperation I felt from Francis. I pushed against her shield, but it didn't yield, and I hesitated at using more force. These were allies, not the enemy, and I couldn't afford to become too spent.

"You won't get into their minds," Willis said, coming close to the bars. "As you can't mine. We've been practicing since you were here last."

Their shields did seem to be stronger than most I'd seen, but would they really keep Delia out? I didn't know. They would Ava, but she couldn't break through any shields the way I could.

I glanced at Mari, debating. "You have to," she murmured.

They certainly weren't going to drop their shields if I asked politely, but that didn't make what I was going to do any more fun. I pushed my thoughts toward Willis, focusing on his eyes. He was right that I couldn't get though on my own, but in a half dozen strokes, my imaginary machete broke through the swirling black wall.

Look at me, I told him. *I'm not your enemy.*

Instinctively, he obeyed and just for a moment, I allowed my illusion to falter on my face. He blinked and said, "Do it again."

No. They may be watching. Tenika sent me. I was about to explain who I was, but caution urged me to silence. I had no idea if our eventual escape would be successful, and I didn't want Delia finding information about me, even if only from his unconscious mind. *Tell the others to drop their shields. We have things to tell you.*

Francis jumped to her feet and tugged on his arm. "Fight her!

You can do it. We know that animal can keep her out." Her eyes shot daggers at Mari as she spoke, and I realized Francis had met Lew Roberts before. What had he done to her that she called him an animal?

"Look." Mari tugged at my sleeve, and I turned to see cockroaches, beetles, ants, and other assorted bugs crawling under the door and from the cracks between the silver sheets on the walls. Even a small mouse squeezed from an impossibly tiny space.

Francis was a summoner. A variation of the sensing ability, a summoner could send out a call that was irresistible to lesser creatures within range. I wondered if she realized she was even doing it because the bugs might be creepy, but there wasn't enough of them to be a danger to us. Plus, if there was something shielding the compound, she wouldn't be able to reach beyond it to find more little soldiers.

Ignoring the bugs, I turned back to Willis. *Is there a camera inside here? Is there anywhere we can leave weapons for you?*

Several more seconds passed as he contemplated me. His thoughts wavered between wanting to accept me at face value and fearing Delia was toying with him. But he did think about cameras, and what I'd mistaken for the smoke alarm was actually something more. Great. At least it was behind us.

There was also a planter of fake greenery near the lab where they had been depositing things they might use in an escape. Silently, I relayed the information to Mari and Oliver.

"So, are they going to drop their shields?" I asked Willis aloud. "Or do I have to help them?" I took out my gun to make a good show in case someone was monitoring the cell.

Making a sudden decision, Willis turned to his companions. "You heard the lady."

"What! Are you crazy?" Francis asked. "I don't care if they shoot me a dozen times and beat me senseless, I'm not letting her anywhere near me." She spat at us, but the spit passed through where Mari's shoulder appeared to be, the man she was impersonating being a good half foot taller.

Francis stared, a horrified expression on her face that told me she was even more afraid.

Dragon stood and gripped the bars. I stepped back, knowing he'd have to touch me to use his ability. Fire licked around his fingers, but did nothing to the metal. "What are you?" he grated. Everything about him was pale, from his hair and skin to his eyes.

Willis touched his shoulder and the fire died. "Do it." To Francis he added, "Let the bugs go."

Their shields dropped slowly and hesitantly to the sound of tiny scurrying feet, and I knew it said a lot about their trust of Willis that they did it at all. Knowing Delia, I wouldn't. Then again, I hadn't been tortured and held prisoner for three months as they had.

Images came from them all at once. Dragon who longed for the woods he loved, Mandalyn who'd asked Guenter to father her child rather than allow her body to be used by the Emporium, and Guenter who had fallen so much in love with Mandalyn and his unborn baby that for the first time in his six hundred years of life he feared death. Francis, who was expecting a baby from the genetically altered sperm of Lew Roberts, the man Mari was impersonating, who both feared for and loved the child she carried. And Willis, who worried he'd just betrayed them all.

Tenika sent us, I told them, trying to focus in spite of the deluge. It was like being in the middle of a room with numerous large-screen TVs all playing at high volume. Only they were streams of sand thoughts instead of TVs, and far more realistic. To my surprise, fear wasn't the dominating emotion; determination to endure won hands down.

We've figured out how to impersonate them, I continued. *We're working on an escape, but have been unable to make headway until today. We'll leave weapons in that planter. Maybe you can find some way to keep them with you.*

They had a place, I realized from the thoughts. Behind one of the silver plates they pried from the side wall of their prison at night when the cameras wouldn't pick up the sight. I smiled at how

Willis had first distracted me with the planter so as not to think about the real hiding place. My admiration turned to pity when I realized they had collected only one butter knife, a pair of scissors, and a piece of sharpened wood. Not much against assault rifles.

Do you know anything about a sixth prisoner? I asked. No one did. *Well, keep an ear out. We'll be coming again, but I can't say when. Just be ready. I'm sorry there wasn't time to get a cell phone we could leave you.* Ours held far too much information to leave within Emporium territory, especially since we would have needed to bypass the safeties to allow the prisoners access. *But I'll be able to contact you once I'm inside.*

You must be Ava's granddaughter. This from Willis, and I sent him a private affirmative response. Delia or no, maybe he deserved that much.

Raising my shields around my own mind, the cacophony shut off. "Come," I said to Mari and Oliver. "I've seen enough here."

Oliver rushed to open the door. I went through first and both guards outside came to attention. "I will see the director now. But we'll stay only a short time." I glanced at Mari.

"Twenty minutes," she said.

Not a lot of time to scope out the rest of the building, but it would have to do.

"This way." The Indian motioned forward. "Dr. Tunns is in the lab."

"Are there cameras in the hallways?" I opened my mind, once more pushing through his shield. Did it seem marginally thicker than the last time or was it my imagination? Maybe I was growing tired.

"Only near the sealed exits and the hallways outside the lobby. We also have cameras in the lab and in the cells. I can order more if you wish." He was telling the truth as he knew it.

"No, that's sufficient." As we approached the hallway with the planter outside the lab, I added, "I want to see the director alone. My companions will wait out here and you will join them once you show me inside."

He leaned over to open the door, glancing at my companions. "As you wish."

I swept through the door after him, as Mari and Oliver readied to dump weapons into the planter. There wasn't much more than a gun and knife for each prisoner, along with a couple of extra magazines, but these were far better than a butter knife. I didn't know how Willis and the others would retrieve them, but they had apparently worked out a system of sorts.

An Unbounded waited for me in the lab behind a desk, a woman, which shouldn't surprise me but did, given what she'd done to Francis. I had to remember that Dr. Tunns was an Emporium agent first and a doctor later. I saw in the Indian's mind that Delia had met her before so I didn't ask for an introduction.

"Delia," Dr. Tunns said, standing as I approached. Nearing Delia's age, she could have been my own mortal grandmother, from the white gray hair to the gentle wrinkles around her eyes. "Nice to see you again."

So we were on a first name basis, were we? I couldn't see any sign of her first name in her mind.

"Wait," I told the guard as he started to leave, wanting to be sure that Mari and Oliver had enough time to do their thing. "I need a drink of water."

"In that cupboard," Dr. Tunns said. "Please sit," she added to me, indicating a chair in front of the desk.

"I prefer to stand. I won't be here long."

"I thought you weren't coming for another week."

I watched the guard remove a bottle of water from the cupboard. "I wanted an update."

"I sent an update already." The reply was casual but there was steel in the doctor's voice that told me she'd known Delia a long time and didn't exactly trust her. Her shield was thick; I'd need the machete.

"I wanted a *personal* update," I amended. "And I was in the area."

The woman inclined her head in acknowledgement as I took the bottled water from the guard. "I'm sorry we don't have cold water in the lab."

"That's okay." I uncapped the bottle and drank before nodding at the guard to leave. "Well?" I prompted, unsure how to continue. I'd broken into her mind but there was nothing in her current thoughts that would do me any good. Almost as if she was purposefully thinking of mundane things to frustrate Delia, and too many questions about things I should already know would reveal my subterfuge.

Dr. Tunns sighed. "The two women are progressing nicely. For the one, we are almost assured of a sensing Unbounded, given the mother's summoning ability and the father's genetics. If the boy Changes, of course."

"You are sure it's a boy?"

"It's early yet, but the tests give every indication. I know you'd hoped for a girl, but that's one thing we can't do with one hundred percent accuracy yet. The other is a boy, too. We're about to begin postconception experiments on him in the hopes of increasing his chances of being Unbounded, but it's a dubious process. The pregnancy will likely terminate before the fifth month. But at least then we'll be able to start over with altered sperm. We had no idea she'd turn to one of the other prisoners in her effort to thwart us. Renegades of her generation are generally more conservative."

"You mean you messed up."

She stiffened. "As you told me the last time."

"What about the rest?"

"We sent ten altered samples of the pyro's genetic material to headquarters. Two have already resulted in pregnancies. We verified your findings that one of the combat Unbounded had an ancestor who was a blaster, so we're working on enhancing that aspect of his genetic material now before we send it along. In all, things are proceeding exactly on time."

"Any sign that we've been detected by the Renegades?"

"None that have been reported to me."

"Very well." I drank more water and took a step toward the door.

"As for the other, he's a capable technopath, but he has a strong sense of right and wrong and he's decided we're wrong."

I set my foot down carefully. Was she talking about the new prisoner who'd so far been kept away from the others? I couldn't pass up the opportunity to learn more.

"I am having about as much luck as his previous doctor," Tunns continued. "Which basically means no progress. Maybe after a few sessions with you, he can be put to use, but in light of your experiments with mind manipulation, I believe that too much force will render him useless for anything but his genes. I guess in his case nurture completely dominates nature." She sighed. "At any rate, in today's world technopaths are invaluable, so that makes it worth keeping him alive for his genes alone."

I wanted to ask who the man was and what we'd been trying to convince him to do, but I should already know all those things.

The doctor bent over and began typing something on a laptop that was connected to a large monitor on her desk. "You want to visit him now? I'll just check to see if he's awake. He went nuts on us earlier and we had to sedate him. I left a light on so we could observe him."

I moved around the desk so I could see the monitor. A live picture on the screen showed an unconscious man sprawled on a carpeted floor. I stared, blinking to clear my vision. *No, it can't be.* The light was dim, but I was certain I wasn't mistaken.

"Looks like he's still out," said Dr. Tunns. "With how much they gave him, I'd be surprised if he wasn't. However, he should be awake within the hour, or maybe two, if you want to wait." She gave me a mirthless grin. "Or would you prefer him unconscious?"

I wanted him any way I could get him, but without a private way to contact Ritter to gain more time, I couldn't agree. "I can't today," I said. "But I'll be back." I wanted to tell her not to mention my visit to anyone, but I couldn't think of any excuse that would fly. We'd have to come back for the hostages before Delia's next visit and hope that in the meantime she didn't become aware of our deception. "This is an unofficial visit anyway," I added. "I mostly wanted to check on the Renegade prisoners." I tore my eyes away from the screen and forced myself to walk toward the door, where I hesitated. "That reminds me. Please see that the prisoners have pillows and blankets. I want them to equate my visit with a reward. Besides, it's cold in there and we don't want anything to happen to those babies, do we?"

The director had climbed to her feet and followed my path. "The babies are fine, and given the rate of Unbounded regeneration, they won't feel the mothers' discomfort, but I agree that at this point we won't gain anything by depriving them further. Maybe it will actually help them become more compliant."

I shrugged and watched her open the door. "It's worth a try." With blankets the prisoners would not only have more privacy but more places to hide their weapons.

Out in the hallway, Mari and Oliver stood opposite the guard. Mari's mind screamed with relief at seeing me, but her voice was calm. "We need to leave now, Triad Vesey."

I nodded at the director. "Thank you for your report, Hattie," I said, finally discovering her first name in her thoughts.

"Next time we'll have refreshments here for you," she replied, her tone and her thoughts making it obvious that she did not appreciate the surprise visit.

How would Delia react to that? With anger? Amusement? The woman seemed to expect something, so I opted for amused disdain. "Make sure the tea is imported then. Americans still haven't realized the value of good tea."

I turned and preceded the guard down the hallway. This was it. We either would get out without trouble, or the rest of the guards would be waiting in ambush.

Stay alert, I warned the others.

Mari hurried to match my pace, steering me to the left when the hallway merged onto another. It was all I could do not to increase our pace because I'd suddenly begun to wonder if whatever was preventing me from contacting Ritter outside might also prevent Mari and me from shifting if it became necessary.

After a few torturous minutes, we arrived at the foyer. As we entered, I was able to maintain mental contact with the Indian guard, though the large guard waiting inside was closed to my probing. My anxiety increased. Something was definitely odd about this room.

One foot in front of the other, I told myself. There was no reason to believe the guard thought us anything but what we had presented ourselves to be. He and all the rest knew Delia, and I expected that would make them cautious about reporting her visit at all.

As we crossed the foyer, I scanned the monitors and other equipment on the long front desk. Was something there generating a field that strengthened mental barriers? Or perhaps created one? Strange that it didn't seem to make a difference to the mental connections I already held with those who'd entered the foyer with me. Once again, I wished Stella were here so we could pinpoint the equipment that might be responsible.

The second guard opened the outside door. "I'll call them down at the gate to let them know to have it open."

That made the gate sound farther away than fifty yards. "Very well," I answered, biting back the thank you that came to my tongue. Delia Vesey of the Emporium Triad did not thank anyone.

My heart thudded dully as I emerged into the cold night and realized a car was already at the gate. My thoughts flew across the empty space, searching for Ritter and finding him on top of the building. He hadn't told me he'd found a way up there without being seen by the cameras or guards.

I guess we both kept secrets.

We're leaving, I said, pushing through his shield. *Everything is fine.*

His relief filtered to me. *Cutting it close,* he responded. He had no way of knowing I received his thought unless I acknowledged it, and for now I decided to let him stew a bit.

We passed the other car on the way out, and once the gate was shut behind us, Oliver collapsed on the backseat, letting his illusions fade. I did the same, experiencing a great release.

"We did it!" Mari picked up speed as we drove down the street. She glanced over at me. "What's wrong? You look worried."

I was more than worried. "You were right," I told her. "I saw the new prisoner and he looks exactly like Patrick Mann."

CHAPTER 13

EVERYONE WAS SUPPOSED TO MEET BACK AT THE SAFE HOUSE, except Jace and Cort who had stayed behind to watch the compound, but I had Mari drop me off a few blocks away. After so much time in everyone's thoughts, I needed to be alone for a while, and it wasn't likely we would do anything more tonight. I'd filled Ava in already on the phone, and they could do without me for an hour or so.

It was after one-thirty in the morning, but many of the bars were open and people still roamed the streets. Some walked casually in loud groups, while lone people or couples walked quickly, darting glances around to make sure they weren't followed. This wasn't a high crime area, but it was dark and anything could happen in such a big city. I absorbed through my pores as I walked, refilling my depleted reserves. I caught the faint flavor of peanuts and fried scones, an odd combination, but this was New York City after all. I wandered aimlessly for fifteen minutes, my mind shut tight against everyone. Only the life forces burned in my mind, alerting me if anyone neared.

My body healed quickly, regaining strength every second.

The curequick no longer hummed in my veins and I missed it. *No more for you,* I thought. Not if I didn't want to end up like Ritter's adopted son, who was in a high security institution in London recovering from curequick addiction.

I soon found myself back at the safe house. Pulling my strongest shield over my mind so as not to alert Ava of my presence, I punched in the code and put my palm on the reader next to the door so it would open. The computer would inform Stella I was there, but she wouldn't tell anyone. I rode the elevators up past the eighth floor, the last four of which were empty and not yet refurbished. Tenika hadn't seen a point with her group so decimated, but one day they would need the space. Unless whatever the Emporium planned was more far-reaching than even we guessed.

Out on the roof, my acrophobia slammed down on me, as though the sky overhead had fallen on my shoulders. I forced back the fear, pushing it into the shiny black box in the corner of my mind. The weight lifted, but I knew it was still there, waiting to pounce if I relaxed my vigil. That was okay. I'd learn to deal with it, and I'd keep visiting rooftops forever as long as it meant I could make myself function despite the fear. I would not allow my flaw to endanger any of the Renegades.

I walked steadily to the edge, clear to the wrought iron fence encircling the entire rooftop. There had once been some sort of garden here, but it was lifeless now, the raised boxes of soil growing only a few hearty weeds. Someone had also kept pigeons in one corner, and it was to the old coop I headed, using a crate to climb up. The roof was flat and sturdy enough to hold my weight, though the creaking of the wood seemed to hint otherwise.

I sat crossed-legged, breathing in the searing cold that made me feel strangely alive. *So what do we know?* I mused.

Patrick Mann, or someone who looked like him, was being held by the Emporium. But Patrick Mann was also on television at the same time the new prisoner had been brought to the compound.

What else?

The vice president worried that his son was different.

I pondered that over for a minute. Maybe Patrick Mann really was different. Maybe he wasn't Patrick Mann at all. But when had the exchange taken place and how had the Emporium pulled it off? We knew they didn't have an illusionist. And not even Dimitri had heard of a shape shifter in all his thousand years.

I closed my eyes trying to search my own memories. Something bugged me about Patrick Mann, something that had occurred at our meeting. If only I could place it in my mind.

A clunking against the side of the coop brought me back to awareness. I reached for a weapon before I saw Ava's head appear. "I thought I would find you here."

I shook my head. "I almost shot you."

"Sorry." But there was little of repentance in my fourth great-grandmother's voice. She was completely dark to even my life force radar, which I had left partially unblocked to alert me to anyone nearby, so I knew she had intended on finding me before I had a chance to make myself scarce. Why she wanted me wasn't immediately clear. I could break through her shield because she'd had me do it several times during our practices, but I wouldn't do it without her permission, even if she'd purposely tried to surprise me.

"We've found something." Ava settled beside me, the coop groaning in protest. "You know that baby who was put up for adoption at the same time the Manns had their child? Well, the adoption agency was none other than the one the Emersons used to adopt their son five years later. The coincidence of a Hunter adopting a potential Unbounded in New York and using the same adoption agency as a woman giving birth in Massachusetts in the same hospital where the future vice president's wife also happened to be having a child is not likely. So Stella dug deeper. She was unable to break into the agency's files, but she talked again to the birth mother and compared all the public adoption records around that time and others that weren't quite so public. She found the baby. His name is Howard Obstfield. He's in Virginia now, grown with three children of his own. My guess is the DNA will prove he's really the Mann's child and not that birth mother's."

"How soon can we test his DNA?"

"I've sent Marco to get that started, but as far as I'm concerned there's really no need. Obstfield's on the city council in Fairfax and well liked for his integrity, so we have plenty of good photos of him. He's a dead ringer for Mrs. Mann." She tilted her head. "That is, if he'd been a female."

"If the Emporium was going to give the Manns a baby with Unbounded genes, why get this other woman involved?"

"Our best guess is that she was one of their legitimate birth mothers, and they were using her labor to mask their presence at the hospital. Since the baby the Emporium gave to the Manns would have come from within their own ranks and not from a mortal birth mother, they would have needed to do something with the Mann's child. When the birth mother's baby ended up dying, we believe they simply put the Mann baby in his place."

"One less adoption to set up." Emporium Unbounded would certainly never deign to raise a child they knew for certain would be mortal.

"Right. Anyway, a day after these births, a premature baby was found dead in a Dumpster in nearby Rhode Island."

I wondered if the baby's death had been completely accidental, or if the Emporium had caused the birth mother to deliver early so they could be at the hospital to take the Mann's child.

Ava sensed my concern. "For what it's worth, they found heroin in the baby's blood."

That didn't make me feel much better. "So if Howard Obstfield is the Mann's biological son, the Emporium obviously put that Unbounded in his place—or a baby they hoped would Change. But then who do they have in the compound? Or does he have a twin?"

"I don't know, but twin Unbounded are extremely rare. Less than one percent of the regular rate for mortals, due to the gene's natural inclination to choose the strongest possibility of individual survival." Ava sighed and stared out into the night. I followed her gaze. Lights gleamed all over the city—from tall buildings, cars, traffic signals, and billboards, some blinking off or on with a curiously beautiful randomness. If I opened my senses, all the life forces of the people stacked on top of one another in such an enclosed place would make it seem as bright as day.

"Could the Patrick Mann at the fundraiser be an illusionist?" I asked.

"All our intel says the Emporium doesn't have anyone with that ability."

I let a few minutes pass until I remembered the other thing that bothered me. "Back at Emerson's when we met that sensing Unbounded, Lew Roberts, I thought I saw Mari shot, but afterward she was fine. I didn't feel her shift out of the way or anything, though maybe she blinked in and out so fast there was nothing to feel."

Ava's eyes found mine. "Show me."

I opened my mind a crack so she could slide in. During our practices, she hadn't yet been able to break through my shield, though I'd shown her repeatedly how I did it. She also couldn't make anyone hesitate in place or move a limb. I believed the effort I'd expended in Mexico cracked something inside me, allowing me to delve deeper into my ability. But it might be because Dimitri's mother had the sensing ability, and maybe receiving the gene from both sides made me stronger. Given the continuous assault from the minds around me, I wasn't completely convinced it was for my good.

Keeping the rest of the world out, I shut my eyes and remembered the scene at the Emersons' townhouse. I knew Ava would be studying the sand stream of my thoughts as I pushed back to the correct memory location.

Wait, she said in my mind. *Show me that shield again.* She meant Lew Roberts' shield. *I've never seen anything like that. So strong. And that cord . . . it seems he's mentally shielding his partner as well.*

It was thin enough to cut. I let my contentment show through.

Doing so might have been dangerous, she countered, and I remembered the black snake-like thing in Patrick Mann's mind. *We'll have to practice making that shield,* she added.

I have a theory on that. I think the more you block someone who's actually trying to get through, the stronger you become. I bet Roberts' repeated contact with Delia is what made him that strong.

Maybe. We'll have to try it with the others. I was able to get through Dimitri's shield yesterday when we were practicing in the car. It took a long time, but I did it.

That he allowed her to try showed the degree of trust between them. I wanted to ask her about that, but now wasn't the time.

We'll talk about this later, she said. *Go on.*

I continued to the place where I'd left Mari unshielded and then to where she'd stumbled as if shot. Ava had me replay it three times, the third with her hand on my face. When she pulled away, my eyes opened. "Well?"

"She was shot and she didn't shift. You blocked her."

I blinked. "What?"

"You threw out a shield." She shook her head back and forth as if unable to believe it herself. "The bullet hit Mari with enough force to knock her over but didn't penetrate." Her head swung back and forth. "I've only dreamed of doing something like this. I want you to teach me."

We spent the next hour practicing shielding each other and trying to break down shields, until our fingers and toes grew numb with a cold so intense that even our regenerative properties couldn't keep us from feeling miserable.

"Your shield is getting stronger," I told Ava. "I couldn't get through those last two times, even using the machete. That supports my theory."

She laughed. "Or you're just getting tired."

There was that. We unfolded our legs and with effort climbed down from the coop. "What about that thing in Patrick Mann's mind?" I said. "Any theories yet?"

"I assume it's there to hide whatever information he knows about their plan so that even if he falls into our hands, we can't pick up on it before it's too late."

"Then we have to try to see what's inside." If Stella could locate him, I was sure Ritter could help me get in to see him. Surely Patrick wouldn't be as unreachable as the vice president himself.

Ava frowned. "Maybe, but we'd better see what Cort knows about it first."

Warmth welcomed us as we entered the stairway leading to the roof. By the time we'd reached the elevator, I could already feel tingling in my fingers as the heat returned to my extremities. I stared at the buttons for a minute, wondering where to go. I wanted to get our prisoners out, find Patrick Mann, and learn the identity of his lookalike—all my thoughts dividing down each path until I couldn't think about any of them clearly.

Ava decided for me. "The others have gone to bed, so this can wait until after workout tomorrow morning. We'll all think better after a little rest."

My exhaustion seemed heavy now that she'd spoken. Of course, it had been a long day, what with getting shot and having to pose as Delia. My bed suddenly called to me, as Ava punched the button to the third floor.

We met Ritter and Dimitri in the hallway, deep in conversation. Seeing Dimitri made me wonder who was watching Brody Emerson with Keene, but I knew they'd have it covered. "I've heard from Senator Pearson," Dimitri said, looking up as we approached. "She confirmed that the rumors about President Stevens are true. He is incapacitated. Some kind of a stroke is what they told her, and no one knows if he'll recover. She says they are stalling for now, but if something doesn't change, they'll have to make an announcement to the public."

Which would put Vice President Mann in charge. Did that fit into the Emporium plan? "Isn't there anything you can do?" I asked.

"Not unless I examine him, and Senator Pearson didn't think

that would be possible. But since she is so close to the First Lady, she's going to see what she can do to pull a few strings." Dimitri shook his head. "There might not be anything I can do anyway."

Ava touched his arm. "You have to try. Especially if this is part of the Emporium plan."

What was it we were missing? Two Patricks, a sick president, and a vice president who despite my dislike of him seemed to be honorable. Not to mention a Hunter with an Unbounded son. What was the Emporium planning? I felt it should be obvious, if I could only fit together the pieces.

Ava and Dimitri were staring at each other. Ava, who looked only a few years older than my thirty-one, and Dimitri, whose physical age was around fifty. There was an intimacy between them that seemed to have nothing to do with their obvious attraction for each other. Was this what others saw when they looked at me and Ritter? Or was that all in my mind?

Well, I did have the weapons he'd given me and that meant something, though I still didn't know what I would do with the knowledge. My gaze shifted to him and found his eyes, dark and unreadable, leveled on my face. Heat ignited inside my veins.

"Guess I'll turn in," I said.

Ritter walked with me to my room, coming inside for the second time in as many days. As soon as the door was closed, his hand went up to cup my face. "You feel like ice."

I didn't feel like ice. Fire spilled from his touch through my skin. It reminded me of the towel he'd used to clean my arm the night before. The next instant I was kissing him, my mind flaring with need. I wanted to feel his lips hard against mine and his tongue on every inch of my body. My exhaustion fled.

"Erin," he murmured. His hands slid around to my back and up to my arms. I let him push my coat to the ground with a heavy clunk and stepped closer.

He picked me up and this time I didn't protest at being carried. Crossing to the bed, he laid me down, sinking next to me. He kissed my mouth, trailing over my face and down to my throat.

My arms went around him, pulling him closer. His hand slid to my stomach and around to my leg, my bodysuit feeling like a mountain between us.

He met the resistance of a knife and I heard it hit the ground. Two more knives and a pistol were next, followed by my boots, my backup pistol, and the ballistic knife. Then his own shoes. His mouth found mine again, and my arms went under his shirt, feeling the heat of his flesh. His mind was open and not only could I feel what he was doing to me, but I could feel what touching me did to his emotions, what my touch did to him. The flames threatened to consume me with pleasure.

I pushed the thoughts toward him, wanting to share it all with him. He groaned and a new thought entered his mind. Me with a stomach full of his baby.

Suddenly the thin material of my bodysuit was too little between us. Ritter had asked me once if I was ready to have his child because that's what an Unbounded relationship meant, and in his mind I could see he knew what the next step would bring. Not only was he ready for the leap, he welcomed it. He'd been waiting hundreds of years.

Ritter might want that, but did I? I was already mourning my brother Chris and his two children, who were too far removed from the direct gene to have any chance of Changing. I was thirty-one and in a hundred years, I'd look thirty-three and my niece and nephew—and probably all of their children—would be dead. It was an unnatural thing for children to die before their elders. How many children would I bury?

I was about to push Ritter away, but he began kissing me again. The hard lines of his body felt right against mine, and I was liquid under his touch. One hand slid over my stomach to my thigh. His lips met mine, his tongue exploring my mouth. In principle I understood the horrifying concept of burying mortal children, but my body forgot to behave whenever he was around.

No, I had a choice. I did. And I would stop him soon. But for now, I was going to enjoy his touch. *I need this.* Besides, I hadn't given him my answer to his weapon offerings, except for temporarily killing Brody Emerson with the ballistic knife he'd given me last week, and Ritter had enough intelligence to understand I'd used the knife without realizing what it meant. Maybe being here so close to him would help me figure out what to answer.

I heard a soft clink and realized that the long gold chain he wore with the rings of his little sister, his mother, and the woman he was to have married had come out from beneath his shirt. The memories he carried shouldn't bother me but for some reason they did. He wasn't still hung up on their deaths as he had been when we'd first met, and I knew he no longer dreamed of the woman he'd loved, but I didn't want her old band anywhere near his heart. Stupid. She was dead and couldn't compete against me. Even alive, she'd never heard of anything like the Unbounded, and if she met the man Ritter was now, she wouldn't even know him. Not like I did.

His hand burned a trail up my side, finding yet another knife, the tiny one Keene had given me. I expected to hear another thump as he tossed it to the ground with the others, but he paused, looking it over. My body felt cold without him pressing so tightly against me.

"What's this?" he asked, his voice deceptively soft.

I saw in his mind that he knew the switchblade hadn't been in our arsenal, and besides, he'd trained me on all my weapons. "Exactly what it looks like. But watch out. It's coated in poison. Keene thought it would—" I hadn't even finished before he was rolling away and coming to his feet, his shield clanging into place around his thoughts. I lay flat on my back, watching him, my head raised. I was still inside his thoughts, but I pulled out. *If that's the way he wants it.*

He set the knife carefully on the bedside table. "Did you use it?"

I flopped my head back on the bed and groaned. "No, I didn't use it, but wouldn't you rather me use it than get killed? This isn't a game we're playing." He didn't respond, so I turned to my side, propping my head up on my hand and bent elbow. "Look, Stella told me about the weapons, but you have to understand it doesn't mean the same thing to me. Three months ago, I hadn't even heard of Unbounded, and certainly not their mating rituals. In *my* world a man asks a woman out, and when he wants to propose something, he uses his mouth."

Ritter stared, his eyes glittering under the single light I'd left on by the door. In two swift steps, he was back on the bed next to me, pulling me into his arms as if I weighed nothing more than a small child. His lips fell to mine, his shield dropping, and once more fire consumed my mind and body. He kissed my mouth, my eyes, my neck, my ears, and every inch of my face until my body sang with his touch. I was soaring and I never wanted to return to earth.

All too soon he drew away. "Okay, I used my mouth." There was a little quirk to one side of his lips that told me he'd purposefully mistaken my meaning.

"Arrrr!" I collapsed back on the bed. "So not what I meant."

That's when I noticed there were only two rings on his chain, those belonging to his mother and sister. The other ring I'd dreaded seeing was gone. What had happened to it? I couldn't pretend it didn't have something to do with his feelings for me. A lump formed in my chest. I'd told myself I didn't want a ring from him because it would be impractical to wear, but the part of me that had been so recently mortal thought it might be nice to have one on the days we weren't in battle.

Ritter smiled fully now, amusement in his eyes. "Oh, you know you loved it." He strode to the door and yanked it opened. "I'll see you in the gym at four."

As the door closed firmly behind him, I groaned again. He was such a ridiculous, egotistical jerk! Yeah, I'd enjoyed it. A lot. So had he. Neither of us could deny the chemistry between us, or how we felt when we were together. There was an intrinsic satisfaction at being close to him that couldn't be found anywhere else.

I chuckled into the quiet of the room. Well, two could play that game, and I'd make my next move as soon as I took a shower and got some sleep.

CHAPTER 14

RITTER CAME AT ME WITH A SWORD, AND I FLIPPED OUT A SAI, blocking him, careful not to have my fingers over the guard. My arm reverberated with the shock. He wasn't holding back, but then he shouldn't since I was channeling his ability. His height and extra weight meant that I'd never be likely to beat him, but I could hold my own in this controlled setting. Occasionally, I even got in a lucky strike.

I'd spent most of the workout under my own steam, because that was the way I progressed the most, but Ritter wanted to make sure I also had practice channeling while fighting. He'd made me channel Jace instead of himself during part of the workout so that I could become used to fighting my own battle while also being aware of Jace's fight going on separately. It was the only way, Ritter insisted, that I could overcome the weakness the double vision naturally created.

I had even tried channeling two abilities at the same time, but that was a complete failure, so I was limited to my own and one other. Still, it was more than most Unbounded had. Ava had so far been unable to channel any of the others' abilities.

She mused that I might be the only Unbounded alive who could channel at all.

"Good," Ritter said at last, lowering his sword. Sweat ran from both our bodies. Around us, the others were stepping away from each other and putting down their weapons. Ritter lifted his voice. "Great workout. Hit the showers."

Only Jace seemed disappointed that the workout was over as he walked toward the row of curtained showers in the adjoining room. Oliver made no show of hiding his happiness at being finished, which was generally the case, but today he'd made decent progress. It was as if his usefulness at the compound had made him more receptive to the demands upon him and his future as a guardian of humanity.

I began gathering up the inordinate amount of weapons we had trained with that morning. Ritter hadn't been with me the entire session because he was in charge of everyone's training, but next to Jace he pushed me the hardest. This morning Dimitri and Mari were missing from our numbers, having relieved Jace and Cort at the compound shortly before the workout. I knew Ritter planned to join them soon, but I hoped to convince him to go with me to find Patrick Mann. Discovering what that black snake contained might be the only way we could learn what was going on. I wished I could figure it out without breaking into what I was sure was Delia's little concoction, but what choice did we have?

Soon only Ritter and I were left in the workout room, and we finished putting back our bo staffs at the same time. I hadn't looked into his thoughts, despite channeling his ability, which had taken every bit of my willpower, but I could feel the heat from him now as our eyes met. I smiled and reached out, running my finger along the base of his throat, slick with sweat. His eyes burned.

"Hey," I said, making a show of looking at the moisture on my finger, "I'm going to talk to Mann. I'd like you to come."

His eyes narrowed. "And if I say no?"

"I'm still going." I loved the way my response made his surface emotions even more apparent: frustration, anger, desire, and admiration. This last surprised me and made me feel a little guilty.

"I'll have to talk to Ava first. We need to make sure the compound is covered. And don't forget that we need a plan that will get our people out before the real Delia visits. Or everything we learned last night for our surprise attack will be forfeited."

I nodded. "Any idea about why I couldn't get inside that guard's shield in the lobby? Or reach you once I was in the building?"

"No. Cort took readings after we left, and he's hoping to analyze them."

With his scientific ability, Cort would make a connection if anyone could. "If we could get through whatever it is, I could warn Willis and the others when we're coming in. Maybe I could anyway if I made it to the roof like you did last night." My stomach clenched at the thought of the climb that was likely involved, but I kept my voice calm.

I didn't fool Ritter because a tinge of sympathy rolled off him. "We'll see," was all he said. A good thing because anything more might drive me to do something irrational, like going up there by myself.

Maybe he knew that, too.

There was a shift inside me, but I didn't understand exactly what it meant and I tried not to let it make a difference. "I'm going to shower." I stood on tiptoe and kissed him until his sympathy turned into something quite different. When I pulled away neither of us was calm. But we were both grinning.

"We'd better hurry or there'll be nothing but cold water left," I said as I started toward the showers.

"That's okay. I think I'm going to need some."

I laughed at the teasing in his voice, glad he wasn't going to let my acceptance of Keene's gift stand between us. Of course that didn't mean I was off the hook. Ritter wasn't a man who'd wait around forever. His eyes dug into my back all the way to the showers.

Ten minutes later as I stood before the mirror in front of my shower stall combing my hair, Keene came rushing into the narrow room. The switchblade he'd given me seemed to burn a hole in the back pocket of my jeans where I'd put it only seconds before. I glanced at Ritter where he stood down a few stalls, but his eyes were on Keene's face. "What's up?" Ritter asked.

"It's the Hunter, Davis Emerson. He contacted me fifteen minutes ago and I came right here."

That meant Keene hadn't been here at the safe house last night because with only four floors in use, we could get anywhere within five minutes. Had he been watching the Emersons all night?

"His Hunter friends," Keene continued, "the ones he called in to help protect his son, figured out what was going on, and apparently they've disappeared with him. Emerson believes they plan to take him to their local headquarters and kill him."

My stomach lurched. "Oh, great. Just great." Taking my Sig from the metal shelf attached to the bottom of the mirror, I tucked it into the holster at the back of my jeans and pulled down my red shirt to cover it.

"What happened to watching him?" Ritter emerged from his shower stall fully dressed, his hair wet. He reached for his weapons.

"Tenika's people took over early this morning," Keene said. "A bunch of cars left twenty minutes ago, but they saw only Emerson's friends. No sign of Brody. Probably threw him in a suitcase."

I winced at the image. "I'm taking it Emerson wants us to go and get him."

Keene nodded. "I don't know that he trusts us exactly, but we seem to be the only Hunters not out to kill his son. At least not permanently."

"Good thing I removed the memory of Mari using her ability, or he probably wouldn't have called us at all. What does he expect us to do with Brody after?"

"We certainly can't let him go back to Emerson." Ritter finished placing his last weapon in the depths of his clothes and came to join us. "Between the Hunters and the Emporium, he's not safe there."

"Emerson knows that." Keene shook his head. "Actually, he wants us to contact the Renegades and give his son to them. I guess faced with the choice between you guys and the Emporium, he's choosing you." It didn't escape me that once again Keene avoided placing himself among our ranks. He might have thrown in with us, but he still had reservations.

"It's the only possible choice," I said. "Good thing Emerson's smart enough to know that. And Tenika's group can certainly use Brody here."

"Where's this Hunter headquarters?" Ritter started for the door.

Keene moved to join him. "According to Emerson, it's more of a meeting place than an actual headquarters. A rented house in Goshen. About an hour drive from here. Lots of open space from what I hear and not many people."

Perfect for disposing a body.

Ritter reached for his phone. "I'll call Ava and fill her in while I grab some supplies. We may need heavy firepower."

"Heavy firepower?" Jace emerged from a shower, still dripping, a towel around his waist, his blue eyes radiating excitement. "Count me in."

Ritter nodded. "I'll need you and Cort. I know you've been up all night. You can catch a nap on the way."

"What about Mari?" I asked. "Her shifting may come in handy."

"She can't shift in without having been there first, and can only get herself and you out. We'll need something more." Furrows appeared on his forehead. "In fact, Oliver may be the biggest help. He could project that SWAT team like he did before. Hunters hate law enforcement for the most part."

Jace kicked at the ground. "Man, just don't play it up too much or he'll be insufferable."

Amusement chased across Ritter's face, but he made no comment as he turned away. "I'll meet you all in the dining room. You can grab something to eat if you want, but make it quick. I won't be long."

Jace grabbed his clothes and started back inside his shower stall. "Be right there."

That left me alone with Keene, or at least in semiprivacy, his green eyes intent on my face. His hair had fallen forward and obscured the scar on his face. Was that what was different about him? Or was it the switchblade burning in my back pocket? I could tell he wanted to say something, but he wouldn't. The next move had to be mine. I tossed my towel into the hamper, removed my coat from the open rack near the door, and followed Ritter out. He was already halfway to the arsenal in the main room, but I didn't think I imagined the glance of relief he shot in my direction.

I needed a few extra magazines myself, but I didn't need to ask. Ritter would come prepared. He always did.

I headed for the elevator, Keene close on my heels, and before the elevator shut, Jace ran toward us, a mound of weapons still in his hands. We waited for him and I held his jacket as he tucked guns, knives, and other odds and ends in his specially made blue jeans that Stella must have found for him. Even his dark green T-shirt had a few subtle pockets, one of which held a backup pistol under his arm.

Keene laughed. "You remind me of your sister."

"You don't carry so many?" Jace finished dressing and reached for his jacket.

"Oh, I carry enough, but I've learned my real strength is in my hands and feet." Keene spread out his fingers.

"That makes sense." The elevator arrived on the first floor and Jace started toward the door. "How are you feeling anyway?" he asked Keene. "I miss sparring with you."

Keene's hand briefly brushed his middle where I imagined his bandage still encircled his chest. "I'm feeling good. Thanks."

"You shouldn't go with us today," I said as we left the elevator.

He gave me a flat stare. "I am going. Remember, I'm the one who knows the secret handshakes."

"Can't we just blow them up?" Jace looked over his shoulder at us.

"Only if we want the whole city to hear," Keene said. "Though it might save us trouble in the long run."

I snorted. "It may come to that. While Brody Emerson may not know how to use his blasting ability, he might discover it really fast. Remember how Oliver discovered his ability when the Emporium attacked us in Oregon?" The Unbounded sense of self-preservation was unparalleled.

"Oh, I really hope so." We couldn't help but laugh at Jace's exuberance.

Cort and Stella were having breakfast when the three of us entered the dining room. They listened as Jace eagerly explained about Brody Emerson's abduction.

Cort abandoned the rest of his meal. "I'd better grab a few things." He didn't look as if he'd been up all night, but maybe he was accustomed to going without sleep.

"Did Ritter mention me going?" Stella asked. "I'm waiting for word from Marco on the DNA results in Virginia."

"No." I didn't feel like eating, but I grabbed a couple slices of bacon.

Stella arched a brow. "You look like you didn't get much sleep."

I was about to comment on my relationship issues with Ritter and Keene, but given what Stella had been through with Bronson, it would only sound like whining. "I slept well enough, though I might have overdone things a bit during workout."

She laughed. "That's nothing new."

Jace had gulped down three helpings of his favorite omelet by the time Ritter and Ava came into the dining room, Ritter with a large black duffel bag in each hand. "If you see that we need more manpower once you get there," Ava was saying, "I can ask Tenika for backup."

Ritter nodded, but his face showed no concern. For all their nastiness and violence, Hunters were mortal and that meant we knew their weaknesses. Unfortunately, we couldn't really afford another unexplained bloodbath, and we certainly wouldn't kill them unless it meant saving Brody Emerson's life. The mortal officials in this area were already on high alert. That didn't stop Ritter from tossing Jace a smaller bag that I knew carried drug evidence we hoped not to have to plant.

Cort met us in the garage as we were loading Ritter's black Land Cruiser, a mini laptop in his hands and a wireless headset that I knew was linked through his phone to Stella's neural receiver. We threw the rest of the gear into the back and piled in. I rode shotgun next to Ritter in the front, leaving Cort and Keene in the second row of seats and Jace and Oliver in the third. Jace didn't look happy, but for once Oliver wore an almost pleasant expression.

Cort cleared his throat and leaned close to the front seat. "Erin, I thought you'd like to know what I found out about the readings at the compound. Stella's running them through a series of analyses now, but from what I've seen so far, I believe they've created a machine that acts very much like a mental shield, only instead of using the human mind, it's powered by electricity. They must have wires circling the entire building. Ingenious, actually. I tried to rig something similar myself back in the day, but electricity was scarce when we first invented it. And later there were so few sensing Unbounded that it hardly seemed necessary. The downside for us is that they can crank up the output so that even you can't penetrate it. But at least until we invent another type of power supply, the device isn't practical for them to carry around. Meaning they can't use it to protect an individual."

I turned to look at him. "So, cut the electricity and the shield vanishes?"

"Yes. It would also become weak during any sort of fluctuation. I suspect that was why you could occasionally sense the prisoners from outside."

"It didn't seem to affect me when I was connected to Oliver as we passed through it. But I was disconnected from everyone outside."

"That's right. It's a barrier and as you pass through, it'd cut you off from those outside, or inside if you were heading through the other way, but if you're already connected and you go inside together, you should maintain status quo. In fact, as you pass through the ten or twenty feet of the shield, you might not be able to disconnect from someone near you. Certainly, you wouldn't be able to put up a new mental barrier of your own. The good news is that with Stella's analyses, I should be able to replicate the shield. It'll make a fine addition to our safe house in San Diego, one that's important given that Roberts guy you ran into at Emerson's. There could be more like him."

"What about other gifts? Would it block those?" I meant Mari specifically, but I didn't have to spell it out for him.

"It didn't affect Oliver, and that is closer to what you do than Mari's ability."

"But wouldn't that be part of the status quo you were talking about?" This from Ritter, who had been following our conversation. "His illusion was already in place as they went inside."

Cort paused to think. "I really can't say, but you're probably right. As for Mari, she might simply fold space and go past it, or it also might not come up on her mental screen as a place that even exists. We'll have to experiment."

"We need to get a hold of that equipment," Ritter said.

"That would make recreating it significantly easier." Cort glanced down at his computer and back at me. "But of course our first priority is getting our people out."

"And discovering what's going on with that Patrick Mann lookalike." I frowned before adding, "I wonder if the one I met is a technopath like the man they have prisoner." A niggling thought pushed at me, but I still couldn't place it. I needed to go back over the whole encounter with Patrick Mann.

I hadn't come to any new conclusions by the time we arrived at our destination an hour later, Ritter having shaved off fifteen minutes from the GPS estimate. Jace had his head back and was snoring noisily, while Oliver stared out the window. Keene was also napping, but Cort was still wide awake and working on his computer.

We focused on the narrow, one-story building nestled quietly among a row of small businesses, each separated by a few parking spaces or short stretches of grass. The Hunter insignia of a man with a rifle splashed across a neon sign on the roof of the building, and below this was another sign with the words: *Freedom Means Protecting Yourself.* Fewer than a dozen cars lined the wide street in front. In all, it didn't look impressive. With any luck we could break in, get Brody Emerson, and be home in time to learn where Patrick Mann was having lunch.

"Uh-oh." Keene pointed at the building next door where a group of people were arriving at what was obviously a church, if you judged by the huge cross on the steeple. So far there were only a few men and women, but it was Sunday and more would likely be coming as the morning progressed.

Ritter edged the Land Cruiser down the block just past the Hunters' meeting house. He looked at me. "How many are inside?"

I was already trying to get a feel, but the life forces were so close that some were hard to separate. "The place is deeper than it looks, or they've spilled out onto a backyard or something, but there's at least twenty." A van drove up in front of the house and three more emerged. "Twenty-three," I amended.

"Those guys don't look old enough to be in the Hunter Circle," Keene said. "That means they've probably sent out an alert to all the Hunters in nearby towns. Can you find Brody?"

I nodded. "Someone is lying down with a group around him. Must be Brody." I pushed harder. "Yeah, it's him. He's conscious—and scared."

"If you can access his ability," Jace said, apparently having awakened with our conversation, "you could gather the energy from nearby and make an explosion. I bet if you piggyback your ability, you could reach even farther to pull in more energy than he can."

The idea was interesting. "I usually have to see it done first to channel an ability. Remember, he only learned who he was yesterday."

Jace smirked. "You mean after you killed him. Bet he remembers that."

I glanced out the window. "What about the church?" More people were arriving now, and even this early a little boy was playing on the strip of grass between the two buildings. Sabbath music trickled into the air.

Ritter followed my gaze. "I don't like the idea of experimenting here, but better a small explosion with enough power to cover our escape than a bloodbath where innocents are caught in the cross fire. Every single Hunter in there has at least one gun."

"Don't they know they're in New York?" Jace said. "I thought owning a gun was practically a felony here."

No one laughed. Restrictive gun laws were a concern to us because it left citizens even more at risk of being trampled by the Emporium once they took control. An unarmed nation is a nation at the mercy of its own government and lunatics.

"I need to get closer to see if using his ability is possible," I said. "There're too many thoughts in there for me to try anything from here. Anyway, the overall feeling is ugly. I think they plan to do more than just kill him." I swallowed hard.

"So let's go in and join them," Keene said.

I blinked at him in surprise. "What?"

"I'm a Hunter in good standing, remember? You, Jace, and Oliver are the only ones here not in their database, which they study as thoroughly as any Bible. I say we go in and assess the situation. If Cort and Ritter get close enough to the building, you should be able to communicate with them while we're inside."

We all looked at Ritter, whose frown showed concentration. "No," he decided. "Any little thing will set off that mob. The four of you against all of them is too dangerous."

"What if we all go in?" Cort closed his laptop and put it under the seat. "Oliver can mask you and me so they'll let us in, and together all of us should be enough to get Brody out."

I should have been offended that the addition of only two would make such a big difference, but I'd seen both of them fight.

Cort wasn't as good as Ritter, but he was still a far cry better than I was without channeling the combat ability, and he made Oliver look like a child. The three of us with Jace were a fair fight against twenty-three Hunters—as long as we could keep from getting shot. If Keene were at full capacity, I'd say the fight would be grossly unfair for the Hunters.

Again Ritter considered the odds and apparently found them acceptable. "Okay, we go in. Close enough for Erin to easily channel Oliver's ability, but in two separate groups so we don't appear to be together. Then when I give the signal, Oliver will project his illusion of the SWAT team. As the Hunters scatter, Erin and Keene, you get Brody out while we provide cover."

"Let's just hope they don't start shooting when they see the SWAT team," Jace mumbled.

Keene frowned. "Unless you know the handshakes, the Hunters won't let you in."

"I know them," Cort said. "At least the ones that were current three months ago. We can run through them again to make sure."

"I may have to drop your cover to make the police appear." Oliver's face was slightly flushed.

"I could take over," I put in. "Or help you call up another SWAT team."

Ritter shook his head. "I want you to concentrate on masking Jace at least until we get into the crowd. They may have a camera in there recording who arrives, and I don't want him identified later."

My stomach lurched. I understood what Ritter was saying. Despite his show of maturity at the compound last night, neither of us was confident that Jace would keep a low profile today.

"I also want you ready to mask Brody if needed," Ritter continued. "Walking him out might be our best plan."

"Wait, what about me?" Oliver asked. "I don't want to be in their files, and if I'm covering Ritter and Cort, I can't mask myself."

"You'll be wearing a disguise," Cort assured him. "You won't be in their faces like Jace will, and they won't be on the lookout for you like they are for us, so it'll be more than enough. Most of them aren't very bright."

"We'd better hurry," I said. "Brody's more afraid now. I— something feels odd in him."

Keene grimaced. "They're probably telling him exactly what they're going to do to him. They like to scare their victims first."

Ritter put the Land Cruiser in gear, driving to a mom-and-pop store two doors down and pulling around behind. The store was closed on Sunday in this small town, but our vehicle didn't look out of place. From there we could see that the Hunter meeting house did extend farther back than it appeared from the front. All the windows there were shuttered.

"I wish Mari were here to keep the engine running," I said, as Jace reached behind him for the bag carrying the bulletproof vests.

Ritter arched a brow and tossed me a handful of magazines and a silencer for my nine mil. "She can find you. Call her."

I shook my head. "I'd rather not experiment with her coming this far."

"She did it before in the jungle." Jace shrugged on his vest and replaced his coat.

He was right, but there were a lot more variables in shifting across several cities than through a jungle, weren't there?

"Text her." This from Cort.

I studied him a moment, remembering Oliver's passionate rendition of him. Did he look at Mari as a woman or an experiment? Or a friend?

I opened the door and climbed from the Land Cruiser, going around the other side so that I was between the SUV and an outcropping of the store. Ritter and Cort kept watch, their guns ready. Making sure there was plenty of space between me and the Land Cruiser, I pulled out my phone and texted Mari. *Can you come here? We need a getaway driver. It's about 70 miles.*

I counted heartbeats as I waited for a return text, but a soft pop and the slight displacement of air told me she hadn't bothered.

"Hi guys." She flipped her long black hair over her shoulder with one hand. "Thank you for getting me out of there. Nothing is going on at the compound, except me freezing to death."

"Well, the Land Cruiser is warm for now." Ritter motioned her inside. "But leave the engine off until you see us coming. We don't want anyone to get suspicious."

"You can turn it on briefly if you need to," Cort added, buttoning his coat so his vest didn't show. "But we shouldn't be that long." I followed his example with my own coat. Enough buttons to hide the vest from casual observation, but not so many that it would prevent me from reaching backup weapons. I'd already put the nine mil in my pocket.

"Are we taking the earbuds?" Jace climbed from the Land Cruiser.

"The earbuds and radios won't be any use in that crowd," Ritter said. "Too obvious. Just watch me for the signal. Erin will communicate anything that might change."

Seconds later Keene, Jace, and I emerged in front of the store and strode down the sidewalk. The others would follow after we got to the wide porch in front of the meeting house. No more cars had arrived outside, for which I felt grateful. I wore a dark wig from the supplies, and Jace sported nerdy glasses and had slicked his hair back under a cowboy hat. I went further with Oliver's ability, changing his skin to a ruddy color marked by acne scars. His clothes were straight off a farm and he smelled of chicken poop.

"Chickens?" he whispered. "Did you have to?"

"It'll keep people away," I said. "The illusions aren't tangible."

"I'm going to get you back, you know that."

"Oh, is the smell making you sick?" I mocked. "Let me know if you're going to throw up so I can jump out of the way."

"Erin," he groaned.

I shrugged. This wasn't a party we were going to, and he was my responsibility every bit as much as I was his.

Keene chuckled. "Quiet now. It's game time."

CHAPTER 15

BEHIND US, I FELT RITTER AND THE OTHERS MOVING DOWN THE walk. Oliver's sense of self-preservation had somehow given him a way to extend his illusions to himself as well, because I didn't recognize any of them by sight. Keene reached for the door.

A big blond man with muttonchop sideburns and hat hair stood guard just inside the squat building, a rifle over his shoulder and a pistol at his hip. His hand rested on the pistol as he greeted us, "Welcome, fellow Hunters. Why do you come to this place?"

"To receive the brotherhood and support the Hunter Circle." Keene reached out a hand and they shook. This time I paid close attention, watching as Keene returned several taps with his fingers.

"Do you wish to join the Hunt and protect the mortal world?" The reverent way the man spoke, I knew Hunt was more than symbolic.

"Yes. That is why I've come. To join with my brothers to the end of the Hunt." More handshakes, this time too fast for me to follow.

"To the end of the Hunt," the big man finished, his hand dropping to his side. "You and your guest may pass."

"It's a real one tonight," he added as we came inside. "First we'll cut him and watch him heal, proving his link with the devil. Then we'll do our duty." Blood lust rolled off him, and for a moment I felt as if I'd gone back in time when entire towns gathered to kill helpless victims accused of witchcraft. Or more recently when men in white robes and pointed hats planted burning crosses in front of humble dwellings. Ignorance and racism in all its ugliness.

I'd stopped moving and Keene's hand shot out to grab me. "Come on, dear. We don't want to miss this."

"Oh, you won't," the big guy said. "I'm going to lock the door in a few minutes. That will be the signal to begin. I work for the Hunter Circle. Two of them are here today."

"What about Emerson?" Keene asked.

The man frowned. "I don't know. I think they're hoping he comes to his senses after the evil influence in his house is gone, but he may be cut off and shunned."

Shunned? Really? In this day and age?

Jace grimaced, which made him look quite gruesome with his bad skin. I could feel he was aching to slam his fist into the man's face. "Let's go," I told him as Keene tugged on me harder.

We walked past a desk holding two monitors and down a constricted hallway, lingering to make sure the others got through the guard safely. By the time they caught up to us, we had made our way to a large room in the back. Nearly fifty folding chairs crammed into the space, a makeshift stage and pulpit jutting up insignificantly at the far end. In front of the stage sat a table covered with a white plastic tablecloth, and on top of this lay a frightened Brody Emerson. His arms were tied with ropes to iron rings set into the tiled floor on either side of the table. His feet were spread wide, held in place at the edge of the table by more ropes and rings. The first two rows of chairs had been shoved back into the others to allow people to gather around the table. Besides a middle-aged woman who stood near the edge of the crowd, all the others present were male.

As we approached the table, a boy barely in his teens spat on

Brody. "Dirty scum," the boy shouted. The older man next to him thumped him on the back with approval. Several others murmured encouragement.

These men had families, wives, and children. Many, I knew, would be appalled at similar inhumanities around the world, but for Unbounded their hatred saw no reason. How many of our people had been murdered here? Sacrificed upon this altar? Next to me, Jace's emotions boiled.

Two older men sat behind the podium, their gray heads bowed together as they conferred. One wore a black suit while the other sported jeans and loafers topped by a blue plaid shirt. Black suit was thin and wiry, while blue plaid was tall and thick and looked as if he'd eaten far too many sweets. I pushed my thoughts toward them.

"Time to bring out the knives," said black suit.

His companion nodded. "Better tell everyone only one cut, so make it count. Mine will be first—his tongue."

Keene was still pulling me forward. I looked around to see Ritter staring after us with the blue eyes of someone I didn't know—a mask created by Oliver. Keene wove us through the Hunters until we stood near Brody's face. His frightened eyes widened further.

"You!" he said. "You stabbed me!" He tried to arch away, but the ropes held all but his head in place. The lights overhead blinked. I could feel energy transferring from them to Brody. Too much. He was already filled to near overflowing, and if he were to somehow ignite what he'd gathered, I doubted any of us would make it out alive.

So much for my flimsy disguise. I pushed into Brody's mind, his barrier long forgotten with his fear. *Shut up, you idiot. Your father sent us. Now calm down. You see that glowing energy? You're gathering too much. Stop it, if you can. I'm not sure how you can expel it without blowing yourself into a million pieces, and believe me, there's no coming back from that.*

I saw in his mind how he was gathering the energy, and it was exactly like the way we absorbed nutrients from the air. Mimicking the flow, I pulled it from him toward myself.

"What are you doing?" Brody screamed.

"Ha," said one of the Hunters near Brody's head. "He seems to be scared of this woman." She should take the first cut." He brandished a knife.

"Thanks, I've got my own." I continued to siphon energy from Brody, and as I did the tension in his body relaxed slightly. Too late I realized that, unable to channel two abilities, I was no longer masking Jace. Luckily, Jace was calm enough for the moment, and his disguise adequate.

Look, I said to Brody. *There are nearly two dozen people here wanting to cut you into little pieces and only six of us to save you. Do exactly as I say. And please don't answer out loud. If you think something, I can see it while I'm in your head.*

The energy humming in my veins reminded me of how I felt when Ritter touched my skin. My eyes went to Ritter now and realization hit, blotting out all thoughts of my feelings for Keene and my worry about my future progeny: I loved this man. I didn't want to lose him. Yet here we were in a room full of angry, frightened men who had permanently and viciously killed numerous Unbounded over the years. We had to try to save Brody, but what it if came at the loss of someone I loved?

"Uh-oh," Jace breathed in my ear. "I think this party is about to get ugly."

The leader in the black suit cleared his throat at the podium. "Hello," he said in a mild voice. Everyone fell silent to listen. "You all know why we are here," he continued. "You know what we must do today. We are the protectors of humanity, and we alone stand between our fellow man and the atrocities these Unbounded plan for them. We were once part of the evil Emporium. We saw for ourselves how they intend to set themselves up as false gods. How they use humans as their slaves until they are no longer needed and then cast aside, even as your parents and grandparents were cast aside. God wants us to protect His mortal children. It's a terrible thing we must do this day, but we will *not* shirk our duty."

A swell of agreement passed through the crowd, but the man at the podium held up a finger. "Our brother Kofford will make the first cut." He gestured to the fleshy man in the blue plaid shirt. "We will get the devil out of this creature, and allow him to repent before we send him to God. Remember that this is for his good as well as ours."

Another murmur through the crowd, this time of anticipation. The air filled with the scrape of knives as they left their sheaths. None of this was lost on Brody. His eyes rolled in terror, and energy flowed into him more quickly. One of the lights popped and went dead. That gave me an idea.

I looked at Ritter, pushing the thought past his shield. *I can kill the lights.*

His gaze flicked in my direction. *Do it. Tell Oliver to get ready to mask Brody. Cort, Jace, and I will see that you get out.* He caught first Jace's eyes and then Cort's, giving them the signal.

Oliver, I said. *When the lights go out, mask Brody. And as soon as you can, call up your SWAT team.* He didn't think an answer but there was a shift in his thoughts that told me he'd heard.

The man called Kofford jumped down from the stage, an insipid smile on his bloated face, and approached the table where Brody struggled. "And the Lord shall cut off the tongue of him who speaks against His people."

Brody screamed, pulling in more energy. I helped, taking it so rapidly through the lights that they all popped at once, plunging the room into darkness except for thin rays that filtered in through the shuttered windows.

"Devil!" someone cried out.

"Get him!" shouted another.

I slashed at Brody's ropes. Knives glinted in the darkness, and he screamed as several met their intended destination. Then Jace and Cort were there, turning the knives on their owners, throwing people back from the table. I couldn't see Ritter, but I could feel him in the general direction of the podium and the leader. In his mind I caught a glimpse of a rifle aimed at his chest.

Move! I thrust at Brody's mind. Electricity bounced in his head, sending flickers of light through my brain. He was close to exploding. I kicked at the man next to me who had raised his knife over his head in preparation to plunge it into Brody's unprotected chest. The man screamed in pain, his knife slicing my arm as it clattered to the tile. I pulled Brody from the table, and we tumbled to the floor together. A glimpse of his terrorized face as we rolled under a window showed that he no longer looked like himself but Kofford, the leader in blue plaid. I had to admit that Oliver had a sense of flair.

The blast of a rifle rose above the screams and confusion. I felt Ritter's mental cry of agony, and the sensation froze me in place. A lamp in the corner switched on, and the leader in the black suit was illuminated. "They are among us!" he shouted, one finger pointed at Ritter, who was being held by two burly cowboys. Ritter heaved, slamming the two men together. Ten rifles aimed in his direction.

Ritter turned, kicking out and moving so fast that he was nothing but a blur. Jace appeared behind three of the men with rifles, and in the next second, they were on the floor. More took their place. I shoved Brody at Oliver. "Get him out of here." I didn't think anyone would stop him. Already several Hunters were fleeing the meeting room. Two more gunshots burst through the cacophony.

Reaching out to Jace, I began channeling his ability, choosing him over Ritter in the hopes that I could protect him better. A rifle turned in my direction and with a twist of a sai that was suddenly in my hand, I blocked, throwing the weapon from the man's hand. Flipping it around, I used the handle as a hammer. *Ritter was wrong. That hold came in very useful.* But only because I wasn't trying to kill anyone. Another opponent took his place, hesitating as he saw me. It was the man who'd offered me the use of his knife. Using the sai, I hooked the arm holding his pistol and twisted it back, feeling the bone crack. With a roar of pain, his knife came toward me, but I stepped easily aside. *Night, night.* I dropped the sai and slammed my fist into his face, feeling a distinct satisfaction as his eyes rolled up in his head and he crumpled to the floor.

"Erin!" Near the door, Oliver wrestled with the man in blue plaid. The real man because Brody Emerson had fallen to the floor, his face alternating between his own and the man Oliver had copied. Oliver wasn't a good fighter under any condition, and his recent training was the only thing that kept him from going under in the assault. I launched toward him, intending to help. No wonder the imaginary SWAT team hadn't appeared. Too bad, because if Oliver had done his job, his opponent would likely be running for cover by now.

Two men rose up to block my path, and a third grabbed my arm from behind. I kicked backwards as Ritter sailed through the air toward the men in front of me. They collapsed to the tile in a tangle of arms and legs. I gave an elbow and another kick to the man behind me. That had the desired effect, and in the next instant I was free, sweeping up my dropped sai and turning to face the man. I tore his rifle away before he could use it, and he slammed down at me with a knife that looked like something from a slasher movie. Twirling the sai until the blade rested against the length of my arm, I brought it up to block. The clang of the knife against the metal would have been music, if I hadn't been slightly off. His blade sunk an inch into my arm. *Ouch.* It'd be a lot easier if I could just shoot him. Instead, I settled for another kick, followed by a hammer punch with the sai. I was still linked to Jace and I could feel my brother's abandon as he used his escrima sticks to free people from their weapons and send them unconscious to the ground.

How many were left? Too many seemed to be moving under the dim light. Another shot filled the space, accompanied by more screams.

Whirling, I nearly fell over the men still wrestling at my feet,

Ritter's arms pumping as he made short work of his last opponent. The blond who'd been guarding the front door appeared behind Ritter, aiming a pistol at his head. I thrust upward with the handle of one sai, jabbing him hard in the throat. He choked and dropped his gun. Back on his feet, Ritter jumped at the man.

I hurried toward Oliver and Brody, but the man in the blue plaid shirt had pulled a gun and pointed it at his doppelganger. The lamp behind me suddenly burst and flames licked up the curtain.

"No!" I shouted. Dropping my connection with Jace, I leapt into Brody's mind, pulling the energy inside me until I felt I would burst. But what power I took from him wouldn't be enough, not if I didn't eliminate the threat so he would stop grasping for it. I felt for my gun, fingers humming with energy. I wasn't going to make it. The pressure continued to rise in Brody faster than I could siphon it off. Since I hadn't any idea of where to put it, that made two of us about to blow.

Then Ritter was there, his gun at the head of the big man in blue plaid. "Go ahead. Kill him. But you'll be next."

Kofford hesitated. Ritter plucked the gun from his hand, and rapped him over the head, knocking him unconscious. Ritter scowled at Oliver. "Where's the SWAT team, huh?"

"Oh, uh. I was fighting with—"

"Now!" Ritter growled.

"Hold it, everyone!" came a powerful voice near the podium. A dozen men in uniforms had appeared there with assault rifles and shields. "Drop your weapons immediately." Rifles and knives clattered to the floor.

"Go!" Ritter grabbed Brody by the back of his shirt and yanked him to his feet. "Oliver, you're the last one out. Erin, tell Mari we're coming." Half-dragging Brody, he jumped toward the doorway. Cort and Jace followed, as well as several Hunters, who seemed more anxious at escaping the police than anything else. I tried to step forward or call out to Mari, but the power pulsing inside rooted me to the spot. My hands still clung to both sai.

"Erin?" Oliver asked.

"Go," I said.

To his credit, he hesitated.

"Go!" I didn't want him here when I blew.

The next instant Ritter was gathering me in his arms and running down the hall. A figure rose up to stop us, but Ritter resolved the challenge with a single kick.

I beat at Ritter's chest. "Put . . . me . . . down. Too much . . . power. Brody's ability . . . going to blow." I didn't want to take Ritter with me. How ironic that I might be the cause of his death.

Ritter slowed, understanding at last. "Break your connection with him."

I couldn't. At least I wasn't taking in any more power, but I couldn't seem to release what I had.

"Find a target," Ritter barked. "Anything. Blast it like a gun!"

There had to be some way to release the power as he commanded. Maybe I just had to choose a target.

We'd reached the foyer where the monitors sat on the desk. That was as good as it was going to get. "Leave me," I told Ritter. "I'll blow the computers."

He held me tighter, his forehead touching mine. "I'm not leaving you."

It was an unreasonable response. He was in charge of the mission and I was endangering it. He should cut his losses. But of course he wouldn't.

I looked at the desk and pointed with a sai, pushing the power toward it. The energy careened through my body in a heady rush. The desk, the computers, and the entire room, burst into flame. Ritter leapt for the door even as the heat became unbearable. An explosion erupted behind us, and we were blown out to the sidewalk in a shower of glass.

Mari screeched the Land Cruiser up to the front walk. Everyone was already inside, except for Oliver, who crouched on the sidewalk, covering his head. Jace jumped out and pulled him inside as Ritter and I found our feet and started running.

Next door, people piled out of the church. "Call the fire department!" someone shouted.

"There are people inside!" called a second person. "Help me break the windows so we can get them out."

Mari stomped on the gas, leaving the destruction behind.

CHAPTER 16

"WHOO-HOO!" JACE SCREAMED. "THAT'LL TEACH THEM TO MESS with us!" His words belied his numerous cuts and bruises, and the already blackening eye. Cort, Ritter, Keene, and I were no better off. Only Oliver had escaped with minimal wounds, and Brody, who'd lapsed into unconsciousness in the back seat with Cort. From the bag of medical supplies on Cort's lap, I suspected it wasn't a natural unconsciousness.

Mari smirked. "Only if your assailants look worse than you do."

"What, you don't think going up in flames is good enough?" Jace quipped.

"That was kind of impressive." Mari glanced back at me, a question in her eyes.

I wasn't about to get into it now, though I'd have to make a full report to Ava. My head throbbed and I felt as weak as a baby. I was glad they'd done something about Brody because I couldn't feel the power in him now. Either he'd found a safe way to release it, or the power had gradually seeped away after he fell unconscious. We'd all been so close to death. The first thing we needed to do when Brody awoke was to help him control his ability or the next time he was frightened we might not be so lucky.

I shivered, though I didn't feel cold, and Ritter put an arm around me. "Pass me a blanket," he told Cort. "And some curequick."

"No curequick for me," I said. The fact that I craved the buzz told me I'd had too much in the past few days. Besides, the power whipping through my body had already given me a high.

Ritter wrapped me in the blanket, but I pushed it off. I felt flushed and I didn't think it was from fever or from three of us being crammed into the middle seat. I felt Keene's eyes on me from Ritter's other side, and when I looked up, there was a sadness there. Or something similar radiating from him. Did he realize that I'd finally accepted my feelings for Ritter back there with the Hunters? That I'd chosen? It felt both good and frightening to even think about so much change. Committing to Ritter was more than a relationship. It meant permanence and family, and I still didn't think I was quite ready, but it was clear that I loved him and maybe the rest didn't really matter.

I looked away from Keene and moved closer to Ritter, which seemed impossible without getting into his lap. Ritter quirked a brow at me, but said nothing. "I'll inject just a little right around your cut," he said. "Otherwise, you'll be good for nothing the rest of the day."

"All right, but no stitches. Just wrap it tight."

"Okay." He tossed a syringe of curequick to Jace in the front seat. "Get Oliver to help you if you need it."

Oliver sat beside Jace, stiff and unsmiling, as though he felt everyone blamed him for our not making it out sooner. But while he should have called up the SWAT team sooner, none of us blamed him for being scared. If he'd admit it, we'd all tell him so, but as soon as his mouth opened, I was pretty sure it would be an excuse or to blame someone else. Oliver might be talented, and his IQ was high enough that he periodically mentioned it in arguments, but his social skills were pretty much nil.

Everyone was quiet as we bandaged our wounds. Ritter sewed up a cut on his leg that made me bite my lip, and Cort announced that he'd need help digging a bullet from his thigh. A few tiny balls from a shotgun had pierced Jace's arm, but they were easily removed, and he was feeling pretty happy after receiving a shot of curequick laced with anesthesia.

"Better pull over while we look at Cort," Ritter said. "And change the plates in case anyone at that church jotted them down."

Mari swerved over with a little too much enthusiasm. "Good, I was getting tired of driving anyway. It's going to take forever to get there. If no one minds, I think I'll just meet you all back home. I can get started on reporting to Ava." She waited less than five seconds before a soft suction of air told us she'd shifted.

"Well," Jace said. "Wouldn't that be nice?"

Cort grinned. "Yeah, she's going to be a pain on the way to the new safe house. Too bad she can't shift there. Something tells me that will be a long trip."

Mari's impatience was a new part of her identity. Before her Change she'd been an accountant, using a machine to meticulously add numbers. Now she added a page at a time with only a glance and folded space as if it were a piece of paper.

Ritter and Keene went to work on Cort's leg, while I leaned over the front seat and checked the bandage on my brother's wound. "Not bad," I told Oliver.

"That guy made it impossible to call up an illusion," Oliver said. "You should have taken over masking that Hunter so I could do what I was supposed to."

"Brody's no longer a Hunter," I countered. "And I was channeling Jace's ability, not to mention making sure Brody didn't blow us all up. Why not say you screwed up and do better next time?"

Oliver scowled. "I wasn't sure when to call the SWAT team, and anyway, Brody was the most important thing. At least I got him out."

I seemed to remember Ritter being the one to carry Brody from the melee, with Oliver still rooted to the spot. But whatever.

"Hey, relax," Jace said. "It's cool. Am I going to drive?"

"No, I am." I took the keys from his fingers.

I slid from the car, my own wounds aching, but needing a little space. The narrow road leading to the freeway seemed to be deserted, and the sun had peeked from the clouds. For the first time in weeks the outside air felt almost warm. Perfect for a short walk where I wouldn't have to smell blood. I began to up my absorption of nutrients to help my wounds heal but found that the power I'd absorbed while channeling Brody's talent had also filled me up well in the nutrient department.

Jace caught up to me after only a few moments. "They're almost finished."

That told me Cort's wound wasn't as severe as it could have been. We'd been lucky, all things considered. If it hadn't been for almost blowing up, it might have even been exciting. "Good."

"Brrrr. It's like ice out here."

I stopped walking. "I feel kind of warm."

He reached over and grabbed my hand, releasing it immediately. "Wow, you're burning."

"Must be left over from that power I siphoned from Brody." Interesting. I'd have to see if he felt hot, or if it was because I wasn't able to get rid of the energy properly.

"He'd be handy to have around in a snow storm. That is, if he isn't traumatized for life after this."

"Even if he is, he'll get over it in a hundred or so years." I took a step forward, but Jace's next words stopped me again.

"Dad isn't my biological father, is he?"

I'd been waiting for him to ask, and in fact I'd been close to telling him myself several times. It wasn't a secret that our parents had trouble conceiving and had gone to a fertility clinic, which was how Dimitri came to be my birth father. Ava had taken advantage of our parents, allowing them to believe the insemination had succeeded, but maybe that wasn't such a terrible thing given my parents' longing for children. They still didn't know the truth.

Jace dug his foot into the small rocks on the side of the road.

"I mean, it's obvious Dad couldn't have more children and besides, we're seventh generation. Without an influx of new Unbounded genes, the likelihood of Change was already practically zero. That both of us Changed would take the possibility into the negative." He blew out a puff of air. "Don't worry, I won't tell Mom and Dad. They went back to that clinic, didn't they? When they wanted to have me. So how do I find out who my father is? It's not Dimitri, I don't think, or he would have said something when you confronted him. Do you think Ava will tell me if I ask? Or maybe you could ask her for me. I'd like to know."

I believed a person deserved to know who their biological parents were, regardless of whether or not they pursued a relationship with them. Except in Jace's case where the consequence of knowing might be fatal. I was afraid that once I put words to it, I'd start something no one could stop.

"Maybe," I said, "Ava has a reason not to tell you."

"You know, don't you?" His words were accusing. "How long are you going to hide it? Until I'm a hundred? Three hundred? Come on, I deserve to know the truth. You know our life. One day to the next he might be dead." A smile quirked his lips, reminiscent of the man whose identity he sought. My stomach twisted.

"I'll talk to Ava," I said. "For what it's worth, I think you have the right to know, but I sure wish you would trust me when I tell you it's not that easy. You may wish you'd never asked." Learning that our mother had been inseminated with the stolen genetic material of Emporium Triad member Stefan Carrington, generally believed to have been used for my conception, definitely wouldn't be the happy ending he was looking for.

"That bad, huh?" He chuckled a little too loudly. "Wouldn't you want to know if you were me?"

I would. But I wasn't Jace. I was impulsive and new at this Unbounded stuff, and even a little bit reckless, but he was all that and more. An innocent in many respects. I didn't want anyone taking advantage of him. "Yeah," I said.

"Okay. Then talk to her."

We walked back to the Land Cruiser in silence, me feeling as though I'd betrayed my brother by not telling him the truth. Since when had I toed the line with Ava in regards to my family? Never. No, I didn't tell Jace now not because of her, but because of my own reluctance. Did I think he'd go over to the dark side?

"So can I drive?" Jace asked. "Give me back the keys."

I jingled the keys in my pocket, hurrying a bit faster. "Nope."

When I had the engine running, Ritter asked, "Has anyone thought to notify Emerson that his son is all right?"

"I'll do it," Keene said.

I glanced in the mirror and Ritter's eyes met mine. I extended my arm to Jace. "Help me pull this coat off. It's hot in here."

The drive back to the safe house went quickly until we arrived in New York City and the traffic bogged down. All of us were moving with less pain after an hour of healing, even Keene, though perhaps he'd stayed out of most of the brawl—I hadn't actually noticed what he'd done there. Or maybe the experimental medicines Dimitri and Cort had given him were actually working.

In the basement garage, we retrieved a gurney and laid Brody on it. He hadn't come to yet, but it wouldn't be long, and he'd be full of questions. I didn't intend to be around to answer. I was determined to find Patrick Mann and make him tell me what the Emporium planned.

Ava and Stella waited for us in the conference room. "So, not as easy as you thought," Ava said, her eyes going past us. "Where's Oliver?"

"He said something about a shower," I told her. Jace sprawled on a chair and rolled his eyes.

Ava ignored him. "Is the boy okay?" she asked. "Brody Emerson, I mean."

"Yeah." Ritter took a seat between Jace and Keene. "But we'd better get Dimitri to look him over soon. He had a bad time of it. We've left him in the hall sedated, so keep an ear out for him."

Ava stepped over to the table, pulling out a chair. "Mari

explained what she knew, but tell me your version of what happened."

I let the others talk while I paced on the side opposite the big wall screen and considered the problem of Patrick Mann. After a few moments, the screen caught my attention. Stella had zoomed in on the picture of a chestnut-haired man, who I recognized immediately as the biological son of Mrs. Mann. He looked exactly like her with his pale, regal face and wide-set eyes. But where her features screamed exhaustion, his screamed energy. A do-gooder if I ever saw one.

Stella noted my gaze. "Following in his father's footsteps as far as politics go, only without White House aspirations."

"So it seems." Next to his picture was a bullet list describing the man, with items such as donations, service, and programs he'd implemented as a councilman. A smaller picture of him with a woman and three children—a boy and two girls—took up another part of the screen.

"Are you okay?" Stella's hand touched mine. Instantly, our minds were connected. Energy like the kind I'd felt linked to Brody Emerson skimmed through my veins. Or maybe it was because of the connection with him that I now recognized it as energy. It pulsed inside Stella's brain . . . leading where? I reached out.

"Oh," I said, drawing in a sharp breath. All at once I knew what had been bugging me about Patrick Mann.

I sat abruptly in the vacant chair next to Stella, making a scraping sound so loud Ava and the men looked over from where they sat at the end of the table. They looked at me expectantly. "Patrick Mann is a technopath," I said.

Ritter cocked his head. "We thought he might be, since the other man he resembles is also a technopath. We've known the Emporium has at least several, so why would that be important?"

"Just now," I said, "when Stella touched me, I connected with her. There are these . . . pulses in her mind, and when I touched them, I followed each one from her brain along a path to an individual nanite. I could see how she adjusts them to keep ahead of her regeneration. I felt the same sort of thing when I was in Patrick Mann's mind. Only it was a hundred times the connections. Or more. His body must be full of nanites." I paused to let that sink in. "Now I'm thinking if Stella can slightly change her appearance with a hundred or so nanites, is it too hard to believe that Patrick Mann—or the man we thought was Patrick Mann—might be changing his entire appearance? If so, he might not bear any resemblance to the real Patrick Mann. And no one would ever know."

"Except the Emporium is far behind us in that kind of research," Cort said. "When Keene was working for them and found out what Stella could do, he was amazed." He looked at his brother for verification.

Keene rubbed a hand through his hair. "Yeah, but I did report it. A couple of years ago, in fact. I think it was one of those tidbits of information you fed me to keep me believing you were still on their side."

"I bet they immediately saw the potential and threw everything they could at it." Stella glowered at Keene, though it was hardly his fault. "Cort and I have been working with some of the others in Europe, and we've made mountains of progress with nanites, but the Emporium has much greater resources."

"We never thought they'd invest so much in something that can only be used by technopaths," Ava said. "Especially when no one in the Triad possesses that ability."

Stella nodded so violently her headset shifted. "A natural assumption. I mean, who cares if a technopath can turn her eyes a different color or is able to tell her body not to ovulate? That hardly has potential to merit a high volume of attention, especially when the effort expended is so great. But they must have had more success with nanites than we've had. Lately, we've been too busy to focus on anything except survival."

"Even with ten times the sophistication of your nanites," Cort tapped something on his laptop, "there would have to be, let's see . . . thousands in your body to change you to resemble, say, Erin."

Stella raised a brow. "Thousands?"

"Okay, tens of thousands." He waved a hand. "Whatever. The point is it wouldn't be easy. There's no way they've had time to create such sophisticated nanites on a self-adjusting level. That means the technopath would have to be directing them at all times and be specifically trained to use them."

"The Emporium has worked for years putting this into place," Ritter said grimly, "so that's not surprising. Apparently, not only have they been churning out babies and placing them in prominent homes in the hopes that they'll be able to control high positions, but they've also focused on technology that could help them worm their way into other places they don't belong."

"That would explain why Brody saw Patrick glowing at the fundraiser," I added.

Jace swore under his breath. "How many of these technopaths do you think they have?"

"Not many," Stella said grimly. "I know of only two, and with Patrick Mann, that makes three."

"Don't forget the other prisoner, who is likely the real Patrick Mann," Ritter said. "We don't know what his ability is yet."

I shook my head. "He's not cooperating, so maybe he isn't with them. We may be able to rescue him with the others. He might even join us. The point is who's the Patrick Mann we met? And what is he planning?"

"I guess," Ava said with a calm that sent shivers through me, "we're going to have to ask him."

I'd been planning on doing exactly that, but now my enthusiasm for confronting him had definitely waned. If the real Patrick Mann was being held at the compound, the Patrick we knew hadn't been raised by the Manns but prepared by the Emporium from birth. He'd be ruthless, well-trained, and amoral. Yet Ava was right. With the president sick and the vice president likely to take over, Patrick Mann was too close to the top of the political hierarchy for our comfort.

Stella's gaze strayed to her monitor. "Vice President Mann has made no secret of his plans to run for the presidency next year. My guess is that this Emporium agent took over Patrick Mann's place in preparation for when his father took charge."

Her thoughts echoed my own. "The vice president was thinking that his son had changed a lot recently. He was worried about it."

"What about the president's sickness?" Jace asked. "Do you think Patrick Mann's identity relates to that? It all feels too coincidental."

"That's what I'm thinking." Ritter shoved back his chair and stood. "Presumably Patrick would have some input in his father's business, but maybe the Emporium Triad got tired of waiting for the next election."

"I still don't see—" I broke off as another idea occurred to me, a terrifying, frightening idea that was too diabolical for the Emporium *not* to have dreamed up.

Ava saw it at the same time I did. Whether because I was broadcasting or because she figured it out on her own, it didn't really matter. "Oh, no," she murmured.

I nodded. "It makes perfect sense."

Ritter stared, his gaze going back and forth between us. "Care to fill us in?"

Ava let me break the news. "I don't know why I didn't see it before. Whoever this Patrick Mann is, I bet he's been in place long enough to learn the vice president's routine. He's not going to try to *influence* the vice president after he steps in for the president, he's going to *become* him."

A hush fell over the room as we all digested the significance of having the Triad control the American presidency.

"Needless to say," Ava took over, "we're not ready for that. We don't have enough people in place to successfully counter any policies he might put into place. This could mean coming out, and once that happens, all bets are off."

"I bet in twenty years mortals will be second-class citizens," Cort said.

"I think you underestimate our will to survive." Keene's voice was hard. "But I agree that more time to prepare would be beneficial to our cause."

"That gives the Emporium just as much time to prepare," Jace said.

Ava sighed. "I believe we can mitigate the damages now that we understand their methods. However, you have a point."

Ritter's mouth drew into a firm line. "It hasn't happened yet, and it's not going to if we have anything to say about it. Let's go have a chat with our fake Patrick Mann."

"Make it a snatch and grab then," Ava said, tapping her hands once on the table. "Use lethal force if necessary, because as much as we want information, we can't allow their plan to continue. Keep in mind that after the attack at the fundraiser, it's likely the Secret Service will be all over him."

I stood, feeling anxious to get going now that it was decided. "Maybe the Emporium will have their guard down because they think he's well protected. I'd rather confront mortals any day."

"Maybe." Ava's pursed lips told me she wasn't counting on it. "Provided, of course that the Secret Service agents actually are mortal and not more Emporium plants."

There was that.

Ava met Ritter's eyes. "Who will you need? Everyone?"

Ritter frowned and shook his head. "Cort and Jace. And Stella to coordinate communications and surveillance. Plus either you or"—he paused, his eyes straying to me—"or Erin. We'll need to know exactly who is in the house."

I glared at him, unsettled by his hesitation. I didn't exactly want to go anymore, but I wasn't about to be left out, either, not when so much was riding on securing the imposter.

"Erin, then. She's stronger than I am." Ava said it without envy, her voice laced with a touch of pride I wasn't quite sure I deserved.

Ritter nodded, so I relaxed and stopped glaring at him. "I'd also like Dimitri," he added. "We may need his ability." My entire body tensed again at the request. If Dimitri had to patch one of us up on the go, things would be bad.

"He's actually gone to the hospital to research some test results that came in from Senator Pearson," Ava said. "She managed to get a copy of the most recent results from the hospital where they have the president. Nothing official, but he wanted to see if there was anything he could do from a distance. He shouldn't be long, though." She hesitated before saying, "You don't want Oliver?"

"No." Ritter's response was short—too short. I knew Ava would want a full explanation later and Ritter would have to report how Oliver had frozen at the Hunters' meeting house. Not that Ava would toss Oliver out, but we'd have to work on his skills before we could depend on him again.

"Mari?" Ava sighed. "I suppose not. If only she could move him herself, it would make things so much easier."

"Ah," Keene said, "but if she had that much power, how would she remember she's still human?" His smirk was just short of disrespect.

Ava gave him a bland smile. "What makes you think any of us are completely human?"

I blinked, trying to decipher her meaning. She'd once voiced a theory about the Unbounded gene coming from a space-faring race that had visited earth, but I'd mostly thought she'd been joking. Now I wasn't so sure.

Cort straightened and cleared his voice. "I've been thinking about Mari. If she's really folding space as we surmise, it's everything around her that's moving, at least in layman terms. So why shouldn't she be able to take someone else?"

"We've tried and she can't." I stood and walked around the table. "We'll have to leave further experimentation for later."

"Agreed," Ritter said. To Ava he added, "I'd also like Yuan-Xin, if Tenika can spare him."

"I'll go," Keene said.

Ritter's gaze shifted to him. "You're wounded."

"I did okay this morning."

I didn't know about that, but he seemed no worse off now.

"Too risky," Ritter said shortly.

Keene's eyes glittered, and he appeared about to say something when Cort interrupted. "If you're planning on me driving the getaway vehicle, which might be a good thing given the abuse my leg suffered today, I could use him as a lookout."

Ritter's nostrils flared. "Okay. But he doesn't go inside. We can't risk anyone who isn't in full form. Confronting the Emporium isn't the same as going up against a few mortal Hunters."

"Of course not." Bitterness filled Keene's voice, though because of his longing to be Unbounded or his hatred of the Emporium, I couldn't guess. I was too busy wondering if Ritter's comment was partially meant for me, a hint to let Ava take my place. I wasn't feeling altogether myself yet after taking in all that power. Heat still filled my body, and although that was better than the constant cold I'd experienced since arriving in New York, it wasn't normal. But I decided if Ritter had a real concern about me, he would have said something earlier. He wouldn't endanger the mission.

Ritter headed to the door. "Stella, I hope you have a location on our imposter because I want everyone ready to go within the hour."

"Oh, I found him," Stella said. "But he's not at a house. It's a hotel. Dress up nice. We need to look the part."

Nice dress and fighting usually didn't go hand in hand, especially as there had been no time to restock my wardrobe after we'd abandoned our last safe house. I'd have to borrow something from Ava's closet, who like all the others, reordered her favorite clothes with a simple click of a computer key.

"Full disguises," Ritter added. "The Emporium knows us all by sight."

My heart thudded inside my chest as I watched him leave. No time to tell him about my epiphany at the Hunter's meeting house. Maybe tonight. But what would I tell him exactly? It wasn't as if he'd proposed.

I was fooling myself, though, because his so-called gifts told me exactly what he wanted—a complete and total commitment for the next two thousand years. Nothing to worry about. Right?

CHAPTER 17

LESS THAN EIGHTY MINUTES LATER, A TAXI CARRYING RITTER, JACE, Stella, and me pulled up at a luxury hotel in downtown Manhattan. I eyed the huge building doubtfully. "How are we even going to get inside, much less grab him?" There was a young doorman outside and I wondered if we'd have to show him our hotel key or something to prove we belonged.

"They have to let us in." Stella smiled sweetly as she adjusted her narrow eyeglasses. "We're visiting a distinguished Russian ambassador." She looked unlike herself, though still completely arresting in her long black wig, fluttery beige dress, and impossible high heels. Far too good to have had time to concoct a cover story.

"I see," I said.

Stella smiled at the doorman, who blushed as he hurried to open the door for her. We all stepped inside. To my surprise, Dimitri was already there, sprawling casually on a couch in the lobby, almost unrecognizable with a longish gray-peppered wig and something odd going on with the shape of his nose. Hovering over him was Yuan-Xin, wearing small spectacles and a fancy gray cap covering black hair that had suddenly grown to his collar.

Both were dressed in designer suits, though Dimitri's was slightly too large.

"Ah," Dimitri said in a heavy Russian accent. "So good to see you, my friends." Standing, he took my hands and pulled me close, kissing both cheeks and then repeating the gesture with Stella. Even Ritter and Jace received a bear hug, which almost made me laugh out loud. Dimitri had actually been born in Russia and it was apparent he enjoyed playing the part.

"Come, let us go upstairs to my suite." Dimitri signaled a bellhop, who relieved Stella and Jace of their large suitcases crammed with computer equipment.

We spoke little as we rode up the elevator to the sixteenth floor. On my recommendation, the others had let their shields drop and had carefully blanked their minds so that if any sensing Unbounded from the Emporium were nearby, their presence wouldn't set off any alarms. A dangerous game to play, but with minds blocked, our life forces would be dimmer, different from the regular mortals around us, signaling our Unbounded connection. It was akin to advertising our identities to our enemies. This way as long as a sensing Unbounded hadn't been personally in the lobby and laid eyes on us, our presence and our natures should go undetected.

Once we were in the room, I'd use my ability to mask everyone completely before they erected their shields so the room would appear to be empty to sensing Unbounded. I wasn't actually sure I could extend to everyone, but as long as we were in the same room, I hoped it would work. At any rate, unless a sensing Emporium agent was watching nearby, we shouldn't be discovered.

The room turned out to be a luxurious suite, with two bedrooms, two baths, a kitchen, and a sitting room that was almost as large as the rest combined. Stella began setting up her equipment after the bellhop closed the door behind him.

I imagined my mental shield pushing out to encompass the room, strengthening it and checking for breaches. "Okay," I said. "You can use shields now."

I crossed the room to where Dimitri stood near the window. "How did you get here so quickly?" I asked, looking down at his broad form. "And dressed like that?"

He leaned closer. "Compliments of Yuan-Xin. Quite resourceful, our New York allies."

"So did you learn anything from the president's test results?" Ever since Ava told me the senator had sent the tests, I'd been curious to know what he'd discovered.

A frown filled his broad face. "There is nothing I can see from the tests except that it wasn't a stroke. The medical history she sent told me a lot more. He's experiencing several organ failures—liver, kidneys, spleen—without apparent cause. Even his heart has been affected. The only thing I've ever seen like it is poisoning."

"What, you mean like arsenic or something?"

"No, I mean something far more subtle. Particularly a cocktail of rosary peas and nicotine that the Emporium perfected in the Dark Ages. Undetectable if given over time, and there is no antidote." He sighed. "What the president needs are several transplants, but unfortunately, it has been going on so long, I doubt he'd survive the surgeries."

Which would give Vice President Mann the presidency.

"At least not without a healer present," Dimitri amended.

Across the room, Jace climbed under the table to connect power cables for Stella, while Ritter and Yuan-Xin talked near the set of couches. Dimitri and I watched them for several seconds before I asked, "You think Patrick Mann had something to do with it?"

Dimitri met my gaze. "The one thing I'm sure of is that he has everything to do with it."

I thought so, too.

"Thank you," Stella told Jace as he crawled out from under the table. She pulled off the long black wig and tossed it behind her laptop.

With a parting smile at Dimitri, I drifted toward Stella. "I'm taking it we're on the same floor as Patrick Mann. What about his parents?"

"They're visiting friends on Staten Island," Stella said. "Junior apparently wasn't invited."

"Too bad for us." I felt hot in the wool coat Ava had given me to wear over her short, blue silk dress, but I was loath to discard the few weapons it concealed. Already I missed the rest of my gear.

"Actually, we'll be more easily overlooked here." Stella put on her neural headset, pushing the tiny metal electrodes down tightly next to her skull. When I'd tried it, the fit was uncomfortable, but she didn't seem to mind. "In a few minutes, I'll be able to control what hotel security sees on their cameras." She turned on her headset. "You read me, Cort? Are you in place?" He must have answered in the affirmative because she nodded. "Stand by. I'll let you know when they're coming. It may be a while."

I looked at Ritter, who was now huddled on the longer couch with Yuan-Xin and Jace. Dimitri was going to join them. Closing my eyes, I reached out past my shield, searching for any sign of Unbounded. Almost immediately, I felt one at the far end of the hall in a room where two life forces lounged by the door—probably Secret Service agents. The shield over the Unbounded's mind was strong, but not a match for my machete. Making it past the shield, I recognized the man I knew as Patrick Mann. He was doing nothing but reading the newspaper. No thoughts of intrigue or treason. Only the shiny black snake undulating in the sand stream of his thoughts testified that something wasn't quite right.

What if I could break into that snake right now and see exactly what the Triad planned? Maybe it even contained the identities of other influential operatives. The undulating construction beckoned to me urgently, and I felt an increasing desire to rip into it with my machete. Only Ava's warning about the snake and my fear of Delia stopped me. Instead, I crouched in Patrick's mind, waiting for what seemed a very long time until he looked up and I could take note of the room where he sat. I breathed a sigh of relief when no one besides the two Secret Servicemen seemed to be nearby.

Who had I expected? Delia Vesey? She was one of the few who would be able to mask her presence from me as I was attempting to do with this entire room. I wished Ava were here so she could see if I was succeeding.

I joined the others near the couches, who were debating the best way to take Patrick Mann without setting off too many alarms.

"I think they'll keep Patrick's abduction quiet for a time," Dimitri was saying. "They won't want to advertise a breach of the Secret Service so soon after the events on Friday. And by then we'll be long gone."

"Agreed," Ritter said. "Once we get him out of the hotel, I don't care what they tell the press. We'll take him to Mexico if we have to."

I settled on the arm of the couch next to Dimitri. "There's just him in the room and two agents, as far as I can tell."

"Then let's go up to the roof and climb down the side of the building to his window." This from Jace, who I was pretty sure had seen it done on a television show the week before.

"For that matter, we could just knock on the door and take out the agents," I put in.

Jace rolled his eyes. "Only if we want the hotel cameras to pick it up."

"Isn't that what Stella's here for?" I smiled at him sweetly. His hair was colored a sedate brown instead of his usual blond, but the blue of his eyes burned brightly. Today those eyes looked even more like Stefan Carrington's, and I knew exactly how I felt about that.

"Well, there are still the neighbors. And anyone else who might be in the hallways." Jace looked at the others. "Wouldn't the windows be the least obtrusive?"

Ritter shook his head. "Better that we wait for him to call room service and take over the cart before it gets to his room. If there's enough time, Stella might be able to place Jace in as a new waiter. Or we can intercept the cart on the way."

"That could take forever," Jace groaned. "I hate to remind you, but he doesn't need to eat. He could be satisfied with just absorbing."

I agreed. He might not eat lunch at all, depending on his normal habits. "The agents might order something. Unless they're on short shifts."

"Maybe Mann will get bored with staying inside and go out," said Yuan-Xin. "Then we can jump the agents and take him."

Ritter nodded. "That would be ideal—getting him to leave the room voluntarily. That way we could take him before he left the hotel. But the likelihood isn't very strong, not with only two agents there to protect him. His father is about to become the president of the United States, and after the attack at the fundraiser, they won't give him much leeway. In fact, I'd be surprised if they don't have a few more agents in the hotel or somewhere close by."

Ritter arose and began to pace, radiating frustration. I understood perfectly. It was disappointing to come all this way in such a hurry only to sit and wait.

"I could call him," I suggested. "Tell him I need to see him. He'd remember me from the fundraiser. I could say I'd recognized him as Unbounded after all and that I needed to talk. Maybe he's new enough—or that arrogant—to take the bait."

"Like he'd believe you'd meet him alone when his buddies at the Emporium have been trying to catch up to you for the past three months." Jace rubbed his hands on his black dress pants, which had to be driving him crazy, given that he hated wearing suits. "He'd know it was a trap. At least I'd know, if it were me."

Ritter turned and faced us. "He's right. Then the guy would contact his buddies. As far as we know, the Emporium has no clue that we're on to him or that we suspect his presence is related to the president's illness. If they had any idea, they'd be here in force." His gaze scorched me, though it didn't linger.

Sheesh. All he had to do was look at me and I was gone. Completely and totally. Did I really have to tell him about the conclusion I'd come to that morning? My emotions felt painted on my face.

"So what's the plan?" I asked, pushing my thoughts away. Later, I would have time to make a decision about how much I would expose my feelings to Ritter. Except if he touched me, I might not have a chance of holding anything back, regardless of the consequences. "I haven't found any sign of Emporium agents. Even if they're able to mask some from me, it can't be many."

"You could knock." Stella's voice came from directly behind me. "If we got Oliver here, you could be anyone you wanted. Maybe Delia again?"

Ritter's lips tightened. "Oliver is unreliable." Meaning Ritter was unwilling to risk my life. I might take the chance, but he was in charge here and the choice wasn't mine.

Dimitri watched Ritter for a few seconds before saying, "Looks like the blind knock on the door might be the way to go after all."

Ritter thought for a moment and started shaking his head just as Yuan-Xin said, "Too risky."

Jace let out a sigh. "I suppose that feeling in my gut is why you guys are saying that?"

"Yep, get used to it," Ritter said, the slightest smile hovering for a second on his face. "Looks like we're going with the room service cart."

"Well, I still think we should check out my roof idea," Jace mumbled.

My turn to sigh. "We didn't bring enough rope."

"Wait a minute, guys." Stella turned from her computer. "I have movement. Two uniformed agents heading up the elevator."

"Reinforcements?" Jace asked.

"More likely a change of guard." Ritter went to look at the monitor, his voice tense. "Unless we've been spotted."

I pushed out my mind, pinpointing the agents as they left the elevator on our floor. "They're not blocking," I said. "I don't see anything that says they've noticed us."

"Yeah, but look at the present they've given us." Without touching her keyboard, Stella brought up a picture of the lobby showing the two agents only moments before. As they passed the check-in desk, one of them locked eyes with an employee, exchanging a slight nod.

"Ah, so the two from the room weren't alone after all," Dimitri said.

"It happens again over here." Stella brought up a second image. "This time with an employee who seems to be watching the elevator."

"If they have those two, they'll be careful enough to have someone near the back exit we plan to use," Yuan-Xin said.

Ritter put a hand on the table leaning over to get a better view of Stella's laptop screen. "Show me the door to the alley." He studied a man slowly vacuuming a floor. "Probably him." He straightened. "We'll have to take care of them all before we smuggle Patrick out. Okay, Jace, get down to the kitchens and report to duty. By the time you get there, Stella will have made sure you are their latest employee."

"Already done," Stella said. "I can't get him the clearance he'd need to deliver room service to Mann because security has it flagged, but once the call is made—if the call is made—we'll give Jace the signal and have him take the cart from the real employee." Her eyes went to Jace. "I'll send the details to your phone."

"The original agents are leaving," I said, having kept track of them, both on the camera picture in one corner of Stella's screen and in my mind. "We'll need to make sure they leave the hotel."

Jace put in his wireless earpiece, followed by the ring that hid a mic. "I assume someone is going into the room with me? Though if there are only two mortals and Mann, it should be a piece of cake. As long as there aren't any others lurking around."

"There could be more hiding their life forces behind shields." I felt uneasy that it was my word they depended on when it was my little brother's life at stake.

That didn't faze Jace. "Then it'd be someone with sensing not combat. If they can't channel like you, they won't be a problem."

If, if, if. I wanted to tell him he didn't know what he was talking about, that Delia was more powerful than he could imagine, but I didn't really have anything but my one meeting with her and my own fears to base that assumption on.

"I've reviewed their video footage since Friday night," Stella said, "and there's no record of anyone entering that room besides Patrick Mann and several different sets of agents."

"No connecting rooms?" I asked.

"None."

I breathed a sigh of relief. It wasn't that I didn't trust my ability exactly, but the fact that I'd been sharing Davis Emerson's mind with Delia's minion and had sensed absolutely nothing had unnerved me more than I'd admitted to myself.

"Regardless, no one goes in alone." Ritter hesitated, his eyes wandering over each of us in turn. "With at least three other agents in the hotel, I'll need someone to help me below, and someone will need to help Jace remove and hide the employee he'll be taking the room service cart from." He glanced at Dimitri. "That's probably you."

Dimitri nodded. "Whoever it is won't even remember the prick of my needle."

"Will you need any help getting out of the building?" Ritter asked Stella.

"No, I'll just take my laptop and my headset and walk out the front door." She patted a five-inch square box. "This will need to stay here to keep their cameras blind, but I'll leave a timed auto erase when I leave, so it won't matter if they find it later." She hesitated a heartbeat before adding, "But we do have another slight problem. I laid down one of my mini bots as we came in, but it stopped transmitting before it even reached Mann's room. I've tried it on various frequencies with the same result and even tried to call it on my phone. Still nothing. That means they've got a signal interrupter inside to prevent anything but hard-wired communications. My guess is not even their own cell phones can call out from that room."

"That could work in our favor," Jace said. "Especially if you can make sure they don't use the hotel phone to call backup."

Stella grinned. "I can do that. Of course, they could always just switch off the machine if they want to use their cell phones.

I imagine it's there so no one can spy on them electronically. That might mean they're expecting us."

"If they were, they'd have a mental shield like the one broad-casting at the compound," Dimitri said. "Erin wouldn't be able to see inside."

"Hmm." Stella didn't look convinced. "I suppose the inter-rupter could be in place to make sure no unscrupulous reporters get their thrills."

"I'll go in with Jace," I volunteered, coming to my feet. "That way I can channel his ability and we'll be doubly efficient. And I'll be able to communicate with you if our radios don't work inside." I'd also be responsible for Jace in case I was wrong about Mann being alone. As I was fairly sure the Emporium wanted me alive, my presence might give me a bargaining tool.

No one else is there, I told myself. *Nothing will go wrong.*

Ritter nodded, his mouth tight. "Okay, but stick to the plan. No variations. Down and out to the back alley. Dimitri will hide the employee and meet you guys in the stairs to help get Mann out. Yuan-Xin and I will dispatch our guys and be there waiting as well. I want it all to happen within three minutes. We can't risk discovery once you go in."

"You want me to remove the employee's memory of seeing us?" I asked.

"Don't waste the time," Ritter said. "He won't see enough of you to matter, and sooner or later everyone is going to know the vice president's son is missing. Let Secret Service muzzle the hotel staff if they don't want the press to know yet."

Jace walked toward the door. "Patrick had better order soon. I swear, if I'm on dish duty, I get patrol without Oliver for the entire next month."

Ritter's lips twitched, but he only said, "Remember that if Mann decides to go out, we'll change to plan B."

Jace paused. "And that is?"

"We jump him before he gets to the elevator and hustle him

down the stairs. You'll be close enough in the kitchens to get the agent at the back entrance."

"Cool." Jace opened the door.

Stella followed him with the cameras down to the front of the hotel and then to the kitchen where the personnel there directed him to the man in charge. Satisfied that Jace was safe, I sat on the couch next to Dimitri to wait. Plan B would be so much more convenient. If only we could get lucky.

After ten minutes, I finally stood and took off Ava's coat before sitting back down. I let a few seconds pass before I said to Dimitri, "How do you keep doing it? All these years." Over a thousand. My mind could barely comprehend living a tenth that long.

"You mean keep fighting against the Emporium?" His eyes were grave.

I nodded. "I'd think at some point you'd just say to hell with it all and disappear. Spend the rest of your days on a beach somewhere, or in a cabin deep in the mountains of some remote village whose name no one can pronounce."

A smile tugged at his lips. "I've actually done both of those things at different times in my life. It never lasts for long. I keep going for my posterity. For the human race. Besides, I enjoy my comforts too much to go native somewhere, and I like working with all of you. We're a family. That's what keeps us going. Family doesn't give up. Not ever."

"So much depends on us. These little fixes." I frowned. "And you also have so many children and grandchildren and other descendants to keep an eye on. Don't you ever get tired? Don't you ever worry that you might miss someone? That you might not be—" Be what? I didn't know.

"Enough?" he asked.

"I guess that's it. I don't know if I could—" Remove myself from my children's lives to protect them, watch my grandchildren die while I was still young. Keep lists of posterity and check up on them when they neared the age of Change, only to induct those who did Change into a secret war that might bring death at any moment—and likely in the most gruesome and painful way possible. So much loss and responsibility.

Dimitri laid a hand on my shoulder, comfort radiating from him. "You do it one day at a time. You use what technology is available and you simply go forward. You let yourself experience joy when you can, and you take time to mourn. It's not as hard as you might think."

"If you had it to do over, would you have so many children?" So many that after a thousand years he wouldn't be able to tell me all the names without one of our genealogical programs.

He chuckled. "Well, it's not as if my genes gave me much of a choice since we can't simply switch off our fertility, but there isn't one I would wish away, and that's a lot more than most mortals can say. I've learned that it's not over until it's really over, and I have unlimited years to wait for misbehaving kids to come around— whether they're mortal or Unbounded." He paused, his smile widening. "Is this about you and Ritter?" He glanced toward the door, where Ritter was deep in conversation with Yuan-Xin.

"Maybe."

He nodded. "It's about time."

"You once told me he might not be ready for a hundred years or so."

"I was wrong. I think you've both delayed enough."

"You're a fine one to talk." Hadn't he and Ava danced around their relationship for much longer?

His brow furrowed. "Whatever are you talking about?"

"Never mind." But there was one more thing. I looked at Dimitri and found him waiting, as though he'd already known there was more. "Jace figured out that his birth was engineered. He wants to know the truth."

"Are you going to tell him?"

"I don't know. I mean, yes. I just don't know when. I'm afraid he won't—" What? That his curiosity and impetuous nature would send him into the arms of the most dangerous man in the world?

Duh.

Dimitri crooked a brow. "Some things you don't get to choose, and you can't protect him from everything. He's a good boy, Erin. He'll find his way."

Yeah, but I didn't know if I could wait a century or two to watch Jace recover from any side trips. Still, Dimitri had a lot of years of experience so maybe he knew what he was talking about. Of course that didn't mean I had to tell Jace tomorrow.

One hour passed and then another as we waited in the hotel suite. Was Patrick one of those rare Unbounded who never ate anything? I pushed into his mind again, wishing I could send him images of thick beefsteaks and mounds of buttered potatoes. Delia had done it to me, put in thoughts that I'd first assumed were my own, but how?

Normally when I wanted to communicate with someone, I simply pushed out a mental thought without much preparation and it appeared almost instantly in the person's sand stream. However, the thought clearly originated outside the person's mind, so I always identified myself if there might be any doubt as to who was doing the pushing. Yet people do sometimes have sudden thoughts that appear for no reason and those don't cause a mental alarm, so maybe the way I pushed thoughts into the stream is what alerted people to my presence.

Tentatively, I formed a picture in my imaginary hand and held it near the sand stream of Patrick's thoughts, working more by instinct than anything else. The idea hovered for an instant, shifted up and down gently, and started to move inside. Belatedly, I realized the stupidity of my actions. What if he suspected someone was messing with his mind? I could blow the entire operation if he called for backup. I reached to take back the thought, but it was sucked inside the stream.

Patrick's reaction was immediate and unexpected. Nausea filled his mind. Okay, so how was I to know he was a vegetarian? Guess that made absorbing rather challenging for him since he couldn't exactly choose not to absorb animal proteins. The good news was that he didn't seem to suspect my presence. Should I try again?

As I considered what else to suggest, he put down his magazine and reached for the phone. "Room service?" he asked. "I'd like to place an order. Vegetable soup and bread sticks, warm with extra butter." I could see the butter melting in Patrick's thoughts, feel his mouth watering. "As soon as possible. Thanks."

Before I could tell the others, Stella was already replaying a recording of Patrick's order.

Ritter shoved in his earbud. "Showtime," he said, approaching the couch. I stood up to meet him. "Our timing will start on your signal, Erin, so let us know when you're about to enter the room and we'll act. Remember, three minutes after you go in I want you at that back door." His voice was normal but worry screamed from the shallow furrows in his forehead. Had he always been this easy to read? Had I only imagined him as a mountain of impassiveness?

"Wait," I said, reaching for Ava's coat.

He hesitated, his eyes going to mine and sending slow heat to my belly. I drew out Keene's tiny switchblade from a pocket of the coat. I'd challenged him to use words that made up communication in the mortal world, but maybe I could use his terms every bit as much as I expected him to use mine. "I won't be needing this."

His hand touched mine, still holding the knife, and at once I felt him around me, exuding a permanence that no longer frightened me. His fingers curled around mine, making my hand into a fist around the knife. "You might need it. You can throw it away yourself as soon as this is over. In fact, I already have another for you." *A better one,* his tone implied.

I grinned. "I see."

With black eyes that looked like molten rock, he drew away and started for the door where Yuan-Xin and Dimitri waited. "Let's go."

CHAPTER 18

IMITRI AND I GOT OFF THE ELEVATOR ON THE TENTH FLOOR, while Ritter and Yuan-Xin continued on to the lobby. Stella directed us down and around several connected hallways to a supply closet, which Dimitri unlocked with a universal key card Stella had created for him. Inside, we donned a couple of uniforms from a rack, tucking our weapons wherever we could. Then we grabbed a laundry basket, threw in a few clean sheets and took the service elevator to the sixth floor where we waited for Jace and whoever would be taking Patrick Mann's order to his room.

Dimitri handed me two small syringes. "In case you need to sedate Mann or if you run into anyone on your way out."

"Thanks." I felt jumpy and nervous, but that was normal at the beginning of a maneuver. Once we acted, the emotion would subside. I reached out, purposely absorbing more nutrients though I still felt full from absorbing the energy from Brody. At least the time waiting in the room had given my body the opportunity to heal completely; my skin had finally cooled and I felt comfortable instead of hot.

Minutes ticked by and finally the elevator dinged, opening to reveal Jace and a young male waiter with a cart—and an older man who reeked of Secret Service. Dimitri pushed onto the elevator, and I slid in next to him. The doors started to close.

"Aren't you getting off here?" the waiter asked Jace. "I thought you pushed the button."

"Yeah, but I forgot the mop." Jace made a face. "Someone's apparently been sick. I don't want to go back downstairs for supplies. It's my first day and I don't want to appear incompetent. They said there's a supply closet on ten, right?"

The waiter laughed. "Yeah. I don't envy you. My first day someone had a clogged toilet and guess who had to clean up a bathroom full of crap? Some rich people are absolutely incompetent when it comes to—" He broke off, apparently thinking better of finishing his thought in front of so many witnesses. "They tip well," he added. "It won't take long before you move up. As long as you are always on time."

"Kind of sad when cleaning up vomit is more appealing than washing dishes." Jace held up his hands. "I think I must have washed every dish in this hotel in the past few hours."

A smile broke over my face before I could help it, and I was glad everyone, including the Secret Service guy, laughed at the comment. I doubted the dishes would free Jace of Oliver, though, even for a month.

Jace held my gaze for a moment and then looked at the agent. His way of telling me the man was his. Fine. I'd let him have his fun. But he'd better keep his mind focused on his vomit story in case any sensing Unbounded were listening in.

The elevator came to a stop. As the door slid open, Dimitri moved toward the waiter, a syringe in his hand. Jace took a step and shoved his fist into the agent's face. Both the waiter and the agent crumpled before the door finished opening. I stepped out to make sure the hallway was clear, while the men piled our unconscious friends into the laundry basket and covered their protruding faces with a sheet. Dimitri pushed the basket into the hall.

"Package secured on ten," I informed everyone through my mic. I didn't mention the Secret Service agent because it wouldn't change the plan and might distract everyone from the bland thoughts they were supposed to be projecting.

We headed for the sixteenth floor. I pulled out my Sig, complete with a silencer, and stuck it under the silver dome holding Patrick Mann's hot bread sticks. Moments later we stood outside his door. I pushed my thoughts into the room, but nothing appeared to have changed.

"They're going to notice the agent isn't with the cart," I told Jace.

"I know." He knocked at the door and raised his voice. "Room service."

"Going in," I told the others. No response. *Radio already isn't broadcasting,* I mentally told Stella, who was the easiest to reach because of her proximity. *We're going in.* I stayed with her until she relayed my message to the others.

The door opened and an agent's gaze flicked over us, suspicion clouding his blue eyes. "Where's my colleague?"

"Holding the elevator," I said. "He didn't want anyone else using it before we're done here."

"I'm going to have to verify that." He took a step toward the hallway, but Jace was already pushing past me, bringing out a tranq gun from somewhere. Before the agent hit the ground, a dart in his neck, Jace kicked out to disarm the second. Meanwhile, I shoved the cart inside and leapt across the room toward the couch where Patrick Mann was still seated, looking casually up from his newspaper.

My gun was in my hand before I knew I'd reached for it. "Get up, *Patrick,*" I said, sneering at the name. "We're going for a little ride." Near the door, Jace's opponent crashed to the ground. "You won't need your friends," I added.

Patrick didn't move, and he was smiling. My first indication that something had gone dreadfully wrong. "So you *did* recognize me the other night," he said.

"Of course. You're the vice president's son." I moved closer as I spoke. If he didn't come on his own, I'd jab him with one of Dimitri's needles and drag him.

"I knew I should have had you detained." Patrick's lip lifted in derision.

"We both know you tried. And that went so well for you."

He waved a hand. "Amateurs. But Delia said it was only a matter of time until you came looking for me. I'll have to ask her how she knew."

Movement from the direction of the bedroom caught my eye. *Jace!* I called out silently, as I dived behind the couch.

Two unknown men burst into the sitting room, dressed in full combat gear, sword hilts rising above their backs. An Emporium hit team. They were followed by an oddly dressed shorter man. Despite his disguise of a padded jacket, long dark hair, and decidedly feminine pale blue skinny jeans, I knew him. Delia's assistant, Lew Roberts, the sensing Unbounded. His shield was as black and thick as before and he was once again shielding his companions, masking them from my mental view. Dimitri had been wrong about the computer-generated shield. They *had* been expecting us.

Bullets flew, the whooshing of the silenced shots sounding deadly and fast. Jace arched as one hit him, even as I pushed out my mental shield to cover his body. The next bullet only pushed him forward as it had with Mari at the Emersons' townhouse. I didn't have time to feel relief as I let off a flurry of shots with my own gun.

One of the men leapt toward me. We crashed with a terrific impact that sent both our handguns flying. He reached for his sword. The instinct of Jace's ability had me rolling to grab one of the end tables near the couch. I tumbled away, bringing it up at the last instant to block the sword as it hurled down toward me.

He slashed again, and I caught the sharp edge of his sword with the table, pushing him off. I heaved the table, flipping it around so the legs went first, hoping to score a blow. In the right place, even a table leg could do serious damage.

"Enough." A gun jabbed painfully into the side of my head. Patrick Mann. I'd taken my eyes off him too long. "Go get the other one," Patrick said to my opponent.

"No!" I reached for the image of my machete, slamming it down on the connection between the two hit men and Lew Roberts. The connections severed and calling up my reserves, I flashed light into their minds. The men faltered, but didn't collapse.

Lew laughed. "Thought you'd try that again. We can't shield them completely, but you'll find besting them won't be so easy this time unless you use a lot more power."

Jace took advantage of his opponent's momentary disorientation and slammed a foot into his chest, knocking him against the wall where his head slammed with a sickening thump. Down, but for how long? The other hit man roared in fury and lifted his sword.

I had the satisfaction of watching Jace use a lamp to wrench the sword from the other man's hand. They began trading punches. Lew raised his own gun and fired, but the shot hit the mental shield I'd erected around my brother and did nothing more than add strength to his last punch.

"Get her out of here," Lew said to Patrick with a grimace. "Be careful. She might still be armed."

"But what about—" Patrick began.

"Now. She's what we need. The other is unimportant. Thurston can take care of himself. Move!"

"Relax. I'm coming." Patrick shoved me toward the bedroom as I struggled.

I thrust light into his mind, but the black snake absorbed it before it did much damage. Patrick swore and shoved me harder, knocking me to the ground. "Don't," he said, spittle falling from his mouth, "do that again." He yanked me to my feet and pushed me once more toward the bedroom door.

I thought about resisting further. A gunshot to the head wouldn't kill me, but it would hurt like hell and put me out of commission for at least a day. Not a wise choice if I wanted to escape. And before I did anything, I had to warn Ritter and the others. They might be too far away to help me by the time they got here, but Stella at least might reach Jace in time. She was amazing in combat for a technopath.

Another thought came immediately after. *I'll discover their full plan and send that to them. My capture won't be in vain.* Releasing my fury, I followed the urge that had pressed ever harder on me since entering the room. The mental image of my machete appeared inside Patrick's mind, and I slammed it down on the undulating snake in his thought stream.

An explosion wracked my mind. Images both raced and fluttered past my awareness. My life. Lives I'd only glimpsed from others. All jumbled together in an unintelligible heap. I collapsed under the assault. A tortured keening filled the room. Was that me?

The detailed plans I'd been seeking were right there—I was right about the information being hidden inside his mind—but I couldn't decipher much of it. Standing in my way was the black image of a robed woman, the edges of her mental outline shining like an eclipse. I knew that outline. Sickness filled my stomach. I had to get out of here!

Patrick's gun shifted to my leg. "Get up or I'll give you something to whine about."

But I couldn't move. Not a single muscle obeyed my command. I couldn't even withdraw mentally from his mind.

Lew's hand stopped Patrick from firing. "Wait," he said in his nasal voice. "Delia wants you to wait."

All at once Lew was in my mind, past any barrier I'd erected. *Ha,* he told me. *Delia knew you would be unable to resist that block in his mind after you saw it at the fundraiser. That's why she added a little something just for you.*

A trap! I needed to warn Ritter. Get them out of the hotel before reinforcements arrived, if they weren't here already.

Oh, you want to reach out to them, do you? a voice said in my mind. *I can help there.* Horror swept over me. It was a voice that had filled every nightmare since my Change. Delia Vesey, whose life and experience made Dimitri look young by comparison. *How nice of you to accept my invitation,* she added. *I know it was unconventional, but I can't wait to continue your training.*

How was she in my mind? She had to be nearby. Either that or she was coming through Lew, somehow forming a link of communication.

Now let's tell your friends there's been a delay. Delia pushed out with me, finding Ritter easily on the main floor. Her range was greater than mine, and I saw that together we'd be able to extend even further. Ritter hefted a Secret Service agent he was stashing in an unused conference room.

Run! I wanted to scream. *Get out! Delia's here.* I pushed the thoughts, but they didn't make it past my own brain.

Tsk, tsk. No spoiling the fun.

Her enjoyment of my torture was all too apparent. I pushed against her will, and when that failed, I tried to bend around her, to reach Ritter on my own. But each way I turned was met with a shiny impenetrable black barrier.

Slight delay, Delia put in Ritter's mind. Not channeling my ability so much as forcing me to do and say what she wanted. *Some annoying hotel guests. But everything's a go. We have Patrick Mann.*

No! I moaned, but Ritter didn't hear.

Delia laughed at my despair. *How long do you think he'll wait before he realizes you are no longer here? Long enough for me to trap him?* Even as she spoke, she directed Lew to order Patrick to pick me up. In my mind, I fought him, but in real life, I was as immobile in his arms as a sack of flour.

My last view was of Jace blocking his larger opponent's right hook as the first man he'd knocked unconscious struggled back to his feet.

In the bedroom, the dresser had been shoved aside to reveal a gaping hole. Stella may have been right about the rooms not connecting, but apparently the Emporium agents had made their own door. It was to this that Patrick carried me. Into another suite and through a connecting door to yet a third hotel room.

Lew opened the door to the hallway. "Did you take care of the camera?"

That's when I noticed Patrick was now wearing something that resembled Stella's neural headset, only smaller. He nodded. "They have control over the cameras already, but I inserted another feedback loop. By the time they discover it, we'll be gone. But how am I going to explain this to Secret Service?"

"No need. I'll come back and clean up the mess, once our reinforcements lock down the hotel. The agents won't remember a thing."

That was an awful lot of cleaning up the Emporium was willing to do, but we'd probably do the same if we had an agent posing as the vice president's son.

Patrick shifted me to his shoulder as they opened a door and headed up some stairs. *The roof,* I thought. *Jace was right about checking out the roof.* Was that the sound of a helicopter?

Delia cursed in my mind. *He didn't buy it. He's heading up to the room. Why is he doing that?*

Because you're not me, I told her, though I didn't really know.

Impossible. You can't have that kind of connection.

Ignoring her, I pushed out. *Ritter!*

He can't hear you, she said.

My world went black.

CHAPTER 19

ARKNESS TUMBLED IN MY MIND, GREEDILY EATING EVERYTHING in its path. Only occasional flashes of light relieved the scenery, but these moments of near lucidity were accompanied by terrible scenes of Jace fighting for his life, of Stella weeping after losing her baby, of Ritter being tortured. Someone was laughing, a horrid, nasal sound that scraped my nerves.

I jerked awake, only to see nothing but more darkness. A hard carpet made up my bed. Where was I? At Emporium headquarters or at the compound? Or perhaps somewhere worse. My first thought was to reach outside myself in search of clues to my location and a way to escape, but I stifled the impulse. First, I had to make sure I was mentally free.

Gingerly, I explored my mind. Was I alone, or was Delia and her assistant poised to control me again? I did the equivalent of mental tiptoeing as I looked around. Everywhere I turned, I sensed soreness, as though the fabric of my mind had been wounded during the mental blast. But no other presence was near, and tentatively, I threw up a shield around my thoughts. The barrier was a weak, flimsy, Swiss cheese kind of thing, but I felt triumphant to have managed that much.

Piece by piece, I repaired the damage, working by feel and hoping I was doing it correctly. Whatever Delia had done to my mind didn't seem permanent. Or would I know if she'd damaged me forever? Others I'd met hadn't known, like Tom, my former fiancé. I'd have to let Dimitri and Ava explore later to see if there was anything the hateful crone had left behind. No way did I want her touch staining me.

Had Jace gotten away? I shuddered as I remembered the dream. If they'd captured Jace, Delia would have one more pawn against me and against her colleague Stefan Carrington. Maybe she would mess with Jace's mind. Was he strong enough to withstand her?

Later, I told myself. Worrying about Jace wouldn't get either of us anywhere. Better to focus on healing and getting out of here. Reaching out, I began absorbing. I'd been more than full before the attack, but now even the effort of thought sent hunger pains raking through my stomach.

Wait, what was that? A small, shiny, black snake coiled in a corner of my mind. I dropped my shield and tried to push it out, but it eluded my grasp. A present from Delia, I assumed. But what was it? A way to control me or to spy on me? A time bomb ready to destroy at some given point in the future?

Regardless, I wasn't going to sit back and let it control me. Time passed as I considered the snake. It seemed to be of the same construction as the one in Patrick Mann's mind, only smaller, as though made for concealment. If I hadn't been lying there in the dark taking careful assessment, I might have missed it altogether.

If I couldn't get rid of it, I wouldn't be able to return to the Renegades, even if I escaped. I would never know if this little present would get them all killed. Then again, if I could hide it, lock it away so that I couldn't access it, maybe Delia couldn't either.

Piece by piece, I constructed another black box like the one that housed my fear of heights. I'd learned to lock it away so that

I could function, so why not the snake? And since I couldn't grasp the loathsome thing, I'd build around it. The construction process was slow and tedious, especially the bottom of the box, where I had to push back the illusion of a floor to build under the snake. When I was done, the seamless box glowed as shiny as the snake ever had. I pushed at it tentatively and found I could move both the box and the snake inside it. I could see no signature other than my own. It would have to do until I reached Ava.

Exhausted, I pulled in more nutrients through my pores, receiving the sensation of alcohol and peanut oil. Well, whatever gave me energy. When I felt strong enough, I left off conscious absorbing to search for any clue to my whereabouts.

A presence glowed brightly not far from me, but the absence of a shield and thoughts signaled an unconscious person. Wherever I was, I wasn't alone as I'd first assumed.

Reaching beyond my immediate vicinity, I found the consciousnesses of the five Renegade prisoners, which meant Delia had me taken to the compound. Why? She knew I wasn't the real biological daughter of Stefan Carrington, but she had gone to lengths to hide this fact and my true ability from him, so she should have taken me to him.

Unless she wanted something more from me.

I sat up quickly, my head spinning. How long had I been here? Had they already performed tests? Impregnated me? Given where I was in my cycle and how long both Unbounded sperm and eggs lived, it wouldn't be impossible, especially as I thought of the two gravid women prisoners they were already monitoring. Bile rose in my throat as I pulled the borrowed hotel uniform skirt as far down as it would go and tucked my knees to my chest.

A quick intake of breath several feet away helped me put my panic under control. "Who is that?" It was a man's groggy voice, one that was familiar somehow.

"My name's Erin," I said into the darkness, "and I seem to be the prisoner of some very nasty people. Guess you are, too. What's your name?" He was Unbounded, that much I could tell, and by the fear and mistrust radiating from him, he had no idea who I was. I suspected he was the prisoner Dr. Tunns had shown me on her monitor, but it was entirely possible that they had captured others since my last visit.

He hesitated. "So you aren't with *them?*"

"No."

"Then what did you do to get tossed in here?" He wanted to believe me, but he was afraid the Emporium was playing with his mind. He half thought I was an illusion his fevered brain had conjured up to torment him.

I had nothing to lose by telling the truth, and it was far easier to remember. "Actually, I was trying to kidnap the vice president's son, Patrick Mann. He's one of them and with the president on his deathbed, the vice president will be moving up. My friends and I were trying to protect the vice president because something about his son isn't right."

"You have no idea." A note of irony entered his voice.

"Oh, yeah?"

"Yeah. Because I'm Patrick Mann."

So he *was* the prisoner I'd seen on the monitor. I scooted closer to him on the carpet. "We kind of figured the other guy was a fake. That was why we tried to grab him. What are you doing here?"

Now that he'd decided to take a chance, the real Patrick Mann was full of information. "A year ago, I decided not to pursue politics," he told me. "I wanted to start an information business of some kind. I'd always loved working with computers, but suddenly I understood everything about them."

"You'd Changed." As a technopath, he'd have made it huge in computer software.

"That's when they first approached me—a woman who claimed to have given birth to me and a man who was supposedly my uncle. They said my father had been killed in an ongoing war involving near immortals and it was time for me to step forward and do what I'd been put in place to do."

"What was that?"

"To become my father." He hesitated before continuing. "I know it sounds crazy, but they've figured out how to use these really impressive nanites to completely change someone's appearance. Not just subtle changes, but a total makeover. I mean, it's easier with people who are the same height and have other similarities, but really they can do anyone."

To hear our suspicions verified so casually astounded me. "So they wanted you to become a puppet president."

"Something like that. They'd find a way to get rid of the president or they'd assure that my father was elected next. Either way I'd step in. Apparently, since I knew my father and politics so well, I'd be able to fool those closest to him for however long they needed. Even my mother. They said it was my duty, a legacy given me by right of my birth."

"I'm guessing you decided not to go along with the plan."

"No. My parents—" He made a choking sound. "I mean, the Manns taught me that it was important to make a stand for what we really believe, even if it came with a cost. Betraying them wasn't an option. I love my parents. I want them to be proud of me even if they never know the choice I made."

"They will know," I said. "We'll make sure of that. But if you're Patrick, who did I just try to kidnap?"

A sharp, bitter laugh. "I don't know. But oddly enough it makes me feel better, less forgotten. They told me my parents hadn't cared enough to look for me, that they didn't accept our disagreement about my career choice and wanted nothing to do with me." He paused and let out a sigh. "I didn't believe them, but after so long, it's hard not to begin to wonder. I mean how could the vice president's son go missing and no one notice? Now it makes sense. Of course they used their nanites to put someone in my place. They were going ahead with the plan, with or without me. And now that we're talking about it, I think I might have some idea as to who the guy is. For weeks straight they had this one man come in and talk to me for hours. Then suddenly he was gone. He was also a technopath."

"He's had a whole year to become you and get to know your father."

"They're going to kill him." The anger in Patrick's voice grated on my ears. "My father, I mean. They never said as much to me, but I know that was the plan after I became him."

"No. We're getting out of here, and we'll stop them. My friends will come for us."

"How will they know where to look?"

With the machine shield in place around the compound, Ava wouldn't be able to contact me, even if they suspected I was here, but I took comfort in the fact that they would eventually come to free the other prisoners. I couldn't tell Patrick that because the room might be bugged, and I didn't want to freak him out yet by speaking in his mind, especially with the possibility that Delia and her assistant were still around.

"They'll come," I said. The belief would be a natural one and wouldn't give anything away no matter who overheard me.

"I just hope it's not too late."

His words sent a chill crawling over my skin. "How long have I been here? Do you know?"

"Well, you weren't here when they brought me back from their so-called therapy this morning, and they usually bring me something to eat once a day around what I think is dinnertime. Or maybe bedtime. Hard to say when they keep me in this room with no windows or light. They haven't come yet."

I forced myself to relax. Since we'd been at the hotel until well after three, if he was right that meant I hadn't been here long, maybe only a few hours.

We sat in dark silence for a few minutes, with me probing for other life forces in the building. Besides the five prisoners, there were four other Unbounded that I could sense, with one of them being the guard outside our room. With another guard watching the other prisoners, that left the director and two others who were either doctors or more guards. That didn't mean Delia and her assistant weren't here, as their impenetrable shields would hide their life forces completely from my view. So possibly six inside. There would also be at least two guards in the lobby where I couldn't get past the machine-generated shields and however many more soldiers around the perimeter of the building. There was no sign of my brother, though they could have taken him elsewhere if he'd been captured.

Unless he'd been really and truly killed. The Emporium hit team definitely meant business and their swords weren't just for looks. The idea sent a wave of nausea careening through my stomach. *No, I won't believe that.* Delia had said Ritter was headed to the room. Both he and Jace had to be okay.

Faint steps outside what I assumed was the door urged me to my feet. I needed to be ready for whatever happened. *Too soon for a rescue,* I thought, but that didn't stop me from wanting it to be one.

Patrick also climbed to his feet, his hand brushing mine like a kiss of frozen snow. "Probably just the food."

"No, there're four people out there, plus the guard."

"How do you know?"

"Later." I was suddenly trying not to panic because I'd only sensed three people out there but I had seen from the guard's mind that Delia and Lew were also present. And now that she was this close, I could feel her impressive shield. Her mental signature screamed out to me. Instinctively, my hands ran over my body, but all my weapons were long gone.

"If they take you," Patrick whispered in my ear, his voice low and urgent, "don't believe anything, even your own thoughts. Some of them can see inside your brain. Not every thought, but they get enough to manipulate you. They push in their own thoughts until you believe they're yours. If I grit my teeth and tense my head until I feel a rushing sound, sometimes I can hide from them—for a while anyway." He was doing it now, and his shield was stronger than many I'd seen. I was sure I could get in, once I was more rested, but it was interesting that he could keep Delia out.

I nodded, though he wasn't able to see me in the dark. I couldn't even be amused at his telling me information about creating shields that I already knew. "Thanks."

Light sliced across the carpet as the door opened, revealing not a room with bars like the one the other prisoners shared, but a simple room with no furniture. The overhead light switched on a heartbeat later, and a tall black man peered in, an assault rifle in his hands. I knew him at once. He was Edgel, the man who blamed me for his mortal daughter's death. When he determined we weren't a threat, he signaled his companions and came all the way through the door, moving to the side of the room, his weapon still ready.

The light was dim enough that it didn't take long for my eyes to adjust, but next to me Patrick was still blinking and squinting. He had healing greenish bruises on his face, which I assumed were from his "therapy." Obviously they'd given up trying to convince him and were now focused on ferreting out any last information about his life that he'd been able to withhold. He did look like his impersonator, but the blue eyes lacked the coldness of the imposter's and his mouth was slightly more generous. It was a mouth that had laughed a lot. He was gentler all around, despite his long internment, and it made him more appealing.

Delia slid into the room as graceful as the first time we'd met, her customary gray dress flowing like a robe around her. Large brown eyes dominated her narrow face. She was a striking woman with a regal carriage even for an Unbounded, but the soft light couldn't hide the age creeping into her skin. The strong smell of an herb came with her, scratching at my nose and permeating the room. I'd forgotten to emulate the aroma when I'd impersonated her, and it felt so strong to me that it was a wonder Dr. Tunns hadn't suspected. Terror bounced off the walls, radiating from not only Patrick but also from the guard still in the hallway.

Lew came in behind Delia, his brown eyes glistening almost as darkly as his mental shield. He'd lost the ridiculous clothing from the hotel, and now wore black slacks and a shirt, the buttons open at the collar. Dr. Tunns followed Lew into the room, her aging face impassive.

"Hello, Erin." Delia smiled and I felt Patrick tremble slightly beside me. I understood exactly what he felt. She frightened me worse than anything I'd ever faced. However, I'd always known this day would come, that she and I would do battle. I'd prepared myself, but I didn't feel ready. I didn't know if I'd ever feel ready, no matter how I reinforced my mental barrier.

"Hello, Delia." I made my voice light. "How nice to see you again. Well, actually, it's not really nice at all, but I tend to lie under stress."

She gave me a thin smile. "Still not ready to accept your fate? It was sealed the moment you walked into your father's office three months ago."

"My *father?* Are you still propagating that story? I guess lying is something you also do well."

Her lips pursed. "As Stefan's daughter, you are safe in the Emporium until he gives the word. I can use that." She took another step toward me, her straight posture loosening. "Look, I realize we didn't get off to a very good start, but you are young and you will have a lot of years to learn that we are doing what is best for all our people, both ours and yours."

"What about the mortals?" I felt her push against my fragile shield and clenched my fists, fleetingly wondering if I could smash one into her face before Edgel shot me. Thankfully, my shield held. Good, she couldn't get inside, not as long as I concentrated.

She waved my words aside. "They will soon know their place."

"You mean when your fake Patrick Mann assumes the vice president's identity after he steps in for the president?" Let her worry about how much we actually knew—not that there was much we could do to stop her.

"I see you've done your homework." Delia permitted herself a small smile. "When I think what we could do together, Erin, it astounds me. You are the only Unbounded alive besides me and Lew who has taken your ability to the next level. I believe it's only the beginning. With study and alterations, we'll be able to make everyone use their abilities to benefit the cause."

Should I lead her on or tell her where she could shove her false camaraderie? The latter was really tempting, but probably not wise given my position. Better to keep quiet. Besides, I found her comment about making people use their abilities interesting. What she talked about was easily attainable to me since Mexico, not by using someone's body and forcing them to act for me as she did, but by channeling their talent and using it as my own. Was she unaware of the possibility? Or maybe it was something she couldn't do. Hope flared through me. I wasn't as strong as she was in mentally controlling someone's physical body, but what if I broke through her shield and channeled her ability? Could I be a match for her?

"It's time to announce to the world that we exist," Delia went on, unfazed by my lack of response. "No more hiding in the dark or pretending to be our own descendants. No more planting drugs to hide our battles or mourning our dead in secret. No more worrying about identification software that could ruin our lives."

Something in my heart twisted at her words. No leaving our mortal families or visiting them in secret to avoid suspicion when neighbors finally notice you don't age. No worrying about the Emporium slaughtering your family.

"We want that as much as you do," I said, "but not at the expense of the mortals. They aren't ready." What I really meant but wouldn't admit was that the Renegades weren't ready to protect mortals from an Emporium suddenly unleashed upon the world. And I was beginning to see that coming out wouldn't make Renegades any safer from Emporium attacks, not if people like Delia and Stefan were in charge. "We won't let you hurt them."

She let out a sigh of exasperation. "Don't you understand yet? They don't have the *right* to decide anything. *We* inherit the world, not them. In a hundred years every one of them will be dead. They are already halfway to dust. Inconsequential."

"In three hundred years you'll be dead as well," I retorted.

Her eyes glittered dangerously, and I knew I'd hit a sore spot. "My legacy will thrive. I have earned rights because of my centuries of hard work, the devotion I have given to our kind. We are gods to the mortals. It is time we take our rightful place as their rulers."

I remembered Keene's statement about the mortals not giving in so easily. "They'll fight."

"Oh, I'm not saying there won't be uprisings. The discovery of that drug in Mexico could have helped us control the rest of the world, but the delay your interference cost us there shouldn't be too detrimental in the overall picture. It's only a matter of a few careful changes in the law, a few more appointments of our people to certain positions. Once we've completely disarmed the mortals and secured our own rights, we'll be ready to make the announcement. We have already invested billions in school education and in medications that will both ease our entry into society and give us a way to control the population. It will only be rough for a short time." She offered a mirthless smile that made me shudder. "Then they will cease to matter. As for overseas, it is high time to use some of that good old American muscle. Mortals are always so willing to waste their short lives on a cause."

She meant war. And not just war but global war, with mortal lives thrown away to further Emporium rule.

Dr. Tunns, who up until now I'd only given cursory notice, pushed past Lew to stand beside Delia. "Are we about done here?" There was no fear in her, but her voice was carefully modulated to show no expression.

"Director Tunns is right," I said. "There must be a reason you came to talk to me, unless you've suddenly gained a conscience and plan to let me go. Let's get on with it already. Why are you here? If you don't have a good reason, maybe I can find a comfy spot on this low-grade carpet and have a nice cold nap while you work it all out."

Delia eyes narrowed. "Oh, I have a reason. You will come with us. Now."

"And if I refuse?" I couldn't resist saying.

"Then I will have Edgel shoot you and drag you to the lab." Her eyes almost begged me to resist.

Dr. Tunns gave an impatient grunt. "Come on."

"Leave her alone!" Patrick stepped forward, finding his voice and his courage. His mind shield was tight, but fear oozed from him so tangibly I was sure everyone in the room felt it, sensing or no.

I hadn't liked the vice president before, but I had to admit that since this whole thing began, I'd changed my mind. Anyone who could raise a man like the real Patrick couldn't be all bad. I put a hand on his. "Thank you, but I want to go. I need to talk with her. Delia and I go way back." Well, as far back as anything I knew about the Unboundaried, or Unbounded as we now termed ourselves. "I will be back for you, I promise."

I felt rather like an idiot making any promise at all, but I couldn't help the assertion. The arrogance was in my genes.

He glared at the others, nostrils flared, resembling the fake Patrick Mann more than he had before. "Okay, but remember what I told you."

"I will. Thanks."

I moved forward as Delia stepped aside to allow me to leave. Dr. Tunns and Lew followed, while Delia and Edgel took up the rear. In the hallway Delia paused and said to the guard who had stayed in the hall during our conversation, "Shoot him." When he didn't move fast enough, she pushed the guard closer to the still-open door. "I don't care where, just shoot him. He needs to learn a lesson."

"No!" I stepped toward the guard, only to have him level his rifle at me. Edgel did the same.

"Lew," Delia said calmly.

In a fluid motion, the slender Lew drew out a pistol and fired through the door. I tossed out a shield in Patrick's direction, but he collapsed, hands gripping his chest. I was too late or too weak. I'd never know which.

And just that quickly I'm inside you again, Delia said in my mind.

CHAPTER 20

I CURSED HER UNDER MY BREATH AND STRUGGLED TO PUSH HER out and repair the damage she'd done to my shield while I'd been distracted, already knowing I was too weak because of the mental explosion at the hotel.

Wait, I didn't have to be strong, not if I used her ability. Unless she could keep me out of her mind altogether. I hadn't been able to get inside Lew's shield at Emerson's, but maybe Delia's connection to me left her vulnerable. Even as the thought came, I pushed it away, replacing it with others. Anger, worry about my brother. Patrick being shot. If I didn't focus too closely on any one idea for long, she wouldn't be able to tell the important ideas from any others in the sand stream of my thoughts.

"After you," Delia said with a laugh.

Against my will, I started walking. My first urge was to fight her compulsion as I'd done the first time we'd talked privately, but I needed to reserve my strength so I let her force me onward.

Delia turned to the guard. "Bandage our guest and give him some tonic. I'll need him well tomorrow."

Anger grew inside me, but I didn't let it take over. *Concentrate,*

I told myself. I knew from my own experience that she couldn't see my ideas unless they were passing in my current thought stream so I was careful not to think about anything that might endanger our rescue plan for the prisoners. Then again, she might try to mess with the stream, forcing it to go as she wanted, to rip the information from me. I had to get her out sooner rather than later.

Her shield glistened like polished black agate, pristine and impenetrable, but there had to be some way in. We were already nearing the lab when I found it, a tiny, almost imperceptible flatness in her shield where part of her consciousness stretched toward mine. A thrust of my mental machete weakened it further, but I still couldn't get inside. Delia didn't react to my efforts, though I knew she must feel them.

"When we brought you here earlier today," she said as we entered the lab, "Dr. Tunns took the liberty of doing a few tests. We now have the results and we're going ahead with a procedure. It will be more comfortable if you don't fight us."

"What procedure?" I glanced between her and the doctor.

Delia looked at Lew and back at me. "We need more sensing Unbounded, Erin. With careful genetic experimentation, we may eventually be able to bring back some of the lost gifts, which has been a goal of ours for decades. In fact, we have experienced a few successes so far."

I was aware of that. Brody Emerson was a prime example, but as far as I knew the Emporium was unaware of his exact ability. "Like what?" I asked, not letting my thoughts dwell on Brody.

Delia only smiled. "This procedure will help us move closer to our goals. Are you ready?" She gestured to a gurney in the corner of the lab that had shackles on the armrests. The end of the bed was lowered as though in preparation for an internal examination. "Lie down."

I fought her now, every step, absorbing from the air as I pushed. One step and then another. One more. Panic filled me. They weren't telling me what they planned to do, but I had a good idea. I felt almost naked in the blouse and knee-length skirt of the hotel uniform.

"I'll just give you something to help you relax." Dr. Tunns plunged a needle into a vial and filled the syringe. Beyond her, I noticed Edgel had taken up position by the door.

I reached out to Dr. Tunns, pushing easily past her shield, and saw what wasn't being said. The solution in the vial wasn't just something to help me relax but to put me out completely, and the procedure was insemination. Lew had received treatments that gave his sperm a higher possibility of engendering Unbounded, and he'd also been taking injections that would enhance the sensing ability in his offspring. More enhancements had been made in the lab and now his genetic material was ready for use.

"I wish we had more time to discuss this," Delia said, compelling me forward, "but Stefan has heard about your capture and wishes to see you tonight." She cast a dark look in Edgel's direction that told me he'd had something to do with informing Stefan. Could it be he didn't want to see me tortured as I'd assumed? "We need to finish this and get you ready to leave," Delia continued. "Don't worry. It's just a little biopsy."

I knew the truth, even if I couldn't sense the lie in her voice. She probably saw in my thoughts that I'd discovered exactly what they intended, but she wanted deniability and unconscious I wouldn't be able to accuse anyone. Even if Dr. Tunns became the scapegoat, Delia's power would protect her. Besides, Stefan wanted more sensing Unbounded, and I had the sick feeling that he'd look the other way, especially in light of how I continued to fight him. The Emporium's breeding program was the reason they were so strong now, and every Emporium member was required to be a part of it.

Delia mentally forced me the few more feet to the bed. Sweat beaded on my forehead as I tried to resist. Dr. Tunns pushed me back onto the mattress, pulling my left arm into the first shackle and clamping it shut. After all the time I'd resisted my attraction to Ritter, in large part because I wasn't ready for the commitment of a family, and here I was about to be forced. By the door, Edgel looked away, no expression on his face. I knew him well enough that even if he didn't agree with what they were doing, his loyalty to the Emporium was unshakable.

A slow smile covered Lew's crunched face, and I could see how much he was enjoying my helplessness. "We could let her stay awake," he said. "She'd prefer that, I think."

"No." Delia's voice was hard.

I scanned the room frantically, searching for anything to save myself. I saw my confiscated weapons on the desk, including Keene's switchblade and Ritter's ballistic knife. Close but too far away to do any good. Even my cell phone was there. Useless now as its self-destruct would have activated the minute they'd tried to turn it on without my fingerprints and the proper codes.

Dr. Tunns neared me with the needle, and I slapped her away. The mental pressure to lay my other arm in the shackle increased. And why not set it down? It was after all, only a small proce-dure that would be over in a little while, and it would benefit everyone, maybe even the whole world by helping to usher in an era of utopia.

Vomit rose in my throat as I shoved the thoughts away. Not mine, but Delia's, so skillfully put inside my thought stream that they felt like mine. I pushed harder against her.

Even as I thought I couldn't fight any longer, the overhead lights flickered once, twice. Everyone looked upwards as they went out altogether, plunging us into darkness. "The generator will go on soon," Dr. Tunns said. "Takes less than thirty seconds."

Ritter, was my first thought, and by the frustration Delia exuded in my mind, I knew she'd heard.

"Edgel," Delia said. "Go check it out."

"Okay." The door opened and closed as he left.

"It's just the storm," Dr. Tunns said. "It was raining when you got here. It's happened before."

Delia wasn't consoled. "I don't like the timing."

I reached for the shackle with my free hand, searching for the release. My hand froze when I became aware of another life force in the building. With a glance at Delia to assure that her attention was elsewhere, I sent out my thoughts, rapidly pinpointing the unshielded newcomer.

Mari.

Erin? Erin? She was thinking so loud, I felt she was in the room.

Hastily, I wove a barrier between Mari and the rest of my brain, not knowing if such a thing was even possible. *Wait!* I told Mari. *Not safe. Shield!*

Her barrier went up immediately. It was strong and masked her thoughts, but I didn't know if it was enough to keep Delia out. Had Delia been too occupied to notice the exchange? Given the rapid flow of thought streams, it was possible, even if my attempt at masking failed. But she would definitely notice the extra life force in the building if she stopped to count.

Well, I'd give her something else to focus on instead.

I jumped from the bed as the lights flickered back on, dragging it a foot. Dr. Tunns grabbed my free hand, but I yanked away.

Lew had his gun out again, pointing it at me. The compelling pressure on my body eased as Delia stepped forward and gingerly stroked my cheek with a finger that felt like paper. "So much energy even now. I really wish we could be friends. But there's someone else in the building, isn't there? One of your friends. Are you going to tell me who, or should I find the information in your mind myself?"

"Probably one of your soldiers," I retorted. I pictured those soldiers in my mind so if she was looking at my thoughts, that's what she would see.

I can always examine your unconscious thoughts, she told me silently.

Nausea clogged my throat. There was too much information I needed to protect from her greedy search—the Renegade safe house, the weakness of the New York Renegades, Brody's ability, and Oliver's as well. They knew about Mari, but not about the safe house we were building in San Diego. Or where my parents lived.

So many lives depending on me. The Renegades would have followed safety procedures from the moment of my capture, but damage would still be done. How much had she already seen in my mind just now as I thought about it?

Spaghetti, bacon, chocolate, shopping for jeans, Ritter's kiss— anything to keep her focus off Mari. My only comfort at the moment was knowing that memories in the unconscious mind were much less detailed and often far more misleading than thoughts seen in the conscious mind.

Delia motioned to the doctor. "Lock the shackle. I think she knows more than she's telling, but all I'm getting is a jumbled mess. I'll have to probe deeper."

Lew pocketed his gun and grabbed my right arm as the doctor complied, his fingers like a vise. "Let's at least get the drug into her. She'll be more compliant that way. Less chance of permanent damage. We need to do the procedure anyway."

I spat in his face. "Is that the only way you can father a kid? In a doctor's office when your victim's unconscious?"

Releasing me, he jabbed his fist into my jaw. Pain reverberated up my cheek.

"You hit like a mortal!" I taunted.

Dr. Tunns slid the needle into my arm held by the shackle.

Desperation had me once again outside the thinner part of Delia's shield, but this time in my imagination I held one of Ritter's sai. I could feel the anger pulsing through my body, reminiscent of the energy I'd siphoned off Brody at the Hunter's lair. Gathering all my energy into the sai, I plunged it into her shield with an upward thrust. It sank clear to the hand guard.

What are you . . . ? Delia began, but this time she was too late. I was inside.

Channeling the strength of her ability, I shoved her from my brain, copying how she made her shield so I could keep her out. I was right that barriers strengthened with practice, but hers also had connections to the electrical paths that ran through her mind, much like the connections the technopaths had with their nanites.

It was brilliant and required less effort to maintain than any shield I'd tried before.

Ha! I sent to her as I used her own ability and energy to hurl a blast of white hot light into her mind before severing our connection.

Delia grabbed at her head, a sharp scream coming from her open mouth. She wasn't the only one affected by my violent mental blast. Next to me, Dr. Tunns collapsed to the ground unconscious and the needle fell out of my arm, the contents of the syringe still intact.

I was already moving, pulling the bed across the room. Lew dived after me, his strong shield having protected him from damage. He went for his gun, but I was faster. My hand came down on Keene's switchblade, flicking it open and throwing it as hard as I could. The blade wasn't long, but I hoped it'd stop him long enough for me to grab my .380 or the ballistic knife. Throwing had never been my forte, but I'd practiced long and hard to become better.

The knife imbedded in his chest, though it probably would have bounced off if he'd been wearing a coat. He laughed, bringing up his gun.

Crap! I thought.

Lew's eyes suddenly widened and he jerked them down at the knife, clawing it out of him with his free hand. He began screaming, still raking at his chest. The gun clunked to the floor. After another wail, Lew followed suit. Smoke curled upward from the blackening hole in his chest where the knife had penetrated.

I blinked. "Uh, that was so not like the poison used on me." I was grateful, though. Keene's little present had saved me.

Another groan from Delia reminded me I was still very much in danger. At any moment she could recover or Edgel might return. As I snatched up my ballistic knife and brought it around to launch at her, she scurried out the door, her dignity gone and her dress fluttering around her.

I reached out to Mari. *Okay, it's safe now.* I threw up a stronger shield around her. *At least for the moment, but we need to get out of here. They suspect the Renegades caused the power failure.*

We did. It was the only way I could get in. Where are you?

Uh, in the lab. I'm a little tied up right now.

Are you alone?

I glanced at the two unconscious bodies. *Pretty much.* I'd barely finished the thought when Mari appeared next to me.

"Wow!" she said, looking around. "I can see you've been busy."

"Our old friend Edgel is going to be back any moment." I tugged at the shackle. "But I'm locked in. Don't know where the doctor put the key. It's around here somewhere."

"So shift out." She leaned over to take a better look at the smoking hole on Lew's chest.

"Oh, right." Channeling her ability, I shifted next to her. "Thanks," I said rubbing my wrist. "How'd you find me?"

She tore her eyes away from Lew. "When Ritter discovered you'd been taken, he pretty much made mincemeat of those guys at the hotel who were trying to kill Jace. Then he somehow managed to shoot a tracking device onto the helicopter that took you. Good thing because your internal transmitter stopped working soon after. They must have disabled it. Anyway, we tracked the helicopter here."

"Impressive. Is Jace okay?"

"Well, he was shot, but he's okay."

"And Ritter?" I stopped myself from finding the answer by examining her thoughts.

She frowned. "I don't know if he's okay, but he didn't look good the last time I saw him. He and Ava rushed off someplace."

He'd left me here? That didn't sound like Ritter, but I couldn't worry about his reasoning now. We needed to get out. I scooped up Lew's gun and shifted to where my own still lay on the desk. "So what's the plan?"

"They left Dimitri in charge. All the rest of us are outside the compound, and the New York group, too. But the Emporium has like thirty men surrounding the building. And those are the ones we could count. It's obvious they're making sure we can't get to you. Anyway, when we first got here, Ritter was all hot to barrel in and find you, all alone if he had to, but Ava took him aside and they exchanged some pretty heated words, and when they came back, he was all calm." She frowned. "Looked like a ghost, actually. But he was calm. Then they grabbed Jace and Oliver and left."

Oliver? I didn't like the sound of that.

"I was supposed to shift in and you'd use my ability to shift out with me. But despite what Cort said about their machine shield, I couldn't fold past it. It makes it so everything inside this building doesn't seem to exist."

"I was afraid of that." I shifted to the door, motioning for Mari to follow.

She appeared beside me. "We used Brody to blow out the electric lines going inside the building."

"And that's when you shifted in."

She made a face. "Yeah, we thought they'd have to call the power company before they could restore the electricity, but a generator kicked on right after I shifted in. Dimitri and Cort warned me it might be a possibility. I thought maybe Brody could destroy that also because it's just another energy source, but now I'm thinking he probably can't get through the barrier since the generator is keeping it alive. So we need to kill the generator ourselves and get out of here."

"Correction." I eased open the door, relieved to see an empty corridor. "We need to release the prisoners, hit the generator, and then get out."

"No." Her hand dropped over mine, still on the doorknob. "Dimitri told me to tell you that you couldn't worry about the others right now. We'll get them when they're moved. Because we've got all our people out there, but it won't be enough against the Emporium's reinforcements. We can pick some of their soldiers off with rifles, but they're wearing body armor and they've driven in huge concrete barriers for protection. We'd need an army to get our people out."

"So what's to stop the Emporium from bringing a hundred men to guard our people when they're moved?" I shook my head. "We have to try to get them out while we can."

"They might die." Mari's voice was scarcely a whisper.

"There are things a lot worse than dying." I handed Lew's gun to her. "Besides, I think I have a plan."

"Oh?"

"In a minute I'll explain. First we have to get rid of the cameras in the rooms where they're holding the prisoners. We'll need a technopath."

"Stella's out there, but you can't channel her ability until we kill the generator."

"Yeah, but I know another one who's a lot closer." I shifted back to the desk and unhooked the laptop that was connected to a keyboard and the large monitor.

"Let's go," I said to Mari, linking our minds. "Follow me."

CHAPTER 21

MARI AND I SHIFTED TO PATRICK'S DARK CELL. HE WAS AWAKE despite the bullet hole in his chest, his shield tight over his mind. "Patrick," I said softly. Pain sluiced off him like water.

He gasped and scrambled away from me. "Who is it?"

"It's me, Erin. I was here earlier."

I felt him relax. "How'd you get in?"

I moved closer and whispered so softly I didn't know if he could hear. "I'll explain later. Right now, I need you to drop your mind shield. I can't risk them hearing."

"You're like *her* then." Disgust in his voice.

"No, because I'm asking. I don't have to."

He considered a moment before dropping his shield. "Okay."

I need you to disable the cameras, I told him. *I know you're hurt, but you're the only one who can do it.* Even channeling his ability, I doubted I'd have enough expertise to do it quickly. *I have a friend here and we're going to help you and the other prisoners here escape.* How we'd do that wasn't exactly clear, but my idea involved taking out the generator, using the prisoners as soldiers, and communicating with the others outside, especially Brody Emerson.

I saw Patrick's consent in his mind and I opened the laptop, fumbling a little with my anxiety. I had no idea what Delia and Edgel were up to, but I didn't suppose it would take them long to regroup. I had to free the prisoners before then.

Mari helped me prop Patrick against the wall. He was cold to my touch. The light from the laptop showed me he'd been bandaged, but his face was pale and drawn. I should have thought to bring him a painkiller because I doubted the guard had given him one. His Unbounded genes would help with that, but a little mortal medicine sometimes went a long way to staving off the pain until true healing set in. Mari removed her jacket to lay over him.

His fingers flew over the keys. I could feel his comfort at the familiarity of the computer. It'd been eight months since they'd let him touch anything electronic.

We need to either disable the cameras altogether or loop in feed from other days, I said in his mind. *Don't say anything aloud; just think the words and I'll see them.* As long as he didn't think about too many things at once.

He shook his head, typing fast. After a moment, he said aloud. "I looped in another room's feed to the lobby desk where they're monitoring everything. They can't hear us now. But I can't do anything with the camera feed. They have them protected and it'd take too long. I can, however, insert my own program that will crash all the cameras. It'll take them an hour to clean and reboot."

"Do it," I said. It would be a clear signal to Delia that someone was in their computer system, so we'd have to get the prisoners out fast. But she already knew something was wrong with what happened in the lab, so maybe it didn't matter. Even as I had the thought, a blaring alarm came from the hallway. "Looks like they're letting everyone know about my escape."

"My phone won't work." Mari stared at the device in her hand. "Crap, I thought we'd at least have that."

I hadn't even considered that she might have her phone. "Delia suspected our people were behind the electricity failure, and she knew someone had come inside. Makes sense that she'd try to block communications." While the phone couldn't get us out of here, it would have been a line of communication with the outside.

"I don't see anything here related to blocking cell phones," Patrick said.

"Well, they have a generator, so whatever's blocking my phone is probably getting energy from that." Mari returned the phone to her pocket. "Can you do anything about the generator from here?"

Patrick shook his head. "Must not be connected to the computer. If I had a few tools and could get to the wires in the wall . . ."

"No time for that," I said. "Look, we'll release the other prisoners and kill the generator. We'll be back for you within the hour."

Patrick's hand shot out to grab mine. "You take care of yourself. If it means everyone else getting recaptured, don't come back for me."

I bit my lip, hoping there wasn't enough light from the screen for him to see the tears in my eyes. "Okay," I said, because that's what he wanted to hear. No matter what, I was coming back. "Are the cameras offline?"

Patrick nodded. "And all their listening devices as well." He hesitated a heartbeat before saying, "Wait. I need to ask . . . before they took me, I had just started dating a girl. She was something really special. I thought we might . . . tell me, does that guy who stole my life . . . do you know if he's dating anyone?"

I thought back to the information Stella had collected, unable to remember. Mari beat me to an answer. "Nope, no girlfriend. Not a surprise when we know his end goal. But apparently it's got a lot of conservatives worried."

"Good." Patrick breathed a sigh. "Smart girl. I hoped she would dump him."

By the emotion peeling from him, I suspected if we ever got out of here Patrick was going to find that girl and explain everything. Since I'd tried to do the same thing with those I loved, I didn't blame him.

"Come on, Mari," I said.

We shifted together, appearing a breath later in a dark room.

"Who's there?" a voice rang out.

I recognized Willis Tyrone's voice, the prisoners' self-appointed leader. Too late I thought about bringing a flashlight. "Erin, Ava's descendant. It's time to get out of here. The cameras and sound have been taken care of, but we still have a few problems."

Light flared from behind the bars as Dragon brought fire to life on his palm. I'd forgotten about him. I'd have to remind him not to burn up the place until we were certain to get out.

"Tell us," Willis urged.

I outlined the situation. "It's not how we planned to come in," I added, "but it's now or never. First we need to get you out of this room, and then we need to kill their generator. That's the only way we can coordinate with our people outside. Plus we have a blaster. If you can hold off the guards until I reach him, he may be able help us take them all out, at least those inside. After that, I can't guarantee we'll get out of the building, but it's a start. We won't try if you don't want to."

"Like hell!" This from Guenter Simon. "We've been ready since the day you came here wearing *her* skin."

"She's here." It was only fair to warn them.

"Good." Guenter again, his voice full of the anger and frustration he felt at not being able to protect Mandalyn and their unborn baby.

"If we take over the inside," Willis said, "that will give us an advantage since we'll have them surrounded. They'll be wedged in between us and our Renegades."

That was one way to look at it. I wasn't as optimistic. If Mari had counted thirty soldiers, there were probably double that number out there. Even though three of the prisoners had the combat ability and the other two had also been trained, we were poorly armed and far outmanned. Still, we had determination on our side, and that had to count for something.

"So how do we open the bars?" I asked.

"The guard outside will have the keys. By the time you get back, we'll be ready." They were already doing something at the back of the cell. Gathering the hidden weapons we'd left for them in the planter near the lab, I assumed.

"I'll start a little distraction," came a female voice. Francis, the summoner. As she spoke, the skitter of tiny feet sounded over the floors. "The guard hates my little friends. They make him nervous."

I reached for Mari, signaling her to get ready to shift. I was tempted to go alone and take care of the guard myself, but while I'd rather have Ritter as backup, two of us were better than one.

Where exactly was Ritter? The question picked at my mind. Probably doing something dangerous. Oliver had better not get him or my brother killed.

Pushing back the thought, I sent my mind to the guard outside the door, and called up my machete to break down his shield. It took longer than expected; despite absorbing as much as possible, all the shifting and mind games were taking their toll on my energy level. He was watching cockroaches, mice, and ants gathering in the hall, moving back as they approached his position. Perfect.

Now, I told Mari, sending her a view of the exact location. She'd been in the hall and so could shift there on her own, but I wanted her behind the guard.

He jerked as the soft *pop!* alerted him to our presence. He was not one of the men I'd seen before, but the sword strapped to his back signaled his expertise. I pointed a gun at him. "The keys, please." Without hesitation, he went for his own gun, but I crashed my foot into his stomach. As he bent over in pain, I pushed deeper into his mind. "Where is the generator?"

He didn't want to tell me, but the sand stream of his thoughts betrayed him, bringing the information to the forefront. The generator was in a little room off the lobby. I jabbed my fist into his face and he fell unconscious.

"Ritter always says we should shoot them," Mari reminded me, removing keys from his pocket, "or he'll just get back up in a few minutes."

As I fired three shots to stop his heart, two more Unbounded skidded around the corner, and I could feel other life forces coming toward us from elsewhere in the building, more than had been inside earlier. Delia and Edgel must have called for backup from the outside army.

"Go!" I told Mari. "Free the prisoners."

We both shifted as the guards fired. I appeared behind them, shooting one but losing my gun as the second anticipated me and kicked it out of my hand. I kicked back, my uniform skirt ripping up the side, and he curled momentarily in pain. But he was combat Unbounded, and if I didn't start channeling his ability, I'd be in trouble. First I had to get through his shield. It should have been relatively easy with my increasing ability, but a mental heaviness weighed me down. Too much effort too fast. I was drained. Could it have anything to do with the miniature snake Delia had placed in my mind?

A tramp of feet filled the hall and more men appeared behind me, Edgel at their front. Reaching for Mari's mind, I dove for my .380, grabbed the fallen guard's rifle, and shifted again to the far end of the hall away from my opponent as the prisoners spilled from the room. "They're coming!" I shouted, letting loose a volley of shots. "Take cover!" More shots erupted around us as everyone sprinted for the next intersection in the hall. Willis, who'd stopped to scoop up the first fallen guard's assault rifle, almost didn't make it in time.

Dragon brought his fire to life. "No!" Willis slapped at his arm. "Later."

"They need more weapons," I told Mari. She nodded and disappeared. I followed her mentally, still connected to her mind. She appeared behind the last guard in the opposing group, her knife slipping into his ribs.

I scarcely had time to register my surprise at her bravery before she was back again, handing over another rifle to Guenter. "You go find the generator," she said to me. "We'll hold them here."

I'd have to channel her ability again to get past the Emporium soldiers and then go the rest of the way on foot since I couldn't shift past the machine created shield. If the soldiers had any idea how important the generator was to us, they'd make their stand in the lobby instead of here in the hallway. At least Delia hadn't guessed that yet, and I'd been using most of my failing strength to keep a tight lock on my mind and on Mari's to make sure she didn't discover our plan.

"Delia's still around somewhere, so put up your shield after I go," I reminded Mari.

"Okay. Just get to the generator."

I shifted.

CHAPTER 22

I APPEARED OUTSIDE THE DOOR TO THE LOBBY, QUICKLY SCANNING the area to make sure I was alone. So far, so good. I edged to the door and appeared inside. One guard sat at the wide front desk, typing furiously on a keyboard. Another stood at attention by the outer door. Apparently all the Emporium soldiers Mari and the others were fighting in the hallway had indeed come from the outside. Were even more slipping though Renegade lines? How long would it be before the local mortal authorities were notified of the disturbance?

Even if notified, I suspected they would look the other way for as long as the Emporium plants inside the organization requested. If only we could go above the regular chain of command and find someone on our side who could help. We were fighting for humanity, and I couldn't help but feel a little resentful that there were so few mortals who were a part of the battle.

I checked the silencer on my .380, glad Ritter had required them for the hotel, even for the backup weapons. I preferred my nine mil Sig, but with the hollow points, this pistol would do the job well enough. I only had two bullets left after fighting the guards in the hall, and I'd have to use those on the man near the door. I needed him out quick before he could signal others outside. The man by the computer would have to check out the sharp end of my ballistic knife.

I hoped I didn't miss.

I'm here, I told Mari, pushing far too easily inside her shield. The weakness of her barrier told me she was distracted. *Get ready for darkness.*

I'll tell the others. Dragon is ready with his fire and can give us some light if needed. But I don't know how long we can hold out. Hurry!

I will. I felt bad that I was in relative safety while they drew the fire, but we had to turn off the generator.

I stepped into the doorway, my connection with Mari immediately severing. Two shots and the man by the door went down. The guy at the computer stood as I ejected the ballistic knife. The blade embedded in his chest with a *thunk!* He gasped as I hurtled toward him. Grabbing his rifle, I slammed the barrel into him, knocking him to the ground.

Now for the generator. I hurried toward the door I'd seen in the other guard's mind, pushing my thoughts ahead of me. No one there. The door was locked, but a quick jab of the rifle butt made the entire latch assembly break through the door frame.

Inside, the noise of the generator was deafening. The machine stood at the far side of the small room, taller than I was and more than double my height in width. No off button was in sight, or cables connecting it to the building's electrical wiring, but there were a dozen dials and switches under a transparent cover that was locked. Upon closer examination, I decided searching for a key was useless since I'd need a degree in electrical engineering to figure out how to turn the stupid thing off. Too bad I couldn't absorb all the energy without Brody's help. But even with him, I'd only be able to take in the power as it was generated. Any faster and the machine might stall, and as long as there was fuel in the tank outside the building, someone could restart it. While I'd seen the location of the tank in the guard's mind, cutting the fuel lines, if I could find them, would be a comparatively minor repair. Better to disable the machine permanently.

Standing as far back as I could in the doorway, I showered the machine with bullets, using everything left in the extended magazine. The generator abruptly cut out. The dials were busted and the outside riddled with holes, but they didn't appear deep. I had to do more. I had to make sure it stayed off.

I threw down the weapons and pushed out my thoughts, the sudden effort making me dizzy. I needed energy—and fast. *Brody where are you?* Did I have enough strength to find him? I'd have to. I was at the front of the building and he shouldn't be out of my reach if the Renegades were near one of our usual observation posts.

There he was, standing near Dimitri under a dark, rain-filled sky. His shield wasn't up or was too thin to make a difference, and without much effort I was looking through his eyes. Lightning flashed in the distance. He was empty of energy and scared, and I didn't want to make that worse. I'd already killed him once, so I didn't think my presence in his mind would be all that comforting, at least without warning. Stretching my limits, I pushed inside Dimitri's shield, my exhaustion making it seem almost like a fortress. Once again, I had to call up the image of the machete. I didn't know why the image gave me more power, but as long as it worked, I would use it.

Dimitri, I said, *it's Erin. The generator is down, but we're outnumbered. I need to channel Brody's ability to destroy it completely and to help us take out the guards.*

Can you do it without his help? Dimitri asked. *He just about blew us all up a while ago when he took out the electricity. He hasn't learned to control it yet.*

That explained Brody's fear. Almost killing everyone twice in a day would be frightening. I was scared myself, though I knew that I could send the power elsewhere if I needed. The trick was making sure I didn't get too full. Or freeze with indecision.

I'll try. But tell him what I'm going to do. People usually can't tell when I'm channeling their abilities, but his is different and I don't know if he'll feel me pulling energy. And wherever you are, there is enough distance between us that I may need his help.

I left Dimitri to explain while I refocused on Brody's mind. Channeling his ability, I reached for one of the two power lines I felt running under the street, happy that there were others in addition to the one feeding into the compound that Brody had disabled earlier.

Absorbing. Pulling in energy. My exhaustion vanished almost immediately, and I felt my skin warm as my body filled. Pleasure flushed through me at the heat. I pulled harder until the fullness became uncomfortable.

Now to find something to help me direct the energy.

Sprinting back to the fallen guard at the desk, I reached for his sword. Electricity arced between my fingers and the blade as I touched the hilt. Stepping only a little closer to the doorway of the small room, I pointed the sword at the generator and released the energy. Lightning sparked from the end of the blade, smashing into the machine and splitting it wide open. Cool.

I felt Brody gasp through our connection, and I realized I'd sent him images of the destruction. When nothing further exploded, he laughed with a relief that echoed my own. Belatedly I realized that if the safety valve on the hidden fuel line hadn't kicked in, I might have blown up half the building.

Thanks, I told Brody. *I just need a little more.*

Again I pulled from the power line. It went dead after a few seconds, and I wondered if someone at the power company had noticed the drain and shut it down. I'd better take as much as I could from the remaining line. I absorbed more quickly.

The lightning's coming this way. The thought came from Brody. *It's attracted to the energy you're taking.*

That's when the second power line died. I guessed that was it. I stopped channeling Brody's ability and reached for Mari. *Coming.*

I shifted, materializing behind Mari in the dark hallway as she peered around the corner. I counted quickly in the dim light offered by Dragon's fire. All our friends were accounted for, but at the edge of the group, farthest away from the intersection, one figure huddled over a fallen one. Mandalyn over Guenter, the small life force of their baby between them, easily seen with the power radiating through me. I wished I had time to try to channel Dimitri's healing ability to ease Guenter's pain, but that would have to wait.

I stepped close to Mari, who, with Mandalyn's preoccupation, guarded this side of the hallway intersection alone. Willis and Dragon were on the other side, with Francis sitting on the floor, a gaping wound in her left shoulder and another on her leg. Her hands tented over her stomach, as if protecting the child who grew inside.

Mari stuck her hand around the corner and pulled the trigger without aiming. "We're out of bullets for the assault rifles, but they seem to be also. I took out three with my knife before they caught onto me, but there were at least seven left. We can't see them in the dark, so it's hard to do anything but fire blindly, but they've moved up. They're shooting from two different rooms on either side of the hallway now." Her gun clicked uselessly. "Oh, and apparently that was my last bullet." She threw the gun aside.

I reached out, feeling for life forces. With the energy boiling inside me, I was strong enough to push back their barriers all at once. So maybe instead of directing the energy at them as I had the generator, I could use it with my own ability. It seemed quite possible and far more effective since I couldn't see where to aim a physical blast.

Night, night, I said. *And Edgel, I'm sorry about your daughter.* Drawing on the power, I let off my mental white flash and the guns fell quiet. Had I killed them? I shoved guilt aside as I detected life forces. They would probably recover. Maybe.

"Okay," I said into the abrupt silence, "they're out. I don't know for how long."

Dragon brought fire to life on the palm of his hand, his pale eyes bright in the flame's reflection. Willis sank to the tiled floor, and I could see he was bleeding from several wounds. "You couldn't have done that before?" he asked.

"Not without enough energy. I needed help from outside." I couldn't blame them. They had no idea how my ability worked. *I* didn't even know half the time.

Willis sighed. "That's it then."

"We still have to get out," I reminded him. "I don't have near enough energy left to do that again." In fact, I felt drained and weak without it to sustain me.

My comment stirred him. "We need to secure the front doors." He motioned to Mari. "First, can you find us some bandages and supplies?" Without responding, Mari vanished.

"We'll need any bullets they have left, Dragon," Willis added. "And make sure they won't wake up."

I wanted to protest, but it was no longer my call. Willis was in charge. Besides, I didn't think one man would be able to slice up that many soldiers on his own. If he did, at least they couldn't try to kill us again.

Dragon moved down the hallway, taking his light with him. Five shots followed. Not enough to kill those who were Unbounded, but hopefully sufficient to put them out for as long as we'd need. I purposefully didn't think about the mortal agents the Emporium invariably had among their numbers. Nothing I could do about their choices.

Mari reappeared moments later with a box of Renegade supplies I recognized as coming from outside the compound. She turned on a flashlight and in silence we began bandaging wounds and injecting curequick as fast as we could. Mandalyn bit her lip, something wet glistening on her cheek, as she sewed up the gaping wound in Guenter's stomach. Dragon returned in time to help me wrap Francis's leg.

"Let's move," Willis said finally, pulling his stocky frame upright.

Guenter had lost consciousness during his treatment and stirred only slightly as Mandalyn whispered something into his ear. With a grunt, Dragon hefted the man over his shoulder.

Willis glanced at me. "You two can shift out? Do it. They'll need you outside."

"What if more of their soldiers come inside?" I asked. "There are other doors to the building."

"I heard them say everything's been sealed but the front." He gave me a smile before putting an arm around Francis.

That's right. I remembered a guard saying something to that effect when I was visiting as Delia. "They could unseal them."

"I'm not saying for you to abandon us," Willis said. "We'll expect direction once we get there. But come along, if you'd rather. Or you can shift out and back in with more weapons. That would help." Lifting a pistol, he started down the hall, half supporting Francis. The others limped after him.

I mentally traced the path they would follow, but could find no moving life forces. Of course there was still the question of Delia. Where was she? Had she escaped to her forces outside? Or was she lying in wait for us somewhere? I doubted the latter was likely. She hadn't lived seventeen hundred years without learning to protect herself.

"Let's go," Mari said.

"I have to get Patrick. I promised. You go outside and tell everyone what's happened in here. See if you can get hold of Ritter and Ava. They might have some ideas of what to do now. I'll take Patrick to the lobby with the others and contact you there."

"You come with me. We can get him later."

"I can't. He's been through too much. I'm going to get him back to his family. Without the shield over the building, I can still use your ability." Though I felt exhausted, I was sure I had enough energy left from the power line to reach her almost anywhere she might go outside. "I'll follow you."

My determination must have been obvious because with a toss of her long black hair, she threw me a flashlight and vanished. I reached after her, channeling her ability, and shifted to the hallway outside the room that was Patrick's cell. No guard, so the man had probably joined the fight at some point.

To my surprise, Patrick's doorknob turned easily under my touch. Why wasn't it locked? There was only one person in the room that I could feel. Lifting my flashlight, I pushed the door open, wishing I had a new magazine for my empty gun.

"Patrick?" I said. "I'm back. Let's get out of here."

I saw him under the weak light, a mound slumped against the wall where we'd left him. He gave a muffled groan.

"And go where?"

Fear slammed my heart against my chest because it wasn't Patrick who'd spoken, but Delia Vesey.

"Wa ohhhh! Unnn!" This from Patrick, whose face turned toward me, silver tape covering his mouth.

Delia laughed. "I knew you'd be back because you promised him when we took you to the lab. You still believe in promises. Guess what, so do I. Here's my promise. If you leave here, my men will make sure Patrick is really and truly killed. We'd thought to use his genes, but we have other technopaths and with his current attitude, he won't be much of a loss."

Shadows moved and I shifted the flashlight to reveal two Emporium hit men looming over Patrick, their heavy swords drawn. I still didn't feel them on my mental senses, so Delia was masking them, and that meant breaking through their mind barriers with my regular ability would be almost impossible unless I concentrated on the link between them and Delia. But even if I severed that, she'd have plenty of time to give the kill order before I could try to stop them.

"I take it you're staying?" Delia turned on her own flashlight, which glinted off the pistol she aimed at my head.

As a soldier, Ritter might say my best option would be to reach for Mari again and shift away, but knowing him as I did, I doubted he'd so easily allow Patrick to be murdered.

If only Ritter were here now. Instinctively, I reached for him— and found him unshielded as if he'd been waiting for me. He was outside the compound and Ava was with him.

Ritter? I asked. The connection was faint and strained.

Relief in his mind, accompanied by self-recrimination that resounded above the aching wounds I felt in his body. *Sorry I wasn't here earlier.*

Through his eyes I saw huge trucks around him, disgorging police officers, SWAT teams, soldiers, and Secret Service. *Who are these men?*

Ava, Jace, and I went to see the vice president. Oliver masked me to look like his son so we could get in. Mann took some convincing, and we sent a couple of Secret Service agents to the hospital, but he came through for us with this army when he realized we were serious about them holding his real son.

There was a question to the thought, and I hurried to answer. *Yes, he's here, but there's a problem.* I sent him images of the freed prisoners heading to the lobby, and of Delia and her soldiers poised above Patrick.

Channel Mari. Shift out! It was an order, as sharp as an ice pick.

She'll kill him if I do.

We'll get to him after we get through these men out here.

You'll be too late. Even if I channeled his ability, I was no match for three Emporium agents, and I didn't have enough power left inside me to break through all their shields. *If I wait for Delia to leave, you can free us both.*

I could see he wasn't happy with the idea. *Okay. But I'm coming for you.*

During my private conversation, Delia had motioned to the soldiers to pick up Patrick, and they'd dragged him to the door, forcing me at sword point to step aside so they could get him into the hallway. "After you, my dear," Delia said to me, taking my flashlight and dropping it to the ground.

Mentally, she was outside my shield—I could feel her like a moth hitting against a light—but I felt confident she couldn't get in, the electricity I'd absorbed earlier having reinforced my shield reserves.

Electricity.

I couldn't break through her shield, either, but maybe with a little more power I could—at least I would try once I got some space between Patrick and those swords. As we walked down the hallway, I reached for Brody and for the power lines. It was harder now because he was further away, but I made the link. No luck. The electricity hadn't been restored.

Through Brody's eyes things now looked different. Objects glowed around bodies and cars and even from some of the closer buildings. *Cell phones? Security alarms?* I wondered. Experimentally, I began drawing them in. I felt Brody's joy as he began helping me, his earlier fear dampened by my success with the generator. He was better at it than I was, and without the power lines, I needed his help. *Yes, pull it in,* I told him. I took it from him as fast as he gathered it. Compared to the power lines, it was a tiny trickle, but maybe I could find enough energy to get through Delia's shield.

There was no glowing from the people I could see around Brody or around the compound, so no one was using an ability. Only Delia glowed as I glanced behind me, not as brightly as the cell phone and the flashlight she carried, but like a candle in the darkness. I tried to suck in her personal energy, willing to risk further depleting myself. Nothing happened. Her shield had to be stopping the transfer.

Something buzzed and Delia reached for her phone. "What? No." The fury in her words made me hesitate in sucking the energy from her phone's battery. "What about a helicopter? I see. Contact our people. Get our cover story ready. We are a simple research facility, and we were attacked. I will—"

With a breath I absorbed the energy and her phone went dead. I was tempted to do the flashlight as well, but for now I wanted to see where we were going.

"Stop!" Delia barked at the guards. "Change of plans. Go to the basement instead. We have a deposit to make."

A deposit?

Reversing their path, the soldiers led us to a staircase I'd never seen before. They let Patrick's feet bump on each stair as they went down.

"Where are we going?" I asked. My connection with Brody strained at the distance, and I let it drop temporarily to preserve energy.

"We've owned this building for many years," Delia told me, "and because of its special properties, it sometimes comes in very handy. The original owner loved the idea of bomb shelters, so he built one here. Of course, from the outside, you can't tell it's there."

I fought down my unease as she led us to a huge furnace, where the guards dropped Patrick on the cold cement floor. He'd lost consciousness and I was grateful for his sake. Delia conferred with her men, keeping her gun on me. When they were finished, the soldiers went to the tall front panel of the furnace and opened it, pulling out the back wall of the panel to reveal a series of ropes. They grabbed onto one rope together, and a section of the cement floor to the left of the furnace began to rise slowly.

"Of course he used a ladder to climb down inside," Delia said as the narrow slab of foot-thick cement reached shoulder height, "and he stored shelves of food, but we don't find those necessary."

One of the guards jumped into the hole left by the concrete and began tugging at something. Delia directed me closer as he opened a metal trapdoor about two square feet wide. A horrible, rotten stench wafted from the dark interior, making me choke.

"What is that?" I asked.

She pushed me closer. When I resisted, she motioned to the soldiers, who grabbed my shoulders and threw me inside. The back of my head banged hard against the edge of the metal opening as I fell into the deep hole, but my training helped me land on my feet.

Inside, the stench was almost overwhelming, and I fell to my knees gagging. What was that smell? Like roadkill. Covering my nose and mouth with my hand, I staggered to my feet again, my head less than a foot from the ceiling. I peered into the darkness, aided only by the dim light from the narrow hole overhead. I couldn't see much, but I had the feeling I was in a small room. Maybe ten by ten feet.

Delia squatted near the opening and directed her flashlight

downward. "I think you can stay here with Patrick for a time and then we'll talk. You'll be surprised what a little solitude can do for your attitude. Or, if you're adamant, you can always end up like that." She shifted the light onto a bulk several feet away from me. A two-foot long mass curled on a blanket, the ends oozing and rotted, the middle looking a lot like a shiny piece of hardened leather stretched over a ribbed frame.

Horror waved through me. "It's human."

Delia laughed. "No, he's Unbounded, of course. Been here over twenty years. Every now and then we open the door to let him absorb a bit just to keep regeneration possible. With my latest mind techniques it might even be worthwhile taking him out and putting him in a bath of tonic to help him regain consciousness. I'll think about it. In the meantime, you'll probably lose a little body mass to him as he instinctively absorbs from you. I'll come back before it gets too bad."

I fought down panic. I'd heard of Unbounded dying of starvation in sealed containers, a gruesome, painful way to die, but I'd never imagined I would see it up close.

"The focus points do everything they can to survive," Delia mused, "including cannibalizing the rest of the body. I had one large woman last fifty years."

I leaned over and retched dryly while Delia laughed. Drops of blood hit the cement in front of me, almost indistinguishable in the dim light. When I touched the back of my head where it had hit the metal edge of the door on the way down, my hand came away wet.

I'm okay, I told myself. Ritter was outside and I would tell him where I was. Or I'd connect with Mari and shift out as soon as Delia started to shut the metal door. Or even afterward as Mari didn't seem to have problems shifting through metal or concrete. No need to act rashly or to embarrass myself by crying to Ritter. Yet.

I pushed at Delia's shield to see if the power I'd absorbed from Brody was enough to break through, but it wasn't. Not even with the aid of an imaginary sai. She was stronger now, apparently having learned from my breach of her shield in the lab. I reached out to Brody, having to expend a precious amount of the power he'd already given me just to link that far. *Hurry,* I told him. *I need more.* I pulled in all he'd managed to gather.

Delia reached down to fiddle with something inside the hole, and a soft hum filled the room. My connection with Brody abruptly ceased.

I pushed out harder, reaching for him. Nothing.

Delia's light shined on my face. "Ah, by your expression, it looks like the generator for this room still works. We modified it a few years ago when we invented the shield technology. It's been useful in dampening a variety of abilities as well as internal transmitter signals, which is helpful in making Unbounded stay where we put them. The fuel for this generator will eventually run out, but not until your friends are long gone. You won't be able to tell them where you are, and even if we hadn't disabled your transmitter, they couldn't have tracked you. Stefan will be grateful I kept you safe."

She drew back and seconds later a bulk dropped through the opening, only slightly ruffling the invisible shield around the bomb shelter. Patrick fell on top of me, knocking me to the cement floor.

"At least you'll have company," Delia said.

I threw my thoughts hard at the shield, using all the power I'd stored. If I could break through a person's mental shield, couldn't I break through one generated by a machine?

Ritter! Agony ripped at my mind, but for a brief instant I felt him.

Or did I?

My vision went dark.

Was the darkness from expending too much energy? Or had they closed the trapdoor? I didn't know. The smell of the leather bundle had grown worse, it seemed, or maybe that was the stench of my own fear.

CHAPTER 23

RITTER WOULD FIND ME. I KNEW HE WOULD. EVERY TIME I'D BEEN trapped, he'd come. I had to make sure I was ready to meet him. Blindly, I rolled Patrick off my body and struggled to sit up, breathing through my mouth so the stench wouldn't gag me. Feeling for Patrick's pulse, I was satisfied that he was just out, not temporarily dead. After removing the tape on his mouth, I forced myself to start exploring my surroundings, avoiding the direction of the leathery mass. There wasn't likely anything around to help me escape, or the other prisoner would have found it, but exploring was better than lying here in the dark, feeling the room closing in around me. Fortunately, I'd never minded small spaces, and maybe that's what would preserve my sanity now.

A quick exploration showed nothing in the room except rows of built-in shelves on one side and a cupboard with ropes that I assumed had something to do with lowering the cement slab from the inside. Nothing I could use to reach, much less try to pry open, the metal door so I could disengage the shield.

My head ached and every muscle in my body protested movement, but I wouldn't give in to despair. I forced myself to mentally reach out to the leathery mass that had once been a man. Sure enough, a dim life force still glowed within him, seeming to increase ever so slightly as I probed. Fascinated, I focused on him until the pounding in my head made me quit.

My heartbeat sounded loud in my chest and despite my determination to remain calm, my anxiety began building. Maybe I'd better try to wake Patrick. Talking to him would be better than going crazy. In the end I decided to let him stay blissfully unaware.

I had no way to mark the time that passed as I struggled not to collapse into a quivering ball of panic. When a faint shout broke the silence, I almost didn't believe my ears. A second shout filled me with hope. I stood and yelled. "I'm in here! I'm in here! Down under the floor!" I tried to reach past the shield, but hot pain slicing into my skull warned that I had overreached my limit.

Then the creaking sound of the metal door and Mari's voice. "Erin, are you there? Oh, there you are. Ugh, what a stench!"

I could tell she was staring down into the opening, but I couldn't see her. My vision was gone, probably because of that last desperate effort to reach Ritter through the generator shield. No wonder I felt like collapsing into a pitiful ball.

"Use my ability to shift out," Mari called. "Ritter's holding off the guys who put you here, but he needs us."

"There's a shield," I said as the shouting and clanging of weapons grew behind her. "Look for a button somewhere—"

Like a breath, I felt the shield wink out of existence.

"What about now? Hurry if you can. We stopped them from putting back the cement slab, but they seem pretty determined."

"Okay, I just need a moment." I began absorbing as rapidly as possible, sucking in nutrients. I wished I could reach for Brody to get more power, but I didn't seem to have enough mental energy to bridge the physical gap between us. At last, Mari's anxious face came into view as new strength restored my sight. The cement slab was only a foot above her head. I shifted.

Instead of appearing next to Mari, I materialized in the hallway near the lobby. As weak as I was, I would do Ritter no good, but here I should be able to contact Brody. Searching, I found him full of energy—and new fear. All around him lightning crackled in the sky, attracted by his pull.

I'm here, I said. *I can take it all.* Energy poured through him into me. *No more now,* I warned Brody. *Don't take in any more.*

I don't know if I can stop.

You have to. Get a hold of yourself. You can do it. I knew what he wasn't saying. That taking in the energy was addictive, an almost sensual high. I'd have to keep an eye on him so he didn't blow up the building.

I dropped our connection and shifted again, this time appearing next to Mari.

"Oh, there you are. For a moment I was worried." She handed me my sai. "We have no more bullets, but they don't have any either. Jace brought these when we first came from the hotel, and I knew you'd want them."

The sound of fighting was louder now, moving our way. A flashlight had fallen to the ground, and humongous shadows danced on the wall near the stairs. I felt Ritter, his mind open to me like Mari's had been, in spite of the danger with Delia around. Where was she? I reached out for her, but if she was anywhere nearby, I couldn't sense her presence.

"You distract one," Mari said, "and I'll get him with my knife."

Hefting a sai in each hand, I reached out to Ritter across the basement, channeling his ability. He came into sight at that moment, dwarfed by his own shadow on the wall. He was beauty in motion, fluid, exact, and deadly.

"Here!" I shouted, running into the fray.

Ritter's thrill of combat, coupled with his relief at seeing me, flooded my senses. Added to the electric energy singing in my brain, it was a heady combination.

A soldier turned to meet me, his sword coming down like a guillotine. I parried with the sai, first with the right and then the left, the lengths of the blades along the inside of my arms.

Next, I twirled the blade out, trying to catch his sword

between the hand guard and the blade so I could twist it from him. He faltered at the last moment, sending his blow toward my other side, but I anticipated and blocked him. It was all the distraction Mari needed. She appeared behind him, one arm wrapping around his torso almost like a lover. He slid to the ground.

Ritter finished with his opponent at the same time. He rushed over to me, carrying a sword in one hand and a sai in the other. He looked like the devil's avenging angel. Blood dripped from several deep cuts on his face, and the coat sleeve on his left arm had been torn completely off to reveal that the arm had been bandaged. Probably a souvenir from his visit to the vice president. The other sleeve and his pants sported numerous cuts.

Without a word, the arm with the sai went around me and his mouth came down on mine, pushing my lips open and kissing me deeply. Need filled me, stirring up more electric currents that made delicious circuits to the most intimate parts of my body. For that moment there was nothing but the two of us. Nothing else mattered.

We came up for breath and his eyes fell over me, taking in my borrowed outfit. "I really hope this isn't where *you* confess some kinky fantasy about hotels." His finger reached inside the rip in my skirt, running up the warmth of my thigh. "Though maybe that wouldn't be too bad. Certainly looks better on you than mine did on me."

I grinned. "How'd you get inside?"

Ritter shrugged. "Oliver masked me until I got through their lines, and then I climbed down through the roof."

"I shifted inside near Patrick's cell," Mari added. "You were already gone, but I followed the light and saw her take you down those stairs. That's how we found you."

I shuddered. "And Delia?"

"We don't know," Mari said. "After they brought you down here, I went to meet Ritter and when we got back they were lowering that cement slab."

"We'd better get upstairs," Ritter said. "I'm hoping to avoid a bloodbath outside."

"Wait. We need to get Patrick." I started back to the bomb shelter.

Ritter lifted the concrete slab higher with the pulley mechanism, but in the end Mari and I shifted down together and brought Patrick up. It was harder with him being unconscious than it had been to shift Jace a short distance, but Patrick also weighed more. Next, we brought up the leathery mass wrapped in the blanket. I didn't know who he was, but we wouldn't leave him here.

Ritter hefted Patrick over his shoulder while I did the same with the horrific bundle. It didn't weigh more than twenty-five or thirty pounds. Was it me or did it already smell less intense? In my right hand I carried my sai. Mari, holding the flashlight, led the way, but I knew her memory would get us to the lobby with or without the light.

When we arrived, we found the freed Renegade prisoners peering out the front lobby door. Guns twisted in our direction. "It's Erin and Mari!" I called out, lowering my burden.

Willis limped over to us, his eyes brightening when he saw Ritter. "Hello, Ritter. Good to see you."

"And you, my friend." Ritter laid Patrick down on the ground and bumped fists with Willis. "I know it's been a long three months."

"It's over now." Willis's voice was hard. He glanced at Mandalyn and Francis, his tone softening. "Well, for some of us."

Ritter gave the women a sympathetic nod and took a step toward the door. "What's the situation out there?"

"We're not sure." Willis walked with him. "A lot of movement, but no streetlights and the rain makes it more difficult to see."

The light situation was my fault, and Brody's, but we'd really had no choice. Feeling powerless without any offensive weapons, I went to the guard behind the desk and retrieved my ballistic knife, cleaning the blood off on the man's pants. Someone had tied him up with rope, so he wouldn't be a problem any time soon.

Ritter's eyes noted the knife as I approached, one brow arching slightly, but he didn't say anything. *Yes, I used your weapon,* I sent to him pointedly through our still-connected minds. *What are you going to do about that?*

He turned back to the glass doors, masking a smile. *Later.* Aloud, he said, "My phone doesn't seem to be working, so I can't call the number the vice president gave me to communicate with him."

"Uh, yeah," I said a bit sheepishly. "I don't think any of the phones are working. Or the radios or anything else that has batteries."

He gave me a sharp glance. "Does this have anything to do with Brody?"

"Don't ask."

I reached out searching for Ava. Her shield was tightly in place, and that worried me. Tonight it looked strong and impenetrable, and I didn't want to weaken myself or her trying to get through, but after all our practice together, I knew if I knocked hard enough to get her attention, she'd recognize me and let me inside. As a sensing Unbounded, she could recognize my signature, as I could hers. Fortunately, she seemed to be waiting for me.

Ah, Erin. Her relief at our safety flickered through my mind. *The army out here is holding fire. We're trying to negotiate, but it's going slowly because none of the electronic equipment is working. And Delia's out here telling lies. She refuses to order her people to stand down. Just hold tight.*

I refocused on the lobby. "They're negotiating," I said to Ritter. "Delia's out there spinning a cover story and holding things up. She's probably hoping her guards have finished burying me in that hole and that they'll have time to recapture and hide the prisoners."

"If the vice president came here to free his son, why doesn't he just fire on them?" Mari let out a sigh of disgust. "He doesn't even know his son's okay."

Ritter's jaw clenched as his face swung to meet our gazes.

"Because I told him not to. We made a deal with them to make a show of force and then negotiate."

"What? Why?" I asked. It didn't make sense, not when we suddenly had the advantage. "We could take out quite a few of the Emporium soldiers once and for all."

Willis heaved a sigh. "Because that army out there can shoot up the Emporium all they want and most of the devils aren't going to die. Eventually, they're going to heal, get up, and fight again. But a whole bunch of those mortals will die if they fight. And they won't come back."

"It's not something we can ask them to do," Ritter added. "Not until they know the consequences. A hundred or so of them for a couple Emporium agents. It's not a good exchange."

All at once I understood. Mortal lives would be the cost, and that went against everything we believed. For now it was our fight—and our death price.

"They have to be told one day," I said. "We can't do it alone."

Ritter nodded. "I know."

The Emporium has given up, Ava told me. *The army had to send someone for more vehicles because none of these out here have working batteries. They're loading the Emporium soldiers who have surrendered into a truck now, but there are only about twenty, and most of them are mortal not Unbounded. We don't know where the others disappeared to. There were nearly seventy at last count.*

They'd probably been given the order to retreat. At least those who weren't unconscious inside the building.

One of the police captains has offered to take Delia to the station for questioning, Ava added. *Probably an Emporium plant, seeing how she's shielding his thoughts. We've tried to intercept her, but they're too surrounded by his officers for us to get near.*

I bet she'd never make it to the station to answer questions. No, she'd be back at her headquarters drinking her favorite herbal tea before we could arrange a working vehicle to tail her. Given the Emporium's wealth and connections, the soldiers taken to the station would likely walk as well.

Ritter laid a warm hand on the small of my back. "Let's go home."

Ritter carried Patrick, while I hefted my smelly bundle once again. Dragon carried Francis, and Mari and Mandalyn helped Guenter, who was finally awake but in need of curequick and a lot of healing time. Willis took up the rear, guarding our exit in case any of the soldiers we'd taken out regained consciousness.

Outside, lightning crackled overhead, framed by turbulent black clouds. I checked Brody to see if he was still attracting the lightning, but he hadn't taken in much more energy. We hurried through the icy rain that was quickly turning to snow. The wetness reactivated the smell lodged in the old blanket, and again I had to breathe through my mouth. We walked past the cement barriers the Emporium had brought in, past the empty guard trailer, and through the open gate. The streets and surrounding areas were littered with police cars, army trucks, and other official vehicles, most of which were no longer working, though replacements were beginning to arrive. Dimitri and Ava and the others waited for us behind an armored truck. Cort and Dimitri took Patrick, while Keene relieved me of my smelly burden, wincing as he peeked inside. All of them looked beaten and worn, and I knew the fight out here hadn't been any easier than ours inside, at least not until the cavalry had arrived.

"Where's Jace?" I asked.

"He's at the first aid tent in the parking lot behind the next building." Stella pointed down the street, looking as beautiful as ever with her wet hair flattened under a camouflage cap that didn't match the beige dress she still had on from the hotel. "Out of firing range. Once we knew you were okay, he finally agreed to leave. He took two bullets today."

"The infirmary is where we'd better get Patrick and everyone else who needs attention," Dimitri said. "I want to look at their wounds. Keene, bring your new friend, would you?" He motioned to the bundle. "Cort, give him a hand. I know you'll want to document every second of the recovery."

Cort nodded. "He *is* quite a find. Though there's not much we can do for him here. We'll cook up a bathtub full of curequick for him when we get back to the safe house."

Keene's eyes met mine, his drenched hair matted down around his face. Something was different. What was he trying to tell me? A snowflake landed on my eyelash and when I blinked, he turned away.

"Check on Oliver," Ava called as they left with the other wounded and those helping them. "I sent him there, too." Her gaze went to Ritter. "Good call using Oliver tonight. His failure this morning might have set him back years."

Ritter shrugged. "We do what we have to. Let's be honest, he was our only option to get in to see the vice president."

Ava's smile didn't change. "More often than not, that's how heroes are made."

I agreed completely. It was a lot like being tossed into a raging ocean and being told to learn to swim. Oliver might have sunk a little further than most of us at the beginning, but he'd come through in the end. I might even have to thank him. I didn't want to think about where any of us might be at that moment if the army hadn't shown up to scare Delia and her minions.

"I'd like to see Jace." I started to ask for details about his condition when I felt eyes burning into me. Scanning the disarray of vehicles, I found Delia surrounded by officers and staring at us over a police car. Someone had given her an ugly black raincoat, but it took nothing away from her regal stance. I met her stare, fury seeping into me. Lightning sparked from the ends of my sai.

"Erin?" Ritter said, worry heavy in his voice.

I was pulling in energy again using Brody's ability, this time directly from the only available source: the lightning overhead. The electricity filled me in a single intoxicating rush. Power pulsed through my body. I crashed it mentally into Delia's shield, and the glossy blackness split open like a melon.

"Erin!" At the panic in Ava's voice, I looked down to find I was glowing. Heat thrummed through me. It was starting to hurt—like a hundred knives stabbing into my flesh. Or perhaps a bolt of lightning.

Ava banged at my mental shield, and I let her in. Then Brody was there, siphoning off the energy under Ava's direction.

Next time, I promised Delia, as the power faded from me. *Next time I will kill you.* I tried to send a wounding flash to her mind, but the energy was gone and her shield popped back into place, tight and whole as ever.

But not before I sensed her fear.

Dredging up every bit of energy I had left, I held my smile as she hurriedly climbed into the police car and was driven away. Blackness colored my vision.

"Help," I said to no one in particular. "I think I'm going to faint."

CHAPTER 24

AVA AND RITTER REACHED FOR MY ARMS TO STEADY ME AS
I pushed to keep the blackness at bay.

"You okay, Brody?" Ava asked. "How are you with the energy?"

He grinned, his blond hair and sideburns dry while everyone
else was wet, even under their hats. "It's gone. All of it. It went
down through my feet." A new confidence showed in his face.
"Guess the earth was big enough to take it just fine. Makes sense.
Lightning hits the ground all the time."

We all looked down. A jagged inch-wide split marred the street
at his feet, one I was pretty sure hadn't been there a few minutes
before.

He shrugged. "I still have a bit to learn." He looked from me
to Ava, his eyes growing bleak. "I'm not going back to my family,
am I?"

"No," Ava said. "But you'll be busy helping Tenika and the
others here rebuild. You can arrange occasional visits with your
family, but they should seriously think about allowing the Renegades to take your sister as well. We have reason to believe she was
placed by the Emporium just as you were. After what happened

with you, they may not wait to see if she Changes before taking her into custody."

He swallowed hard. "I'll talk to them. Thank you."

I thought he'd be okay, despite his years of indoctrination by the Hunters, but only time would tell. As a psychologist, Tenika could help him better than most. At least Brody no longer seemed angry at me for killing him.

"We'd better get you to the first aid tent," Ritter said to me, his hands running down my arms. "You're shivering."

I *was* cold, thanks to Brody taking every bit of my borrowed energy. There wasn't enough left of my own to hold me up.

"I'll take her," Stella said, moving to my side. "General Whiting is waving at you."

Ritter looked at a cluster of uniformed men near the gate. "Good. Ava and I want to see if we can get back inside the building with our people. It we can, it would mean at least a few Emporium Unbounded we could take to Mexico."

Mexico meant our prison compound and an attempt at rehabilitation for Emporium Unbounded. Or to stand trial for their crimes, the punishment being true death. I still hadn't dared ask the ratio of rehabilitation versus executions, but Ritter had told me that final decisions took up to a century, which gave me hope.

"Well, hurry," I said, wiping rain from my face. "You look worse than I feel."

He gave me a stare that succeeded in upping my temperature significantly. "I'll meet you there."

I watched Ritter and Ava stride toward a tall, uniformed man with a narrow face. Even as they began to talk, five Emporium Unbounded emerged from the front door of the compound, and a shout went up from the watching army. There was no mistaking Edgel in front. Behind him came Dr. Tunns and two soldiers supporting a staggering Lew. Edgel had his hands raised in surrender. I didn't anticipate they'd be in any jail cell long, despite the vice president's participation tonight.

"Come on," Stella urged, taking my arm.

I'd rather shift to the tent, but my head felt stuffed with cotton and the idea of dropping my shield to link with Mari who had gone ahead with the others made me nauseated. I was glad Delia wasn't around or she'd probably already be inside my brain.

Stella put her arm around me as we moved forward. "You okay?"

"Yeah. Except that I might be so far gone that I can't feel the pain."

She smiled and transferred her cap to my own head. "You did a great job."

I stopped walking, pushing wet hair from my eyes. "I'm not afraid of Delia anymore. I know I have to be careful, but I'm not afraid."

She hugged me. "That's good."

I started walking again, but slowly so Stella could lead the way. The first aid tent turned out to be three times larger than I expected, glowing with lights that had either been too far away for Brody to absorb or that had been replaced. Outside, it looked like a Secret Service reunion.

"It's the vice president," Stella said over the underlying hum that filled the area. "And his wife. They've been waiting here for their son. Don't worry. I was here earlier. They'll let us in, but we'll have to leave our weapons in that box by the door."

Knowing Stella, half of the Secret Service agents had probably asked for her phone number.

"Here's another survivor," she announced to the agent at the tent door, making a show of helping me walk. I didn't have to pretend to lean on her.

"Go right in, Miss Stella," he said. "After you both put your weapons in the box, of course."

I obliged, placing my sai and my knife inside. From her coat, Stella took out two guns, four knives, a short saber, and several throwing stars. "The guns aren't even loaded," she whispered with a roll of her eyes. "I used all the bullets outside the compound."

Inside, a wave of heat hit our faces, and I realized that some of the noise outside had come from a generator. That explained the lights and the warmth.

Jace, Oliver, and the released prisoners were lying or sitting on cots, while Mari and Cort stared into a large metal basin in the corner where they had put the shriveled Unbounded. Further into the room was a narrow corridor and curtains making up private rooms. More Secret Service stood shoulder to shoulder down the corridor and in front of the room on the right.

"One guess where they've taken Patrick," Stella said dryly.

"Erin!" Jace started to rise from his cot, but after a few moments of struggling, he groaned and remained where he was.

I went to his side and plopped to my knees to hug him. "You were great at the hotel."

He pushed me away. "Ew. Sorry, sis, but you really stink. Must be that dead guy. Keene smelled the same way when he brought him in."

"Oh, yeah. Sorry." Now that he mentioned it, the rotten smell did seem to cling to me.

"Not dead," Cort corrected, glancing up from the lump.

"I wonder who he is." This from Willis. "He's probably one of ours who went missing."

"We put our supplies in the end room on the left," Stella said to me. "You should be able to find something to change into."

I was about to take her up on that when Dimitri squeezed out from behind the line of Secret Service agents. "Erin, come in here. Patrick wants to see you." He looked at Stella. "And Mrs. Mann asked for you."

"I'll come back in a bit," I told Jace.

We walked down the narrow corridor a couple feet, brushing against the agents, who, to give them credit, didn't even cringe at my smell. The makeshift room was actually supposed to be two, given the curtains tied up in the middle, but even so it was tiny. Patrick lay on a cot in the middle. His mother sat next to him on a stool, holding one of his hands, while his father squatted on the other side. At least there were no Secret Service agents inside, which was probably breaking all kinds of protocol.

"Hey, you," I said to Patrick, trying not to feel awkward with the audience.

"Hey. I wanted to say thanks. Without you, I'd still be in that place." His poor attempt at a smile stretched the fading green bruises on his face. "For a moment, I thought it was all over when they tossed us into that hole."

"You were awake?"

"I was in and out." He paused before glancing at his parents and continuing. "They know about it—all of it. They're going to help, right Dad?"

The vice president patted his son's shoulder before standing. "I can't say I'm pleased with the discoveries I've made tonight, or the fact that my son is some kind of new breed of human, but I am happy to have him restored to me." He shook his head. "There's no way I want people like those who took him at the head of our country. They must be stopped. So, yes, you can bet I'm going to do everything I can to prevent that from happening."

"We'll be moving Patrick tonight," Dimitri said. "For now he'll go to our safe house, but we'll have to fake his death. Otherwise, it will be too hard to protect him. He's pretty well-known here. He may have to go to one of our groups in Europe for a time. But he'll be free to contact you as much as you both determine it's safe."

"Wait," I said. "We need a face. A face for the Unbounded when we eventually do go public. Why not Patrick?"

Patrick struggled to sit up further on his pillows. "I want to help. I'll do whatever I can."

Dimitri thought for a moment. "Maybe. We'll have to talk about it. You'd still have to be hidden and protected until you're needed, but instead of death maybe we can come up with another story that will leave us more options."

Mrs. Mann gave a little sob, but the vice president nodded. "I understand. And I thank you, all of you, for bringing our son back to us." He lifted his eyes to include Stella and me in his comments but refocused immediately on Dimitri. "When you're finished here, I'll take you to the president. I'd like you to save his life if you can."

"He will never recover what he's lost," Dimitri said, "but I will try to save his life. Even if I succeed, it will mean several transplants. He won't be strong enough to continue as president."

Mann's shoulders slumped slightly. "I'll prepare myself for that eventuality, however much I hope it's not true. Thank you for whatever you can do. Regardless of his future position, Kenneth Stevens is a wise man and I believe his advice and counsel will help us through this crisis. Now I'd better see about sending all these soldiers to their beds." To his wife, he added, "I'll be back soon." Nodding to the rest of us, he strode from the room.

"You're in good hands," I told Patrick. "I'm going to change, but I'll see you later."

Before I could leave, Carolyn Mann said something softly to her son and arose. "Can I talk to you?" she asked Stella. Strong emotion flowed from her, the first I'd been able to feel through my shield since my brush with the lightning.

We squeezed out past the Secret Service agents, but instead of returning to the main room, Stella led us through the curtain on the other side of the corridor. "You can get through the supply room this way," she told me. "And you won't have to fight your way through the agents in the hallway." Sure enough, inside the other narrow room was a split in the curtains.

Mrs. Mann reached out to touch my sleeve, holding me in place. "I'm so grateful to you all for finding him." Tears started down her cheeks. "Especially you for going inside that building."

As if I'd had a choice—as least the second time. I felt embarrassed at her praise.

"I love Patrick so much," she continued. "I always have, but I have to say that in those months after he was born, I did feel something . . . missing. Something not related to Patrick. A . . . a hole. I didn't understand it then, but it makes sense now. I wouldn't change what happened, not if it meant losing Patrick, but I . . . I'd like to know who he is." She gave us a watery smile. "My—my other son, I mean. Does he really have three children? Does he look like me or his dad? Do you think . . . do you think he'd ever want to meet us? Not to interfere in his life. Just . . . just to meet him?"

Stella put her arm around Mrs. Mann and she finally let go of me. "I'm sure he would," Stella said. "I'll get you all the information I have. You can be proud of him. He's a good person and a respected leader. A devoted father. He had good parents."

"I'm glad." Mrs. Mann's face bobbed as she nodded, trying to contain her emotion to a level the people beyond the curtains couldn't hear. "I'm so glad. Thank you. Thank you so much for giving me back both my sons."

I hoped the Manns would be able to have some sort of relationship with Howard Obstfield, their biological son, despite the negative publicity it might give Mann's run for the presidency, because Patrick's life would be far from normal. At the same time I felt pity for Patrick losing part of his parents' attention, though I doubted he would see it that way. He'd want their happiness, and he'd be occupied with Renegade business anyway. He would never be able to have an ordinary relationship with his parents.

As Mrs. Mann turned and left, it was all I could do not to lie down on the floor right there and go into a coma. Stella pushed me toward the slit in the curtain. "Go get changed and I'll put out a cot for you near Jace. We shouldn't be here too long. Tenika sent a couple of her people to find some working vehicles. We'll jump-start the others and get going."

"Brody can recharge them," I said. "I mean if he can redirect energy, he should be able to."

Stella made a face as she parted the curtain, stepping into the corridor. "You're probably right. But is that something we really want to mess with tonight? I don't think so. Poor kid's been under enough stress today." She let the curtain swing shut.

That *kid* was my age.

"Oh," she added, popping her head back in. "There's a light dangling from the middle of the supply room. When Brody made the generator stall, they turned them all off before restarting, and it doesn't look like that one got turned back on."

I watched her go with a sigh and pushed through the curtain, but that room was empty. Another slit in a second curtain beckoned me onward. *How far does this tent go back?* Inside the next narrow room, my eyes fell on a six-foot camp table filled with duffel bags. More duffels and a few boxes had been crammed underneath, the supplies stretching to each wall of the room.

A dark figure was already rifling through the bags I recognized as belonging to our Renegades, but I couldn't see who. I stepped across the room, reaching for the chain dangling from what might be a light bulb. The figure turned as I pulled the chain.

"Don't—" It was Keene, and he held a shirt in front of him as the light clicked on. But not before I saw that he wasn't wearing any bandages. His recent scars looked years old, and the older ones had almost faded completely.

My eyes flew to his, which were as dark green as a forest at night.

He lifted his arms and pulled the shirt over his head. "Jace told me I stank," he said without emotion.

I stepped next to him, my hand going out to stop him from pulling the shirt down over his chest. "Dimitri healed you, but not like this." I reached out with both hands to his chest, one hand tracing the length of his newest scar. His heart pounded against my other hand. "You . . . oh, Keene, you Changed! I felt a difference in you earlier but I thought it was because—" I broke off. The variance a person radiated when they first began to Change was easily misconstrued, but that wasn't an excuse for not paying more attention.

He pushed away my hand and tugged down his shirt, as if my very touch burned him.

"Sorry. Am I hot?" My skin had been warm for hours after

the first time I'd channeled Brody's ability. With all the effort this evening, I might be burning, no matter how cold I felt.

"No." He hesitated, a sardonic gleam in his eyes. "I mean, yes, you're hot, but not like you mean. It's better you don't touch me." His wet hair had slicked back when he put on the shirt, revealing the absence of the scar along his right cheek.

"When did it happen?"

"I noticed it yesterday morning, after we got back from Emerson's. It had probably already started inside before that, or I wouldn't have been able to get out of bed, even with Dimitri's healing. I'd nearly stopped hurting by this morning." He rubbed the left side of his chest. "Now the scars are fading, even the old ones." A hint of wonder filled his voice.

"Does Cort know?" At thirty-six, Keene was a year beyond the outside Changing range for a typical Unbounded, but his wasn't the only late Change I'd heard of. Maybe he'd given up hope too early. I didn't dare consider that whatever Dimitri and Cort had given him had influenced his Change.

Keene shook his head. "He might suspect. But no one else knows, and I'd appreciate if you didn't say anything just yet. I spent a lot of years struggling to accept who I was, and now I don't know who or what I am."

That I could understand. His bitterness at being mortal had been one of the things I hadn't liked about him. He should be jumping for joy, not hiding in the dark. Still, I knew he'd come to love the Change, every bit as much as I did. "Why didn't you tell me?"

"Would it have made a difference?"

I hesitated. Would it have made a difference yesterday? Probably not. But three weeks ago it might have, and that's what he was asking. "Maybe," I said.

For a moment I thought he hadn't heard me. Then the words, "That's why I didn't tell you." He stepped past me toward the opening in the curtain. "Goodbye, Erin." He had such a tight control over his emotions that not a hint escaped about how he was feeling.

"Wait. Where are you going?" Concern made my voice rise. He shouldn't be alone, not when so much was suddenly different for him.

"Does it matter?"

"I used your switchblade," I answered. "It saved me."

"Good." A slight smile tugged at his mouth.

"I'd like to be here for you. I know the others feel the same."

He rubbed a hand over his face. "Don't worry. I finally know where I belong, if nothing else. While you guys clean up here, I'll help Chris finish getting the safe house ready in San Diego. Not even Stella and her most powerful computer or Brody with all the energy he can hold will be able to get inside when I'm finished. See you there."

I let him go, trying to take it all in. Keene was Unbounded. All his life, he'd worked hard to make his father proud of him, always falling short because he wasn't Unbounded. Now he'd Changed and the man might never know. He didn't deserve to know. We were Keene's family now. All the Renegades would be happy for him, if he let them. For now, I'd keep his secret.

I pulled off my hotel uniform and retrieved a pair of worn gray sweats from the duffel Keene had been standing over. Likely some of Ava's, since Stella was a little shorter than we were and the legs and arms fit. It wouldn't have mattered if they didn't. I pushed up the sleeves and contemplated how many steps it was back to the main room of the tent.

The next thing I knew, Ritter was behind me, pulling my back against his chest, bringing the outside cold on his clothes. "There you are," he said in my ear. "The cars are here."

"Did we get any of them?" I asked. For Mexico, I meant.

"Four."

It was a pitiful amount compared to their number of soldiers, but it was better than nothing. And we'd freed the prisoners. Not a bad day after all. Even so, we'd have to do better. One of these days, the Emporium was going to announce to the world our presence and we'd better be ready.

I leaned into Ritter. "Fortunately, they also gave us our best weapon in the form of the vice president. And possibly Patrick."

"Yeah, we lucked out on that." Ritter nuzzled my neck. I shuddered, feeling my body respond despite its exhaustion.

"At the hotel," I said, "when Delia told you there'd been a delay. How did you know it wasn't me? She was using my mind, so it *was* me."

"It didn't feel like you." He hesitated before continuing. "There was no . . . you in the thoughts. No sass, no passion, no . . ." He laughed. "No irritation. When I realized they'd taken you, I felt . . ."

I turned to face him, waiting. Had he been sad? Scared? Despairing? I dropped my shield to see if he wanted to tell me that way.

"Angry," he finished, leaning over to place his forehead on mine. "Angry at both of us for taking so damn long. I love you, Erin. I love you like I've never loved anyone else. I want you like I've never wanted anyone else. You make me more crazy, more frustrated, and happier than I've ever been. I feel alive inside again for the first time in more years than I care to count. No matter what we've felt or meant to others, it's not the same. It can never be the same. You were right to be upset when I left for those two months I disappeared. I should have taken you with me, but I wanted you so badly, and you weren't ready. I guess I was . . ." He didn't finish, and he didn't have to. His shield had gone down, and even in my exhausted condition a mental link sprang up between us. "I needed to get my head on straight."

He reached for the long chain around his neck, bringing it up over his head and down over mine, without breaking the connection of our foreheads. "I want you to have this. You know what it means to me."

I knew, but if I hadn't, the emotions of love and loss pouring off him would have told me only too well. I brought my hands between us, fingering the rings, feeling the tiny one that had belonged to his sister and his mother's larger band. He'd carried them for over two centuries, mourning their loss. Now he was ready to let go. There was also a new ring I didn't recognize, with a large stone that felt like commitment. But from the moment I'd realized a relationship between us was possible, I had known he'd settle for nothing less.

"The other is for the mortal world," he said. "I'm relearning that language." He kissed me gently at first, running his tongue along my teeth. I pushed closer and our contact deepened until it felt as if we were one. I loved being in his arms, loved the delicious heat I felt from his hands, the hard lines of his body pressed against mine.

I pulled back to look into his eyes, trying to catch my breath from wherever it had gone. "Okay, Your Deathliness. You win."

"You mean we win."

I laughed. "That doesn't mean you don't owe me that poisoned knife you promised."

"You know what?" He removed my ballistic knife from the folds of his clothes and placed it in my hand along with two smaller blades. "You can have all my knives."

"Hey, how'd you get those past Secret Service?"

"You kidding? That's the least of what I got past them."

I'd just finished kissing him again when the National Guard began taking down the tent around us. We each grabbed a couple of duffels and hurried to the waiting cars where our wounded were being loaded. I still felt like someone had run over me with a truck, but the weight of my knife and Ritter's other gift against my chest gave me new energy.

There were only two things I needed to take care of in the immediate future. One was a discussion with Stella about her comment regarding technopaths being able to use nanites to control fertility, because despite my commitment to Ritter, I wasn't ready yet to have a child.

The other was the matter of the little present Delia had placed in my head. I'd checked on the box, and it was untouched and unchanged. As soon as I recovered enough energy, I'd reinforce the box using what I'd learned about shields from Delia. But I couldn't leave the snake there. I had to know what it meant.

Maybe if Delia had left it there to control me, I could use it to control her.

THE END

TEYLA BRANTON GREW UP AVIDLY READING SCIENCE FICTION AND fantasy and watching Star Trek reruns with her large family. They lived on a little farm where she loved to visit the solitary cow and collect (and juggle) the eggs, usually making it back to the house with most of them intact. On that same farm she once owned thirty-three gerbils and eighteen cats, not a good mix, as it turns out. Teyla always had her nose in a book and daydreamed about someday creating her own worlds.

Teyla is now married, mostly grown up, and has seven kids, so life at her house can be very interesting (and loud), but writing keeps her sane. She thrives on the energy and daily amusement offered by her children, the semi-ordered chaos giving her a constant source of writing material. Grabbing any snatch of free time from her hectic life, Teyla writes novels, often with a child on her lap. She warns her children that if they don't behave, they just might find themselves in her next book!

She's been known to wear pajamas all day when working on a deadline, and is often distracted enough to burn dinner. (Okay, pretty much 90% of the time.) A sign on her office door reads: DANGER. WRITER AT WORK. ENTER AT YOUR OWN RISK.

She loves writing fiction and traveling, and she hopes to write and travel a lot more. She also loves shooting guns, martial arts, and belly dancing. She has worked in the publishing business for over twenty years. Teyla also writes romance and suspense under the name Rachel Branton. For more information, please visit http://www.TeylaBranton.com.